Praise for

The Ironbridge Saga

'A journey. Compelling. Addictive'
VAL WOOD

'The attention to period detail and beautiful writing
drew me right in'
LYNNE FRANCIS

'An addictive, heartwarming book, with an
unputdownable plot. I didn't want it to end'
DINAH JEFFERIES

'*The Daughters of Ironbridge* has that compulsive
page-turning quality, irresistible characters the reader
gets hugely invested in, and Walton has created a
brilliantly alive, vivid and breathing world'
LOUISA TREGER

'Feisty female characters, an atmospheric setting and a
spell-binding storyline make this a phenomenal read'
CATHY BRAMLEY

'Evocative, dramatic and hugely compelling . . . has all
the hallmarks of a classic saga. I loved it'
MIRANDA DICKINSON

The
Orphan of
Ironbridge

Mollie Walton has always been fascinated by history and on a trip to Shropshire, while gazing down from the iron bridge, found the inspiration for her debut saga novel, *The Daughters of Ironbridge*.

Also by Mollie Walton:
The Daughters of Ironbridge
The Secrets of Ironbridge

The
Orphan of
Ironbridge

MOLLIE WALTON

ZAFFRE

First published in the UK in 2021 by
ZAFFRE
An imprint of Bonnier Books UK
4th Floor, Victoria House,
Bloomsbury Square,
London WC1B 4DA
Owned by Bonnier Books
Sveavägen 56, Stockholm, Sweden

A CIP catalogue record for this book is
available from the British Library.

ISBN: 978–1–83877–314–4

Also available as an ebook

3 5 7 9 10 8 6 4

Typeset by IDSUK (Data Connection) Ltd
Printed and bound in Great Britain by Clays Ltd, Elcograf S.p.A.

Zaffre is an imprint of Bonnier Books UK
www.bonnierbooks.co.uk

This novel is dedicated to the memory of Jude Corfield, who listened to her daughter Lu brilliantly narrating an Ironbridge *book and 'heard home'.*

Prologue

August 1861

The child sat down on the bed, shuffling herself back until her little legs stuck out over the edge. Her feet were bare and grubby from dusty adventures outside. She was holding a doll made from scraps of material, a floppy ragged thing that she loved to distraction.

Anny watched her draw the doll to her lips and kiss it tenderly. Beside her, stretched out under the sheets, pale and limp, the child's mother rested her trembling hand on the child's arm.

'Hettie,' said Anny, and the girl looked up sharply. 'Your mama wants to talk to you. Lean down close to her now, for her voice is small.'

Hettie nodded. She looked round at her mother, unsure, then clasped the doll to her breast and haltingly leant towards her mother's face. She glanced round at Anny for reassurance, and Anny nodded encouragement. *Poor child*, thought Anny, *and poor mother*. Martha had been unwell for so long that she had grown strange to Hettie and the child was a little afraid of her. It must break Martha's heart.

Anny sat down on the wooden chair near the door and took up some sewing. She wanted this to be a private moment for the two of them, but she was too worried about Martha to leave her.

'Sweet Hettie,' said Martha and smiled. She lifted her hand and touched the child's face, who watched her mother's gaze with wide eyes. 'I've things to tell you, child. As you are only three years of age, these are things you wonna be understanding now or maybe for a long time, but I mun tell them nonetheless.'

Her body is weak, thought Anny. But her voice was firm, though quiet. Anny guessed she must be using her last ounce of strength to talk to her daughter. It was perhaps her last chance to do so.

'Tell Lizzie,' said Hettie, and carefully placed her doll on her mother's shoulder, resting it against her hair.

Martha smiled. 'I'll tell you both. You were born in this house, Hettie. Born from love and into love. I was born in different circumstances. I never knew my mother or where she came from. All I know is that she died on the iron bridge, handing me over to a kind man who took me in. I dunna even know where they laid her to rest.'

Martha paused to draw a deep breath. *So*, Anny thought, *it was really true; Martha was the baby on the bridge*. She'd heard rumours of this from her mother, but never had it told from the horse's mouth before.

'This man was a good man, a Quaker. He took me in. He and his wife raised me as their own. I couldna been

2

luckier, to land with such a family. I wish you coulda met them, as they were loving folk and they'd've loved you so. But they both were owd folk when they got me and they died afore you were born. They brought me up a good person and that's what your father, Adam, saw in me and he loved me for it. He is a good man too. But he inna here, as you know. And you havna met him yet. But one day, I hope and I pray, he will be returned from that faraway land they sent him to on the convict ship, and he will come to find you. Now listen, Hettie. Listen carefully.'

Anny watched Martha's face, her large green eyes intense. Hettie took fright. She snatched her doll back and clutched it.

'Lizzie scared,' she said.

Anny watched as Martha's intensity faded, replaced by a saddened smile, her eyes glistening in the dim light of the sickroom.

'Dunna fret, my angel,' said Martha, stroking Hettie's arm. 'I didna mean to frit'ee. But you mun mind me, when I tell you this. One day, if your father ever returns, you mun love him with all of your heart. And look after him, as I would, if I were here. He was the happiest man alive the day you were born, and it were never his fault that he were taken from us. He was innocent, Hettie. He did no wrong in this world, only good. You came from good, you came from love, my sweet lass. Never forget that.'

Martha stopped then and closed her eyes, coughing weakly. Anny put down her sewing and came to her. She touched her forehead, which was cold and clammy.

'Rest now, Martha, hmm?' Anny said.

Martha opened her eyes, her gaze hazy for a moment, until she seemed to remember where she lay and what her purpose was.

'No,' she murmured. Then, 'I mun speak. Hettie, my little duckie egg.'

Anny feared the child could take no more of this. She was too unsettled by her poor mother's illness.

'Just hear your mother one more time, Hettie. Then you may go play with Evan.'

Hettie's eyes lit up, then she glanced back at her mother. Anny's eyes pricked with tears as she watched Martha struggle to keep the little girl's attention. *She must be close now*, Anny thought. If only the child were older. If only she understood how significant this moment was. Anny vowed to memorise what Martha Jones said that day so that she could relate it to Hettie when she was older and had need of it.

Martha said, 'I mun tell you, my chick, for it may be my last chance. This life is not about where you came from, but where you are going. Always be good, be kind and treat others as you would wish yourself to be treated. Some are eaten up by hate or revenge. Some rail against the life they have, against the wrongs that have been done. Others meet hate with love and do all

4

they can to build bridges. You must be the last sort, the good sort. Like your Quaker grandparents. Like I have tried to be. Like Anny and Peter and Evan Malone who will look after you when I am gone. Do good in this world. Once all is said and done, what folk need most is kindness. Be good, be happy, my child, my lovely lass, light of my heart.'

Anny sniffed and wiped the tears from her eyes as Hettie, sensing a break in the stream of words, hopped off the bed and ran across the room. Her swift steps showed how glad she was to escape.

'Hush now, Martha,' said Anny, stroking her dear friend's face. Martha closed her eyes, a faint smile about her lips. She had said her piece. She was happy now.

Anny looked up to see that Hettie had not left the house, but was loitering near the door to the sickroom. She moved towards her.

'Give Lizzie to Mama,' said Hettie, and thrust the doll at Anny.

'You are a kind, good girl,' she said and put her hand on the girl's little head, golden brown from the sun. 'Run along to Evan now. He's picking beans with his father, I warrant. Can you pick faster than him?'

'I can, I can!' Hettie yelled. She turned, skipping across the front room and through the open doorway to the dusty ground beyond.

Anny turned back to Martha. As she reached down to place the doll beside her face, she stopped. She drew back and held the doll close. Martha's eyes were half-open, her lips parted and her face as still as a mask.

'Oh, Martha,' whispered Anny. She sobbed as she held the doll to her mouth, tears for her dead friend rolling down her cheeks into the doll's woollen hair.

Chapter 1

January 1875

The sound of their clogs could be heard a mile away or more. It began before dawn, in the milky darkness of a foggy winter's morn. A rumble from afar, that grew in strength and breadth until it took on a more chaotic form. Each wooden clog that made its mark on the ground had nails driven into the sole; they struck a note with every step. The noise grew louder still, as the men and women of the pits appeared from front doors and back doors, from side roads and alleyways, joining the throng on its way to work. If any lucky person were still abed, they would be rudely awoken by the growing clatter of the clogs on the cobbles, ringing and bouncing off walls and windows of every street. Along with this came the chatter of the men and oftentimes the singing of the women. The pit bank lasses would rouse them all into sound, even at this early hour. No wonder they called it the clog chorus.

Hettie Jones could hear the singing from across the way as she pulled on her bonnet and grasped her basket. It was as if they sang only to her, calling for her to join them – and so she did, six days a week. So she had done for the past five years, since she left school aged eleven. For Hettie was a pit bank wench and proud of it.

'Make haste, Evan!' she called, as she went to the door. 'They're a-coming down the bank, singing all the way.'

'I am coming,' he answered grumpily. Evan Malone never did like the early mornings.

'Dunna forget your bait,' said his father, Peter. He passed one packet to Hettie, who put it in her basket, and one to Evan, who shoved it in the pocket of his greatcoat. Peter did the same with his own lunch.

'Ta-ta, Anny,' said Hettie and kissed her cheek.

Anny smiled at her. 'Careful on that pit bank. You know girls can fall down shafts if they're careless with their footing. Mind that's not you.'

'I always do,' said Hettie.

Out she went, Peter close behind and Evan following last, out into the bitter air of a January morning. The path was glittering with ice crystals.

'Jack Frost has been,' said Peter and shuddered.

Hettie drew her shawl closer around her and hurried ahead of Peter and Evan, keen to catch the other women as they came down the hill and onto the path that led by the Malones' house. Today they were singing one of her favourite folk songs. As she passed beside the river, swift and black in its winter dress, she could hear their voices rise above the ramshackle rooves of the houses.

Hettie joined in before she could see them, singing out and trotting forward, her clogs tapping in time to the beat of the song. She glanced back at Evan and saw him watching her. He lifted a hand and gave her a crooked smile. She smiled back and turned the corner to see the women marching forward, their voices raised as one. They all wore the same kind of clothes, an unofficial uniform: warm flannel dresses covered waist-down with a home-made apron, petticoats and thick leggings beneath. Some had greatcoats like the men and others had woollen shawls. Many sported patterned neckerchiefs, and all wore print bonnets and clogs. Their wooden shoes were made locally, cool in summer and warm in winter, and raised their feet up out of the mud.

'Morning, Hettie!' said Ada, her closest friend at the pit bank, falling into step beside her. 'Where's Evan today?'

'Back there.' Hettie gestured, then continued singing along.

'Such a nice face. And tall!' said Ada, looking back over her shoulder as they walked. 'You're so lucky to have such a handsome sweetheart.'

'He inna my sweetheart!' said Hettie. 'We grew up together is all. We're more like best friends than anything.'

'Well, I wish he were my best friend,' said Ada, grinning mischievously. 'I'd like to wake every morning to that face, I can tell thee.'

'Ah, stop your nonsense,' said Hettie and broke into song again.

She did not like to talk about Evan with the girls. They all fancied him and it made her feel tetchy. Growing up together had brought them closer than most. And these days everybody seemed to think that they might one day be wed. The idea hung in the air like a question waiting to be answered. But was it the right thing to do? Would their precious friendship be spoilt if it changed? Hettie did not know. Nobody spoke of it directly. It was just there, as a constant presence. She sang extra loud to stop herself thinking about it.

But somehow she couldn't stop thinking about it. She and Evan had been thick as thieves since before she could remember. They played together the whole of their childhood. Even when Evan's siblings were born, Hettie and Evan didn't play with the others much, instead rushing off to the woods or the river to be alone. Only school and chores took them away from each other. They had their own language that no one but them understood, which infuriated Anny and Peter. They would have crawled into each other's beds each night and slept together if the Malones had let them, but Anny made sure they had separate rooms, which were soon occupied with other babies and toddlers as Anny's new children grew. They were all Evan's siblings, and Hettie was the odd one out.

She was a Jones, not a Malone, her mother dead, her father transported. Hettie had never met her father, Adam Jones. He'd been in Australia for sixteen years now, nine beyond his sentence. Everyone thought he was probably dead. In dark moments, Hettie thought of herself as an orphan. It was such a forlorn-sounding word when she whispered it aloud to herself: *orphan*. But the Malones had never made her feel left out and had treated her as one of the family. And Anny always told Hettie stories about her lost mother and father, so that Hettie could keep their memories alive, even if they were second-hand ones. Once school was done and she joined the ranks of the pit bank wenches, they felt like family, too. And now Hettie was never alone. She loved that; she loved gossip and good company.

They all marched together now, about thirty or so females, mostly young women from fourteen or so up to their early twenties, with a couple of middle-aged women and one older still. The walk was another two miles to the pit and they sang all the way, some breaking off to talk or laugh at a private joke. The roads were glassy with ice and some lost their footing as they went, tipping into those beside them. But there was always a pair of hands to catch and right them. They moved as one, the pit bank wenches.

As the pit workings appeared ahead, the crowd of walkers split, the women all heading right, towards the weathering heaps, and the men heading left, towards the shafts. Dawn was breaking now, as dreary daylight crept over the brow of the mound. The great grey heaps of clay studded with nodules of ironstone loomed above them. This was their place of work, their territory. They filtered in and out of the cabin, leaving their baskets and stopping to warm their hands by the fire. Someone would soon light the brazier that sat atop the bank, so that the pickers up there could have a bit of a warm while they were at their work.

And so it began, the Saturday shift.

The pit bank was a huge pile of weathered clay around thirty feet high. Teams of women and girls would go along it, picking out the lumps of ironstone. Hettie began collecting, still humming the song. She deposited each piece in an iron basket. Once it was full, she pulled out a rag from her pocket – an old cloth of Anny's – then folded it and placed it atop her head. She called Ada, who helped her lift the iron basket and settle it on her head, the folded cloth protecting her scalp and helping the heavy basket to balance. The first day she'd started work, aged eleven, Hettie had come home that night crying at her stiff neck. She hadn't thought she could go back and do it all again the next day. But she did and her neck got used to it. Now she could carry a basket with no hands, in perfect balance.

She walked over to the heaps of ironstone that everyone called 'ranks' and deposited her load. Then, back to the bank and the whole process was repeated.

Yes, it was repetitive, but there was a comfort in that. There were few horrible surprises in her workday, unless a girl fell down a mineshaft, as Anny had warned, or there was an accident down the pit. It did happen from time to time and was usually bad news, the worst. Other than that, it was the kind of job that meant you were free from a bossy overseer or the meddling of other workers. Everyone just got on with it, working mostly in good humour, enjoying the freedom to be in the open air. Many other girls her age were in service, and though she liked the idea of that on rainy days, Hettie enjoyed being outside. She loved the camaraderie and the confidence it gave them all. These were girls who had not been bowed by confinement, and it showed: each had a face in ruddy health, strong arms and thighs. And when Hettie took the corner of her neckerchief to wipe the dust from her face, anyone could see she had clear, peachy skin, bright green eyes like her mother and, beneath her bonnet, shining hazelnut hair. Every girl moved assuredly along the bank. It was honest, simple work and Hettie liked it.

The pit was in full swing now and the bursts of chatter from the girls were accompanied by the sounds from the pit mouth, chains clanking through the pulleys, waggons clattering over rollers. The women periodically stopped to stamp their frozen feet on the solid ground and rub their hands together. Hettie and Ada clambered up to the brazier, now burning brightly atop the bank, and held their hands to the heat, fingers reaching towards the flames as close as they dared. Hettie looked up above the mine, beyond the woods nearby and into the sky. It was glowing with a strange yellow-white hue.

'Looks like snow a-coming,' said Hettie.

'I canna wait till summer,' said Ada. 'Oh, Hettie – you are coming to London with us this year? Have you asked your . . . Anny?'

Hettie thought, *Ada was going to say your parents, your mother or father*. But Hettie had no parents to ask anything of. She tried to push the thought away.

'Not yet. I'm a-thinking on it.'

Ada replied, 'Oh, you mun come! Whatever might be stopping you? I wanted you to come last year, but you wouldna. But you shall love it, you'll see. We shall all take the train to London together. The gardens will be in full fruit and we shall spend our days picking strawberries and the like, packing them in baskets and carrying them on our heads to the markets and carrying our empties back. Then when the fruit is done, we go on to vegetables. Singing all the way. And lots of coin to be earned. And then you shall spend it – or some of it, leastways – on the prettiest dress that the fair ever saw. And in September, at Oakengates fair, we shall be the finest wenches in

Shropshire. You didna go to the fair last year for you didna have a fine enough dress. So you mun go this time, Hettie. You surely mun go!'

'I know all of that,' said Hettie. She turned, pretending she'd spotted some lumps of ironstone a few steps away.

The truth was that she did not know whether to go or not. She loved the sound of it, the annual migration of the pit bank girls to the fruit and vegetable fields west of London, where their skill for picking and carrying heavy loads was put to an alternative summer use. But she was nervous of leaving home alone, without Anny or Peter to look out for her. And without Evan – that was the truth of it. To go a whole summer without her Evan, without seeing his face every morn and night, without his words and whisperings when they walked together, without his shoulder to lean on when they sat in a cwtch, with the other children on the settle, before the fire. Without all of this, she did not know if she had the confidence to leave her home for three months, only in the company of the other pit bank wenches. But she did not want to admit it to Ada, or to anyone. It made her feel silly, to dote upon Evan so, but he was her sun and her moon, and that was that.

Yet the strawberry fields were tempting. She could only imagine how sweet the scent of the air must be in a field of fruit. And the thought of seeing new people and places, of the hustle and bustle of the

London markets, the fruit sellers and the other market folk shouting and cursing, as Ada had told her stories of. It would be thrilling! Hettie had been too afraid last year, but perhaps it was time. She was sixteen, after all, and most of her friends had done it now. And she would have some rum stories to tell Evan when she came back.

'All right,' she called over to Ada, who needed help with her iron basket. Hettie came towards her, slipping a little on an icy patch, her clog skidding down the bank a couple of inches, her breath catching in her throat. But she stayed balanced and went back to Ada, helping her up with her load. 'I'll do it. I'll come strawberry picking.'

'You wonna regret it, Hettie!' cried Ada. 'And what larks we shall have!'

∽

There was a new boy today. Ten years old, trying to look taller than he was. Evan watched him clamber into the chain seat that would take them down the pit shaft. He climbed on beside him, followed by two other men. Evan could feel the new boy's shoulder juddering against his own, shaking and shivering. It wasn't just the cold that gripped the boy – they'd all taken their coats off and left them in the cabin – but it was fear, too. Each one of them was handed a lit candle, stuck fast into a lump of marl. Evan's eyes were drawn to the captivating flames, the only bright thing in this scene of greys and blacks.

The contraption that carried the men down the shaft was called the doubles by the miners. The banksman stood beside it to ensure a decent connection between the hook above them and the chain that carried them down. The bellman gave a quick ring of his bell to signal all was safe and ready for the men to go. All done, the slow descent began. The four candles threw swift, flickering shadows onto the brick-lined walls all around them.

There were four of them riding the doubles today. Evan's father was working above ground, supervising the loading of the coal into the waggons and fixing some of the equipment. Along with Evan and the boy were two of the oldest, most seasoned and sarcastic colliers that ever drew breath.

Boxer, the eldest, a man built like a brick privy, cleared his throat to speak, then coughed and coughed again. All colliers past a certain age had that cough. And one day the cough would carry them off. Everyone knew that.

'I think it be twelve month today since rope last broke,' said Boxer.

Evan rolled his eyes at the tasteless joke, but the new boy began to whimper.

'I believe this understrapper be afeard,' said Socksy, their other companion, a wiry little man with a thin neck but thick arms like two hams.

The boy said nothing.

'He hasna a scrap on him,' said Boxer. 'He'll be dead of hard work afore it's time for bait.'

'Leave him be,' said Evan, gruffly. He had no time for bullies.

'But mon,' Socksy carried on, 'this little nipper needs some advising, dunna he, Scrapper?'

All the colliers had nicknames and this was Evan's, in honour of his habit of falling into scraps with other boys from an early age. And pretty handy with his fists was Evan, too.

'Arr, he do,' added Boxer. 'Listen up, Daff.'

So, the new boy had his nickname already. Daff meant someone shy and a bit wet behind the ears. He'd never outlive that name. The die was cast.

'Now then, lad,' began Socksy, leaning over and speaking in the boy's ear, close enough that the boy must have been able to feel the tickle of Socksy's pro-digious moustache hairs. 'There be only one thing that can kill you down there and that's all of it.'

This was followed by a guffaw of laughter that made the boy flinch into Evan's arm.

'Damp'll kill you,' added Boxer. 'And I'm not talking moist. I'm talking gas. Damps, we call 'em. Stinkdamp smells like rotten eggs and'll make you sick as a dog. Firedamp'll catch from your candle and blow you to bits. But worst of all is blackdamp – it lingers above you, no odour. Just one breath and you're dead.'

Evan decided to tell the boy later about the canaries in cages they used to test for blackdamp. But everyone knew that it came so fast sometimes that the men were dead in their tracks before they'd had a moment to even notice the canary's demise, leastways alert anyone. He wouldn't tell the boy that, though. No sense in scaring him even more.

Boxer and Socksy fell silent now, leaving the boy to his morbid thoughts. Evan closed his eyes. The winder was so steady that it almost felt as if they were not moving. But when he opened his eyes, he saw that most of the brick-lined shaft was above them and they were about to reach the bottom. He felt the speed slacken as the ground came up to them, and then it was time to extricate his legs from the chains and stand firmly on the floor. They were around eight hundred feet down beneath the surface, in a place no human should ever be.

'Off you pile!' cried Boxer.

Evan watched the new boy climb clumsily out of the chains. He tripped, dropping his candle. It hit the floor and promptly went out. Evan took it up, relit it from his own and handed it to the boy, who nodded in gratitude. His face was as white as a sheet as he gazed around at his new surroundings.

The first thing the boy would see was the stables: cut out from the rock was a recess in which a few ponies were kept all year round. Some of them had not seen sunlight for seven years or more. Evan knew that if you touched them their skins were smooth like velvet, because they'd been cocooned down here so long. Evan pitied them, of course he did. Though he sometimes had a short fuse, Evan hated cruelty in all its forms.

He pitied the boy Daff too, who was now gaping about himself and wiping his brow with his cloth cap. The heat was already building up here at the foot of the shaft. It would only get hotter as they went deeper into the earth. The others were taking off their shirts and hanging them up on nails driven into the rock. Evan followed suit and gestured that Daff should do the same. Everyone worked half-naked down here.

Evan had to get off to the coalface and the boy would be taken to his place somewhere else, perhaps to man the doors that kept the airflow controlled, or to pull a waggon of coal in some confined space. Before he went, Evan took Daff aside beneath the timber supports that arched over their heads at the commencement of the tunnels.

'Where's your bait?'

Daff still did not speak, but took a pitifully small package from his trouser pocket, wrapped in newspaper, as Evan's was.

'When you get where you're going, if you can, string it up with a bit of explosive wire, so it hangs above the ground. Either that, or eat it straight away. Otherwise it'll get pinched.'

'They'll take my food? But it's all I got,' said the boy, welling up.

'Not the blokes,' said Evan. 'The mice. And the rats. Watch out for them.'

He left the boy then, not wanting to waste any more time. He had to move along to the coalface and get started. Boxer and Socksy were already heading that way. Colliers were paid by weight, not time, so every minute counted. Evan left Daff clutching his lunch, still pale-faced and terrified. The boy would have to get used to it, that was all. Nobody could do it for him.

As Evan walked away from the boy and down the tunnel they called a 'road', he finally had time to think. His candle threw strange shadows about him, twisting, fleeting things that dipped and swooped like dark ghosts. It was common to think on such things down here, though why a spirit with free rein of the outside would ever bother to haunt a mine was beyond him.

He thought he'd seen one once, flitting between the gravestones at dusk, when he and Hettie used to frequent the ruins of Southover. They did it all the time when they were nippers. It was quiet up there, away from the other village kids. They liked nothing better than to play alone. When the other kids were about, there was always some trouble brewing. The children from different villages, especially those from different sides of the river, were perpetually at war, with lengthy, staged battles taking place all over. Evan was always

21

commandeered for his skill at fighting, though if the truth be known, he'd much rather hang about with Hettie than anyone else.

Most folk avoided the ruins of Southover, saying that it was indeed haunted. But Evan couldn't stay away; it fascinated him. He knew it was the place where his brother Owen had died when Evan was still in his mother's belly, the brother Evan had never known. His parents never spoke of it, but Evan had heard the gossip, the story that Owen had loved a girl from the King family and it had been the death of him. He'd died saving her from the burning building.

Though he never knew Owen, this fact alone raised him to the status of hero in Evan's eyes. He often wanted to ask his parents more about his elder brother, but every time his name was mentioned, his mother's eyes would fill and his father's would cloud and Evan could not bear to see the pain in their faces, still fresh after all these years. So he was drawn to the ruins. But since he and Hettie had both started working, they had far less time to spend together. Though they were employed by the same pit, they worked in different worlds, Hettie above ground and Evan below, scouring away at the earth's riches, buried jealously away from man's endeavours.

Evan finally reached the coalface. First, he fetched his tools that he left in a recess in the rock each day, as all the men did. His pick was his own and no man must touch it. All the colliers felt the same about their tools. They were sacrosanct. Each had the owner's initials carved in the handle. Beside Evan's pick was his ringer, a crowbar with a spike at one end and a lever at the other, to break up the coal. He knelt down and shoved them along the ground, holding the candle in his other hand, crawling along to reach his place at the coalface.

It was about three feet high there. He set down his candle and sat on his knees, his clogs beneath him, each arse cheek resting on a clog. It saved his feet from aching too much. But everything else ached, his neck from bending, his back from crouching, his knees from kneeling. Now and again he'd stretch out on the floor and roll around to free his muscles up a bit, then back to it. In five hours he'd stop and eat his bait, there at the coalface. Then another five hours and it'd be time to go and see Hettie.

'Hettie,' he said her name aloud, then checked himself. But nobody was listening. The nearest collier was six yards away, already striking the coalface with his ringer and ignoring all other presence than his own two arms and the coal that spilled forth from his labour. Nobody chatted down here at the face. Nobody had the time or the strength. It was graft, pure graft. And Evan must start his for the day.

He took up his pick and with his sizeable arms, muscles straining, he heaved it at the coalface and struck it soundly. Only thousands more strikes to do and then his day would be done. Out of this godforsaken place and up, up into the waning day and his first glimpse of Hettie since dawn.

⤜∾⤛

Hettie loved her job, but she always welcomed the end of the shift and the walk home with Peter and Evan. All the way back, her mind was filled with her decision to go to London, though she did not speak of it. She was not ready to tell Evan about it yet. Something told her he wouldn't approve. No, it was more than that; he wouldn't want her to go, for he would miss her company terribly. Perhaps even more so, he would fear that she would change, that she wouldn't be his Hettie anymore once her head had been turned by London ways. But that was precisely the reason Hettie wanted to go. She *wanted* to change and grow, to see a patch of the world beyond her own. And she found a kernel of resentment in herself that Evan and the rest of the Malone family might want to deny her that chance.

As they tramped home in the cold, for the first time she found herself thinking, *Nothing ever happens around here. Every day is the same.*

Once home, they were welcomed by Anny with a hot supper and they all shared the gossip of the day. Once the meal was done and they were clearing the table, Hettie took her chance.

She announced to anyone who would listen, 'I want to go to London to pick strawberries this year.'

24

Everyone stopped and stared at her. From their surprised expressions, Hettie could see that Peter and Evan were against it, but Anny was smiling and nodding, showing she was for it. Flora, aged ten, with a thatch of thick red hair, glanced earnestly at both sides. She most likely wanted to go to London herself one day, and would be picking up tips of how to achieve that when the time came. The younger ones, the twins with their blond curls – christened William and Lilian, but known to all as Billy and Lily – were ignoring the debate. They were aged only six and were far more concerned with Billy's set of jacks. They'd lost the ball and were traipsing around the cottage looking for it, whining from time to time and being roundly ignored by all.

'It inna fitting for a girl to go to London on her own,' said Evan, standing with his arms folded, glaring at Hettie.

'There'll be twenty other women with me!' said Hettie.

'A gaggle of wenches dunna mean you'll be safe,' said Peter, puffing on his pipe.

'Is anyone going to help me with these blessed dishes?' asked Anny impatiently, wiping her hands on her apron while the others stood about and bickered.

'But what do you think, Anny?' said her husband. 'This is important. We mun make a decision.'

'Listen to me,' said Anny, and everyone did – even Billy and Lily ceased their search for a moment. Anny was the matriarch of the family and what she said was followed to the letter. 'Hettie is sixteen and shall turn seventeen in July. She is a young woman. She can make her own mind up about these things. What do you want to do, Hettie?'

All eyes turned to Hettie. She raised her chin and spoke clearly. 'I want to go.'

'That's that, then,' said Anny, and went to the sink to pour in water.

'But there are dangers in London,' said Peter. 'You know what they say about girls who go there, unaccompanied as they are.'

'I will be accompanied! I've told you!' cried Hettie, exasperated now.

'But there'll be no man to keep you in line, lass.'

Anny turned swiftly round from the sink and gave her husband such a glare that he coughed a little on his pipe smoke.

'No man keeps me in line, Peter Malone,' she said in a low voice, laced with threat.

Peter shook his head and coughed a little more. 'Oh, I wasna thinking of such as you, my sweet.'

'But Father is right,' said Evan, hunched in a chair by the fire. 'You know what they say about the girls who go to London.'

'What do they say?' piped up Flora, even more interested now.

'Nothing,' said Anny. 'Just idle gossip.'

'Well, that Morrison girl wasna gossip, was she? She came back with . . .'

'With what?' said Flora, eyes wide as saucers.

Peter puffed again, then said quietly, as if that meant Flora couldn't hear, 'In the *family way*.'

'She was always like that, Olive Morrison,' said Hettie. 'Always after the boys. But I inna like that!'

'We know that, love,' said Anny. 'And anyway, Olive's young man came from London and took her there and they married and 'twas all respectable in the end.'

'But we dunna want our Hettie marrying some London feller!' cried Evan.

Anny gave him a sharp, curious look. Evan turned away. Hettie watched all this with interest.

'As I say,' Anny went on, 'Hettie is a young woman now and the decision is entirely hers to make.'

'But Mother,' began Evan, standing up from his chair.

He was interrupted by Billy and Lily, who had had enough of this tedious discussion and wanted to assert their own rights to attention now. Billy piped up, 'We've looked high and low!'

'High and low!' repeated Lily.

'And no ball!' cried Billy, which Lily again echoed. 'The only place we havna looked is the ceiling.'

'What ball?' said Anny, lifting a bowl from the sink and setting it down to drip-dry on the draining board.

A faint knock came on the front door. Only Flora noticed. 'Was that a knock?' she said, and everyone stopped to listen.

After a moment's silence, it came again. Definitely a knock, then another and another. Three knocks, louder this time, more insistent.

Peter said, 'Answer it then, Flossie.'

Flora skipped over to the door, lifted the latch and pulled it open. Everyone heard Flora gasp and they turned to see as a blast of winter air filled the room.

Hettie was behind the door when she saw Flora's face turn, with a touch of apprehension, to her mother. 'It's a mon,' said Flora in a small voice and stepped back from the door. She was usually chatty with strangers, and it was unlike her to be afraid.

'My God,' said Peter, his pipe held motionless, smoke spiralling from it in the cold air.

'Who is that mon with the long beard?' asked Billy, and Lily added, 'Proper long beard.'

Hettie stepped round to look at the man at the door. He did indeed have a very long beard, dark and bushy and threaded with grey. He wore a thin coat unsuited to the January cold. His trousers were muddy at the knees and ragged at the ankles, atop filthy boots. He wore a grey waistcoat and a chequered shirt, a grimy neckerchief knotted about his neck. On his head was a battered brown hat pulled down low over his ears, hiding his eyes in shadow.

'Come in, mon. Come in,' said Peter, who was now striding over to the door and reaching out to place his hand on the man's shoulder. He obviously knew him.

But, Hettie thought, *who is he?*

She turned towards Anny, to see if she knew the man. Anny looked white as a sheet. Then she glanced hurriedly at Hettie. The look was piercing, as if she had seen something in Hettie's soul. Hettie felt a sudden surge of confusion and alarm. What was happening?

As the man stepped into the room, nodding at all of its occupants, Anny moved towards him. When he looked at Hettie, he stopped and stared at her. He removed his hat and now Hettie could see his eyes. Black eyes, so dark and intense they gave her a shock.

The man looked at Anny, gestured to Hettie and said, 'Is this my girl?'

My girl? she thought. Then the knowledge came to her like a slap. This man was her father. This dishevelled, roughshod man was her own father, returned from certain death in Australia.

'That it be,' said Anny, placing her hands on his shoulders and guiding him over to the table. He sat down, never taking his eyes from Hettie. She stared back at him, unable to speak or move. He went to place his hat carefully before him on the table, but hesitated and put it on his lap instead. Perhaps he thought it too filthy to sully the Malones' table.

He turned his face up to Anny and asked, 'Where is my Martha?'

The younger children stood around like wax dummies, watching the man's every move.

Hettie saw Anny's eyes fill with tears.

'She's gone,' said Peter, and patted the man on the shoulder. 'Thirteen year ago now. She didna suffer. A short illness. We've kept Hettie ever since. She's been well looked after.'

The man turned and looked at Hettie again, pain in his eyes. Then he looked away and his head fell. He buried his face in his hands.

'Everyone,' said Anny, 'this man is an old friend of ours. His name is Adam Jones. He's Hettie's father.'

Chapter 2

Queenie looked out of her bedroom window at the swaying trees beyond. The temperature had not risen above freezing that day, and the branches were still draped in white. Queenie was swathed in blankets and shawls, with slippers made from fox fur. Sitting around was what she mostly did these days, and Jenkins kept the fire stoked up, but Queenie always felt cold, the kind of cold that went down to her bones.

She shivered and shifted in her seat. Just the same old trees to look at, nothing more. She had been in this house, the old brickmaster's place as many still called it, for sixteen years now. She had grown accustomed to it since the loss of Southover in the fire, torched by those errant brickmakers who had defied the Kings and destroyed the seat of their power. *But, as ever, the Kings were not to be beaten*, thought Queenie proudly.

She had led this family back to success – for three years after the fire, at least. Then her health had taken a turn for the worse, and against all of her better judgement, she had had to hand over the running of the business to her daughter-in-law, Benjamina. For thirteen years the woman had been in charge, and Queenie had to admit that she had done well. Very well, if truth be known. But Queenie would never let on that this was the case. She had always disliked Benjamina, and she knew the feeling was mutual. Now that Queenie was a very elderly woman herself, she knew that her daughter-in-law's deepest desire was for her to die. She should have died years ago, she knew that; ninety-six was a ridiculous age to attain. But here she still was, a needle in Benjamina's side. That fact at least pleased Queenie.

'Meeting soon,' came a voice, and Queenie turned to see Jenkins shuffle in. 'It's your meeting with Benjamina soon, and after that it'll be time for dinner, so you'd best look lively. Did you hear what I said, woman?'

'I heard you quite clearly,' replied Queenie in a haughty tone, 'but seeing as it is a weekly occurrence and I have not yet lost my mind completely, I was well aware of the fact already.'

The two women glared at each other, then their eyes softened. They had played this game of back and forth for so long that it was in their very blood. Behind the bickering was true closeness. Rose Jenkins, her beloved lady's maid, who had been with her for decades, had always stood by her, through thick and thin; she was Queenie's only friend in the world. Queenie was always aware that it was a business arrangement,

32

that Jenkins was paid to be there. But in her softer moments, she liked to think that Jenkins had at least a portion of the regard – and dare she say, even love? – that Queenie had for her, after all these years. Queenie watched her approach with real fondness. Jenkins stopped and coughed, then coughed again. It took her several moments to recover herself, moments that Queenie spent encased in a creeping fear.

'Jenkins, that is the third time this week I have seen you overcome in this way.'

'Overcome? It is but a winter cough. I'm fine. Don't fuss me.'

'I don't know how many times I've told you – I've lost count – but you are too old for this job. You must retire and let me pay your pension. It will be generous, you know that.'

'I don't want to retire,' said Jenkins and huffed. She came to Queenie's chair and rearranged the blanket over her knees, tucking it in to ensure Queenie's legs were fully covered. 'And what would I do with a pension? I have no children to leave it to. And who would I talk to, down in Worthing or Weston-super-Mare or wherever it is old spinsters go to stay in cold boarding houses before their imminent death?'

'My dear, you are seventy-five years of age. You are often breathless. I worry for your heart.'

'Oh, there's nothing wrong with my heart. You know I have old Dr Fitzgerald check it every so often, as you pay him handsomely for it. And besides, I have Clayton to help me now.'

'Yes, you do. But you must allow her to do more.'

'How can she do more? I know she's young, all of twenty-five. And of course, being my cousin's child, she comes from good stock and would never be one to shirk work. But she's Benjamina's lady's maid, not yours. She has enough to do. I let her do the heavy work – not that there is much. I manage the rest. I am quite capable of working for a good few years yet, Miss Alice, you mark my words.'

'But you should not be working any longer. You should be resting,' said Queenie, gently placing her hand on Jenkins's own.

Jenkins gave Queenie's hand a quick squeeze, then went to her hair and fiddled with it, though Queenie knew it needed nothing. Jenkins's reluctance to retire and leave her bathed Queenie in warmth. Perhaps Jenkins needed Queenie as much as Queenie needed her, after all.

'I don't want to rest, Miss Alice. I'd be horribly bored. Now, I'll go and tell the girl to bring your tea.'

While she awaited her tea tray, Queenie made the decision to give Jenkins a week off all duties and insist that Clayton tend to her needs, whenever Benjamina could possibly spare her. Even though she could afford to hire as many new maids as she liked, utilising Benjamina's maid would madden her so very much, and this fact brought Queenie great pleasure. She was still grinning about it when Jenkins came back.

In fact, just to annoy Benjamina further, she told Jenkins to stay and have a cup of tea with her and not fetch the younger Mrs King just yet. That jumped-up shop girl could wait.

Presently, Jenkins got up and said, 'I'm off to get the dog botherer.'

Queenie smirked at Jenkins's nickname for Benjamina. How they both despised her! They always had done, since she was brought to the house by her unwise son to be his wife when she was aged just seventeen. She had only her beauty to recommend her, with no sense and no class. Benjamina had been a shop girl that Ralph had found in Shrewsbury, for heaven's sake. Hardly a suitable match for the King heir. But his first wife had died giving birth to their second child, and he had been heartbroken by it. He wanted this new wife to cheer him, and Queenie had not been able to find reason enough to prevent it. He had insisted and Queenie had let him win.

From that day forward she had begrudgingly put up with the child – for that is what Benjamina had been, more or less, when Ralph brought her home. She had been only a few years older than Ralph's own children, Margaret and Cyril. They were only twelve and fourteen then; now, both of them were dead and gone, just like her son.

Her memories were interrupted by the entrance of Benjamina, followed by Jenkins. Benjamina wore a midnight-blue silk dress with a bodice far too tight for her age, with a sizeable bustle at the back. She was carrying a sheaf of papers to make her look important. Queenie noted with satisfaction that her hands looked far older than her face, belying the age she took such pains to hide. But Queenie had to admit that Benjamina was an extremely handsome woman. Few would guess she was in her late fifties.

She took a seat opposite Queenie, perched on the edge due to her bustle, which made Queenie smirk. It was definitely one of the more ridiculous current fashions.

'Firstly, the weekly figures,' announced Benjamina imperiously. There was never any small talk between them. Queenie listened carefully to Benjamina's summary, although she'd already seen the figures herself; she had these sent to her regularly, as she liked to be prepared. Benjamina was wittering on now about how well everything was doing, as if it were all down to her and her alone, as if there were no workers labouring from dawn till dusk to bring this success about.

'I am sure you'll agree, Queenie, that the running of the companies has improved vastly since my late husband's day. His inept handling could have landed us in the workhouse!'

At this mention of her son, Queenie sighed. So many of her family were gone now. Her son Ralph had died of illness brought on by lazy living. Though she had had little feeling for him during his lifetime, she did regret his early death. Her grandchildren also both died young, Margaret lost in the fire and Cyril killed in a railway accident fifteen years ago, over in America. He had gone there after the fire, eager to escape the aftermath, and had been accompanied by Queenie's beloved great-granddaughter Beatrice.

Beatrice was Queenie's great love, but her mother's death in the fire broke her for a time and she would not stay in a place that plagued her with memories. She had told Queenie that there was a boy she loved, one of that Woodvine family, the Malones by marriage. He'd saved her life the night of the fire, but died himself in the burning house.

Queenie's eyes filled with tears, not for Owen Malone, though she was grateful to his memory for saving her darling Beatrice, but for Beatrice's absence. She had been resident in America for sixteen years now without a single visit home, and nothing Queenie wrote to her could ever persuade her to come back. Beatrice wrote letters to Queenie every three months to the day. She was a loyal child that way. But she would not come back. She'd once written to Queenie that she felt haunted by Ironbridge and all that had happened there, but somehow the ship to America had left those spectres lingering at the port, unable to cross the ocean.

'Queenie?' said Benjamina.

Queenie looked up to find the woman staring at her. 'Yes, yes, I am listening,' she said.

Benjamina raised her eyebrows to no one but herself, which annoyed Queenie intensely. Benjamina went on, 'I must now move on to another matter . . . one I know you dislike to discuss, but it must be said.'

Queenie knew what was coming; they had the same argument roughly once a month or so.

'Go on,' Queenie simply said. She liked to watch Benjamina work herself up into a lather.

'I do believe that the letters you receive from your great-granddaughter are a bad influence upon your decision-making.'

'Ah,' said Queenie and smiled. 'It has been a little while since you attacked Beatrice. Please do elaborate.'

Benjamina shifted in her seat. 'Attack is entirely the wrong word. Rather, I advise. Beatrice is a kind soul but she has been in America too long. Her brain has been addled by the talk of freedom they adore over there. Things work differently here in the old country. I know how fond you are of her, but her ideas are not suited to our way of life. She has encouraged you to change the business and include a philanthropic wing to our work – which is admirable, certainly, but it makes no sense in business terms. It is costing us dearly, and I fear it will place our business in a dangerous position if we continue in this same vein.'

'You cannot scare me into changing my mind,' said Queenie. 'You've never succeeded in scaring me, Benjamina, and you never will.'

Benjamina shifted forward in her seat. Was that meant to assert dominance? Queenie wondered. It just made her look even more precarious, as if the bustle would shove her off the chair imminently. 'I strongly advise you to disregard Beatrice's advice. You won't like me saying it, but it has to be said. You must cease this sentimental clinging to the ghosts of the past.'

At the mention of ghosts, Queenie glanced around. No ghosts here – not for years. She had not had a sniff of the spirit of her old maidservant, Betsy Blaize, since a few months after Beatrice had left.

Many years ago, Blaize had been raped and impregnated by Ralph senior, Queenie's husband, and Queenie had stood by and let it happen. Since Blaize's death when she was just sixteen years old, her ghost had visited Queenie continually, cursing her and the Kings for their actions and berating her for not protecting her daughter, the baby on the bridge. But then, sixteen years ago, Queenie herself had saved the husband of Blaize's daughter from certain death: her intervention in the trial of Adam Jones had led to him being sentenced only to transportation, not death, for organising the arson upon Southover. And she had done more than that for her fellow man, much more: once Queenie had heard from Beatrice that she was never coming back to take over the King business as Queenie had desired, she had decided to run her business in a new way, dealing with their workers in a more humanitarian fashion and devoting any surplus profits to charitable works. Since that decision, the ghost had stopped its visits.

Three years after the fire, Queenie heard from Jenkins that Blaize's daughter Martha had died, and that her child Hettie continued to live with Peter and Anny Malone. Queenie had arranged for Jenkins to take money to the Malones several times, to help with Hettie's upbringing, but it was always refused and returned. On each occasion, Queenie expected the vengeful ghost of Blaize to appear and berate her, but it never did. Either the spirit was satisfied or Queenie's former madness had passed. She was never quite sure where the truth lay, in supernatural causes or the vagaries of her own mind. But the ghost was gone, for good it seemed, and that was a comfort to Queenie.

She had become a better person in the last sixteen years, not only at the ghost's behest but also at the urgings of her darling Beatrice, who had told her again and again that things must change. Queenie had ensured that Benjamina continued her charitable business practices when she took over, and it was something they argued about incessantly. Benjamina did not have Queenie's reasons to be soft in business, and fought against Queenie's directions. But Queenie believed with all of her heart that if the Kings ever returned to the cruelty of their past, then the ghost would surely appear again, lighting up Queenie's room at night with its unearthly glow and bringing disaster to the King household once more.

'Queenie! Please concentrate!'

Queenie recalled where she was and who she was talking to. She might have been nearly a hundred years of age, but she still had a voice, and a strident one at that. And she still had her wits about her. 'If you wish me to remain present, then you must stop repeating your empty phrases like a trained mynah bird. The charitable contributions will remain as long as I am alive. And it would serve you well in the eternal here-after, Benjamina, if you thought of others more than yourself. You never know who is watching.'

Benjamina looked queerly at Queenie. *She thinks I am mad*, thought Queenie. *Let her. I know I'm right about this one.*

'Is that all, Benjamina? I do believe it is time to prepare for dinner. You may go now.'

Benjamina got up in a huff, Queenie smiling serenely until she'd left the room. Once the door closed, she felt spent. It was a tiring business, thwarting Benjamina. But Queenie was determined she would continue these weekly meetings – to the very day she died, if she could.

It gave her great pleasure to aggravate the woman at every possible opportunity.

∾

Hettie stared at the man. Flora, Billy and Lily all turned and gaped at her. She felt their astonished scrutiny and glanced at Evan. He was watching her, too, but with pity in his eyes. She hated it, this sharp attention on her. She wanted to run away and hide. Could this mess of a man really be her long-awaited father? He looked about a hundred years old and he smelt terrible. Now the door was closed and the icy air had gone, the unwashed stink of him wafted about the room and sickened Hettie.

Still, she knew that something was expected of her, so she stepped forward. The man lifted his eyes and fixed her with his dark gaze.

'Pleasure to meet you, sir,' said Hettie, her voice croaking a little in the middle, her mouth suddenly dry.

'I have dreamt of this moment for many a year,' said the man. She could not bear to think of him yet as her father or even as the fabled Adam Jones she had dreamt of when she was a young child. She was ashamed of him, she realised, and ashamed of herself for being so.

'Let us feed you and water you and get you to rest,' said Anny. 'We can talk more in the morning. Children, this man has travelled thousands and thousands of miles to be with us this night, and he must be sorely tired. You must all be quiet and get an early bedtime and leave him be.'

'But I wanna talk to the mon!' cried Billy.

'And ask about his beard,' added Lily. 'Are there sparrows living in it?'

Billy whispered loudly to Lily, 'I think I saw a spider in it. Also, he smells like pig dung.'

'Off with you now,' said Anny, and shooed the little ones away to their room. She tasked Flora with sorting them out, then came back to the main room, giving a concerned glance to Hettie.

Hettie was rooted to the spot, unable to move or speak. Her father was sitting with his eyes drawn to the fire that danced in the fireplace. He looked half-delirious. Hettie guessed he must be exhausted.

But then, abruptly, he sat upright, turned to her and spoke.

'I know my arrival will be a dreadful shock to you, Hettie. My appearance is not what I'd have hoped for my first meeting with my daughter since her infancy. But I want you to know that underneath this filth, these soiled garments and this crow's nest of a beard, is a father. A father who once loved you more than life itself, though you wouldna recall it, being just a babby when I saw you last. I have been through the circles of hell since then, and I have much to tell you, if you wish to hear it. But for now, I would like to eat and drink. I am exceeding weary from my journey.'

'Yes,' said Hettie, nodding. She was taken aback by this eloquent speech, which she had not expected from such a rough exterior. 'You must eat and drink.'

She still could not move, but she saw Anny was fetching bread and meat from the shelves in the larder and bringing it to the table. She thought a drink of milk would be good sustenance for the man – her father, as she must now think of him – and she managed to move her rooted feet to fetch him one. She walked to the jug and exchanged glances with Evan, who came to stand beside her.

'Are you well, Hettie?' he said, kindly. His eyes searched her face. Evan always understood her. He would know how shocking this moment was for her and how important.

'Quite well, thank'ee,' she said quietly and poured out the milk into a mug.

She took it to her father and placed it beside him on the table. He looked up at her and somewhere in the midst of that bushy beard, there came a smile. His eyes softened as he gazed upon her and she could not help but smile back.

'Thank'ee.' He nodded at her, taking up the mug and downing it almost in one gulp.

'You're more than welcome,' she said, taking up a seat on the other side of the fire, not far from Evan. She could still feel him watching her.

Peter and Anny went about their chores as her father solemnly ate his food. Bits of bread stuck in his beard, which he brushed off from time to time. Hettie knew he must want to eat in peace, but so many questions were racing about her head, and she felt she would burst waiting to ask them. So the three of them sat in an awkward silence, Evan, Hettie and her father, watching him eat, or staring into the fire, or glancing at each other.

When all three of the younger children were in bed, Anny invited Adam to sit by the fire in Peter's chair, the most comfortable one of all. Anny continued bustling about with jobs, while Peter found a spare pipe for Adam and together they lit up and puffed. Evan and Hettie watched all this with interest.

Then, Adam spoke again. 'Daughter, I suppose you would like to hear the story of what has happened to me these past years.'

'Yes!' said Hettie, then checked herself. She hadn't meant it to come out so eagerly.

'Good,' said Adam. 'For there is much to tell.'

'Are you not too tired, Adam?' said Anny, bringing him a steaming mug of tea to enjoy with his pipe.

'I find myself revived,' he said, a twinkle appearing in his eye, which made him look ten years younger. Hettie realised with a jolt that this man was probably the same age as Peter, or thereabouts. He must be in his early fifties, though he had looked ten years older than that when he first appeared at their door.

Anny settled in a chair with her knitting. Evan stood by the fire, leaning against the mantelpiece, watching Hettie watch her father as he began his story.

'I was transported on the *Palmerston* in November – the eighth of November, 1860. I'll never forget the date. There were just over three hundred souls on board. Most were sentenced to life imprisonment, some to seven years, like me, others to twelve or more. We left from Portland. There were some passengers on board, too, pensioner guards, wives and children, as well as soldiers and us convicts. I treated every man on that ship as an enemy until I had hard proof they were not. Eventually, I became friends with one man, Henry Adkins. He'd also been sent down for arson – he'd been convicted of firing a haystack, which he said he hadna done, just as I didna commit my crime. His sentence was ten and mine was seven, so I counted myself lucky.'

He paused for a moment, clearing his throat and breathing heavily. Hettie wanted him to rest and was about to say he should, when he started up again. She supposed it was more important to him to get his story out.

'We arrived in February in Western Australia at the Swan River colony. It was a rural place, small, like a village. The houses were little, made of brick or stone, some laid out with gardens and allotments for growing food. Some of the main thoroughfares had proper roads, but most of the place was paved in loose sand. It blinded you in the bright summer light and turned to mud in the infrequent rain.

'Convicts were stationed at a low, long, white building called the 'Establishment', where all the chain gangs were housed. We worked on road building at first. Later on construction of buildings, docks and bridges. Sometimes one of the other men tried to escape. Sometimes they were caught and received the lash, but most of the time the punishment was the land itself. There was no sustenance or comfort in the bush, and all escapees starved out there, or else returned to the chains to accept their punishment and survive. My friend Henry Adkins tried to persuade me to escape with him, but I saw it was senseless. They brought his body back some weeks later, a bag of bones, starved to death. They laid it out as a warning for all to see. That near broke my spirit, I tell you, but I persevered. Writing home was all that kept me going at first. I wrote to Martha again and again, but I never received any reply. Perhaps they never arrived. I don't know. I always tried to hope so. The thought that Martha had disowned me was too much to bear.'

'We never received a thing,' said Peter, in astonishment.

Anny's eyes were shining with emotion. 'How terrible,' she muttered.

'Well, I'm happy to know I wasna ignored and 'twas but a quirk of fate my letters were never answered.' Adam sighed. 'After four years, I was eligible for a pardon and was allowed to work as a wage earner for free settlers for the next three years of my sentence. I was given my ticket-of-leave. But the money I'd earnt was nowhere near enough to secure passage back to England. I worked for sheep farmers around and about for another four years before I was finally able to apply for my Certificate of Freedom. As soon as I had it, I saved up some money to board a ship to eastern Australia.

'It was difficult to find much work there. The people were prejudiced against convicts. I struggled for a while in Sydney before I returned to Western Australia, seeking the old masters I used to work for. I lived as simply as I could and I saved as much of my wage as I could manage without starving. I saved up for the passage home for the next five years.'

'It can't have been easy,' said Anny.

Adam shook his head. 'It weren't. I had to master my loneliness and desperation, remembering always that my goal was to return to my Martha and my child. My money was stolen twice, and I had to start saving again from scratch. But eventually I got there and bought my passage. It took four months for the ship to arrive. I came straight to Shropshire from the coast, walking mostly or hitching a ride on a waggon here and there.' He glanced at Peter and Anny. 'I've no money left, I'm sorry to say, so I canna offer you payment for your kindness to my girl.'

'No payment necessary, mon,' said Peter.

Hettie had listened to the whole narrative in awe. To think that this man, her father, had been alive all this time, when she thought he must have died; had been thinking of her all this time, when she thought he cared not; had been plotting his return to her and her mother all these years, when she thought she was an orphan and would never see a parent again in this lifetime. And here he was, alive, well-spoken and intelligent, sitting before her, large as life.

She stood then. She moved towards him and leant down, placing her hands on his shoulders. He gazed up at her with a kind of reverence, as if she were an angel descended from heaven to greet him. She leant down, trying to ignore the stench of his trials that lingered about him, found a bare patch of his skin on his weather-beaten cheek and kissed him there.

'Welcome home, Father.'

Chapter 3

Queenie awoke with a jolt. Before she opened her eyes, she knew. She had felt precisely this way before. It was many years ago now, but the mind never forgot such an experience. Her eyes were still closed, as she was too afraid to open them. It couldn't be *her*, could it? Surely not, after all these years?

Queenie willed herself to open her eyes to a slit, just wide enough to see if that same spectral blue-white light came through the crack in the curtains. It did not, but it did emanate from somewhere else in the room. She snapped her eyes shut again and screwed them up. Why now? What had changed?

There was nothing else for it but to look at her intruder.

There she was, standing by the wall, gazing straight at Queenie. She looked just the same. Queenie knew from before that this spirit never changed, never aged. The beautiful pale face of the spirit of Betsy Blaize stood before her, regarding her with ice-blue eyes. Queenie stared, getting used to the sight of her again. There was a time, just after the fire, when the ghost had been with her so much of the time that she became a silent companion. In a curious way, it was good to see the spirit again, like meeting an old friend. But her presence was always tinged with malice, and Queenie began to feel queasy. She knew that her appearance in the past had foretold dreadful events.

'Hello, old friend,' she said wearily to the ghost.

The spirit nodded slowly, never taking her eyes from Queenie's.

In the absence of an utterance, Queenie spoke again: 'I know not where you go when you are not with me. But wherever you have been, you may or may not have been watching my actions these last years. I wish you to know that I have been the very model of charity. I have directed my businesses to give some of our profits to those in need. I have also acted far more kindly to our workers. I had assumed you knew this and approved, and that this is the reason I have not seen you again.'

The ghost was not one for conversation. She continued to stare at Queenie, her eyes unreadable. Queenie felt a twisting inside her and wondered if the ghost was causing it. She knew there was more she wanted to hear.

'As for your child, the woman died young, I'm afraid. Perhaps you have met her again in your realm – who knows. I suspect you will not tell me. You only seem to speak in riddles. Or curses.'

Queenie involuntarily shuddered at this last word and pulled the covers closer to her chin. The ghost's presence and the cold room made her shiver. She was tiring of this interruption to her sleep.

'Since then, I have sent money to the Malones on a regular basis, as they kept your grandchild and have raised her. But that Anny Woodvine hates us Kings and will not take a penny from us. There is nothing I can do about that. The woman is as stubborn as a mule. Perhaps you should visit her instead, spirit.'

Queenie was warming to her theme now and felt a certain smug superiority over this silent ghost. But at that moment, the ghost moved swiftly to the bedside, making Queenie gasp with her sudden approach.

'*The child will cross the bridge. The child will make one house from two. The child is the answer.*' The spirit was close to Queenie now, her flowing white hair subtly shifting in the spectral air, her eyes piercingly blue.

'You said those words to me before, many years ago. But you were wrong. This did not come to pass. The child Beatrice went to America and never came home. And she most likely never will. So perhaps you are not such a powerful seer as you think, Blaize.'

'*Fool!*' cried the ghost, in such a screeching yet hollow wail that Queenie felt as if a poker had been thrust in her ear. Surely the house would wake at this unearthly sound. But nothing stirred. *I must be finally losing my mind*, Queenie thought.

'I am ninety-six years of age,' she said quietly. 'Please do not berate me, spirit.'

Queenie felt a waft of warm air on her cheek. When she turned, the ghost was inches from her face.

'*The wrong child*,' she said and pulled away, standing up, seemingly taller than ever, glaring down at Queenie.

'But . . . which child is it, then?' Queenie muttered.

'*Child of my child.*'

With that, the ghost fixed Queenie with a last stare, then faded from view, its eyes the last to go, leaving a bluish tinge to the air. Then it was gone.

Queenie stared at the space where the ghost had stood. Then, everything went black.

When she awoke the next morning, she realised she must have fallen asleep within seconds of the ghost's departure. She went through the motions with Jenkins all morning and was quite relieved when Jenkins went for a walk into town and left her to rest. Finally, she had a moment's peace to think.

Child of my child, the ghost had said. That must mean Martha's child. Hettie, her name was. Well, the child was well looked after. One couldn't ask for more devoted adoptive parents than the Malones. They were good people, Queenie knew that. And the child had lived a good life with them. She was now a pit bank girl, Queenie had heard. How would this child cross the bridge and make one house from two? What did that mean anyway? And why was the child the answer? What was the question, indeed?

When Jenkins returned in the afternoon, she looked more sprightly than usual. Queenie was happy to see that the week of rest had done her old friend no end of good and she looked more hale and hearty than ever.

'I bring news from town,' said Jenkins. 'Some interesting gossip concerning the Malones.' She settled down with a shawl of Queenie's that required a hole sewing up. Her fingers were still nimble, and her needle moved more swiftly through the fabric than her age would suggest.

Queenie turned to her, seated in her chair by the window as usual. News of the Malones after last night's visitation made her skin prickle. 'Spit it out, then,' she replied.

'They say that Adam Jones has returned from Australia.'

Queenie stared. 'After all these years? How many is it?'

'Seventeen years this summer since the fire. Everyone thought Jones must've died out there, so long past his sentence he was gone. But he's back, large as life.'

'Hettie's father . . .' Queenie muttered, her thoughts elsewhere, with the spirit's words.

'He is staying with the Malones for the time being. He came back a week ago. But they say he looked like nothing on earth when he appeared at their door. Anny

Malone has cleaned him up since, shaved his beard and so forth, but he came back stinking of drink and has been seen drinking the afternoon away at various inns hereabouts all week, setting up unpaid accounts all over town. The Malones have had to fetch him and half carry him home.'

This does not bode well, thought Queenie. The ghost's sudden reappearance must have something to do with it. The father come back, drinking himself silly. What must the child be going through? Yes, this was why the ghost had come back. Something must be done.

'Send money to him,' said Queenie.

'What?' said Jenkins, looking up from her sewing, her needle held mid-stitch.

'You heard me, woman. Send a goodly sum to him.'

'But he will drink himself to death with it!' cried Jenkins.

'Send it,' Queenie said. 'Then tell Benjamina to come to me. I have something to discuss with her.'

Jenkins put down her sewing and muttered her way out of the room.

As Queenie waited for her daughter-in-law to deign to come to her, Queenie made a decision. It was something she'd been toying with for a while. Now she knew it was the right time. The ghost's appearance and Jones's return told her that. She had a plan to put in motion and she would need Benjamina's assistance.

There was a brief rat-a-tat-tat on the door, quickly followed by the woman herself. She never waited after her knock and only did that from time to time, after Queenie had complained that she mustn't barge in.

'What is it?' asked Benjamina with impatience. 'I was about to set off for an afternoon tea.'

Queenie was not fazed by her bullying tone. 'Organise an architect to come and see me. The finest in the county.'

'Whatever for?' scoffed Benjamina.

'We are going to rebuild Southover.'

∞

Benjamina spent her entire time at the afternoon tea in a fit of grumpiness after hearing Queenie's latest hare-brained scheme. The woman was getting far too old to be permitted to make decisions about the family finances. Rebuilding their old family home was pointless when they had plenty of room in the old brickmaster's house where they now lived. Here was yet another example of why Queenie should have taken retirement years ago and left everything to Benjamina.

Wasteful old fool, thought Benjamina as she mounted the stairs to her room to take a short nap before dinner. Entering her room, she expected her little dog Drina to welcome her, but discovered that the maid had not yet brought the dog back from her afternoon walk. If it wasn't troublesome old women, it was troublesome maids that plagued Benjamina's life. She could hear one of the stupid girls outside calling Drina's name.

Finally, there was a knock on the door and in came the scurrying sound of Drina's feet on the carpet, music to Benjamina's ears.

'Where have you been, you naughty little thing?' said Benjamina, scooping up the dog and fondling her velvety ears. Then she peered at the servant over Drina's bobbing head, as the dog panted in her arms. 'Why did it take so long? Where have you been?' This was one of the tweeny maids and not her own lady's maid, Clayton, who had been requisitioned to help Queenie while Jenkins was resting. Another ridiculous decision that made Benjamina hopping mad, and meant that other things in the house went awry.

'Begging your pardon, ma'am,' said the maid. 'When you let the little dog run about the grounds on its own, it does run off into the forest and chase squirrels and suchlike. It inna easy to get it back in. It dunna wanna come back.'

'Don't be an idiot,' snapped Benjamina. 'Of course she wants to come back. This is her home and I am her mistress. Next time, keep an eye out for her and don't let her go into the forest. She could be taken by a fox or heaven knows what. Just after my husband's death, one of my dogs was strangled by a worker that came out of those woods. Do your job with the same care you would take with an infant. She is that precious, do you hear me?'

'Yes, ma'am,' the maid replied, her eyes frightened at Benjamina's harsh tone. Benjamina could not even remember this one's name. Servants seemed to come and go far too quickly these days, getting themselves pregnant or uppity and finding other jobs. It was almost impossible to find a decent maid. And this one was a bit too bold for Benjamina's liking.

'Get away with you. Get out.'

Benjamina shoved the door shut with her shoulder, right in the girl's face. She knew it was a common gesture, but the girl had angered her. And she had her hands full. She buried her face in Drina's soft coat and kissed, kissed, kissed her dear one.

'You are my baby, my perfect little baby,' she said. 'Yes, you are. Yes, you are.'

Drina whined then barked. This was Benjamina's fifth King Charles spaniel, after Chloe and then Phoebe both died in quick succession when young; then the unfortunate Louise, murdered by one of those cruel strikers from the brickyard. Then there was Nancy, who caught distemper from a fox. And now there was Drina, the dear thing. Drina was the liveliest of the lot, and barked too much for everyone's liking. But Benjamina took pleasure in their annoyance. She adored Drina and disliked everyone else in her house. Drina was the only one that loved her and was loyal to her. Drina was her only friend in this cluttered prison of a home.

She kissed Drina again on the top of her soft head and whispered, 'I love you, little one. More than anything.'

The dog heard a sound outside and wriggled free of her mistress's grasp and ran to the bedroom window, staring pointedly upwards. She hopped up on a chair, then the dressing table, knocking over two items of Benjamina's toilette. She sat at the edge, where she had a perfect view out of the window, and whined and yelped at something down there, something of great import in a dog's world. But Benjamina felt too indolent to move. She lay back on her bed, full of her tea, feeling despondent at her dog's rejection.

She knew she was utterly alone in the world, a widow for seventeen years now. For all his faults, at least her husband Ralph had been hers. When she was given to him at sixteen, she had lost her freedom but gained money, lost her mother but gained a husband. Benjamina had come from nothing. Or rather, her father had left them nothing after he drank himself to death.

He had been of the middling sort, with ambitious merchant parents who educated him and spoilt him. He was set up with a hat shop, mostly catering to men. It was a tidy little shop in a good street in Shrewsbury and it did very well at first. But her father had a taste for gin, and it ruined him. It was a common occurrence in her childhood to be awoken from her bed in the middle of the night and dragged downstairs by her mother's hot, sweaty hand, then shoved under the stairs in a tight cwtch. Together they would hide in the cupboard there, to avoid her father's violent rants. He would find them and pull out her mother, beating her about the head until he collapsed in a drunken stupor.

He left when she was fifteen years old, thank God, and they heard some months later that he had died in the street. *Good riddance.*

It was a great relief to be free of the man. Benjamina and her mother lived in glorious liberty for a while. But they were saddled with debt that grew like mould. Her mother ran the shop adequately, but custom was down and getting less and less by the month. Fashions were changing, as Benjamina noted; she had a keen eye for the latest style. Waists were pinched in and hats were tall, but her mother continued to stock old-fashioned hats and recommend styles that were sometimes of the last century, let alone fit for the new decade of the 1830s. The younger male customers fell away and only older men appeared in the shop. Some days it seemed they only came to flirt with the proprietor's delicious daughter.

There was something about being a shop girl that seemed to invite all manner of indecent proposals. Benjamina laughed them away in her girlish manner, but soon realised it was the only power she had. She would woo clients and flatter them, trying to inveigle them into buying the more expensive items. It sometimes worked – but at other times, she only received a groping for her troubles. And all the while, the shop's profits were dwindling and the debt was rising, and the shadows under her mother's eyes darkened daily.

One day, a middle-aged gentleman with a pot belly came in and seemed struck by lightning when he saw her. His goggle-eyed fascination was disarming, if not rather alarming. Through conversation with her mother, the man revealed that he was widowed with two children not much younger than Benjamina. He fawned over her mother, who giggled like a schoolgirl, then kept glancing at Benjamina in a meaningful way. Benjamina did not like the look of those glances, not one bit. She disappeared into the back room, and was called upon to return. The gentleman introduced himself as Ralph King, an ironmaster from Ironbridge. The workings of iron and all such industry revolted her; she imagined it to be tainted by hard, manual work and the stink of chimneys. But her mother seemed delighted with this pompous fool, who returned the very next day and flattered them both by buying far too many handkerchiefs and two new hats. She did not want this man as her new father and was amazed her mother seemed to consider sacrificing her own freedom for this fat idiot.

But after a couple of visits, it became clear that another plan was afoot. And her mother would not be the one who made the sacrifice.

'Princess,' her mother had said to her, the name her mother always used with her when she wanted her to do something. 'My beautiful princess. You shall save us. You will marry this King and become his queen.'

'No, Mother! I hate the man!' Benjamina had cried, tears streaming down her face.

But her mother flourished the mounting bills at her and said, 'Do you want to see me in the workhouse before the week's end? That is what'll happen if you don't grab this gift from providence. It is up to you, princess.'

Benjamina married Ralph King when she had just turned seventeen. He promised to pay a lump sum to her mother to save the shop and off Benjamina went to Ironbridge with her husband, who was older than her own father had been when he died. They went to a large house on a hill surrounded below by the muck of industry. There lived two children who she knew immediately hated her. News came after a few months that her mother had died of a weak heart. She went to the funeral with her husband, who closed down the shop and sold the assets, pocketing the profits. Back they went to the big house in Ironbridge.

She was seventeen, owned by a man she disliked, forced to live with two unpleasant children who looked at her reproachfully whenever she spoke. And there she was, the lady of the house. Except that there were two others who ruled that house, and they did so with an iron fist. Her father-in-law, Ralph senior, who ran the business and assaulted the household maids whenever he got the chance. And his wife, her mother-in-law, Queenie. She could see that Queenie despised her from the first moment they met, even more than silent, boring Margaret and petulant, sulky Cyril. She had no words of comfort or advice from a soul in that house from the moment she arrived. She had never felt so alone, even as a child hiding in the cupboard under the stairs, her hands over her ears, cowering in terror that one night her father would murder her mother and then start on her. This loneliness was worse, a slow, creeping malaise that weighed her down, like the heavy burden of her husband's body on top of her each night.

Thus she decided there was nothing to do but embrace this new life, as desolate as it might be. At least she could enjoy the comforts of wealth. She used all her fashion acumen to purchase a new selection of the latest clothes, an ever-evolving wardrobe of which she was very proud, knowing how fine she looked in her exquisite gowns. She purchased a King Charles spaniel which she named Chloe – the name of the heroine in the first play her new husband had taken her to. She had never owned a dog before and this animal adored her, whatever she did or said. She had never known such fierce loyalty from any living thing and she could not have enough of it. Her spaniel became her only love and she petted and spoilt it from dawn till dusk, her only friend in that friendless house. Her husband she satisfied each night as he wanted and simply closed her eyes while it was happening, thinking about the shop or her dog or fine silks and ribbons or whatever else she could fill her mind with to escape the dreadful pounding of his flesh into hers. Worse even than this nightly misery was the thought of bearing a child. She had not one maternal bone in her body and she dreaded the time when a baby would come. But each night, she douched herself as her mother had once taught her, and it must have worked, or else there was something broken inside of her, as a pregnancy never appeared, much to her relief. After a while, she began to feign illness to avoid the nightly chore and he deferred to her at first, whining from time to time. Then she made it very clear she did not want him to come to her in that way at any time, day or night. At first he railed against her, shouting and stomping his feet, at which his jowls would wobble and his cheeks would go purple with rage. But eventually he gave up. He did not have it in him to attack her. He was not a violent man like her father. She was grateful for this at least.

And so decades passed, a life of indolence, fine things to eat and lovely things to wear and the love of small dogs who devoted their lives to her. From time to time there was a dalliance with a passing gentleman, the most notable of which was the artist Jake Ashford, who bedded her on the chaise longue on several passionate occasions when he was supposed to be completing her portrait. He never finished the painting, or even really started, as to everyone's amazement he chose the tedious little Margaret and ran off with her to Paris. Benjamina had had no particular designs on Jake herself, but she hated Margaret for taking him from her. She enjoyed their sexual encounters and the danger of fornicating in the drawing room, where a servant could walk in at any time. All her misplaced passion from the lonely years came rushing out into her lust for Jake Ashford. And then he was gone, off to a new life in France with that little harlot, her stepdaughter. The only satisfaction was that, according to the house gossip, Margaret left him with the daughter still in her belly and he died a while later.

She had once been envious of Margaret, for those brief months of happiness they must have had after the elopement. At least Margaret had tasted love for a while. Benjamina had never loved anybody, apart from her mother, and she was long gone. Now she had only a selfish, spoilt dog for company.

How pathetic! She scolded herself inwardly and stood up. She knew what the answer to loneliness was. It was power. It burned inside her like a perpetual furnace, this desire for power. It was the only desire she had left. Sex was dull, her beauty had faded, children or true friends she had neither (only acquaintances for whom she cared little), and her family was a joke to her. Hated and hating, she had whittled herself down to this one purpose: to be the ruler of the King business and household. For the past thirteen years, she had run the businesses and done an excellent job. The King fortune was stronger than ever. She had found her calling at last, after years of pointless existence. At the age of fifty-nine, she was an icon in Shropshire, an independent woman operating in a man's world, fully capable of anything a businessman could do.

But it was still not enough. Queenie held Benjamina's future in her hands. When Queenie's husband, Ralph senior, died, he left everything to Queenie in his will, not trusting his son to manage anything properly. And this meant that when Ralph junior died, Benjamina inherited nothing from her husband. It all still remained in Queenie's ownership.

Since Benjamina had taken over the business, Queenie had agreed to pay her a salary for her work. Benjamina had been careful with this money and stowed it away in the bank and in safe investments, so she certainly had a good stock of cash when she needed it. But Benjamina wanted her rights. She deserved it. She was owed it. She had married that oaf and put up with him for all that time. And, since all of Queenie's children and grandchildren were either dead or, as in Beatrice's case, refused to be a beneficiary, Benjamina had now been named as the sole heir of the King fortune in Queenie's will. But the old woman had lived till ninety-six! And still she seemed to show no signs of going anywhere. She had usurped Queenie and ruled in her stead; all of the other Kings were either dead or gone. There was nobody left to inherit but herself. She would have it all.

'Come, Drina,' she called and the dog looked alert, leapt down and followed her. Benjamina walked across the landing and knocked on her mother-in-law's door. Before she took her nap, Benjamina intended to argue with Queenie about this ridiculous decision to rebuild the old house. She knew she would not win the argument and that Queenie would go ahead with it anyway. But she loved to antagonise her, and she knew that by causing a row about it, and having her yappy little dog in the room, she'd successfully ruin Queenie's evening. Queenie did not like dogs, so Benjamina often brought Drina along to Queenie's room, just to watch her distress as the dog gambolled about, disturbing the peace.

How she loved to lord it over Queenie. And how she hated the old harridan and could not wait for her to die.

Chapter 4

Sitting by the fire with Hettie, watching the flames flicker, chatting about the latest gossip from the pit, Evan knew this was the best moment of his week. It was unusually quiet in the Malone household, as his parents were out with friends celebrating a new birth, wetting the baby's head, as they said. The younger children were asleep in bed. Hettie was darning some of Flora's socks and Evan was stretched out in his father's chair, the soles of his feet turned towards the heat, his eyes watching the flames and the lamplight play across Hettie's face and hair as she laughed at his jokes and bent her head to see her stitches.

Adam Jones was out too, thankfully. What a relief it was when he left their home. He had gone out every day since he'd received the King money a week ago. And though Evan was relieved to see the man leave, his return was always fraught; he had come back every evening drunk as a lord, much to Hettie's shame. After her father turned up that night a fortnight ago, he had been quiet for the first few days, sleeping a lot and talking little. But soon, he started going out drinking at the local taverns every single day. Each time he came home was worse than the day before. Hettie took charge of him, marshalling the drunken fool to his bed in the boys' room. Evan now had to squeeze into a narrow bunk with Billy, and more often than not, he'd lie awake and listen to Adam snoring, stinking of beer, dreaming of God knows what and calling out in his sleep, interrupting the rest that Evan so desperately needed to get through another day at the coalface. To his credit, Adam had given a portion of the King money to Evan's mother for housekeeping, but the rest he was drinking away and it made everyone uneasy. Hettie seemed to accept it. She clearly didn't want to discuss it, but Evan could hold it in no longer.

'It's nice, this,' said Evan.

'Yes, it surely is,' said Hettie, smiling.

'We dunna get much time to just be, me and you.'

'No, we dunna these days.'

'Indeed. These days . . .' Evan hesitated. He knew what he wanted to say, about Adam Jones, about how he was spoiling things. He didn't want to ruin this peace they had tonight with talk of that man, but it was so hard to get Hettie alone these days, he felt he couldn't miss this chance. 'Since your father came back . . .'

He saw Hettie's mouth purse, as if she were steeling herself for what was to come next. How could he say it so that it didn't sound like a criticism?

'It's a kind of miracle, really,' he said, hoping that's what she'd want to hear.

'Thank the Lord,' said Hettie, not lifting her eyes from her sewing.

'A marvellous thing,' Evan went on, pretending to sound as if he was merely musing, not planning. 'And I am proper pleased for you, to have your father back. I am, truly.'

'I know it,' said Hettie, still not looking up.

'But I mun confess . . . I do miss our old times. You know, the times we'd spend like this or out on our walks. But since your father's return . . . and dunna get me wrong, I know how important it is for you two to get to know one another. And like I said, it's a marvellous thing.'

Hettie said nothing in reply and Evan avoided looking at her. If he did, he might lose his nerve to continue.

'But the truth is, you've changed, Hettie. You used to want to spend all your time with me, but now you're always with him.'

It came out wrongly. He didn't mean it that way. He sounded like a jealous child.

'I think I might turn in,' said Hettie, stabbing her needle into a sock and putting the sewing aside.

Evan sat up, pulling his legs in, resting his elbows on his knees. 'Dunna go, Hettie. I'm sorry if . . .'

'I'm tired, is all.' She glanced at him, her eyes shining.

'Please, Hettie, dunna go. These times with you alone . . . well, they are precious to me.'

'And to me,' she said and looked at him again. He was sure she had tears glistening in her eyes and it shamed him. 'It's a pity you spoilt it.' She stood up then and turned as if to go.

Evan stood too and reached out to her, touching her arm. 'Dunna go, Hettie, please! I am sorry. I just wanted to . . .'

She turned abruptly back to him and now he could see anger in her eyes. 'You were right about one thing. It is marvellous to me to have a father return as if from the dead. And I'll do everything in my power to look after him and make up for the years we lost. I'd hope you'd understand that. And what that means for me.'

'Course I do! But he's . . .'

'He's what? A broken man? Wouldna you be, after what he's suffered? Wouldna anyone?'

'Yes, course, but it's the way it pains you I canna bear. The drinking . . .'

A sound came from behind them and stopped their argument. It was Flora, appearing at the door, rubbing her sleepy eyes.

'I woke up,' she muttered. 'Bad dreams.'

'Come on, Floss,' said Evan and went to her. Flora often suffered from vivid dreams. She was a clever girl with an active imagination which spilled over into her sleeping life and often caused nightmares. Evan was used to it and always knew how to solve it. 'Let's get you a sip of milk.'

He put his arm about his sister's narrow shoulders, and she rested her head on him as he led her over to the kitchen table. He was aware that Hettie had sat down beside the fire again and taken up her sewing. That was good. Perhaps once he'd got his sister back to bed, he could make amends and regain the lovely atmosphere of earlier, before he'd ruined it. He sat Flora down at the kitchen table and fetched her a splash of milk in a mug. Somehow, tasting some goodness like that always chased her dreams away. He'd done it for her since she was a little nipper and she always came to him when she was upset at night. She was a sweet child and loved him simply, as he loved her. They had a knowledge of shared ancestry that made their love pure and effortless. Certainly, they annoyed each other from time to time, as all siblings do. But their love was quiet and ever-present, never questioned and never a trial.

As he watched Flora sip her milk, he glanced back at Hettie. She was his first love, his first companion, thrown together as infants and as thick as thieves ever since. There was nothing simple about the way he loved Hettie. Everything about their friendship, their relationship was intense and urgent. It pained him and delighted him equally. And it confused him terribly.

He had always known that the love he bore Hettie was not like the love he bore the rest of his family, but it was only these last few years he had truly understood that he loved her not only as a friend but as a girl, as a young woman, as a companion – and one day, he hoped as a lover and wife. The thought of marrying her had filled his mind for months, if not years. He was sixteen now and he could ask her. It was constantly in his mind.

It wasn't simple, though. Where would they live? If they stayed at home, no doubt they'd be given the boys' room and Billy would have to go in with Flora and Lily. It could work, for a while, but they'd have no privacy and it would start married life off badly. He kept meaning to sit down and work out how much money they both earnt at the pit and see if they could have afforded their own place. But something stopped him from doing so.

As he watched her now, sewing by the fire, he realised that what stopped him was fear. He was terrified that if he had everything in place, he would have to ask her to marry him and there was the alarming prospect that she would say no. If that happened, how could he continue to live with her, knowing she had rejected him? How could they possibly remain the friends and companions they had always been? It would be intolerable. Every couple of weeks or so, he'd look at her and think, *do it. Ask her.* And then he would turn away, afraid of what her answer would bring.

Flora finished her milk and looked up sleepily at her brother, a white rim along her top lip.

'Come on, Floss,' said Evan and led her back to bed. He saw his littlest sister Lily asleep on her front, knees tucked under, bottom in the air. Her quirkiness made him smile. He looked in on Billy to find him in the exact same position as his twin.

He knew that he took his love for his siblings for granted. They were part of him and would always be there. But his love for Hettie ran faster in his veins. There was little peace in it. It was flighty, unobtainable as a butterfly; if you caught it, you'd crush it. He'd always been afraid he'd lose her one day. And now, her father had returned like a ghost from the past, raking up old feelings and opening old wounds. His presence was splitting the family and separating him from Hettie.

Somehow, he needed to show Hettie that he understood how important Adam's return was to her, but also that she needed to realise he was not her responsibility. Adam was his own man and he would have to learn how to stand on his own two feet; she did not need to be at his beck and call. Surely if he explained this to her calmly, she would understand.

He went back into the front room. There was Hettie, still seated by the fire, and Evan was about to make his reasonable speech, when the front door was flung open and in stumbled Adam Jones.

Immediately Hettie was up and by his side. The man was incoherent, muttering something about bones and blood. Everything the man said, did and was felt hateful to Evan. He knew he ought to help Hettie, as Adam slumped against her and she fought to assist him. But he was too resentful and self-righteous, slumping instead into his father's chair by the fire and staring into the flames. He ignored the two shuffling figures beside him as they headed for the boys' room. He heard Hettie shushing Adam, getting him into bed as quietly as she could so that he didn't disturb Billy and the others. *If he wakes the little'uns, I'll tear a strip off him*, thought Evan.

Presently, Hettie came back in. She fetched a glass of water and took it back through to her father. Then she appeared again and said, 'I'm off to bed.'

'Please dunna go yet, Hettie.'

'I am tired. I must sleep,' she said and drew a trembling hand across her eyes.

Evan went to her. He wanted to reach out and take her in his arms, but he didn't. He couldn't. He was too afraid she'd push him away.

'*He* is making you tired, Hettie. It's not right, what he's doing. He's wrecking you. He shouldna be spending King money on drink like this. He should be using it to set himself up in a new place, a new life. Instead of drinking it all away. It inna fair on you!'

Hettie looked up at him, her eyes fiery. 'Show some charity, Evan Malone! He's been through hell. He relives it every waking moment and every night in his dreams. He's just found his family again and it tortures him daily, what he lost. He's finding his feet now. He'll stop drinking once he's settled, you'll see. Show him some kindness, for my sake if nothing else.'

It was an eloquent speech. Hettie had always had that gift.

'I'll do it for you,' said Evan, trying to say the right thing. Yet he couldn't help adding, 'But not for him.'

She shook her head at him and left the room. Evan knew he could've made himself more agreeable to her. But he was headstrong. And he was convinced he was right about this. He did not believe that Hettie's predictions of her father's recovery would ever come to pass. Adam Jones was broken beyond repair and he would bring Hettie down with him.

Well, Evan thought, *I won't stand by to see that happen. Not ever.*

∽

A week later, Anny was hurrying along High Street with her three smallest children, eager to get home and out of the cold after a long day's work.

'Come on now, no dawdling,' said Anny, turning round to see Flora daydreaming with her head in the clouds, as usual, while Billy and Lily were conspiring over something in Lily's hand. A swift look confirmed it was a woodlouse, which Anny batted away onto the road.

'Mother!' cried Billy.

'Mother!' echoed Lily.

'I said, no dawdling! We need to get home so I can get on with chores. Now, everybody stop at the roadside and wait for this carriage to go by. Then hold hands . . . and go.'

The four of them hurried across the street, filled with late-afternoon shoppers and strollers, farmers driving animals, workers walking home weary and children picking pockets, given half a chance. They approached the iron bridge and Anny put down her basket, empty of the pies she'd just sold and delivered, to look for the toll in her own pocket.

At that moment, she heard a commotion nearby. She looked over to see a couple of burly men manhandling a fellow out of the Tontine Hotel bar. Immediately she realised it was Adam Jones. They pushed him forward and he lost his footing, landing on his outstretched palms and losing his hat in the process.

'Blast that man,' Anny muttered. She turned to Flora. 'Here, watch the twins and my basket. Do not move, you hear me?'

'Yes, Mother,' said Flora, her eyes wide as she watched the forsaken figure of Adam Jones grovel in the dust.

He managed to right himself before Anny reached him. He lent down to retrieve his battered hat, but Anny got there before him and swiped it up, thrusting it at him. He looked at her blearily. He used to be such a handsome man, thought Anny. Dark, good looks. Now what she saw was the alcohol he consumed every day swimming in his red eyes. His skin was patchy and aged, no doubt from years of Australian sun. There was pity in her heart for him – of course there was – but it was fast running dry.

'Come on.' She tried to keep her voice kind, but it wasn't easy.

'Dear Anny,' he muttered and let himself be led by her, acquiescent as a sleepy toddler.

Anny linked arms with him and marshalled him to the bridge. Flora's eyes were wider than ever, the twins watching warily, holding tightly onto each other's hands. Flora picked up Anny's basket and followed, chiding the twins if they lagged behind.

She's a good girl, thought Anny; she could usually rely on Flora to do the right thing. How utterly thrilled she'd been when she had her, late in life, her first girl. She'd been immediately besotted with her, tiny little thing she was, with a shock of red hair. Evan and Hettie paired off and disappeared much of the time, leaving Anny to adore her first daughter in peace. Then the twins came four years later and were such a joy to her. Her brood, just as she'd wanted, as her mother had once wanted and never achieved; Anny had been an only child. Until recently, everything felt like it was coming together nicely. Her little'uns were growing fast and true, and Evan and Hettie were near coming of age, ready to start their own lives soon, maybe even their own family together. Anny and Peter had always felt they seemed made for each other.

But then this happened: this man she now struggled to keep upright as they crossed the bridge, receiving disgruntled or disapproving looks from passers-by as they did so. This ghost from their past who'd returned. A cuckoo in their happy home.

As they struggled on down the roads towards home, Anny inwardly scolded herself for thinking of him that way. After all, Adam Jones was family, in a way. His first wife, Juliet, had been Peter's cousin, and even after her death and Adam's remarriage to Martha, Peter and Adam had remained close. And since he had been away, he had been through so much suffering, it was almost unimaginable. Anny herself had had her own stint in prison and knew the horrors of it. It had never left her, despite it being decades ago now. She dreamt of it some nights and woke in a panic. And if she felt this, after just months in prison, how must Adam feel after all those years? She knew he had nightmares, too; they all knew, as he had woken up shouting, waking the whole household. Hettie would get up and go to him, infinitely patient with her new-found father, stroking his brow and soothing him back to sleep. The poor girl was half asleep on the way to work these days, with her careworn evenings and sleepless nights worrying about this man. Hettie was always a kind girl, a thoughtful one, who wore her heart on her sleeve and cared for all living things. Now she had a new parent to care for, she seemed to pour all her love into the man, despite his absence most of the time at the local taverns. He was still a good man underneath, Anny was sure, but a broken one. She could see it was exhausting for Hettie, and she knew that Evan did not like it. He was restless and grumpy much of the time these days; he seemed jealous of Hettie's attentions to her father, though Evan must know it was wrong to feel that way. Anny knew her son better than anyone else did and she could see the envy seething in him. Peter was struggling with his presence, too, though he felt obliged to keep him there for the sake of their family ties. And the little ones were scared of Adam Jones.

In their small house there were three bedrooms for seven occupants, and now an eighth who slept in with the boys. It was overcrowded, to say the least. But it wasn't just that. There was a change in the atmosphere of the home, which before had been good-natured and busy. It was as if a cloud had arrived over their house, a dark cloud that cast shade across their daily existence. This man and his drinking had brought it. For her own part, as sorry for Adam as she'd always been, for his wrongful conviction and the terrible years he had to spend away from home, there was still a stone of resentment buried inside Anny. It was lodged down deep, but she could still feel it there: Adam had been with her son Owen the night the burning King house fell upon and killed him. Adam had led him there and Adam had been out cold on the ground when Owen went into that burning house. She knew it was wrong to blame him, but in Anny's mind Adam Jones had let her son die. She could never forgive him for that, whatever the rights and wrongs of it were. It was a primal, unreasoned hatred that she had buried when he had been away, had disappeared and was assumed to have died across the oceans. But now he had come back, as if from the land of the dead. An uncharitable thought came into Anny's head; she tried to brush it away, but its stain remained: Adam Jones should never have come back from Australia. It would've been better for everyone if he had died out there.

Arriving home, she ushered Adam into Peter's chair by the fire and stoked it up, adding precious coal to heat the room. The twins fell to playing and Flora helped her mother set the table and prepare the dinner: slabs of fidget pie for all with stewed apples from a jar for afters. Anny boiled up turnips to go with the pie and soon the house was filled with the scents of good food. Adam dozed in the chair – Peter's chair, Anny thought sourly.

Then the clog chorus signalled that the missing members of the household were about to appear, and soon enough, there they were, red-cheeked from their cold walk home and eager for food. Peter, Evan and Hettie came in as one, laughing and joking, but the moment they were inside, Hettie immediately went to her father dozing in his chair by the fire, and all amusement ceased. Peter and Evan removed their coats and scarves in silence and Anny felt irritated, yet again, that this man threw a shroud over their lives by his very presence.

She served up dinner and everyone took their places at the table. Hettie woke Adam, who came meekly and sat beside her, waiting quietly and bleary-eyed for his food. Unlike usual family dinners in the days before, this one was subdued; even the twins did not complain or bicker much as they used to. Everyone stared at their food and passed the odd pleasantry. But the stink of alcohol emanating from Adam was enough to put anyone off their dinner. Anny had had enough of it.

'This has to stop, Adam Jones.'

Everybody halted, mid-chew. Adam looked up vaguely.

'I said, this has to stop. D'you hear me?'

'Now then, Anny,' began Peter, but Anny shot him such a glare. It stopped his mouth and instead he shovelled another forkful of pie into his face, blackened with coal dust.

'Now then, nothing. Are you listening to me, Adam?'

Adam looked up from his dinner and managed to fix Anny with a stare. The deadness in the eyes arrested her for a moment and she regretted her tone. But she had something to say and she knew it needed saying.

'We all know you've been to hell and come back. I cannot imagine the trials you have suffered to bring you to this table this night. But we have all been through trials. We have all suffered losses, some too painful to mention.'

There was dead silence around the table now. Even the twins were transfixed.

'But life goes on. It must. And we have moved on. We have forged new lives and not mistreated others or ourselves while we have done so. But you, Adam Jones, are making our lives a misery.'

'No, Anny,' began Hettie, her eyes shining with tears, her voice cracking with emotion. How hard it must be for her, caught between the family who raised her and this new addition, her blood father, a wreck of a man who brought her nothing but trouble. But she must hear this, decided Anny.

'Yes, Hettie, it needs to be said. Your father must change his ways. No more drinking. No more. He's been drinking daily for weeks now and it's going to ruin him. If he stops now, he has a chance of recovering his strength, of being able to work some day and be useful. Only if he gives up the drink will he have a chance of regaining his life.'

Adam spoke then. His voice was low and gravelly, cracked with despair. 'Regain my life? My life, you say? I had my life wrenched from me. My freedom, my youth, my wife. Everything was stolen from me. And I was hurled across the world and left to rot there for a decade and a half, beaten and abused, tortured in the unbearable heat and forced to wear the chains all day and all night, until they chafed me to the bone. It was no life, it was a living death. I had a life once, here. But everything was taken from me.'

It was a stirring speech which affected everyone. A stifled sob came from Flora, tears rolling down her cheeks. Hettie looked as if she were holding back tears, trying to be strong, in that stubborn way she had. But Anny was undeterred, though her voice was softer now.

'Not everything was taken from you, Adam,' she said. 'You have Hettie. And she is worth more than gold.'

'Truth,' said Evan and the twins nodded their joint agreement. Hettie's eyes were filled with tears now too, and she could not look up at those around the table, so her tears fell straight into her lap, splashing onto the backs of her hands.

Anny went on, 'And you owe this girl a father. She is the best of people and she deserves the best father you can be. So far, since your return, you have failed her. Now is the time to step up and change that. No more drinking, get yourself well, get yourself working and earning, find yourself a place and make a home. Because you will not be staying here forever, and that is a fact.'

It rang harshly, but Anny knew it was right.

'I have found a place,' said Adam, his chin raised in defiance, his eyes coming to life now. 'If you had but asked, you'd've discovered it.'

'What place?' asked Peter, his voice uncertain yet tinged with hope.

'A place down yonder, along the river. An old butty has offered it to me. I just need to find the first month's rent and I'll be gone there, dunna you fret. It has two rooms, one for me and one for Hettie.'

Anny hadn't expected that. It was out of the question, of course. Adam should go – he could go to hell for all Anny cared right now – but he would not be taking Hettie with him.

'A room for me?' said Hettie, her eyes shining.

'Oh no, that will not be happening,' said Anny. 'Hettie lives here. Her home is here.'

Adam fixed Anny with a hard stare. 'She is my daughter and she will come with me.'

'It inna right,' said Evan, his voice higher-pitched than usual. The twins followed the argument agog, turning their heads in perfect synchronicity to each speaker in the argument. 'Hettie mun stay here, with us.'

'Nobody should speak for me, but me,' said Hettie. All eyes turned to her. Anny knew she was headstrong, but hoped against hope that the girl would see sense. Living in some hovel with a drunken father was not the place for her. Anny wouldn't allow it.

'Hettie, dear,' Anny began.

'No, please, Anny,' Hettie went on. 'Please let me speak. I made a promise many years ago, that if my father returned, I would look after him. You were there, Anny, when my mother asked that of me. You told me about it, in great detail, after the event, as I was

85

just a little'un then. And I made my promise. I feared it would never matter, that I made that promise, as I was sure my father was dead and gone, never to return. But by some miracle, he has survived and he has come back to me. I must honour my mother's wishes and go with him.'

The tears were rolling down her cheeks now, her chin quivering as she raised it, in just the same gesture as her father's. Anny's heart broke to see this brave girl squander her affection in such an undeserving place. She glanced at Evan and saw in his face that his heart was breaking too, at the thought of losing his soulmate, his Hettie. His anger a moment before seemed all turned to pain. Love like that was the mighty river behind the dam and any crack would send it charging through.

Anny said gently, 'Your mother would not have wanted this for you, Hettie.'

'My Martha?' cried Adam. 'How dare you speak for her! She was my wife.'

Anny stood up from the table. She was not having this. 'How dare I? *How dare I?* Only that I nursed Hettie into the world and nursed Martha out of it. Only that I tended to her all the days she had left, after you'd gone and she came to live with us, when she fell onto hard times. Only that she was the best friend I ever had and I was hers. Only that I raised her daughter as my own. Only *that*, Adam Jones. I think I have earned my say in this matter.'

Hettie stood up then. She was about to speak when a knock came at the door.

'Who the devil will't be this time, Mother?' piped up Billy, and Lily added, 'Who the devil?'

'Hush, you two,' said Flora. Peter stood and went to the door.

Anny saw it was the errand boy from the King house. What was he doing here again?

'For Mr Adam Jones,' said the lad, and handed over a package of brown paper. 'From old Mrs King, over at the old brickmaster's house. With 'er compliments.'

And with that, the lad was gone.

Peter shut the door and stood holding the packet for a moment. Anny could see it had a crimson wax seal on it. She knew those packets, for they had come before. The ones for her she had always turned away, every single one. But when one came two weeks back for Adam, he had taken it greedily and kept it without comment. She knew that quite a bit of it had gone on drink, as well as some to her. She hadn't wanted to take it, but she had no choice; Adam's bed and board needed funding somehow.

Now Adam stood up and took this new packet quickly, tearing it open. Inside was a suede purse filled with coins. It looked double the amount he had previously received.

He snapped the purse shut and pushed it into his pocket. Then, he looked up defiantly at Anny, his eyes clear and black now. 'Now you shall see how I will make good for Hettie. All of you. I will take her to this place and we shall make a life. I thank you, Anny, and you, Peter, for your hospitality these past weeks. But now it is time for me to go.'

'Tonight, Father?' said Hettie, wiping the tears from her face with her neckerchief.

'Yes, child. I shall go tonight and see this mon I know and take possession of our place, my dear. Tomorrow you shall bring your things and live with me there. How does that suit you, eh? You have a father of means now, with this.' He patted the purse in his pocket, and it chinked with coin.

Anny had no argument left. Adam had his money and his daughter's devotion. What could she say to that?

'He will go out this night and drink all that money away,' said Anny, folding her arms firmly.

'I will not.' Adam spoke loudly and deeply, his voice shocking the little ones, who cuddled up together in fright.

'We've heard that before,' said Anny, knowing she had lost the argument now, but too stubborn to give up, for she knew she was right.

Then Hettie spoke. 'I will only come with you tomorrow, Father, if you promise me that you will not drink again. Will you promise me that, as I once promised my mother I would take care of you, if you ever returned?'

Adam took a step towards Hettie and placed his hands on her shoulders. Whatever argument Anny had faded as quickly as it had erupted, as Hettie looked into her father's face, awaiting his response.

'On my life, I promise you, my darling daughter, that I will never take a drink again.'

'Then I shall go with you, Father, and we shall make a home together. And it shall be neat and clean and proper and good.'

The children were overcome at this vision of contentment, and Flora broke out into a little peal of applause, while the twins cheered. It created a festive atmosphere as Hettie and Adam hugged and she kissed him on the cheek. Peter looked approving too, though there was a wary look in his eye.

Evan and Anny did not join in the celebration. As they glanced at each other, his eyes were willing her to do something. He shook his head faintly at her and Anny knew he could not bear to see Hettie go with this man. But what could they do? The decision was made.

Chapter 5

'We are only down the road,' said Hettie, pulling out a hankie to wipe Flora's tears. 'Only a short, brisk walk. You can visit whenever you wish.'

But everyone knew that Hettie's new home, the place her father had found for them, was a tiny hovel and there would be no room for visitors there.

'Or I will visit you, often,' said Hettie, and tried to beam a smile at the Malones, gathered as they were in the front room. Billy and Lily were crying too, clinging onto their mother's skirts. Peter was trying to look supportive and Anny was fussing over the little'uns, unable to meet Hettie's eye. Evan was standing at the kitchen window, his back to her, refusing to be a part of this.

Anny ushered the fretting twins towards her husband, then came towards Hettie. The look they gave each other was fraught with meaning. Anny folded Hettie into her arms and Hettie thought she might sob. She had to fight to stop herself from breaking down. She wanted to be with her father. Of course she did. She wanted to look after him and tend to him, to make that plan of his recovery, of which she'd spoken to Evan, come true. But the stark fact of leaving her home and her family was upon her now and she could hardly bear it. To leave her loved ones and live elsewhere, with a man she barely knew, was a hard, cold choice, but one which she felt was impossible to refuse.

After a tight hug from Anny that Hettie never wanted to end, Anny withdrew and held Hettie at arm's length, her hands firmly about her shoulders.

'You are a brave girl,' she said, nodding resolutely at her. 'A good and kind girl. You have made your choice and I admire you for it. But Hettie, know that you are part of this family and you will always have a home with us here, whenever you need it. Know this in your heart.'

'I do know it, I do,' said Hettie and felt her eyes fill. She had to look away then, or she knew she would bawl like a baby. It was daft, really, all this emotion. She was only moving to the other side of town. She would still see Evan and Peter at work. But it was more than that. It was leaving home, giving up comfort and security for the unknown. Partly the idea excited her, but it also terrified her.

A new life beckoned, and she did not know if she was up to the challenge.

The truth was, Hettie's new home was a dump. It did have two bedrooms as promised, thankfully, but the main room consisted of a dirt floor and an inefficient range that was choked with soot to begin with. It took Hettie a whole day to clean it out and get it to burn without billowing smoke. The house itself had been thrown up by some canny developers looking to make some quick cash, and was built with walls as thin as paper. One night Adam put his foot through a wall when he came back drunk and angry, bitter at the world and all its miseries. Peter came to fix it for them, shaking his head at Adam, who scowled at him and then tried to pay him for his trouble, which Peter refused. Adam always seemed to have a coin about him, which then disappeared before the end of the day, spent on everybody-knew-what.

Money kept arriving from Mrs King, and Adam gave some to Hettie and kept the rest for 'sundries', as he called it. He was drinking still, of course. He had broken his promise. But he told her that he was in constant pain from his old injuries, aching all over every day due to the physical hardships he had suffered. A little drink took the pain away, he explained, and he was too ill to work. Hettie's wages and the regular packets from Mrs King kept them just about afloat.

Hettie soon gave up hope of him seeking out productive work that would keep him from the taverns or drinking great pitchers of beer at home. He didn't get as drunk as he used to, but it was more that he was slightly inebriated all of the time, rather than sober in the mornings then roaring drunk in the afternoon. After a few weeks of this, Hettie could hardly imagine him sober.

She cooked for him every night after returning from work. He did the washing well enough on Mondays and the ironing on Tuesdays; he had a real talent for that. He told Hettie that for a time in Australia his legs had been injured and, unable to do the construction work at the colony, he had been put on laundry duties for a few weeks, cleaning all the clothes of the prisoners and their masters at the Establishment, the building in which they were housed at the Swan River colony. He had tried his very best at it, to provide the cleanest, smartest laundry he could under the circumstances, so that they'd keep him there and not make him go out in the chain gangs on the roads again. But it had not turned out that way, and he was sent back out as soon as his legs recovered. Other than that peculiar skill at laundry, he was not much good at anything else around the home. He swept up a bit, but the rest of the cleaning and house care was done by Hettie on Sundays.

Anny had told Hettie she could come home any time she wanted to, that she didn't have to live like this. Oh, how tempting it was: Anny's motherly care and her excellent cooking; the children's laughter; Flora's sweet companionship; and last but not least, Evan. The first few weeks she missed Evan's presence like a hunger. She still saw him part of the way to and from work, but it wasn't the same as cwtching with him before the fire of an evening. She missed her family desperately. Evan came to see her on Sunday afternoons, but she was often too busy with housework to go for a walk with him. She could see the resentment, too, in his eyes when she talked of her father or when Evan saw or spoke to him. His disapproval of Adam became too difficult to bear and at last she asked Evan not to come anymore if he couldn't be civil and find a place in his heart for her father. He hadn't been back after that, too proud to agree to her demands. But Hettie could not abandon her father. He had nobody else. And she had promised her dead mother.

Getting used to the idea of having a father at all had been difficult, but it had had its little joys. The Malones only saw the broken drunk her father presented to the world, but over the months they lived together Hettie began to see a different side to him. In the evenings, after they had eaten and tidied away, they sat before the fire, Hettie mending, patching and knitting, Adam puffing on a pipe and telling Hettie stories about the time before he was sent away. He told her all about her mother Martha, how they met, what a good wife she was, how beautiful she was and how Hettie had inherited her bright green eyes. He spent a whole evening telling her the tale of how Hettie was born, how Miss Beatrice came from the big house with the lady's maid Jenkins, who fetched the doctor and saved not only her mother's life but Hettie's own. Hettie liked the sound of Miss Beatrice and was curious about the suggestion that she and Evan's dead brother, Owen, had had a forbidden romance. Adam related to her all the events of the brickmakers' strike, the way the Kings behaved so shabbily, his friendship with Owen and the bitter sadness of Owen's death and Adam's subsequent arrest and conviction.

Hettie had heard snippets of these stories from the Malones, but it was an eye-opener to hear someone else's version of events. Certainly, Adam came out of it as the hero of the day, in Hettie's eyes, at least. This was despite the fact that Adam tried to blame himself for the failure of the strike and also for Owen's death. Hettie chided him for this; as far as she could see, her father had done his very best and bad luck had caused the results, not bad judgement or bad acts on his part.

He also told her about his time in Australia. He spared her the most grisly details, and instead told her of the beauty of the strange land in which he found himself for all those years. He described to her the spectacular red sunsets that glowed across the wilderness that surrounded them. He told her about the strange creatures of the place that sounded like something from a storybook – an animal which kept its babies in a pouch on its tummy; a bird that laughed and laughed; a little bear with fringed ears that lived in gumtrees. The stories filled Hettie with wonder and a desire to travel. She knew she would most likely never sail the seas and visit anywhere as exotic, but she knew she wanted to see something beyond Ironbridge one day.

The first step towards this was her trip to London to pick fruit and vegetables from late May to August. Her father was against it. This was the only thing that Adam and Evan agreed upon. But Hettie was adamant; she'd told her father again and again that the money she earned would be considerable and would help improve their home. Secretly, she intended to keep a chunk of it to buy herself a pretty dress, as Ada had suggested back in January. All the unmarried girls who came back from London did this, spending their hard-earned wages on the best dress they could afford to wear to the Oakengates fair in September. She couldn't wait for that.

But her mind was conflicted about the trip: the truth was, she was afraid to leave her father. He drank steadily these days, but was still able to perform some domestic duties and remain civil. She hoped this was because of her calming influence. But with her gone for three whole months, would he have the self-discipline to maintain the house, keep cooking and cleaning for himself, and not drink himself to death? She worried about that most of all.

Before she went, she had a quiet word with Peter and asked him to keep an eye on her father, and Peter agreed. She knew she couldn't ask this of Anny or Evan, because they would have refused. She just hoped her father could keep himself from misadventure for those twelve or so weeks.

∽

The night before she was to leave for London with the other pit bank girls, Hettie could not sleep. The thought of leaving her home without Anny or Peter for the very first time and travelling by rail to London to live there for three months, was too thrilling to induce rest. She lay awake in her bed, listening to her father snoring behind the thin wall that separated their rooms.

The next morning she was up with the lark and kissing her father goodbye while he was still sleepy. He roused himself as he saw her pick up her carpet bag and head to the door.

'Hettie, wait!' he said groggily and hauled himself up and out of bed, standing unsteadily.

'Father, I mun go. The girls will be waiting for me.'

'Will you write to me, child?'

'Only if you will write back in return, Father.' She hoped that the incentive to write letters might keep him on the straight and narrow a little.

'I surely will. You have brought me back to life, my love.'

'Nonsense,' she said and took his hand. 'You are doing that all by yourself. Promise me you . . . will . . . take care of yourself?'

She wanted to tell him not to drink too much, but he hated it when she mentioned drink, as if it were a figment of her imagination. He had a large capacity for self-deceit.

'Course I will. You too. And dunna get yer head turned by any of these London folk. They be no better than you or I, with their fancy ways. Do your work, earn your wage, mind your business and come home to me as soon as you can.'

'I will, Father. Dunna fret.'

She kissed him again and he threw his arms around her, squeezing her tight, nearly knocking off her bonnet.

She withdrew and left him standing there in his nightshirt. She gave him a smile and a nod, before taking her luggage and leaving, closing the door gently behind her so as not to vex him. His head was always fragile in the mornings. The moment she stepped into the street, she realised how much she had been looking forward to escaping that little house – and her father – and this wracked her with guilt as she walked along the way to meet the others upriver. But there was no reason to feel guilty, she knew that; she was going to work, not for a holiday. It would be hard work, no doubt, so she had nothing to feel bad about. But she fairly skipped along as she approached the meeting place on the corner not far from her old home, where Ada and the other pit bank girls were waiting for her.

Chapter 6

'Come on, slow coach!' cried Ada as she saw her friend approach. They all had a bag each and were wearing warm travelling clothes. It was early, and despite being the end of May, there was a bit of a nip in the air. She fell in with Ada and they walked together, gossiping about this and that. Before long, they reached the railway station at Coalbrookdale. They queued up at the ticket office window in a gaggle, all talking at once and fishing in their bags for the money to pay for their tickets.

From here, they were to take the train to Wellington, change there and get the train to London. Both the train to Wellington and the next to London were not too busy and they all found a seat with ease. The open sides of the second-class carriage gave a marvellous view of the countryside and villages they went past, which fascinated Hettie. She'd never been far beyond Ironbridge in her life. But the lack of windows also made this morning journey distinctly chilly, and Hettie drew her shawl around her and cuddled up to Ada to keep warm. She was thankful it wasn't raining that day.

There was an atmosphere of excitement and anticipation amongst all the women. There were about twenty of them, many around Hettie and Ada's age of sixteen or so, with a couple of older women who had done the trip many times and knew the route inside out. The eldest and the one thus seemingly in charge was Nora, a woman in her early forties who had a sharp tongue and kept the women in line as they changed trains at Wellington. As their train swayed around a long curve and began its approach to Paddington, Nora called to the girls to pay attention.

'Now listen, wenches. When we get to Paddington station, it'll be sniving with folk bustling about hither and thither. We mun stick together. Find yourself a butty to keep an eye on you or a couple of butties. We need to cross the station and find a train on the GWR line that stops at Hayes and Harlington. You hear me? Hayes and Harlington. That be the one we need. So, choose yer butties now to keep an eye on and we'll soon be off.'

Hettie and Ada immediately linked arms and nodded. As the train pulled into the vast station, Hettie's eyes filled with wonder. She looked up at the massive arched structure built with iron girders that might have been cast at Coalbrookdale – who knew? It was the largest building she had ever seen in her life, let alone entered. It gave her a thrill to move along under its lofty curved ceiling and see the pigeons flap about up there.

As the train slowed to a halt, the next wonder was the people. There was a veritable army of people outside, filling the platform. There were many minutes of pushing and shoving to alight from the train, while others tried to fill it at the same time. Hettie grasped Ada's hand so hard she feared she might break her bones, but she was terrified of losing her grip and not being able to find her way back to the other women.

As they made their way along the platform, Hettie gazed up at the signs hanging above them signalling all manner of rooms beyond: cloakroom, general offices, gentleman's lavatory, telegraph office, and so on. Paddington felt like a village in itself, complete with inhabitants and shops and businesses all its own. The crowds of passengers moving hurriedly to and fro along the platform were joined by dozens of railway workmen and men in uniform, who she saw were porters being paid a penny here and there to carry bags. The turmoil of noise and movement assaulted her ears and confused her eyes, as bells rang out left and right and the sound of hundreds of folk talking and shouting and laughing filled the steamy, acrid air. She still held tight onto Ada's hand and made sure she kept her eye on the bobbing feather in Nora's hat that moved a few feet before them, weaving its way through the crowds to the ticket office for them to queue up yet again to purchase the ticket for their next train.

That achieved, they headed back into the melee and finally reached the correct platform, expertly sourced by

Nora. The train to Hayes and Harlington was waiting for them there. Again, hordes of people filled the platform. Everyone wanted to get into the carriages furthest back from the engine, pooling there at the near end of the platform. The train stood empty and Hettie soon realised everyone was waiting for some signal to climb aboard, fidgeting and jostling to get the best position to do so.

Suddenly a loud bell rang out and everybody moved. There was a great push towards the nearest carriages. Hettie saw Nora's feather bobbing away along the platform and she followed it, Ada grasping her hand as tightly as ever. All the carriages they passed were soon filled, so the women continued their way forward and most of them ended up in the very first carriage at the other end of the platform, right next to the engine itself, about which lolled the driver and his men, smoking cigarettes and winking at the females. The rest of the women climbed into the next carriage along.

Once in, they managed to sit on the wooden seats more or less together, with the odd seat taken up by another passenger, all of whom looked disapprovingly at the gaggle of wenches with the funny Shropshire voices filling up the seats around them. Nora popped out onto the platform and into the next carriage, then returned, carrying out a total headcount to make sure they were all there, then sat down herself. Hettie was relieved they had all got through the station in one piece and that nobody was lost along the way.

It was not long until the train set off and Hettie soon realised why nobody wanted to sit near the engine. The carriage filled with smoke, which billowed in and out of the open sides. Ashes floated on the air and landed on their clothes, some still hot, which left black burn marks on the skirts and cloaks of some. As the train picked up speed, the smoke and ash were not as bad, but still rolled in from time to time and made them all cough and brush themselves down. Her excitement at the newness of taking the train soon changed to annoyance that the conveyance was such a mucky, tiresome way to get about, so unlike walking or hitching a ride on the back of a waggon, as she sometimes did at home. Horses left their dung in the road and always smelt ripe and earthy, but at least they didn't throw burning coals at you. What was more, the train bounced around and jerked the passengers to and fro quite violently at times. At one point, one of their girls fell forward into the lap of a woman opposite, who cursed her clumsiness, at which the girls all laughed. It wasn't their fault after all, just the rough riding of the train.

After what seemed an age, and was in fact most of a day's dirty, crowded, exhausting travel, the train pulled in to Hayes and Harlington station, and Nora shepherded all the girls towards the doors. Coming out onto the platform was quite a relief. The day was waning but still warm in the late-May sunshine.

The women all gathered and Nora led the way again, walking out of the station and onto a long straight road lined with houses, along which the women began to walk in pairs or threes. The sun beat down upon them and Hettie removed her cloak and threw it over her arm. The sun on their faces felt good, and she was so relieved to be out of the train and away from the madness of the railway stations. She imagined what it must be like for folk who worked every day in London, who had to navigate their way through that chaotic bustle every morning and every evening, just to get to and from work. She had never been so grateful for her walk to the pit. Even on the coldest, rainiest mornings, she would rather do that than ride in those infernal trains every day.

The houses soon thinned out to be replaced by fields and farms. They walked for about an hour or so, taking glugs of water from bottles they'd brought with them, as well as bites of food. Hettie had eaten all of her bait on the train journeys, and she was so weary and hungry now that she wished she'd kept something for later. Ada kindly gave her an apple to eat, which tasted so sweet after the trials of the day.

At long last, Nora turned back and said, 'This be the place!' They turned off the main road, walking up a dusty path bounded on one side by a long row of apple trees, and thence through a gate to a collection of several wooden huts that stood empty with their doors wide open.

'Home sweet home!' said Nora, and went straight into the first hut. Hettie followed her, along with Ada behind and a friend of Nora's called Edna. There was straw on the floor and that was all, with enough space for four to sleep. Hettie had been told to bring a blanket and something to rest her head on. She'd found a small flattish cushion at Anny's that would fit in her bag. The girls deposited their bags, took off their hats and cloaks and went back outside.

So, this motley collection of huts was to be their home for the next three months. It was basic in the extreme, but Hettie found herself grinning from ear to ear. What an adventure! Nora and another woman had fetched some pots to cook in. All the women pooled the food they had brought with them to find a goodly collection of potatoes, onions and leeks, as well as a bit of bacon and some apples. There were two trivets in one of the huts which they brought out, collecting sticks to make fires underneath. Nora had the matches and set up the campfires, while others helped peel and chop the vegetables. They used a standpipe nearby for the water. They soon had a hearty stew of vegetables and bacon bubbling away. Some of the women had little leather bottles from which they swigged and passed round from time to time. Hettie recognised the smell of alcohol all too well, so declined when it came her way. Her father's predilection for the stuff had turned her off for life. Instead, she went to her hut and collected the bowls and spoons she and Ada had brought with them and took them back to the others. The stew was ladled out and they sat quietly and ate it quickly in great mouthfuls; they were all so hungry. Hettie was shattered, filthy from the journey, footsore and achy – yet sitting there cross-legged on the dusty ground with those twenty or so women shovelling stew into their mouths that May evening, she felt she had not been so happy in years.

∽

In the morning, Nora was outside the huts at first light, calling everybody to wake up. Hettie had worried that sleeping on the hay would be so uncomfortable that she would toss and turn all night, but she had been so shattered from the day's exertions that she did not even remember falling asleep. The women prepared themselves with a quick wash from the standpipe and pulled on their dresses and aprons brought from home. Some had been made from flour bags, and the manufacturer's name could be seen emblazoned across it: SAMPSON FLOUR. They all wore bonnets and neckerchiefs to protect their heads and necks from the afternoon sun.

Once up and ready, they travelled out to the strawberry fields in horse-drawn carts. There was much good-natured chatting between Nora and some of the other old hands and the men who drove the carts. Hettie realised that they were probably old friends; Nora had been coming here annually for years. It also dawned on her that she had agreed to this job without asking one question about what the work was actually like. She suddenly felt a little nervous about it.

'Ada,' she said as they trundled along a dusty road, bordered by hedges beyond which lay orchards and fields on both sides. 'What do we actually do all day? What will our duties be?'

'We'll be picking the strawberries and packing 'em into pottles first.'

'What's a pottle?'

'It's a little basket, shaped like a dunce's cap. We put all the fruit in there, then pack those into round baskets. We'll be hoeing the fields, too, scuffling for weeds. Some of us will be sent to carry the big baskets on our heads to market on some days. We sell the pottles there then bring the baskets and money back to the masters here. They pay our wages at the end of the week. Later in the season, we'll be picking other fruits and hoeing the vegetable fields as well.'

'How far is the walk to the London market?'

'Oh, a good ten mile. Takes about three hours or so.'

'Danker me!' cried Hettie. 'I had no clue it was such a trek.'

'Ah, well, 'tis easier than the picking, which fairly breaks your back after a few hours. I always like to go to the market, and you must too, Hettie, for it is rare fun.'

'Fun? Walking for miles and miles there and back?'

'But just you wait till you see the market. Full of interesting folk and some nice-looking lads, too! Even more handsome than your Evan. You'll see . . .'

Ada winked at Hettie, who sat quietly for a moment. She was so busy thinking about the London markets that she barely registered what Ada had said about Evan. It would be good to see the world, and she was used to walking to and from the pit every day, though it was not half as long a walk as this. Either way, she'd had her curiosity piqued by Ada's account, and wanted to go into London very much.

Once they'd arrived, the women got down from the cart and went through a gate into the strawberry field. It stretched out before them, the brown earth dotted with what seemed like thousands of bright red spots, fringed by green leaves rustling in the breeze, seeming to crawl across the land in low mounds. To the right was a rough structure, a three-sided shed, where could be seen the large round baskets and conical vessels Ada had described for packing the strawberries into for market. Also piled up were smaller baskets that Hettie guessed were for carrying with them in the fields to pack the picked fruit into before it was transferred.

Hettie followed the others as they went to the shed and collected their baskets, then fanned out into the fields and began to bend over to pick the strawberries. She was sorely tempted to snack on them, but had been told she must not taste even one, so of course she did not. But how she longed to feel the sweet taste of a strawberry on her tongue! The sun was soon up and it was warm, threatening to be a proper hot day. Now and again, a worker would traipse back to the hut and take a drink from a standpipe there and rub some cold water across her face and neck. Hettie followed suit. Soon, her basket was full and so was Ada's. Hettie watched as Ada took the fruit carefully from her basket and packed it into the pottles, then into the big baskets.

'You mun keep the very best strawberries at the top,' said Ada. 'These are called the toppers, because that's where we put 'em. It makes the whole pottle look fairer to the customer. The little squished ones we put at the bottom, which wonna be seen before the pottle is bought.'

'Clever,' said Hettie and followed suit, picking out the best strawberries from her basket last in the process.

The first morning was long and increasingly hot. Ada had been right about the picking; after a few hours, Hettie's neck, shoulders and back were aching. She watched a selection of women go off before lunchtime to the markets and envied them their escape, though carrying the heavy baskets full of laden pottles on their heads for ten miles would certainly not be easy. But she knew she wanted to be chosen one of these days. She'd carried iron baskets of ironstone on her head for years – not for ten miles, admittedly, but she hoped that strawberries and wicker baskets would be lighter, at least.

At lunchtime, a man from the farm came on a cart and brought baskets with cheese and bread in and beer to drink. Hettie found she was ravenous and ate quickly.

After lunch, she went back to the field and carried on, her body protesting against the constant bending and righting, up and down. There had been conversation and a bit of jollity in the morning, but now, in the heat of the afternoon, with everyone growing weary, all the women picked silently. The sounds were not of chatter but of their labour, accompanied by the soft sigh of the wind through the orchard trees beyond the hedge.

Then, into this came a new sound: a melody. Someone was whistling a tune. Hettie looked up to see which woman was so cheerful, but it was none of them. She looked in the direction of the music and saw a hat, bobbing along atop the hedge that bordered the field. Then, a man appeared. He stopped, not pushing through into the field, instead leaning on the gate. He was a gentleman, anyone could see that, with his morning coat, ascot tie, smart trousers, waistcoat, pocket watch on a chain, and felt hat with a band – every inch the city gent. So what on earth was he doing here near Isleworth, leaning over a gate into a strawberry field?

Hettie looked away, aware she was staring. But she soon glanced back and saw that he was watching them all of them, the women picking the strawberries. Then he looked directly at her and she swiftly looked away. He had dark eyes which had a way of picking

111

you out and pinning you to the spot. She looked back again and he smiled at her, then reached down and fiddled with the latch on the gate. He was coming into the field! Perhaps he was an overseer, maybe the landowner.

Hettie fell to working even harder, in case he should come and scold her for not picking his strawberries quickly enough. He stepped into the field, closed the gate in a leisurely fashion and strolled along the edge of the field to the packing shed. He nodded to the workers there, who nodded back. Then, Hettie heard the women around her start to mutter and giggle. They too were aware of the gentleman and some were making comments about him.

Her hut mate Edna called out, 'Tell us the time then, Master!'

Hettie envied her the nerve to shout at a gent like that. Hettie would never have dared. The man smirked at her and began to approach. As he came closer, Hettie could see those dark eyes again. They turned with interest from girl to girl in the field, nodding and smiling.

'Good afternoon, ladies,' he said, stopping at the edge of the field and removing his hat in a salutatory gesture.

'Ooh, ladies!' said Nora, and laughed sarcastically.

'I can see by your dress that you are from Staffordshire or Shropshire, perchance?'

'Yes, Shropshire,' said Nora, sounding a little wary of him now. 'What be your business here?'

'I happen to study the lives of working women all over our great country. I'm particularly interested in seasonal labourers such as yourself, who spend part of the year here and the rest elsewhere.'

'What is there to study about us?' Nora replied, bending down to pick more fruit and toss it into her basket. 'We bend down, like so. We bend up, like so.'

Hettie was awed by Nora's fearlessness. She was always mouthy at the pit with the lads, but this was a gentleman and a London one at that. Yet it seemed to have no effect upon her. Hettie resolved to be more like Nora, if she ever had occasion to.

'There is much to study, my dear,' he went on, unfazed. 'I'm fascinated by all aspects of your lives. From the details of your labour, the skills you demonstrate, the manner of your dress, your travel habits, et cetera, et cetera.'

The girls had stopped their work now and stared at the man, one and all. One or two had giggled at first, but now all smirking had passed and their faces were quite serious.

The gentleman spoke again: 'Are there any pit-wenches amongst you?'

'Aye!' cried Edna.

There was a general nodding and mutterings of, 'That be true.'

Nora added, 'We all be. Every one of us. Most of us have worked on the pit bank most of our days.'

'And you travel here in the summer months, when pit work is slack, is that right?'

Everyone nodded and agreed.

'And what do you do with the money you earn here?' he went on. Then turning to Edna, he said, 'Do you use it for a dowry for your sweetheart?'

Edna giggled and it was infectious. Lots of the girls tittered then and some covered their mouths in embarrassment. Nora was not smiling, but Hettie could not help it. The gentleman had a wicked little grin on his face and it had set them all off.

'No, sir,' managed Edna between snorts of laughter. 'Leastways, not yet.'

'And you?' said the gentleman and turned his eyes directly on Hettie. She felt rooted to the spot. Was he really talking to her?

'Me, sir?' she said quietly.

'Yes, my dear. What will you spend your money on?'

'I shall give it to my father,' Hettie said, straightening up. It was the truth and it pained her, but she wanted to give an honest answer. She knew no other way in life but to speak the truth.

'And buy a pretty dress for the fair,' said Ada, a saucy look on her face.

The gentleman said, 'Ah now, that is far more interesting. You wish to impress the young men at the fair, my dear?' he said to Hettie, looking at her directly again. She could see now that he was quite young, perhaps only in his twenties. She had to look away from those eyes. There was something dangerous about them.

'I might buy a dress,' she said quietly. 'But if I do, it shall be for myself. It inna to impress boys.'

She surprised herself by speaking back to the man, but he seemed impressed with her response. He stepped closer to her, wending his way into the field itself to stand before her.

'Quite right,' he said and smiled. 'You are young. Have you come here before?'

'My first year,' she said. 'And this be my first day in the field.' The other girls were muttering now and falling back to their work, glancing at Hettie and the man as they continued to talk.

'Even though you've just arrived, I suppose you must be heartily sick of strawberries after eating them all day, my dear.'

'Oh no, sir. We inna allowed to eat the fruit.'

'You've been picking strawberries and haven't tasted one? Not one?'

'No, sir.'

'Well, then, we must see what we can do about that.'

He looked about him, then turned from Hettie and walked over to the packing shed and had a quick word with one of the women there. He passed her some coins and she gave him a pottle. He brought it back. Hettie watched him approach her and glanced at Ada, who had a sly smile on her face.

Ada whispered behind her hand, 'He be sweet on you, Hettie. Sweets for his sweet!'

'Hush your noise, Ada!' said Hettie, then turned to see him holding out the pottle to her.

'For you, my dear. A whole punnet for you to eat yourself.'

'I canna take a gift from a stranger,' said Hettie, shaking her head. 'Thank'ee all the same.'

'Thank'ee, thank'ee! What a charming phrase! Oh, but you must, my dear. And I am no stranger now, for we have been talking. Please, do take it and share with your friend, if you like. I can see she wants some.'

He smiled at Ada, who was agog at the idea, eyeing the large, juicy toppers. So, Hettie took the pottle and nodded a thank you to the man. She passed some to Ada, who grabbed a couple and immediately started munching away. Hettie offered one to the gentleman, who shook his head and said, 'No, not for me. All for you, my dear. It is a crime that you should have to pick these beautiful, ripe fruits all day and not have the pleasure of partaking in them. Please, go ahead.'

Hettie felt embarrassed now, eating in front of this gentleman, and wished she could save them for later. But he was waiting for her, and it seemed rude to disappoint him. So, she took a strawberry and raised it to her mouth, blushing all the while, then took a bite. The soft sweetness exploded in her mouth and filled it with pleasure. A little juice escaped and she had to wipe her lips with the back of her hand. The gentleman looked on appreciatively.

'Does it taste good?' he said.

Hettie's mouth was filled with strawberry, so she merely nodded.

'I'm so glad. You girls work so hard, you deserve a treat.'

Hettie swallowed down the fruit and said, 'Thank'ee again for your kindness, sir.'

'The pleasure was all mine,' he said, smiling. Then he fished about in his inside pocket and brought out a little silver case, which sprang open as he touched a clasp. Inside was a pile of tiny pieces of card. He took one out, put away the case and handed the card to her.

'Can you read?' he said, with no hint of embarrassment about asking such a personal question.

'I can indeed, sir,' Hettie answered, with some pride.

'Good. Then you'll see my name and address on there. If you ever come in to central London, or if you ever find yourself in any kind of need of assistance, I hope you will consider me an old friend and seek me out.'

Hettie thought it unlikely that this might ever come to pass, but she merely nodded and held the card awkwardly before her in one stiff hand, the pottle of strawberries in the other. Above the man's address in London, the card was headed with three words in flowing, elaborate script: *Laurence Maxwell Ripley*.

'Good day, Miss . . . to whom do I have the pleasure of speaking?'

At first she wasn't sure what he meant, then worked out he must be asking for her name.

'Hettie Jones,' she said.

'Well, then, Miss Hettie Jones, I bid you and all you ladies farewell, until next time,' he said, removed his hat with a flourish and gave a little bow.

Hettie watched him walk away, then heard Ada snort with laughter the second he had gone through the gate and disappeared behind the hedge, the only sign of him being his hat bobbing along the path away from them.

'Ooh, he was all over you, Hettie!'

'What rot!' said Hettie.

'A gentleman admirer! I never did!'

'Oh, do stop your noise!'

Ada took another couple of fruits from Hettie and laughed again, staring at her now.

'You like him! I can tell! You be all crowsty about it. A sure sign!'

But their argument was abruptly ended by Nora calling out across the field for them to get on with their work. She approached and added rather spitefully, 'Now the King of England's gone, you might have time to pick some fruit, eh?'

Hettie put down her own fruit to save them for later. She took another look at the gentleman's card, then placed it carefully into her pocket, hoping it wouldn't be too damaged by the time she had the chance to look at it again that evening. For she knew she would be looking at it again, and again.

She went back to picking, trying to fall into a rhythm of it in order to take her mind off the extraordinary meeting she'd just had. But she couldn't stop thinking about it, about the sweet, luscious taste of the strawberries, the pure white, clean and unblemished card, and about the gentleman with those eyes, Mr Laurence Maxwell Ripley.

Chapter 7

The days and nights went on just as the first one, long hours in the field, short hours in the evening, then sleeping the sleep of the dead at night. Hettie bonded with the others in her sleeping hut and they told each other long stories of the boys they loved and hated. Hettie did not once speak of Evan. It seemed wrong. Ada mentioned him from time to time, with a twinkle in her eye, but Hettie did not react. Evan was private to her, nobody's business but her own.

After a month in the fields, Hettie was chosen to take the fruit to market. Much to her annoyance, she was not permitted to go with Ada, who had been chosen to go another day. Nora was there, and two other girls who Hettie did not get on with so well. She felt out of sorts about the whole thing and was not looking forward to it.

Mid-morning came and she was called to the hut to load up. The large baskets were filled with pottles and she put a folded cloth on her head – the same kind she always used for carrying the ironstone, but this one was new and clean, brought from home. The basket was weighty but no more so than the ironstone. It fitted quite comfortably on her head and off they went, Nora in front with the other girls, Hettie behind, alone.

The day was warm but not sweltering. Even so, it was a hard trek from the market gardens near Isleworth to the busy streets of central London and their destination, Covent Garden. They walked down long lanes flanked by fields, that soon gave way to more and more housing, more and more people, as the way grew wearier and hotter. Hettie's neck began aching about halfway and got worse and worse by the time they walked through the busier streets of the city. But the sights she saw fascinated her, and took her mind off the pain.

Ironbridge and the surrounding towns were busy, especially on market days, but London was something else. The people flowed through it like a river, a mucky, jumbled river full of flotsam and jetsam. Hettie wondered who they all were, where they were all going, what they were all thinking. There were hawkers and pedlars and costermongers everywhere, who Hettie and the others had to manoeuvre their way around, stepping into the gutter at times in order to avoid them. Hettie's biggest fear was that she would lose her balance and the basket would topple, so she steadied it with her hands from time to time, whenever she had to avoid people barging past.

The street sellers were fascinating though, selling all manner of goods: cough lozenges, dolls, buns, pipe tobacco, combs, ornaments, flowers, books, chirping birds in cages, healing ointment and harmonicas. There were street musicians on every corner, playing everything from accordions to penny whistles, and there was one boy in a cap too large for his head strumming quite tunefully on a full-size harp.

Also evident on the streets was the appalling poverty of the metropolis. There were people grovelling on the ground for scraps outside eateries and being kicked or stepped on by passers-by. Hettie saw a mother with twin babies sitting almost comatose on some steps, the babies crying weakly and the mother as thin as a sapling. Hettie felt sickened by it and looked away. She felt very fortunate that she had her family and her friends to support her, and that she lived in a small town where people looked out for each other, not in a sprawling, uncaring city like London, as thrilling as it was to walk through its streets.

At last, after over three hours of walking, Nora announced that they would soon be approaching Covent Garden market and that they should, as ever, remain together at all times. Horses clip-clopped by, jingling their harnesses, pulling a bewildering variety of vehicles behind them in the streets. As they passed by, they threw up great clouds of dust that lingered in the warm air and settled on Hettie's clothes and face and irritated her eyes. As the market drew nearer, the roads tapered and thus grew busier and more chaotic. The passages leading to the main square of the market were very narrow indeed, causing vendors to jostle and argue with each other over space. Hettie held onto her basket in alarm, lest all should be lost. Yet, eventually, they were allowed to pass through and into the market proper.

It stretched out across the piazza and was a sight to behold. Every manner of fruit and vegetable could be seen, ranged on stalls peopled by noisy sellers. The air was filled with the thrum of humanity, pierced by the calls and songs of the vendors shouting out their wares and their bargain prices. Two girls laden with flowers in baskets strolled past her, one singing out 'Two bundles a penny, primroses!' while the other called, 'Sweet violets, penny a bunch!' The scent of the flowers, as well as that of a thousand foodstuffs, mingled with the sharp notes of soot, smoke and the stench of animal dung and foul mess in the street gutters all about. Hettie felt her eyes widen like saucers as she struggled to take in the rambling madness of it all, as well as keep her wits about her and follow Nora and the others to their spot.

It turned out their masters had a stall at the western edge of the piazza, so they negotiated their way through the thronging crowds in that direction to find a sleepy and wrinkled old woman selling the few pieces of fruit she had left, and who was very pleased to see them. At last, they could remove the baskets from their heads and place them down onto the stall. The little old lady had looked half-dead when they arrived, but she soon perked up. As she reorganised the stall, she lifted her chin and began to sing out, 'Ripe strawberries! A groat a pottle, today. Only a groat a pottle, is what I say!' The voice that issued from the old woman was high, sweet and clear as a bell, and Hettie was surprised at the pure, angelic sound issuing from such a wizened vessel.

Nora told the others to wait there while she bought them something to eat. Hettie passed the time by watching the buyers of London flock past to haggle with the sellers, easing her neck ache by rubbing it with her sweaty hand. Covent Garden was quite the spectacle, and she was glad she'd seen it.

Ada had told her about the young men hereabouts, and Hettie looked out for them. Opposite was a collection of flower stalls and a group of men busied themselves in hats and caps, brown jackets or waistcoats and shirtsleeves, picking up blooms and placing them in baskets to take to other stalls or deliver to girls who carried them about, singing. Their faces were weathered and bronzed by the outdoors, unlike Evan and the other miners who were pale from working underground. They looked healthier for it, just as Hettie and her fellow pit-wenches and strawberry pickers did – working outside gave you that healthful glow. Ever since Evan had started working down the mine, Hettie had had a dreadful fear of the underworld, as she called it, when they talked of conditions under-ground. 'How goes the underworld?' she'd say to him, when they were walking home of an evening. 'Deathly and dull,' Evan would reply.

Evan . . . the thought of him gave her an ache in her belly, made worse by her hunger. Where was Nora with their food? She watched the flower boys move with ease and confidence, one catching her eye and winking at her. She turned quickly away. He was a good-looking lad; they all were. But they could not hold a candle to her Evan. Or indeed to Mr Laurence Maxwell Ripley.

Nora returned with slices of pie filled with some indeterminate pale meat, probably some sort of offal. They were tasty and hugely welcome. She also got them beer to drink and apples to put in their pockets for later.

That done, it was time to start the walk home. At least their baskets were lighter now, empty save for yesterday's pottles which they stacked up inside. The walk back was easier, of course, with less weight, but Hettie's feet were wearier. She thought about her bed on the straw most of the way out of the city and into the suburbs, looking forward to the moment when she could acquaint herself with sleep again. There was some idle chatter with the others, but the three of them knew each other better than they knew her and she felt too tired to make the effort with conversation and yet also disappointed that none of them tried to engage with her. But mostly, she was too drained to think. She plodded on, following Nora's striding gait, as ever.

They were about two miles or so from Isleworth when she heard her name spoken aloud, her full name, preceded by the word 'Miss'. It was so odd to hear that she thought she must have imagined it and almost dismissed it, until there it came again.

'Miss Hettie Jones?'

She turned around and saw that the gentleman, Mr Laurence Maxwell Ripley, had appeared behind them and was striding up to her. She knew she ought to be polite and say how do you do, or some such thing, but she was so astonished to see him again that she merely stared at him.

He stopped before her and gave her a quizzical smile. 'I am addressing Miss Hettie Jones, am I not?'

'Why, yes,' she managed, her voice dry from not talking or drinking since London. She cleared her throat.

'I knew it was. I never forget a face, certainly not one as memorable as yours. It's Mr Ripley, from some weeks ago. I visited your field and gave you my card?'

Hettie stared at him. Then she realised that Nora and the others had not seen her stop; they were far ahead of her on the road towards the fields.

'I mun . . . I mun go,' she said, and turned to trot off in their direction, feeling a fool for such a graceless exit – but in truth she had not concentrated on the walk to London and so was afraid she would lose her way back.

But Mr Ripley soon caught up with her. 'I assume you are returning to the fields from London?'

'Yes, sir,' she said, peeking at him, then immediately looking away. Those eyes. He was not a tall man; in fact, he was exactly the same size as her, slight of figure, with black hair that emerged from his hat in dark sideburns and a few locks that escaped across his forehead from under the brim.

'Please, call me Max. It is not my given name, but a corruption of my middle name. Everybody calls me Max.'

Hettie said, 'I canna call you that!' His boldness with her had given her an ounce of courage to answer him back. What was he thinking, accosting her in the street and asking her to call him by a nickname? She was glad she wasn't in Ironbridge. Imagine the gossip!

'Of course, of course. My mistake. Mr Ripley, then? That is proper, surely.'

'If you say so,' she said, hurrying to catch up with Nora and the others.

'Miss Jones, I was wondering if I could talk to you as we walk. I was actually on my way to visit your field to discuss something with you ladies when I saw you. A happy accident.'

'Discuss what?' she said.

'I believe I mentioned to you something of my work.'

'I didna think gentlemen did any work,' she said and smiled at her own cheek. She was warming to this now, talking to a gentleman and giving him a bit of trouble about it.

He chuckled. 'Well, yes, you are quite right. It certainly is not work in the sense of what you achieve each and every week of the year, Miss Jones. Indeed not. But I do my best to make myself useful in the world. As I mentioned, I am studying the working women of England. Their work, their habits, their dress, and so forth. I am interviewing as many as I can and making sketches of them, as well as taking notes on everything I can find out. I was wondering if you would allow me to ask you about your work as you walk back to the fields.'

'If you're strolling the same way,' said Hettie, 'I canna stop you.'

She glanced at him and they shared a smile.

'Splendid!' he said.

The last few streets of the village near the farmland thinned out and soon they were on the long, dusty path back. As they walked, Mr Ripley asked Hettie a series of questions about her work at the pit, the hours, the conditions, and so on, as well as detailed queries about how they travelled to Isleworth, their working times and what they did in the evenings. She liked the timbre of his voice; it was quite low and mellow and it took her mind off her aching feet. He seemed genuinely fascinated by her kind and yet was not overly enthusiastic, remaining a little reserved, which made her want to please him more, to bring forth his praise. From time to time he said extraordinary things, calling the pit-wenches 'courageous women' and describing the walk they did to Covent Garden market with the baskets full of strawberries on their heads as 'the stuff of heroes'.

After a while he returned to the subject of her work on the pit bank.

'And how do you find it, Miss Jones? Is it not a hardship to be outside all through the winter?'

'I like it fine,' she said. 'It is healthful, being outside. And we wrap up proper warm when we need to.'

'Did you know that a few years ago there actually took place a government enquiry into the degradation of women working on the pit bank?'

'The *what* of women?' Hettie had had some schooling and thought herself quite bright, but she had never heard that word before or anything like it.

'Ah, forgive me. The report complained that the women should not be working on the pit bank, as it was shameful. In some parts of the country women wear trousers to do this work, and it was felt by some to be immoral. They feared the women mixing with the male miners could become indecent.'

'I dunna understand all of what you said, but I think it a good job for a woman. I canna fathom why some people hundreds of miles from us want to stop it.'

'There was a concern that women working outside in such jobs would become too independent and unfeminine.'

'And what is wrong with being independent? A woman at home has to work every day of her life without a helping hand, and yet at work she is expected not to be able to look after herself? Sounds like rot to me. But will they win? What shall we do without our jobs if they do?'

'No, indeed. The enquiry found in favour of allowing women to continue. The report showed no evidence that women working on the pit bank were . . . how to say it . . . lacking in morals or decency.'

'How could they think it? All us pit bank women are decent and upstanding! And if we didna work there, we might end up in the workhouse, or worse. Many of our number are the children of miners and some are widows of miners, who wouldna be able to keep their own children if they didna do this work.'

'I agree with you. It was a badly conceived enquiry. We can only be grateful that common sense prevailed. After all, why should any woman be prevented from earning an honest wage? I for one am delighted to see women working outdoors. It's healthy work, better than being cooped up inside. I do believe women should indeed have been banned from working underground in the mines: it is indecent to be in mixed company down there with so much . . . well, to be frank, so much nudity.'

Hettie felt her cheeks colour. Everybody knew that miners stripped off to work in the terrible heat down there, but it was too much to hear the word 'nudity' from this gentleman in general conversation. He seemed to sense her embarrassment, as he glanced at her and coughed nervously.

'My opinion is that pit bank wenches such as yourself have a perfectly respectable profession. It is a joy to see you all so hale and hearty and full of confidence and independence.'

'I agree,' said Hettie. 'And I'm proper glad those fools who tried to stop it were beaten!'

'Me too, Miss Jones. Me too.'

They were now nearing the farm gates that led to the strawberry fields. Hettie would have to finish her shift there before she could rest. She felt exhausted all of a sudden, and realised that the entire time she had been talking to the gent, she had not noticed her sore feet or her weariness. She had been transported to a different world for a short time in her monotonous working day.

'I mun go now, sir,' she said, noticing that Nora and the others were eyeing her coldly. It seemed they did not approve of her conversing with such a man. *Most likely just green with envy*, thought Hettie.

'Miss Jones, I want to thank you for your kindness in talking with me today. Your answers have provided an excellent level of detail for my studies. I am so very grateful.'

'You're welcome,' said Hettie quietly, allowing herself now to look him square in the face. She wanted to look at those eyes for a long time.

'You have my card. Remember what I said. If you ever are in need of assistance, please do not hesitate to get in touch. It would be my pleasure to see you again.'

'Thank'ee,' she said, and bobbed a curtsey.

'Oh, Miss Jones, please. There is no need to do that. We are equals, you and I. In fact, I would propose that you are my superior; I play at working, and yet you are the true worker. You labour to bring us not only the iron from the earth but also the fruit of the land. I have great admiration for the working women of this country and that is why I study them. Thank you again.'

'Hettie!' cried Nora. Her face looked like thunder. 'Hurry up, child.'

'Coming,' called Hettie. She did not wish to displease Nora and the others, but oh, how little did she want to go back to the field and end this conversation. 'Goodbye then, Mr Ripley.'

'Farewell, Miss Jones. Until another time, I hope.'

He smiled at her and she smiled back. Then he turned away and walked back the way they'd come.

Hettie rushed onwards to join up with Nora, who gave her a sharp look and said, 'Evan Malone wouldna like the sight of that, you all familiar with a gent.'

Hettie's cheeks burned as she walked on. She wanted to argue with Nora, but she knew that Nora was their self-appointed leader as well as her hut mate, and she didn't want to get on her wrong side. The truth was that nothing was set in stone with Evan, was it? People just assumed it. And anyway, the gentleman had a professional interest in Hettie – that was all. And now it was done and she would never see him again.

As they reached the gate to the field, she turned to look at him once more. She saw him, Mr Lawrence Maxwell Ripley, strolling away down that dusty road, banked by fields of strawberries on one side and orchards of apple trees and gooseberry bushes on the other. The late-afternoon sun ahead of him hit the trees and made them glow, his shadow lengthening behind him.

All this was burned into her memory like a painting – a moving one, filled with life and longing.

Chapter 8

September 1875

It was the first week of September and the sun was rising over a still, clear day that promised much. Hettie was up before the sun that day; she had her chores to do before she could thoroughly wash all the dust and grime from herself in good time for leaving for the fair. She made her father a breakfast of eggs and yesterday's bread and roused him from his sleep. She encouraged him to breakfast well, as he often did not eat again until the evening. He had grown worse while she'd been away in London, and had been resentful and needy at first when she returned. But she'd now been back a full week, and he was growing kinder to her and was drinking less. She was pleased to see his progress.

'Come on then, Father,' she encouraged him, brushing off the suit she'd bought him especially for the fair. Her own new dress hung in her bedroom, pristine, ready to make its debut out in the world.

Once he was ready, she said, 'You scrub up well!' and her father grinned.

'Go get yourself ready then, wench,' he said. 'I canna wait to see you in your new frock. You'll be the belle of the ball.'

She smiled and went into her room. There it was, her London dress, as she thought of it. The money from all her summer work had paid for a few things around the house, as well as her father's suit and this dress. It was worth the months of labour to see him handsome and smiling. It was also worth it for the experience of being away from home and seeing the world through new eyes. She was now someone who had left their town and journeyed to bigger, brighter things, and coming back to Ironbridge somehow made everything at home look small. Hettie didn't think this in a critical way, but suddenly the parameters of her experience had widened and she felt her life as it had been was narrowed.

And the summer of work had also brought something else: Mr Laurence Maxwell Ripley. She could not stop thinking of him, although she knew it was pointless. She only met him twice, and it was months ago now. But she had never met such a person and she knew he had turned her head.

She had not been to see Evan and the rest of the Malones since her return. Indeed, she had not seen them now in person for several months. She had moved on from them and their sphere of influence so much since she'd left for London and she felt like a different person, a new creature, emerged from the cocoon of her Malone years. She was blossoming into a fresh incarnation.

Now, Hettie stood in her bedroom, gazing at her new dress. It was made of panels of dusky pink and pale green, with neat little pink roses on green backing here and there. The bodice hugged her frame snugly, with an open neck suited to the warm weather, fringed with green ruffles. The skirt was formed of layers of material, alternating pink and green, with an underskirt striped in both colours, a slice of which could be peeked at the front. There were two large green bows, one at the lower back and another beneath the bust. The sleeves were three-quarter length and close-fitting. The whole dress was fashioned from a fine cotton, which made it light and easy to wear in the summer heat. She could not afford new shoes to wear with it, and the walk to the railway station and from there around the fair would make them impractical anyhow. So, Hettie had polished up her best boots to a shine instead.

She dressed her hair simply, held up at the sides and front with pins, while the rest tumbled down her back. She was proud of her light brown hair and her green eyes and wanted to show them off today. The colour of her dress enhanced them. She took it down from the hanger and laid it out on the bed. It was the most precious thing she had ever owned. And she was thrilled she had bought it with her own money, earned by her own hands. She stepped into the skirt and buttoned it at the waist, followed by the bodice, which she fastened all down the front, loving the feel of the tiny buttons slipping through the holes, each one decorated with a single pink rose bloom. They were the most beautiful buttons she had ever seen, let alone worn.

She had no full-length mirror to view herself, so she took a hand mirror to hold at various angles to see the shapes her figure made against the drab background of her room. What she saw thrilled her; she was indeed a new person in this stunning dress. She felt a stab of nerves at the thought of being seen in public in such fashion and how it would surely bring the gaze of others, something she'd never craved before. She hated to be the centre of attention in anything, but she was proud, too, that she would be a beauty at the fair, and who knew what that beauty would bring her?

But there was a kernel of disappointment that Mr Laurence Maxwell Ripley would never see her in this dress. He'd only seen her in her dowdy work clothes with the home-made apron and her hair in a mess from her labour. But she must put thoughts of him from her mind today and focus instead on enjoying the thrills of the fair.

She left her room and went to find her father, whose face looked pained.

'The image of your mother,' he said with a choked sob. 'The very image!'

'I am so happy to hear that,' she said, and gave him a kiss on the cheek.

'She would be so proud.' He dried his eyes, smiling broadly now as he looked her over again. 'And so am I. My beautiful girl.'

She linked arms with him. 'Come, let us go out and make merry.'

They took the train to the fair. It was worth the small expense, as she did not wish to muddy her dress on the long walk. They strolled arm in arm to Madeley Market station, where they caught the train that went through Stirchley and Mallinslee before arriving at Oakengates Market Street station. The carriages were stuffed with fairgoers, the men in their Sunday best and the ladies in their new dresses. Hettie found many a face turned towards her, the women in approbation or envy, the men with something else in their eyes. Her dress was demure, but it hugged her figure perfectly, and she felt their eyes trace her curves. Her father spoke to some of the other men on the train, while she looked out of the window, keeping her thoughts to herself. She had not seen Evan for months, and wondered what he'd make of her. The thought troubled and excited her in equal measure. For all that the London gentleman had turned her head, another part of her still wanted Evan to think she looked nice.

From the station, it was a short walk to the fairground. All paths were thronged with fairgoers and a noisy hubbub of excited gossip. The Oakengates fair was held at the same time as the Wakes, a series of entertainments that took place over several days in September. The fair was the highlight for most people, a feast of superior food and drink, attended by every family, every lad and lass, every labourer and maid alike, folk coming in from all over the county. Some workers were given the full day off work for the fair, and those who were not would rise early, so that before dawn on the day of the fair a passing field mouse would be surprised to see plough-men out on the fields completing their work, so that they could finish early and attend the fair.

All along the main street, Hettie walked arm in arm with her father, who was beaming his pride at every passer-by. They saw stalls set up with every sort of good thing to eat for sale. There were little cakes, oranges, hot sausages and buns, with many a stall selling different varieties of ale and sweet drinks such as ginger beer and lemonade. They stopped and bought some gingerbread to munch on, one of their favourites.

The throng thickened as they approached the entrance to the fair itself. The air was filled with the sounds of celebration: music emanating in waves across the ever-warming late-summer air, mixing and jangling with the shouts of sellers and the air of hilarity from the revellers. Hettie scanned the crowd for the Malones. She'd received a message through a mutual friend that they would all meet at the coconut gallery at some point during the morning, and Hettie was eager to see them, if a little anxious, too. She had missed them all over the summer, and she wanted them to see her new dress.

But before they found the shy, her father spent a few pennies taking her on a roundabout, which whipped them round at quite a rate and made Hettie cry out in delight, her father laughing heartily. How good it was to see him laugh! She caught a glimpse of the whole man he must once have been, before life took him up so roughly and broke him.

From the raised height of the roundabout, Hettie spotted the coconut shy, and after they'd finished their ride she led her father in that direction. The Malones were not there yet, so Hettie bought her and her father a strawberry ice in a glass cup each, which they licked out until not a vestige remained, handing the cups back to the stall when they were done.

'Hettie!' called a deep voice, and she turned to see a tall young man walking towards her.

She was astonished to realise it was Evan. He had had a phenomenal growth spurt over the summer, and now his sixteen years – soon to be seventeen in October – looked more like twenty. He had turned into a man in her absence. He looked inches taller, his voice had lowered considerably and he had the hint of a pale beard about his jaw. His blond hair was thicker and darker, his neck bulged with a prominent Adam's apple that she had never noticed and his legs looked longer and broader. As he strode towards her, she could not take her eyes from him. He too was gazing at her with intention and fascination. He looked her all over, his eyes bluer than ever in the sunshine. She was so thrilled to see him she could not stop herself, and threw her arms about him. He laughed and hugged her back, hard and urgent. She stepped back, alarmed at her rash behaviour, unbecoming to her smart dress. But nobody around them seemed to care; everyone was too busy with their own merrymaking.

'Hettie, my dear!' came Anny's voice, and soon the whole Malone tribe were upon them, the twins hugging her waist, Flora touching her hair and the tiny roses on her dress with a grin. Anny and Peter gave her warm hugs and kisses, and many a pat on the shoulder was given to Adam, who Hettie was proud to see stood beaming and chatting good-naturedly with Peter. *Perhaps this will be the turning point*, thought Hettie, *the moment where Father sees the error of his ways and stops drinking forever*. Perhaps they would look back on the day of the Oakengates fair as the time when everything changed for the better.

'Come with me,' said Evan, taking her hand. Hettie nodded eagerly, and a quick glance at her father in the company of the Malones reassured her that he would be in good hands. She could go and have some of her own fun. Evan pulled her onwards, into the heaving crowds, his large, manly hand clasping her own, warm and sticky in the rising heat.

'Where are we going?' she said, and Evan replied, 'You'll see.'

Then there they were at the swing-boats, which rocked back and forth at an alarming height and pace.

'Is it safe?' she asked Evan.

'Course,' he said and squeezed her arm.

While they waited for the current ride to finish, they suddenly became aware of each other and Hettie stepped away from him slightly. There was an awkwardness between them, different from the distance they'd had since she left, the opposite of their childhood closeness. There was something in the air that vibrated with meaning. It was attraction. Hettie looked up at him, now so much taller than her. He was no longer just her Evan – he was a young man and he was staring at her. When their eyes met, a message flashed between them, so exquisitely painful she had to look away.

'Your dress . . .' Evan began. He was never very good with words, and she waited patiently for him to form them. 'Your dress is the prettiest thing I ever saw.'

'Thank you,' she said and did a little curtsey, which made them both laugh and broke the spell a little.

Then, the swing-boat man called for new customers as the ride came to an end and its occupants dismounted. Evan took Hettie's hand to climb in. She did not need it, being a pit bank girl who clambered on steep slopes in all weathers, but it was nice to feel his hand again. They snuggled up on the slatted wooden seat and were joined by another pair opposite, a young courting couple. Before the boats began to swing, the young man opposite had his arm around his girl and was whispering things in her ear that made her giggle. Hettie glanced at Evan and they both burst out laughing. They were embarrassed and amused, but there was also a hint of envy as they glanced back at the couple, just before the boat began to move.

As it rose higher and its angle grew steeper, Hettie found herself reaching up to grasp Evan's arm. He swiftly drew it out and around her, pulling her in close so her head was beneath his shoulder and the whole length of her frame pressed into his side. The thrill of the ride mingled with the thrill of their closeness. How much Evan had changed was foremost in her mind. She had gone to London and left him a boy. She had returned to a man. The boats went higher still and she felt his arm clutching her closer. The females in the boats were squealing, the men laughing or cheering. The air rushed past Hettie's face, taking her breath away, while the feel of Evan holding her made her feel safe. She did not turn her face to look at him, as the ride made all small movements impossible, but she felt his presence course through her as the boats reached their top height and speed. She held onto him tightly and though the ride made her feel giddy, she wished it would never stop and she could stay in his arms with a good excuse for doing so.

After the rush of the swing-boats, her head felt light when she stepped out onto solid ground again. Evan smiled at her and she found herself laughing; she felt as if she had been drinking ale. Evan laughed too and took her hand again, leading her off into the crowd.

They stopped at a stall selling sausages and bought some with onions and bread, a delicious, hot, spicy treat. They ate noisily, talking about the local gossip, Evan giving her some choice facts about lads and lasses he saw passing by, telling her what she'd missed while she'd been in London. Their awkwardness was waning now, replaced by the ease they once had, but peppered with their physical awareness of each other. How good it was to be with him in this easy way again.

'So, how was strawberry picking then?' he asked, polishing off the last of his food and wiping the crumbs from his mouth.

'It was proper hard work. Nearly broke my back, all that bending and carrying. And walking ten miles or so to the market with the basket on your head. And standing in the hot sun in the fields all day. The huts we slept in were proper simple, just straw on the floor.'

'Sounds like hell,' said Evan.

'Not really. It was hard. But it was fun, too, messing about with the other wenches after dark. And going into London was proper jam!'

Evan made a face and said, 'I always thought London sounded like a drodsome place. Just the word sounds horrible.'

'Oh, it had its bad points, surely. There were some poor souls in the streets that looked like ghosts, so thin they were, with eyes that looked black and wide, like holes in their faces. Fair broke my heart. You dunna see that round here in the same way, except at the work-house perchance. There's a fair amount of those around. But the market was full of life and the living. All sorts of colour and noise and smells, and people from all over. It was something to see, it truly was.'

'Sounds better here,' was all Evan wished to say on that matter.

Hettie felt disappointed with his response. She wanted to impress him and delight him with all the details. But he was not interested. Or perhaps it was something else.

Then he said, 'You meet anyone there? Anyone turn your head, eh?'

Hettie knew he was just teasing her, but an image of Laurence Maxwell Ripley leapt to her mind and she felt her cheeks go hot.

'You did!' he said, looking more closely.

'I didna!' she cried, and turned away. 'Who would I meet working in the fields all day? Dunna be daft.'

'You were blushing.' He stepped round her, so that she had to face him. 'Did you meet someone?'

'I've given my answer. Now stop badgering me, Evan Malone! Let's see more of the fair.'

She grasped his hand and led the way this time, straight to the shooting gallery. It would be good if Evan could impress her with his aim. It might take his mind off what had just happened. But Hettie could not stop thinking of it, of Mr Ripley and of Evan. She had built the gentleman into an object of perfection in her mind, but Evan was Evan, and she knew that what she felt for him ran deep. Watching him raise the weapon and expertly hit the target, winning her a posy of artificial flowers, Hettie felt a thrill. Mr Ripley had those dark eyes, but Evan had this body, a body that worked hard and showed it in its curves and dips. Looking at his strong arms made her feel a little faint, and she had to look away.

They strolled on as the sun rose higher in the sky, passing by clowns, an Aunt Sally and a test-your-strength machine; men boxing and women dancing; boys assaulting people with water pistols and screaming with laughter at their antics. For a while they watched a man walking on a high wire with a net beneath him, which was thrilling and bizarre. Hettie could not believe her eyes; it seemed impossible that a person could walk on something so narrow. She laughed with Evan and they held hands and talked. All in all, a perfect day.

They were strolling back towards the coconut shy to see if the other Malones and her father were there when a commotion broke out nearby and a man fell to the ground before them.

'Ignore it,' said Evan, manoeuvring her gently out of the way as the man scrambled on the floor. 'Just some drunken fools.'

But someone was shouting at the man, who was standing up now, brushing himself off and shouting back. Hettie looked up to see where the noise was coming from. There, beside a beer stall, upon which was a nine-gallon cask of beer and a mess of dirty mugs, was her father.

He was pointing at the man on the ground and cursing him in the most filthy language, worse than any miner on a bad day. His face was distorted with anger and beer, his cheeks a deep red, his eyes swimming, his movements erratic. The horror of seeing her father that way in front of everyone at the fair rooted her to the spot. She knew she should go to him, but she dreaded having to admit to all around them that he was related to her. The day had been wonderful, her dress was beautiful and Evan was everything. And now, here was her only kin making a spectacle and ruining everything. A drunken fool, as Evan had said, before they realised her own father was involved.

Evan seemed to read her mind, as he always had. 'I'll deal with him. You go.'

'No,' she said. 'No.'

She couldn't desert him. She'd promised her mother. She went to him, Evan behind her saying, 'Hettie,

147

Hettie.' But she went on, pushing her way through a gaggle of other drunks holding mugs of beer, which slopped this way and that. One man tripped sideways as she came through and raised his voice at her, lurching towards her, his beer sloshing up in a great splash which landed right on Hettie's front, soaking her green bow and staining her bodice a dirty brown. She stopped and looked down at her dress in horror. Her beautiful dress – ruined!

Things moved very quickly then. The man was in Evan's grip within a moment and she looked up to see Evan land a fist on his cheek. He was floored in an instant. She saw her father's face, confused and alarmed, raising his mug and shouting about how it was just a bit of fun. She grasped his mug and threw it to the ground, then took his arm and manhandled him out of there, ducking the men, who were now in a chaotic fist fight. Evan was in the centre, taking no prisoners, punching out every man that came near him.

'Evan!' she cried, trying to hold her father up. He now looked like he was going to collapse. He lurched forward, nearly toppling her, then fell onto all fours and vomited copiously onto the ground. People walking by gave him a wide berth, laughing, shaking their heads, gasping and complaining. Hettie felt as if she would die of humiliation.

She looked round to see Evan step away from three men groaning on the ground, wiping his hands on his waistcoat. He always had been handy with his fists. Now he was tall and strapping, he had finished them off with no trouble.

Hettie stood, her dress stinking of beer, her father still coughing up half-digested beer which ran in rivulets through the dusty ground, his new suit wrecked as he grovelled there.

Evan took her arm and said, 'Go find Mother. I'll deal with him. And after this, you mun leave this fool forever and come home to us. You've done your best by him. But home is where you belong, with us. With me, Hettie.'

Chapter 9

The trees lining the road up to the Southover plot were dressed in rich autumn colours. Copper-coloured leaves drifted down as the carriage climbed the hill. Queenie regarded the outside world largely with mistrust these days, yet she was surprised to find that she'd enjoyed the feel of this short journey, from her present home to her real one – for that was the way she thought of Southover: her proper home. It had belonged to her long-dead husband's family, but she had made his family, his name and his legacy all her own, and so she had made Southover her own. The loss of it in the fire went deeper than anyone else knew, and the wound still smarted.

And so, for reasons known only to herself, she had made the decision in January to have Southover rebuilt, and now was the time to inspect its advancement. The carriage's progress up the gravel drive and onto the sweeping frontage of the house was like something from an old dream. How many times she had once done this, and how much she had missed it when it was gone years ago! Jenkins climbed out of the carriage first and came round to open the door for Queenie.

'Do you want to stay in the carriage?' said Jenkins. 'You can see things from there. No need to fuss yourself.'

'No,' said Queenie, firmly. 'I wish to see my house with my feet on the ground.'

Jenkins made a face, which could have been annoyance but which looked a little like pain. Queenie knew Jenkins thought this trip was a bad idea; the weather was unseasonably cold for October, and she had told Queenie to wait until the house was fully finished in the spring. But too much of Queenie's life was left to others to manage and she wanted to do this for herself, to see the progress of her house with her own eyes. She had been looking forward to it for a long time.

Jenkins put out her hand and helped Queenie down the steps onto the gravel. The ruins were long gone and in their place were new foundations, with new walls rising brick by brick. Local bricks, from the King brickyard, of course. Some of the fancier bricks and tiles for patterning around the doors and windows were purchased from her old associates, the Elkins, at their yard that specialised in such designs. The layout of the new house would mirror that of the old one. The architect had tried to convince Queenie to go with a more modern design, but she would not be turned. She wanted the same house, an exact copy, as if the old one had never burned down.

Walking slowly towards it, leaning on Jenkins's arm, she found herself smiling as the shape of her beloved home was forming before her. The builders and other workers had stopped their work and lined up on the gravel with their hats and caps in hand to receive her. She waved them away and said, 'Continue with your work.' They did so, looking relieved that none of them were required to speak to her.

She watched their progress with interest for a while, Jenkins beside her, adjusting Queenie's shawl to keep her warm. The bricklayers fascinated her. She watched them scoop up the mortar and slap it down, placing the bricks so carefully, so perfectly. There was such skill in building a house, yet these poor fellows would never be rich from their skills, as impressive as they were. Queenie made a mental note to instruct the site manager to raise their wages for this job, the surplus of which she would cover. *Always appeasing the ghost of Blaize*, she thought. Or was it that she had truly changed and become a better person? Either way, she was proud these skilful men were making her home, and she wanted them to be rewarded justly for their sacred task.

She moved on and performed a tour of the whole house, walking around it twice to get a feel for how far the building work had come. It would surely be ready for them to move into in the spring. Ah, to see the clouds of white blossom on the hawthorn trees from her bedroom window again – that would be quite something. She pictured it all as she ambled around her own grounds. The garden was overgrown and needed some brutal care. She would engage gardeners soon, to clear the growth of weeds and begin again. Regrowth, renewal and new life all felt like gifts at this late stage of her life. The thought of it made her smile again as she rounded the eastern corner to arrive upon the gravel drive once more, Jenkins beside her for support.

After a while, Queenie's legs began to tire. She was delighted with the progress of the building, and had seen enough. She turned to Jenkins to instruct her to take her back to the coach.

But Jenkins did not seem to hear Queenie's command. She had let go of her mistress's arm and was standing oddly bent over, staring at the ground.

'What is it?' asked Queenie, with alarm.

Jenkins's hands came up suddenly and clutched at her chest. Her face crumpled into an expression that fluctuated between fear and extreme pain.

'Help!' cried Queenie. 'Help us!'

The coachman came running, as did two of the builders. But they were too late to catch Jenkins, whose knees buckled beneath her as she fell forward onto the gravel. Queenie cried out and felt a rush of faintness come over her. She could not kneel down beside her friend to help her. All she could do was cry out, 'Help her! Help her!'

One of the builders was talking to Jenkins, asking her what was wrong, but Jenkins was still clutching at her chest, grimacing, and could not speak.

The coachman stepped over to Queenie and said, 'Come with me, Mrs King. Let's get you safely back in the carriage, eh?'

'But Jenkins!' Queenie cried.

'I can help her better if I know you're safe and sound, ma'am. May I escort you to the carriage? And then we can fetch help and get you home at the same time.'

Queenie was too upset to reply. She allowed herself to be taken by the arm over to the carriage and helped onto the step. Before she got inside, she turned back for another look at Jenkins. Two builders were leaning over her as she lay helplessly on the ground.

'Go straight to the doctor's house,' she told the coachman. 'Do not take me home first.'

'But ma'am . . .' he replied.

'Do as I say!' she said, as loudly as she could manage. She felt feeble and breathless, as if she might pass out at any moment. He helped her onto the seat and closed the door.

Soon they were off, and as the coach rattled across the gravel, Queenie sobbed at the thought of Jenkins left there with only strangers for company, in her hour of direst need. She closed her eyes and slumped against the side of the carriage. She was so upset that she could not bear to look outside.

When the carriage came to a halt, she prepared herself to face the doctor, but saw instead that they were at home. She heard the coachman calling into the house for help. Her anger boiled up that he had dismissed her orders and taken her home instead of helping Jenkins first. She was fully prepared to raise her voice at him or even raise her fists.

But the next thing she knew, she was in someone's arms. She was being carried. A man was carrying her. It was the most extraordinary sensation, of being weightless and helpless, like a child carried by a parent. What on earth was happening?

Then, there was nothing for a time. The next moment of consciousness was waking at night. She called out for Jenkins, wondering if she were still doubled over on the ground at the building site, nobody to help her as the builders would have gone home for their suppers and sleep. But a voice came, and hands. It was not Jenkins. It was Benjamina's maid Clayton, who was talking soothingly, stroking Queenie's forehead. So she closed her eyes and slept again.

The morning came greyly, a thin strip of light through the curtains that someone had not closed properly. Everything was wrong. Nothing was right without Jenkins here. And where was Jenkins? That fool of a coachman had better have got the doctor to her without delay. Jenkins would be recovering there, perhaps, or here, at home. For it was Jenkins's home as sure as it was her own. The woman had devoted her life to this family, to Queenie. Surely Benjamina would have dealt with it all fairly, ensuring the most senior maid in the household was taken care of appropriately.

'Clayton,' said Queenie, her voice dry and almost silent. She cleared her throat and tried again.

The door opened and in came the young woman. She had a nice face. But it was not the right face. She went to the curtains and opened them a few inches to let in more light.

'Now then, ma'am,' she said softly. She came to Queenie, helping her to sit up slightly against her pillows. She held a glass of water to Queenie's lips without even being asked. She seemed to divine that she would be thirsty. Queenie sipped the water gratefully.

'Where is Jenkins?'

'Oh, ma'am,' said Clayton, and her face fell. 'I am ever so sorry, ma'am.'

'No,' said Queenie. 'No!'

'Please stay calm, Mrs King. You need to rest.'

'Where is she? Where is Jenkins?'

'She's with the undertaker, ma'am. The funeral is tomorrow. You've been asleep on and off for two days yourself. I am so very sorry, ma'am. They said it was her heart gave out.'

'Rose,' whispered Queenie.

'She's at peace now, ma'am,' said Clayton. 'Take comfort in that.'

'Rose Jenkins. My oldest friend.'

'Let me fetch your breakfast, ma'am. You'll feel so much better once you've had a bite to eat.'

Queenie turned away from Clayton's young, pitying face and stared at the gap in the curtains. Through it she could see that fog had engulfed the house, as if they were at sea. Her head felt light and airy, as if the fog had wended its way inside her mind as well. She felt utterly lost.

∽

Queenie was incapacitated for over a week, her strength seemingly lost with Jenkins. She slept for the first day, then spent the next one half awake, half asleep. That evening, she was possessed with a sudden fear and called for Benjamina, only to tell her as clearly as she could in her weak voice one thing: that Jenkins must be buried in the King family plot. She said it three times to Benjamina, to ensure the woman listened properly. After this, she told Clayton that she did not wish to see Benjamina again until further notice.

Queenie was not well enough to attend the funeral. The knowledge that she could not say farewell to her friend brought a mild relapse. She would speak to nobody but Clayton. She turned her face often into her pillow and wept. Nothing consoled her. She simply wanted to die. There did not seem any point in continuing with this pointless, overlong life if Jenkins was not there to share it.

And the cruelty of not being able to help her in her final moments or even say goodbye to her at the church was too much for her. She was glad at least that she had ensured Jenkins would be buried in the family plot, which was still situated in the grounds of Southover, tended carefully by a servant from the house. Thus when she recovered she would at least have the meagre comfort of being able to visit her friend's grave whenever she wanted in her own private grounds. Soon, Southover would be her home again and she would be close to Jenkins forever. She would insist that she was buried next to her when her own time came. Queenie thought of the ghost's curses, how frightened she had been of them, how worried she had been for the risk to her life at moments, over the years. Now, she felt that her long survival, living to nearly one hundred, was the curse. Lying there in her bed, too weak to move for much of the day, she wished now that she had been killed in the fire with Margaret. What good had come from her life since then? Nothing good. Beatrice and Cyril had left, never to return; Benjamina had taken over the business; and Jenkins was dead and gone.

All she had now was Clayton. Benjamina's lady's maid had worked for the family for just over a year. She was in her late twenties and had come with impeccable references from another good house in Wrockwardine. She was a relation of Jenkins, her cousin's child, and that was a comfort to Queenie. Clayton was not pretty, but rather handsome. Tall, a squarish face, mousy hair in a neat bun, small brown eyes that seemed to comprehend meanings swiftly and strong hands that were quick and capable. When Jenkins had needed rest, Queenie found that Clayton had filled in admirably. She possessed all the cleaning, mending and styling skills a lady's maid required and, best of all, she was sympathetic. Heaven knows how she found working for Benjamina, who was petulant and demanding. In the terrible days after the loss of Jenkins, Queenie turned to Clayton and put her life utterly in her hands. And the young maid took great care of Queenie and helped ease the passage into her new life without her rock. Queenie was grateful beyond words.

Yet, as Queenie's health and strength recovered, a plan began to form in her mind that would hopefully mean she would not have Clayton by her side for much longer. It would be a wrench, but Queenie knew it was what she needed to do. Someone demanded it. Or rather, something demanded it.

So, two weeks after Jenkins's death, on a chilly Saturday in November, Queenie wrote a letter, sitting up in bed, and had it sent. Then she told Clayton to prepare her favourite green day dress and matching shawl, for she was to receive a visitor on the morrow, first thing in the morning.

'Yes, ma'am,' said Clayton.

'And prepare my beige dress for this afternoon, as I do believe I am strong enough to venture for a walk to the graveyard today.'

'But ma'am, it is bitter cold out, and you have only walked about this room these past days. You've not even been down the stairs yet. I think you best stay in bed a while longer.'

'No,' said Queenie. 'I need to visit my dear friend. It has been two weeks since her passing and I have not visited her grave yet. I imagine the stone has not been put in place as yet, but I would like to see her resting place at Southover. Tell the men to get the carriage ready for after luncheon.'

'Southover, ma'am?' Clayton said, doubtfully.

'Yes, Southover, of course,' replied Queenie, a little tetchily.

'The grave of Rose Jenkins is not at Southover, ma'am.'

Queenie stared at her. 'Of course it is. I insisted upon it to Benjamina.'

'I am sorry, ma'am, but Jenkins was laid to rest in the town. Many old friends from Ironbridge turned out for her. It was a fine service. I omitted mention of it, ma'am, as I wanted to avoid upsetting you.'

'What? What? But she should be on King ground! This is terrible!'

'Please, you'll make yourself ill, ma'am!' said Clayton, stepping towards Queenie, her hand outstretched to placate her.

But Queenie would not be calmed. This was the worst injury Benjamina had inflicted upon her yet. How cruel could a person be? How *dare* she!

160

'Send Mrs King to me immediately,' said Queenie with more strength and resolve than she'd had in weeks.

Clayton nodded and left the room, while Queenie sat bolt upright in bed, seething. Her anger gave her strength, but woven through her anger was also a burgeoning sorrow, that her bosom friend was in a town plot with all those strangers, abandoned by the Kings at her last hour. It was almost too much to bear.

The door opened and she steeled herself for the showdown with Benjamina. But it was only Clayton.

'Mrs King wishes me to inform you that she believes you are yet too weak to receive visitors, and will delay her visit until such time as you are fully recovered. She said she wished to have no part in delaying your recovery.'

Clayton said all this with a blank look on her face. Queenie could not yet read her with accuracy, but she was certain she detected a note of judgement in Clayton's voice.

'So, she hides from me,' muttered Queenie. 'Well, she will rue it. She will rue all of it. Mark my words.'

Chapter 10

Hettie received the letter from old Mrs King on Saturday evening, on her return from work. Her father had already broken the wax seal and opened it, which she scolded him for.

'It was a letter, is all. I didna know it was for you, until I saw Dear Miss Jones at the top. I didna read the rest. I have some honour, you know.'

'I know, Father,' she said.

Hettie took the letter and read it quickly. It summoned her to a meeting with Mrs King at the old brickmaster's house the following morning at eight. She was curious, of course, but regretted that she would lose the luxury of her Sunday-morning late sleep.

'What is it, then?'

'Old Mrs King wants me to come to a meeting with her tomorrow morning.'

'Whatever for?' Her father's voice was low and his face was fixed in a scowl.

'It doesna say.'

'That woman,' said her father, taking a deep puff on his pipe, leaning against the mantelpiece as if for support. 'She was the death and the life of me. Her family took my freedom away, but she begged for clemency for me and saved me from the noose. I hate her and I am indebted to her in the very same breath.'

'I know, Father. Dunna fret. Maybe it is regarding this money she's been sending. Perhaps she is to stop it and she'd rather inform me than have to deal with you directly, who knows? It is most likely for the best, if so. I do believe it may be time for you to look for work.'

It was something she'd wanted to raise with her father for a while now, and she was glad to have this letter as an excuse to bring it up again.

Her father sighed, staring into the fireplace. 'You know my nerves are not up to working, my dear.'

Hettie came to him and put a hand on his shoulder. 'I believe that your nerves would do better out of this house and out of the taverns and in the fresh air.'

'And what sort of job would anyone give me, an old convict?' he replied, bitterly.

'I dunna have an answer to that, Father. But you wonna know until you look.'

He grumbled some unintelligible response to this, and she chose not to ask him what. She had just finished a long shift on the pit bank and she was tired. This week had exhausted her. She'd had another argument with Evan last Sunday and it had been hanging over her for days. He had told her again that she ought to leave her father once and for all and come home.

Evan meant well, she knew that, and it was hard to keep disappointing him. But she could not seem to make him understand that she would never abandon her father. It wasn't only the promise to her mother that stopped her, but the fact that this man, however trammelled by circumstance he may be, was her only kin on this earth. After her mother's untimely death, she had grown for the past thirteen years without a member of her true family about her. She had nobody she could look at and say, *this is where I come from, this is who I am*. The Malones had given her the best childhood an orphan could desire, filled with love and acceptance. But this man, this broken man, was part of her, and she was part of him. She'd rather die than leave him.

∞

The next morning, she was up and about long before her father, dressing in her Sunday best for this unexpected meeting with Mrs King. She carried out her early chores and put out a breakfast of boiled eggs and a little bit of ham for her father, before leaving the house quietly.

She was out in plenty of time and did not need to hurry, so walked in a leisurely way along the river, over the iron bridge and through Benthalledge Wood towards the old brickmaster's house, the King residence. Walking along the woodland path, deserted on this Sunday morning, she felt at peace amidst the sound of birdsong and the river burbling away beyond the trees. It was quite a while since she had been alone, and an age since she had walked through a wood and had the time to listen to the sounds of nature. Her life always belonged to other people and other things – her work, her father, her responsibilities. She had little or no control over anything she did. Walking in this quiet place, hearing the birds singing and seeing them flit from branch to branch, she felt some envy for their freedom. They were masters of their own fate, and best of all, they could fly away from everything whenever they wanted.

With this thought in her mind, she saw the King house edge into view. She swallowed nervously as she rounded the house and went to the servants' entrance at the back; she knew full well it was the appropriate door for someone of her low status. As she recalled her reason for this peaceful walk, her stomach lurched with nerves. What could old Mrs King want with her? Surely it would only be about the money. Hettie murmured a little prayer, hoping that it was not bad news. She was too tired to face any more drama in her life.

But something told her that any dealings between the Joneses, the Malones and the Kings never ended well.

Inside, the house was grand but not overly so. She liked the jolly look of the chequerboard tiles in the hallway. She followed a maid up the stairs, but did not know the girl, who was a few years older than her. The maid had given her a swift look of dissatisfaction when she had presented herself. At the top of the stairs, the maid went down a corridor, then knocked lightly on a door at the end of the landing.

'Enter,' a voice said.

The maid went in and Hettie followed. It was a large, bright bedchamber, sparsely furnished. In an armchair by the window sat a very old woman, her face deeply lined and wrinkled, her ice-white hair swept away from her face in a chignon, her shoulders slightly humped and her body wrapped in a shawl and blanket. But her eyes were bright and piercing, staring now at Hettie. She had never seen Mrs King, because the old woman hardly ever ventured out these days, but Hettie presumed this must be her. Her penetrating gaze was disconcerting, but Hettie tried her best to face up to this strange meeting and stepped forward when the maid introduced her as Miss Jones.

Another woman came in at that moment, a more senior maid. She gave Hettie a quick up and down glance, then gestured that she should sit in a chair that had been placed opposite Mrs King. Hettie did so, and the two maids left the room.

Hettie finally raised her eyes to look again at Mrs King, who it seemed had not taken her eyes from Hettie.

'Miss Jones,' said Mrs King. Despite her advanced age, her voice was as clear and strong as her gaze. 'You have your mother's green eyes.'

This was a shock, to hear her long-lost mother spoken of by a stranger. Was she allowed to speak? She imagined so, since she had been summoned by name for an audience. 'Thank you, ma'am,' she began meekly, then took courage and continued, 'Did you know my mother, ma'am?'

'I met her once,' said Mrs King. 'She was heavy with child – with you. She had the most extraordinary green eyes, and you have inherited them. In fact, you are the spitting image of her. It is quite disconcerting.' She paused. 'I suppose you have little memory of her.'

Talking to this local dignitary was peculiar enough, but speaking of something so personal was even more so. But it was welcome to Hettie, somehow, as she had always had a hunger to talk of her mother – and here was another person, outside of the Malones and her father, who had known her first-hand. 'I have some pictures in my head, ma'am. Little things. Passing things.'

'I suppose that such early memories must be mingled with dreams and wishful thinking, so that the thoughts one possesses could be seen as unreliable. You may have a recollection of your mother that has been placed in your mind by what others have told you, or even what you wanted her to be.'

It was a complex utterance, but Hettie believed she had the gist of it. 'I think that is true, ma'am. I think dreams can feel real. So it inna always easy to tell 'em apart from the waking world.'

Mrs King smiled and nodded her head approvingly. 'Good. Good. You are a clever child. I was hoping you would be. Your father was always a very intelligent man, so it seems you have inherited his brain, as well as your mother's looks.'

Again, Hettie did not know quite how to respond. 'Thank you,' she said, as she perceived it was a compliment, though Mrs King's voice had a slightly disparaging tone to it when she mentioned Hettie's father.

'Now then, I have some business to discuss with you. My lady's maid, Rose Jenkins, died recently. She was my maid for decades and her loss is keenly felt.'

Mrs King stopped and looked down at her hands. Hettie felt the old woman was overcome with emotion, which seemed peculiar for a lady to have when talking of a mere servant. As the silence continued, Hettie felt compelled to speak. 'Sorry to hear it, ma'am.'

Mrs King recovered herself and looked up again at Hettie. 'That is the reason I have summoned you here today. I wish to offer you the role of my new lady's maid.'

Hettie stared at the old woman, so shocked she could not speak. Her, Hettie Jones – pit bank girl and strawberry picker – a lady's maid, one of the most senior female servants in the house, second only to the housekeeper? Hettie had no idea how to respond.

'I understand this will come as something of a surprise to you, to say the least. You have had no experience in service. I understand that. But I will ensure that you will receive training, not only from my current maid Clayton, but from the entire staff and also from myself. I will ensure that you are paid well. I would estimate it will be almost twice the wage you currently receive as a picker at the mine. And of course, the conditions will be vastly superior, working indoors with me as opposed to out of doors, facing the elements day in and day out.'

This was not the time to protest how much Hettie enjoyed working outside, how much she liked the freedom of it. And how she had always dreaded the fate of service, cooped up in a house with masters and mistresses bossing you about all the livelong day, with the starchy smart uniforms and the bowing and scraping. She'd never seen service as something to aspire to and had always been glad of her job.

But now, this extraordinary offer was being placed before her. And more than anything, her first thought was spoken as a question, a loud, piercing question that needed to be answered before she could even entertain the proposal that was being put before her.

'Why me?' she said suddenly. It almost shocked her that it came out aloud, rather than in her head. She wished she could take it back, as it was the height of rudeness. But it was out there now, and so be it.

Mrs King smiled. 'That is the pertinent question, and you have hit upon it instantly. A clever girl, as I said. So, why you, Miss Jones? The answer is a complex one and you will understand it more as time goes on. I promise you that in the end all will become clear. But for now, what you need to know is that I require a lady's maid and I have a notion to train one up. And since your family has links to mine, from regrettable events in the past, I feel that offering you the position will serve to mend those rifts, or at least attempt to. I would urge you to consider my offer carefully. It will change your prospects in life immeasurably. It will provide security for your future. And, though this will make no difference to you presently, I am sure, it will make a very old woman very happy indeed.'

Hettie did not know how to respond. All of the information had landed in her lap with a thump, and she felt pinioned to the chair by it. Mrs King seemed to perceive this, as she continued to speak.

'It will not be an easy decision. There is much for you to consider. Go back to your nearest and dearest and discuss it with them. I will offer one warning to you, though. There will be factions about you that will try to talk you out of accepting this position. I won't mention names, but I think you know how certain families around here feel about the Kings. I would counsel you to listen to all arguments, but remember, make your own decision based on your own needs, desires and aspirations for your future. All of us only possess one gift, and that is life. It is your choice what to do with your life. Please have that in the forefront of your mind when you make your decision. And it is your decision, Hettie Jones. It is your life.'

Hettie knew Mrs King must be referring to Anny and the Malones. Who else could it be? She knew Anny would hate the idea, and so would Evan. Her father might, too, although the position it gave her and the money it brought might tempt him – and he quite liked to be on opposing sides to Anny over any issue, merely out of resentment. Hettie knew there would be arguments ahead.

But Mrs King was right: this was her decision, her life.

'Thank you, ma'am,' she said, as Mrs King watched her closely, a slight smile about her wizened lips. 'It is a very kind offer. I will think about it, proper careful.'

'That is all I can ask. Consider it well. Will you come to see me again next Sunday at the same hour, to give me your answer?'

'I will, ma'am. And thank you. Again, I say thank you. I never had such a meeting in my life. And such … consideration. I hope … I inna being rude or … unladylike in my manners. I am in a bit of a shock, that's all.'

Mrs King smiled more broadly now. She seemed genuinely pleased with Hettie, though Hettie herself had no idea why. 'You have behaved perfectly, my dear. Now off you go and have a good think about it. Let the decision be yours and yours alone.'

Hettie thought of her determination to go strawberry picking and how it had been opposed by Evan and Peter. It was Anny who had counselled her then, who had told her she was a young woman now and that the decision was her own.

'It is my decision, ma'am,' she said with some pride. 'And I shall make it myself.'

'Good girl,' said Mrs King. Her eyes were twinkling now as she smiled at Hettie. And Hettie couldn't help but smile back at her.

As long as Hettie could remember, this old woman had been an object of awe and contempt, known as the 'owd witch' or even the 'owd bitch', and other awful insults that the townsfolk and in particular the Malones had often been heard to throw at her from afar. And now she, Hettie Jones, was sitting quite cosily with this local legend, sharing a smile. Hettie found herself basking in the wonder of it. As each day came, you never knew what might happen by the end of it. And this day, this meeting, and this offer might well change Hettie's life forever.

Chapter 11

After the meeting with Mrs King, Hettie went straight home and told her father. His eyes lit up, especially when she told him her wage would be double that at the pit. It seemed like a dream come true, except for the fact that it was an offer from the Kings. That name had resounded in the house like a curse throughout her life. She knew she would have to discuss it with the Malones and get their views on it. They knew far more than her about the Kings, and she needed to hear both sides.

'My advice is dunna go and talk to 'em about it,' her father said. 'This is a once in a lifetime chance, wench. Gifts like this dunna come along twice. It'll be the making of you. This is your way out of labour and poverty. You wonna be young forever, and the pit bank and the fruit picking is a younger wench's way of earning a crust. This lady's maid post will be easier on your bones and your back. But mark me, the Malones will try to talk you out of it because Anny Malone hates the Kings. By God, I hate them too, but old Mrs King did save my life, and I owe her that. Besides, if she feels enough guilt about us and what happened to give you this job, then I say we grasp the opportunity with both hands.'

Hettie agreed, but she still wanted to hear the Malones' views. She walked over there that very afternoon, apprehensive of how her news would be taken. She was greeted with good cheer, as she had not seen them all for a while. Evan in particular was delighted, and greeted her in a somewhat awkward fashion, yet his eyes were sparkling at the sight of her.

But as soon as she revealed her news, the mood dropped with a thud. Anny's face was like thunder. Peter shifted uncomfortably. The children watched with wonder as to what would happen next. Evan shook his head in disbelief.

Anny said, 'None of us will ever work for the Kings again. We made this choice years ago.'

Hettie wanted to say, *But I'm not one of you.* She didn't really mean it, not in a cruel way. These people had been all the family she'd had or needed from her earliest memories. But this feud with the Kings was not her battle to fight.

'It's a good chance for me,' Hettie said.

'You canna do it,' said Evan, folding his arms.

Hettie had never followed Evan's advice, and she wasn't going to start now. 'That will be my choice,' she said firmly.

Anny came to her across the room and took her hand, looking into her eyes feverishly. 'Listen, lass. I know that us telling you not to will make you wish it more so.'

Hettie shifted uneasily. Anny knew her so well. Of course she did. She was her second mother. Hettie hated to disappoint her. She could feel tears pricking in her eyes.

'But that's no reason to do it,' Anny went on. 'The Kings are poison. I know that's not what you want to hear. I know you think a great opportunity has come to you and you'd be a fool not to take it. But those Kings . . .'

Anny's eyes glistened with tears. She dropped Hettie's hand and turned away to Peter, who came to her and took her in his arms. Anny was the towering strength of the family, and to see her like this upset Hettie more than anything.

'Anny, please,' she said.

Peter held his wife and said to Hettie, 'The Kings' money is blood money.'

Hettie knew the stories, of Anny's imprisonment after a false accusation of theft from Cyril King, who had wanted to bed her and wed her but instead took out his revenge on her; of Owen, Evan's older brother, who was worshipped as a saint by the Malones, how he'd died when the King house crashed down on him as he saved a King girl from the fire at Southover. It was a bitter legacy indeed.

'I know there is hatred for the Kings. I know terrible things have happened. But good has come from them too. The Kings' money paid for the doctor who saved my mother when I was born, which saved me too. And Mrs King saved my father's life.'

'And look what he's done with it!' said Evan. 'Drunk it down the drain!'

'Dunna speak ill of him!' cried Hettie, shocking all those in the room. Even the children stopped fidgeting. 'I am sick and tired of having to explain my father to all of you. He is what he is. But most of all, he is my father. He is my kin. I never had kin in my life, not in the life I remember, leastways. You all have each other. You always have. The Malones are like . . . are like a kind of castle. You have the walls to keep others out and keep you safe inside. And I am grateful you kept me safe within these walls for all those years. I know you raised me as your own and loved me as your own. I will always be grateful for that, believe me, to my dying day. But my father is my kin and I will never desert him.'

Anny had recovered enough to leave her husband's arms and turn to Hettie. 'Nobody is asking you to, love.'

'Evan is!' said Hettie, pointing at him.

'And so I am!' he said. 'You shoulda left him at the fair and never looked back. I told you that then, but you never listen.'

'Because he is my blood! Because I come from his blood! Blood makes all the difference. Blood is everything!'

She didn't mean it to hurt, but she could see it did. The Malones seemed to shrink from her then. It felt like the final step away from them, on a journey she had begun the moment her father turned up on their doorstep all those months before. She regretted it, but there was a part of her that desired it, too. She felt she was finally moving towards something of her own, after years of being the cuckoo, though she was never, ever made to feel that by them. It was something she had put upon herself, and now she felt ready to fledge and fly.

'I am so sorry to bring any of you heartache,' she said, holding back the tears that would surely come. 'First by leaving you to go and look after my father. And now this post I've been offered. But you mun see that I have a life before me and I mun make of it what I will. I love you all. I hope you know that. But I mun go now and forge my own path.'

She turned to go to the door, but Evan caught her arm as she passed. His eyes were wide, imploring. 'Dunna go, Hettie.'

'Try not to hate me,' she said, and stared at his hand until he removed it from her.

'Hettie, that will never be,' said Evan, and the emotion in his voice nearly broke her will.

She looked back as she opened the door. The children were shifting about uncomfortably, and Anny and Peter would not look at her. She could not look at Evan again.

She left and closed the door gently behind her.

∽

Hettie gave notice straight away and had to work one more week before she was permitted to leave. The pit bank girls greeted her news with equal amounts of incredulity and resentment. She knew then that they would never again be her friends. Her closest pit bank companion Ada seemed the most resentful of all, immediately transferring her affection to another girl on the bank, leaving Hettie to see out her week's notice largely alone. There was no celebration, no grand goodbye. At the end of her final shift, she slunk off home. That Sunday, Hettie arrived at the King house just before lunchtime. She was shown to her room by a sullen tweeny maid who had no interest in speaking to her, let alone making her feel in any way welcome. All the maid said when they reached the room, which was next to Mrs King's bedchamber, was, 'Jenkins's room.'

Hettie knew that Jenkins had been Mrs King's old lady's maid, and she felt she was trespassing.

Unpacking her carpet bag in this room was a strange sensation. She had few things to unpack: two day dresses for Sundays, underclothes, two hats and shawls, a spare pair of boots, some items of toilette and a book of poetry for children that Anny had given her on her tenth birthday. It was a precious item; she liked to read the poems when alone and be taken back to the days of childhood, before the pit bank, when she still went to school and played with Evan in the ruins of the old King house. And now she was working in the old brickmaster's house for Mrs King. Could she have predicted such a turn of events? Never, not in a thousand years.

Once she'd unpacked, she wasn't sure what to do next. She had been given no instructions. She put her ear to the door that separated her room from old Mrs King's, to see if she could hear if the lady was in there. She did not have the nerve to knock on the door and enter as yet. She sat on her bed for a while and waited, growing increasingly nervous. Should she go and ask someone what to do? Would that be a black mark against her?

Then, the door opened.

'Jones, is it?'

It was Mrs King the younger. Hettie knew her by sight. She was a beautiful woman, old – not half as old as old Mrs King, but still old to Hettie – yet she was still a fine woman.

'Yes, ma'am,' said Hettie, standing up abruptly and giving a quick dip of a curtsey.

'I am Mrs King. I am in charge of all the servants.'

'Yes ma'am.'

Mrs King looked at Hettie's feet, then slowly worked her way up to Hettie's face. 'So, this is the new lady's maid.'

Hettie didn't know what to say to that.

'Come with me.'

'Yes, ma'am. Thank you, ma'am.'

Hettie was trying to be as polite as she could, but she felt something was off about this Mrs King. She seemed to sneer at Hettie and make her feel small.

She took Hettie to meet the other servants in the kitchen. Everyone stared at her. Nobody smiled. Young Mrs King told Hettie everybody's names, but in her nerves she couldn't take in a single one. Hettie was told to sit near the top of the table, next to the butler, who grimaced at her. Surely there was some mistake and she should be further down. But Mrs King made it clear that the lady's maid must sit near the head, as she carried that privilege due to her high status in the servants' hall. A titter went around the servants. Mrs King smirked too, then left, sweeping her skirts out of the room.

Hettie sat down to a lunch of mutton stew, with tapioca for pudding, and nobody spoke to her. When Hettie stood up to help clear the table, a young maid with black hair grabbed Hettie's arm and said, 'Excuse me, *miss*,' then kicked her sharply in the calf, throwing her arm down and leaving the room afterwards.

It all happened so quickly that Hettie just stood in shock, unable to respond. Nobody seemed to notice or, if they did, they didn't say a word.

As Hettie left to mount the stairs to her room, she saw the girl again, who gave her a vicious smile and spat out the words, 'Pit-wench', as if it were poison on her tongue.

Hettie hurriedly fled up the servants' staircase to her room – or rather, to Jenkins's room. She sat on her bed and felt the tears pricking in her eyes.

'Dunna cry!' she scolded herself in a harsh whisper. She was determined to be strong. But as she waited in her room, again unsure what she was supposed to do next, she felt the tears begin to roll down her face. She brushed them away smartly and told herself to get on with it. She stood up straight and marched across the room to the door and, after a brief, trembling hesitation, she knocked firmly on the door.

After a moment, she heard a voice say, 'Come in, Jones.'

Hettie opened the door to see Mrs King sitting up in bed, smiling.

'Come closer, Jones.'

Hettie walked over towards the bed and stopped at a distance she felt was respectful.

'I am glad you've arrived. Have you had luncheon?'

'I have, thank you, ma'am,' said Hettie and curtseyed.

'No need for any of that nonsense. You never need curtsey to me again, do you understand?'

'Yes, ma'am.'

'Now then, I don't suppose Mrs King the younger has told you a thing about your duties. She does not approve of you, as I'd imagine you've guessed. But never mind that. She is of no consequence. You are here at my behest and you answer to me. Understood?'

'Yes, ma'am.'

'Now then, this afternoon you are free to make yourself comfortable in your room and not to worry about any duties for today. Your training will begin on the morrow. Later you will be visited by a seamstress to measure you for your uniform. Attend dinner after that downstairs, and in the morning Clayton will wake you and talk you through your duties. Any questions?'

'No, ma'am. Thank you, ma'am.'

'Good, good. Leave me now. Clayton will tend to me today. Tomorrow is the beginning of everything.'

'Yes, ma'am,' said Hettie and curtseyed again, then stopped halfway and said, 'Sorry, ma'am.'

'Off you go, Jones,' said Mrs King.

Hettie left and went back to her room. She sat again on her bed, puzzling over the conversation. Had she done well? Mrs King seemed to have something of a twinkle in her eye after she did that ridiculous half-curtsey. She seemed to be tolerant of Hettie's inexperience, far more so than anyone else in the house. Hettie wondered what this Clayton would be like, and tried to remember if her name had been amongst those in the servants' hall.

When the seamstress arrived, she was brisk and businesslike, with no time for conversation. Hettie stood stiffly as the woman measured her all over. That was the only person she saw for the rest of the day, sitting in her room, staring out of the window or flicking through her poetry book. A young maid fetched her for dinner without a word. Again, nobody spoke to her at dinner and she was too nervous to attempt a conversation. She went upstairs in silence and retired to her room for the night. At least nobody had kicked her this time.

Lying awake in bed, Hettie suddenly felt very alone. She knew nobody here, she had not been met with kindness, and she had no idea what she was supposed to be doing. She felt as if Ironbridge were a hundred miles away. She wondered if she'd made a terrible mistake. But she told herself that change was always hard, and change was also good. She'd get used to it. She'd do her best.

⌀

The next morning, she woke up very early. She was wide awake in the darkness. She had had a dream about Mr Laurence Maxwell Ripley. It had been a kissing dream and Hettie had awoken sharply, wishing for that moment between sleeping and waking so that she could drift down into it again. But she knew it was over and she was here, in the King household.

She tried to hold onto the image of Mr Ripley from the dream. She wondered what he would think of her new post, if he'd find her half as interesting now she was a servant, as he seemed to be much more fascinated with the rougher trades. She felt proud that she had attained such a position, but she was confused, too; there was a part of her that knew she had not been given it through merit, but instead some old debt, wrapped up in her father and mother and the Malones and all the secrets of the past. Despite her rise in fortunes, she had begun to think that her destiny was more than ever not her own. Here she was, sleeping in the next room to old Mrs King; soon she'd be tending to her every need. But she took comfort in the fact that her doubled wage would secure her future and her father's retirement in comfort. She just hoped he would be able to keep off the drink in the meantime. She missed her pit bank friends and Evan and the Malones, and she hated the fact that they disapproved of her working here. But she also felt excited that her life had changed so very much. It just showed that you never could tell what was waiting for you, just around the corner.

Then, she heard footsteps outside her door and a light knock.

'Yes?'

The door opened and in came a young woman, a few years older than Hettie. She recognised her from dinner last night, but they had not spoken, though the woman had looked at her curiously a few times.

'I'm Clayton, Mrs King the younger's lady's maid. I'm here to talk you through your duties. I'll give you a few minutes to get yourself dressed and then I'll be back.'

'All right,' said Hettie, then paused, as she did not know whether to call another senior servant ma'am or by her surname, or what. But Clayton didn't wait to correct her and shut the door swiftly.

Hettie scrambled up and got herself dressed as quickly as she could. She had brought her Sunday best winter dress to wear in her first few days, before a uniform could be organised. She brushed her hair and washed her face and made herself presentable.

Then Clayton came back and Hettie's instruction began.

'They tell me you have never worked in service, so I shall go over everything in detail with you and assume you know very little. Does that sound fair?'

'Very fair,' said Hettie, and smiled.

Clayton did not smile back. She went on, 'Firstly, you must rise just before your mistress and carry out your own toilette first. I will knock on your door each morning to wake you. Your first task will then be to look over your mistress's clothes that have been worn the day before, check for any stains or mending needs and put them away or aside for later work. If your mistress has been out, it may be necessary to remove mud from hems or boots, but since Mrs King rarely goes out, you will usually be spared this task. But all shoes need a regular clean, despite lack of use. Kid leather boots need a polish with a sponge dipped in milk to keep their shine.'

Clayton paused and looked at Hettie.

'Thank you,' said Hettie, unsure of what was required.

'Do you have any questions so far?' said Clayton, looking peevish.

'No, not really. You make it all very clear. Thank you for that.'

Clayton said, 'You're very welcome,' and there was a hint of a smile. But as soon as she'd said this, she seemed to regret it and she set her mouth firmly in a straight line again. It was peculiar. It felt almost as though she'd been told to be horrid to Hettie, but couldn't go through with it all the way.

Then it occurred to Hettie that perhaps this was exactly what had happened. Old Mrs King had said the younger Mrs King didn't approve of her. Perhaps that was why all the servants were mean to her; perhaps they had been ordered to be so.

Hettie listened carefully as Clayton went on with her instructions. There was so much to learn and remember, Hettie felt her head begin to swim with the enormity of it all. Once her mistress was awake, she must bring her the breakfast tray and either draw her bath, if required, or prepare her jug and basin for washing.

Then came assisting Mrs King in dressing and styling her hair, which was past shoulder length. Since Hettie had always had long hair, she had some experience of putting it up into attractive styles, as she often did on Sundays. But she had no idea of the fashions for ladies of advanced age, other than what she'd seen Mrs King sport so far. Hettie would need to learn what products her mistress required on her hair and how to keep it looking shiny and bright white. It must be washed with a mixture of rosemary water and borax, then, once the hair had been thoroughly dried, an amount of pomade must be applied. Clayton said Mrs King also liked to use a variety of creams and other potions on her face and body and Hettie needed to learn which was which, as well as order the ingredients for most of these and con-coct them herself. Hettie must also ensure the reorder-ing of such essentials at regular intervals.

Once Mrs King was washed and dressed, Hettie must then tidy the room. Clayton explained that this would normally take place after the mistress had left the room for the day, but that Mrs King liked to sit in her arm-chair and look out at the woodland and was quite happy for her maid to clear up about her and chat. The dress-ing table, toilette table and linen would need attention. Combs would need to be cleaned but not with water, as this would damage the teeth and make the tortoiseshell rough; they required the use of a comb brush, a small object made specially for the purpose and kept with the range of other brushes Hettie would need. Her mistress's hairbrushes must be cleaned carefully, in water that had a little soda dissolved in it, the bristles cleaned thoroughly but not left for too long in the liquid in case they turned soft. When it came to her mistress's clothes, Hettie must learn the particular care for materials such as tweed and silk. Some would need laying out on a table and brushing, others a light beating with a handkerchief to remove dust.

Though the laundry was done elsewhere (by people like Anny), Hettie would need to sort the clothes to be sent out and reorganise those that had been sent back. She was also expected to keep a written inventory of all items that left the room and a record of costs of laundering those items, so that the household was never cheated on its bills. The same went for the costs of cosmetics. Hettie was given an accounts book for this. She was glad Anny had ensured she'd been educated, or this part of the job would be far beyond her. Clayton told her that Mrs King often dropped food down the front of her garments and that these stains needed careful attention by the maid immediately and were not to be left for the washerwoman to deal with. The room would need airing once a day as well, especially after the mistress had used the commode, the clearing away of which was also Hettie's duty.

All items used must be cleaned, the wash basins rinsed of soap scum, fresh water and clean towels replenished. Though Hettie was not responsible for dusting every tiny object, as another maid would do this, she had to ensure the room was spick and span at all times, with not one spare thread or hair to be seen on the carpets or furnishings. It was also necessary to keep a strict inventory of every object in the mistress's rooms, to keep an eye on any thieving servant who might remove small objects of value thinking their absence would not be noted.

Once the room was inspected and tidy, the mending work began: darning stockings and other jobs for the needle and thread. Clayton said that most lady's maids had to be tolerable seamstresses and milliners, able to even make outfits from scratch if necessary. This alarmed Hettie, who had never made a whole outfit, though she had mended her own and her father's often enough. But luckily, as Mrs King rarely left the house and never attended events these days, new outfits were rare.

In a way, old Mrs King was the dream mistress for a lady's maid. She afforded so little wear and tear on any of her items. If she did leave the house, her bonnet or hat must be either brushed or dusted with a feather plume before putting away. Any clothing items that had feathers or flowers would need adjusting; perhaps the feather might need recurling with a warmed knife or any crushed artificial flowers would need amending with a pair of flower pliers. Again, these were to be found in Jenkins's armoury, left behind in her room to be passed on to the next lady's maid.

Once all of these tasks had been carried out – or even while doing them, since Mrs King rarely left her rooms – Hettie's other main duty was to provide companionship for Mrs King. Her life was to be wedded to that of her mistress; she was to be on hand at any moment of the day or night. A younger mistress would be out of the house for periods of time, but not Mrs King.

Clayton also explained that Mrs King was still mourning the death of her previous maid, Jenkins, to whom she had been very close.

Clayton added, 'You will never replace Jenkins. She was here for decades and many said they were more like sisters than mistress and maid. But you can do your best to be civil and solicitous at all times, listening to Mrs King's complaints or stories and nodding or providing comment if asked.'

Hettie said, 'I've heard of Jenkins.'

'She is well known,' said Clayton. Then, after a moment's hesitation, 'She was my mother's cousin.'

Hettie nodded. 'She was there when I was born.'

Clayton gave her an inquisitive look and asked, 'How did that come about?'

'It was in the strike days. Anny Malone –who raised me after my mother died – she told me that Jenkins came with the young lady of the house when my mother was in labour. Things had gone bad and they didna think she'd live, nor me. So they fetched a doctor and the Kings paid for it. I was born and my mother didna die and nor did I.'

Clayton frowned. 'But why would Mrs King pay for a physician for the likes of you? No offence.'

Hettie thought about it. 'I anna got a clue,' she said and smiled. 'It is a story from before my memory and I've often thought of it, how the Kings helped me.'

The Kings had also done far worse to those she loved, but she wasn't going to mention that to Clayton.

Clayton eyed her curiously. She hesitated, then said, 'Anyway, I cannot stand around here talking to you all day.'

'I'm Hettie, by the way. What's your first name?'

Clayton drew herself up and said haughtily, 'First names are not required for lady's maids. The under-servants should call you miss, and your mistress and I will call you Jones.'

'I know that,' said Hettie, smiling. 'But I'd be grateful to know it anyway.'

Clayton shook her head to dismiss such silliness and walked to the door. But she stopped, turned and said quietly to Hettie, 'It's Kezia. Kezia Clayton.' Then she left.

Kezia's instructions had taken up much of the morning. Luncheon was quiet and miserable; Hettie was universally ignored. In the afternoon, she sat with Mrs King, who asked her to read to her from an old novel from the last century. Hettie was a good reader, but she struggled with some of the words. Mrs King didn't seem to mind, and was soon napping in her chair anyway.

Hettie took the opportunity to acquaint herself with the tools of her job, all tidily packed away by Kezia in Jenkins's room. She made a mental note of each brush and what it was for, reminding herself to ask Kezia of the ones she'd forgotten.

Mrs King slept a lot that day. Hettie watched as Kezia helped her mistress get ready for dinner. Hettie saw how gentle Kezia was with Mrs King and was touched. Kezia had a tenderness about her that was lovely to watch.

Lying in bed that second night, wide awake with fretting when she should've been sleeping, Hettie decided she would make a friend of Kezia Clayton if she could. For whatever reason, the other servants all seemed to hate her, and the one who'd kicked her had chosen Hettie as her mortal enemy. Nobody spoke to her at mealtimes and she was universally shunned. Kezia Clayton was the only person other than Mrs King who had shown her a moment's kindness.

The varied and innumerable tasks of a lady's maid, and everything she must learn, were daunting, but more worrying still was the feeling that she had come to a house that wanted her out of it. She had no idea why. She'd never felt this way before. All her life she had been surrounded by love and affection: at the Malones' house; at school, where she always had plenty of friends; at work, where the camaraderie of the pit bank girls was rough but constant; even with her difficult father, who despite his problems loved her truly. Her childhood feeling of being a cuckoo at the Malones' house was magnified a hundredfold in the King household. She missed them all and pined for a kind word, a gentle look, someone who was glad to see her.

'Jenkins!' came a call from the next room. 'Jenkins!'

Her mistress was calling. She threw off her bedcovers and shrank from the winter chill as she padded across the floor to the connecting door between their rooms.

Hettie went to her and asked, 'Can I help you, ma'am?'

Mrs King, eyes screwed shut, held out her hand. Hettie didn't know what to do with it at first. A maid or a pit-wench didn't go round touching the hands of dignitaries like Mrs King. But as well as being an upper-class lady, Mrs King was just a person, an old woman who needed someone's help.

So Hettie took her mistress's hand and felt it relax in her grasp. Mrs King sighed contentedly. Hettie stroked the old lady's hand, papery and cool to the touch. She waited there, quietly, until Mrs King fell peacefully back to sleep.

Whatever fears and sorrows Hettie had, one thing was clear: old Mrs King needed her and wanted her. And she would do her best to serve the lady well, whatever the rest of the household did to thwart her.

Chapter 12

Evan Malone did not like change. He knew this about himself. He never was any good at it. He liked routine. He found it comforting. He liked the fact that he was always woken at the same time each morning by his mother; that he always took the same bait to work; that his work rarely varied from day to day; that the walk home was with the same people as yesterday, down the same streets and past the same houses; that his Sundays were always spent the same way, playing a bit of chess with his mother, helping his father in the vegetable plot behind the house, playing hide-and-seek or pirate ships with the little'uns; going for a walk with Hettie. He liked his routine.

But these days, that last joy was often denied him. Hettie was now working at the King house, looking after the old woman. Evan had not seen her at all in the month since she'd started there. He'd sent a note to her at the King house four times. Three were answered with a reply in the negative, something along the lines of *Not this Sunday. Too tired. See you presently. H.*

But this Sunday, at last, Hettie had agreed. Well, she had her caveats, but in theory, she'd be there: *Meet you at Southover midday. Only if the weather be fine. Otherwise not. H.*

Evan hoped the weather would hold. It was a foggy winter morning on the way there, but as he arrived, at least a half hour early in his enthusiasm, the fog began to lift and a weak late-November sun threw a yellowish light over the Southover building plot. The place was empty of workers, being Sunday, and so they would have privacy.

Evan wondered if Hettie was avoiding him or if she really was simply too tired. The agony of not knowing gnawed at him. They had fallen out over her father, and now this. He felt as if unseen forces were moving against him when it came to Hettie. Once her father appeared from nowhere, the special place Evan had held in her affections was supplanted by this ghost of a man. Nothing Evan could say or do would shift her from him. It seemed that Adam Jones could have set fire to their house with Hettie in it and she'd still forgive him and take him back. Evan knew it was madness to compete with a girl over her father – but he could not help himself. Adam Jones was bad news, the worst kind. A good man gone bad, no good now to himself or others, especially Hettie. Evan tried to understand, tried to support her in her decisions, but he missed her too much. He wanted her back in the safe embrace of the Malone family; he wanted her home. He wanted *her*.

And now this, the job with the Kings, was fate moving against him again. His mother had said as much, many times over the years, bemoaning the curious fact that the Malones and the Kings seemed destined to be tangled up like wool forever, however much they wrangled with the knots. Evan knew he could not contend with that; he couldn't fight decades of feuding between these two families. And now Hettie had happily stepped into that muddle and embraced it, working not only for the Kings, but with the head of the whole nasty heap of them, Mrs King herself! What was she thinking?

He had to pull her out of it, somehow. He had to make her see that her fate was doomed if she stayed beholden to those forsaken bastards, as his mother often called them, out of the earshot of the little ones. But he'd have to be clever about it; if he told her outright what to do, she'd never listen. Hettie Jones never did take orders from Evan Malone; never had, never would.

These were the scrambled thoughts that plagued his mind as he sat on a stone bench, covered by years of creeping moss, in the grounds of Southover, awaiting his love. For she was his love, Hettie Jones, and now they were both seventeen years of age, he felt ready to declare it to her.

And here she was, crunching up the gravel drive towards him. She was dressed well. Her wages must be good, or else the Kings had given her new things. She wore a dark maroon dress striped with grey. Around her shoulders was a thick shawl the colour of red bricks. She wore gloves. She'd never had such smart walking clothes, and it made him swiftly glance down at his own Sunday best and find it wanting. His suit was handed down from his long-lost brother Owen and had been mended many a time by his mother, the patches showing clearly if you looked close enough in a good light.

I inna good enough for her now, he thought, hope-lessly. But at that moment, she raised her eyes and saw him, giving him such a beaming smile that he forgot his previous doubts. He took off his hat and rose up to meet her, grinning all the way.

'Well, inna you a picture!' he said as he walked briskly towards her.

'And you, Evan.'

'Oh, I dunna think so. You've seen this old suit a hundred times.'

'But you look well in it,' she said, still smiling.

'Shall we take a stroll about the grounds?' he asked. He was suddenly nervous. He knew what he wanted to ask her, what this meeting was for, but he knew he'd have to work up to it gradually and he needed some mileage to get there.

'I am tired,' she said, and sighed. 'Do you mind if we sit here a bit instead? I need the rest.'

'Yes, surely,' he said, minding his language, trying to echo her new voice, tinged with a new properness about it that she'd never had in her pit days. She must be learning by listening to the Kings. Another sign she was slipping away from him.

They sat beside each other, a good twelve inches between them, so unlike their younger days when they'd sit in a cwtch beside the fire at home.

'Tell me about your new post, then,' he said, turning slightly so that he could see her face. He felt suddenly all fingers and thumbs and did not know where to put his hat. In the end, he placed it on the ground beside the bench. He needed his hands free for later, he hoped.

'It is good,' she said and nodded. 'It is a lot of work. I am up with the mistress and tend to her needs all day. And she dunna sleep well at night. I'm often in and out, as she calls for help. She can sleep in if she wishes, but I mun get up at the usual hour and carry out my duties. But I mun say it is easier than the pit bank and the strawberry fields, by far. Much, much easier.'

'I warrant it is,' said Evan, watching her face. Her eyes were greener than ever, her lips plumper and rosier. She did have shadows beneath those pretty eyes, but she looked even more beautiful now than she did in his imagination. Her light brown hair was down, over her shoulders, silky and thick. She must have washed it that morning. How he longed to touch it.

'And you? How is your work? I think of the pit and my days there. As hard as the work was, I miss it. I miss it something terrible.'

'Do you? How can that be? It sounds like a proper lollocking job you got there.'

'Oh, it inna idle or easy, by no means. But not back-breaking. No, it's other things I miss.'

Hettie looked away, towards the half-built structure of the new Southover. He couldn't see her face but knew her of old, knew every nuance of her moods and reactions. He knew she was upset. He reached over slowly and touched her arm gently.

'What is it, Hettie? Tell me.'

She turned back and he was right. Her eyes had filled, and one fat tear rolled down her cheek and dropped onto her shawl.

'I inna wanted there.'

'But why? Mrs King asked for you herself!'

'Mrs King likes me. She is kind to me. Very kind. But the others. Everyone. They all hate me. I dunna know why.'

'Oh Hettie, how could anyone hate you? I canna fathom it!' How he longed to wipe her tears away. And then kiss her better. When they were little, they had kissed on the lips all of the time. They had cuddled and held hands. But when they reached a certain age, it stopped and they grew wary of each other. How unfair it seemed that now he wanted to kiss those lips so very much, there seemed a barrier between them thicker than a castle wall.

'They have taken against me. All the other servants. Except one – Kezia Clayton, her name is. She is Mrs King the younger's maid. She is that kind to me, it gives me some small comfort. But she's shy about it, as if she's been told not to be nice to me.'

'Who woulda told her that? And why?'

'I dunna know. I think maybe Mrs King the younger. She looks at me as if I were a crawling thing beneath her dainty feet. I know there's no love lost between the two of 'em, the elder and the younger Mrs Kings. Maybe that's the reason. But the worst is one of the younger maids. She is proper vicious with me. How I do hate her so!'

Hettie's tears were drying up now she was warming to her subject. It was good to see her old feistiness return.

Evan asked, 'How so? What does the wench do?'

'She pinches me and kicks me, pulls at my cap or my hair. She spreads lies about me amongst the other servants, saying dreadful things about me ... saying ... I am easy and lie with the messenger boy or whoever I fancy.'

Evan felt the rage boil up in him. He wanted to kill this maid. How dare she hurt his girl! And to say such things about Hettie! She was pure as spring water and no mistake. 'I shall murder her,' he said in a low voice.

Hettie reached and took his hand. It was a thrill to feel her touch. 'Dunna say such things, Evan. I tell you this because I have nobody to talk to. I need you to listen and do nothing. I must fight my own battles. And I will win them, one day. I am kind to everyone in the house, sweet and gentle with them all. I will win them round, you'll see.'

'But it makes me proper furious, Hettie, to hear of you being hurt. All it would take is to see if this girl had a brother . . . I could sort him and sort her too with one strike.'

'You'll do no such thing, Evan Malone!' Hettie's voice was raised. She let go of his hand and he regretted his outburst.

'I just want everything in your life to be good,' he said, taking her hand again.

She squeezed it and replied, 'I know, I know. But what I need is for you to listen to me when I need it. And to be my friend.'

She was looking right at him now, right into his eyes. All it would take was one swift movement and his lips would be on hers. But he faltered. She had said 'friend'. That was not what he wanted. He struggled over how to reply, but he was not quick enough. She was speaking again.

'And my father is suffering from my absence.'

Oh, not her damned father again! he thought. But Evan had to look sympathetic or she would shun him. And besides, he knew all about it. Everyone did. Adam Jones had been seen to frequent the inns hereabouts again in the past month, something he'd all but given up under Hettie's care, preferring to drink at home instead – still enough ale to make him merry but not like he'd put away when he was at a tavern.

'I know it,' said Evan. It was all he could muster.

'I was wondering . . . if you could look in on him from time to time.'

'You ask much of me with that, Hettie,' he said. He forgot for a moment that he'd intended to be everything she needed, so that he could ask her to be everything he wanted. 'I mean, I will if that is what you ask of me.'

She looked at him a little quizzically and replied, 'Of course that is what I ask of you – I have just this minute asked it! You are in a queer mood, Evan. What is the matter?'

Was now the time? Her hand was still in his. He squeezed it again, for courage, and she squeezed back.

'I have a question for you, Hettie.'

'And what is it?'

Did she really have no clue? He looked searchingly into her eyes. And there was a flutter there and she looked away. He could not read her so well these days. He did not know what it meant. But now was the time. He might not get another chance for a long while.

'Hettie, I wish to see you more.'

'I am so busy, Evan. And so tired.'

'Not like that. I wish to . . . well . . .' He faltered. Could he come out and simply say it? 'I wish . . . I wish you and

I were children again and could play in the ruins here as we used to.'

Hettie turned from him and took her hand away. She smiled at the memory. He had lost his nerve and the moment had passed.

'Happy times,' she said, still smiling. Her eyes scanned the new building work, perhaps recalling their childhood antics as she looked.

'They were the very best,' he went on. 'Just me and thee, galloping around like ponies. Free as birds. Careless as the wind.'

'Oh yes, Evan. That we were.'

'And could be again . . .' he tried. She turned to him, that same little arch of her eyebrows showing her curiosity. 'If . . . you were not so far above me now, Miss Hettie Jones, lady's maid. If that were not who you are now, one day we coulda been married. And be together always, with a brood of little'uns to bring us joy.'

Ah, how clever he had been! Surely she would turn it round now and make it right.

'Yes . . .' was all she said, and she looked away again. That wasn't supposed to happen. Then she added, 'It's a lovely idea . . . but . . .'

But? She trailed off and left him desperate. 'I dunna like the sound of that *but*.'

'We're a bit young to be talking of such things, I reckon.'

'Too young? Many folk around these parts are married off by now.'

'And my post . . . I'd have to give it up. And I only just started it. And learning the ways of it. And it is a great chance for me, Evan.'

'So . . . so you'd rather work for that forsaken family than . . .'

'Than what?'

'Than marry me!' he blurted out, infuriated now.

She looked round at him. 'Evan, you haven't asked me to marry you.'

'Well . . . I . . . not in so many words, lass, but . . .'

'You see, you inna ready for it neither. Even if it seems a lovely idea.'

'You have changed,' he said, annoyed at himself now, more than her. She was right. He should've prepared it properly, with a speech all ready for her. She deserved that and so much more. He was a fool to think a shabby suit was enough for Hettie Jones. 'You woulda never said *lovely* in former times. You woulda said *proper jam*.'

'You're right. I have changed. I inna the girl I once was. I've new responsibilities now. To my father. And to Mrs King.'

To hear the name King in the midst of his marriage proposal was more than his short temper could bear.

'Over me? And us, all of us?'

Hettie sighed and shook her head. 'Dunna start a row now, Evan. I dunna wanna fight with you.'

'It's just ... we all feel ... me and Mother and Father ... we all think you need to show ... more ... be more ...' What was he even saying? He needed to stop this and get back to the matter in hand, to marriage, to his love for her. But she had angered him and now his mouth was running and he couldn't pull back.

'Grateful?' she asked, and her eyes turned cold on him. 'You want me to be more *grateful* to you all?'

'No,' he said, exasperated. 'But, well, yes! You've gone and left us and ... you dunna seem to ... wanna know us no more.'

'I'm here now, aren't I? And anyway, how do you want me to show how grateful I am? Shall I get myself on bended knee? Whip myself with a cat o' nine tails, such as my father had on his back in the colonies?'

'Agh, wench, you are so vexing!' That was that. He had lost his temper now and she had caused it. Impossible girl!

'Since I dunna agree with every little thing you say, Evan Malone, then I am vexing.'

'You surely are! I came here today to ...' Her face softened now. But he could not finish his sentence. He could not take more rejection. 'Never mind.'

'You came here today to be my friend. So, please honour that. Do not box my ears. I have no one to talk to down there. I must listen and follow orders. I have not one friend in my new world, not a true friend. Not like you. Will you be my friend, Evan?'

So, now it was her asking the question, and it was not the one he wanted to hear. But how could he refuse her simple, plaintive request?

'Course. Course I will. Always. You know that, Hettie.'

'And I thank God for it. For you. Thank'ee for listening. And for coming. I mun go now. I need my rest before tonight and another round of fitful sleep.'

She stood up, and he knew it was done. His chance was gone.

They walked down the hill together in silence. She seemed lost in a dream, staring ahead as he glanced at her. At their parting of ways, they said farewell, without a hug, without the kiss he had been dreaming of for weeks. All that was gone. He had come to Southover to make her his bride, and he left there with nothing.

Except her friendship. He did at least still have that. And it was a prize he valued more than any treasure.

Chapter 13

Christmas came and went and the dark days of January followed. Much of this Hettie spent with her mistress in her room, reading to her or listening to her stories. Over these past months, old Mrs King had transformed in Hettie's eyes, from the old witch some people in the village felt she was, to a warm, clever and witty person for whom Hettie genuinely cared. She was constantly amazed at how sharp her mistress was; she was ninety-seven years of age and frail of body, but her mind was all there. She did get a little tearful at times, especially when she reminisced about the past, as she had done more and more in recent weeks. She told Hettie stories about her son Ralph, her grandson Cyril, her granddaughter Margaret and her great-granddaughter Beatrice. One afternoon, she shared stories of her childhood with Hettie. She had been a child in the later decades of the eighteenth century, a time that seemed impossible to Hettie to have lived through, it was all so long ago.

'Something you might not know about me is my real name. Do you know it, Jones?'

'No, ma'am. I only know you as Mrs King.'

'Once I married I became known as Queenie, because I ruled this place and this family like a regent. But before that, I was Alice Hinton. That was my true name. I had a sister, Selina. She was beautiful and kind. And told wonderful stories. I loved her very much. But . . . well . . . she died.' Her voice trailed off and her eyes clouded.

Hettie said, 'I am sorry to hear that, ma'am.'

Mrs King shook her head and forced a smile. 'Oh, it was ever so many years ago now. Well, let me tell you something. When we were children, Selina and I had a piano teacher come to the house called Miss Simkiss. She was an elderly lady, but very sharp and a talented pianist. She was kind to us, though she could be a bit of a taskmaster. One day, Selina and I were permitted to visit Miss Simkiss at her home. It was a terraced house by the river towards Buildwas, painted white with a magnificent wisteria that climbed gloriously across the façade. The house was neat and tidy and comfortable. Two cats lived there – now what were their names? Ah yes, Pusskins and Smudge! Extraordinary how I can remember such useless information from eight or nine decades ago. Another woman lived there, too, another Miss Simkiss. We were introduced and the lady bid us good afternoon.

'As our teacher poured us glasses of cordial in the small, homely kitchen, I remember thinking how much I pitied Miss Simkiss, that she was an old spinster, that she had never found a husband and had to live with her sister, poor old thing. We went back out into the pretty garden and I sat quietly with Selina and the Misses Simkiss. We listened to the birds chirping and the river flowing and the breeze ruffling the uppermost branches of the trees. The two old women were at peace and completely at ease with each other and their surroundings. I found myself yearning for such peace, though I did not understand why. It was as if a knot in my stomach had unravelled itself, and the relief was immense.

'I was too young then to understand it, but years later I have looked back on those ladies, after they were long dead, and realised that I had envied them. They had mastered the art of living. To have stayed with my dear sister Selina forever, in a tidy little house, with pea plants and wisteria, with two indolent cats and that perfection of peace – no husbands, no fathers, no children, no grandchildren to spoil it – that would have been the best life I could imagine. How happy we would have been! Selina and I, alone in perfect companionship. If only my life had been that way.'

Hettie listened with fascination. Throughout these conversations about her mistress's past, Hettie would listen or ask polite questions as Mrs King spoke. She often talked fondly of the past, but sometimes spoke with true vitriol when she described her husband, son or grandson. For the female members of the family, she had nothing but praise, and sometimes she would weep a little, for the death of Margaret and for Beatrice's absence. Hettie realised that, whatever terrible things the Malones and Anny's family, the Woodvines, had been through due to the Kings, Mrs King had suffered too.

Mrs King turned to look at Hettie. Her eyes were shining with tears, an apologetic smile on her face. Hettie knew that if she said a kind thing now, Mrs King would weep. But perhaps that was not what she needed, to be exhausted by tears and regret when she had so little energy already. So Hettie only said, 'Keep your chin up, ma'am.'

Mrs King shrugged her shoulders and smiled wider, then jutted her chin out and said, 'Is that better?'

'Much better, ma'am.'

They sat in companionable silence after that. Hettie knew she would never replace Jenkins. But she was proud that she seemed to bring some scrap of comfort to this extraordinary lady in the winter days of her life.

∞

It was the most curious feeling. When Queenie awoke that February night, she was aware of the cold first. It always crept into her bones in the middle of the night, no matter how many blankets Jones gave her. Sometimes she felt weighted down by bedding, as if she could not move, but still the cold would come for her. But this morning, something else had crept into her body, something new and foreign.

She opened her eyes and found there was a fogginess there. It must just be sleep in her eyes, she guessed. Lying on her right side, she went to raise her left hand to wipe it out and found that her left arm was immobile. Again, just sleepiness, she thought. She tried again. But her left arm would not move, nor her left leg. She opened her mouth to speak and said, 'Beatrice.' She hadn't meant to say that name. She'd wanted to say Jenkins, even though she knew it was Jones she wanted, her dear Jones, her Hettie. How fond she'd grown of the girl since she'd started there a few months before.

'Jenkins,' she said. 'Cyril,' she said next, now alarmed. Why on earth would she be calling for him, her grandson who had passed away? And besides, she was only whispering. If all these people she'd called had been standing at the other side of the room, they would not have heard her.

'Blaize,' she said next and then felt truly frightened. She would never willingly summon the ghost of the long-dead servant. Oh, if only Jones could hear her!

She tried again to move her left side, and nothing happened. She lay there for some time in a state of terror. She stared across the room at the doorway to Jones's room, as if glaring long enough would wake the girl. But her eyes were still foggy and the doorway shimmered, the door jamb beginning to waver and undulate like a snake. She closed her eyes and felt a sudden rush of dizziness, so disconcerting that she opened them again.

She decided to stare at the pillow, as its comforting whiteness blanked out everything else.

She must have slept eventually, for when she came to daybreak had lightened the curtains.

'Jones,' she said, relieved to hear the name she intended to say and also that her voice was stronger. 'Jones!' she called again and this time she heard, at last, movement from the next room.

In came Hettie, her light brown hair in a long plait over her shoulder, her green eyes shining in the early-morning light. For a moment, Queenie thought she was Martha Jones, come back to haunt her. It seemed her room was filling with ghosts.

'Morning, ma'am,' said Hettie, going to the window to draw open the curtains. 'We have both slept in a little today. I am so sorry. I should've been up by now. Please forgive me.'

'Jones, I am ill,' said Queenie.

Hettie turned to her and came closer. 'In what manner, ma'am?'

'I cannot move anything down my left side. Help me to sit up. I have been trapped like this for hours.'

Hettie rushed to her then and put the back of her hand against her forehead. She then grasped Queenie's shoulder and turned her body to lie on her back. What a relief it was to be off her side. Her right arm felt numb from being underneath her so long, but feeling was coming back to it. Her left side, however, was still useless.

When Hettie looked down and saw Queenie's face, she gasped.

'Help me sit up,' said Queenie, and now that her face was freed from lying on her side, she realised that the left side of her mouth was not moving. Only the right side was forming the words. Hettie tried to pull her up, reaching to drag an extra pillow behind her head. She was propped up now at least – not fully, but enough to feel a touch more dignified.

'I shall send for the doctor immediately,' said Hettie.

'What is wrong with my face?' said Queenie.

'The left side . . . has dropped, ma'am. I shall fetch the doctor, do not fret.'

Even in the shock of the moment, of confirming her fear that something was very wrong with her, she was pleased to hear that Hettie was learning to speak more correctly, losing the *dunna* of her previous self and using the standard form of *do not*. Queenie had been training her well these past months, not only in the duties of a lady's maid, but also in the correct etiquette for ladies themselves. Only Queenie knew why she had begun this process of transforming Hettie. And now Queenie had woken up incapacitated and – who knew? – perhaps that much closer to death, she was content that her work on Hettie was well under way. She might not have much time left to complete her plan.

The doctor had been sent for and Queenie rested her eyes while she waited. The dizziness had gone, at least.

Hettie, now dressed in her smart maid's uniform, fed Queenie her breakfast of porridge with honey. Queenie could have used her right hand, but had little vitality to move and was glad of Hettie's help. The girl was kind-hearted and never spoke too much. She had adjusted to this new post and her new life with decorum, fortitude and a willingness to learn. Her manner was gentle but never cloying. As she thought on Hettie's good qualities, Queenie realised that tears were streaming down her face.

Hettie took a handkerchief from her sleeve and dabbed at Queenie's face. She looked into Hettie's green eyes, smiling with compassion, and said, 'Thank you.'

Hettie merely nodded, but a moment passed between them, a knowledge that the maid was more than a maid and the mistress was more than a mistress. It made Queenie's heart sing, even in the midst of her distress.

A knock on the door announced the arrival of Dr Fitzgerald, physician to the King family. He was looking old these days. Indeed, he was around the same age as Jenkins had been and probably should have retired by now. But Queenie trusted nobody else with her health. In he came, placing his hat on a side table as he crossed the room to her bed. One look at her face and he nodded. Hettie took away the mostly finished bowl of porridge and stood at the end of the bed, awaiting instructions.

'Mrs King,' said Fitzgerald softly, offering her a pitying smile. 'What an odd state we find ourselves in this morning, hmm?'

'None of that,' said Queenie. 'Tell me my prognosis.'

'I'm glad to hear your speech is normal. As acerbic as ever.'

He carried out an examination of her body, looking into her eyes and taking her pulse, then asking her to move certain things she couldn't move on her left side, but could on her right.

'All done, dear lady,' he said at last, and stood up. 'I shall have a word with your daughter-in-law and give her instructions. You must rest now for many days, until you feel better.'

'First you shall tell me the prognosis, as I have asked.' The paralysis of half of her face made talking awkward, but her voice was as clear as it could be. She did not wish that Benjamina should have any say in what happened to her. She wanted the truth, so that she could plan accordingly.

Dr Fitzgerald sighed, then sat down on the bed and crossed his legs and his arms. He then looked Queenie right in the eye and said, 'The prognosis is not good. You have suffered from a bout of apoplexy. There are some invasive procedures I might try with a younger patient, such as bloodletting, but to my mind, considering your great age, the kindest approach would be to leave you be. It is highly likely that you will have another bout within weeks, days or even hours, and that the next one will be fatal. So I believe the best course of action is to make you as comfortable as possible and ensure you have your affairs in order.'

Queenie had feared this, but it was almost a relief to hear it, to know the facts. She hated being in ignorance more than almost anything. Now she knew exactly what she must do.

'Thank you, Fitzgerald,' she said and gave what must have been a lopsided smile.

The doctor smiled back at her. 'You've lived a long and fruitful life, Mrs King,' he said. 'And it has been my honour to serve you through these many years.'

'I will join Jenkins soon, and Selina and my babies,' she said and again those tears began to stream down her face without warning. Hettie came over and dabbed at her cheeks.

Fitzgerald had his own moment of emotion, for Queenie knew he had always been sweet on Rose Jenkins and that she had spurned him in favour of her post as lady's maid. Her death must have moved him tremendously.

'Leave me now,' Queenie said. 'Give instructions to Jones here, not the other Mrs King. Jones may be young, but she is more than capable.'

Fitzgerald nodded and took his leave. Queenie saw him talking in hushed tones as Hettie went with him to the door. She lay alone for a moment, as Hettie saw him out. Thoughts rushed in. So, she was to die soon.

To die. To leave this place, to go . . . where? To another place? Or to oblivion? She had never had much faith, though she went through the motions of churchgoing.

Other thoughts crowded in, of those 'affairs' the doctor had mentioned. She must instruct Hettie the moment she came back into the room. Hettie must write immediately to Beatrice, demanding that she come home from America to see Queenie before she went. It was probably a hopeless request, as according to the doctor's prognosis, Queenie might not last the day. But he had mentioned weeks. Weeks could be months – who knew? Queenie had defied all odds living to nearly a hundred as it was. Well, Beatrice must be summoned.

Even more pressing was her need to see her solicitor. She was stupid to have left this so long. She needed to see him immediately, today. When Hettie returned from speaking with the doctor, Queenie would order it. She only hoped that he would arrive before the apoplexy returned and finished her off. She decided that if she began to feel seriously unwell again when she was waiting, then she would have Hettie bring her paper and a pen and she would sign it herself, asking Hettie to write down the necessaries. Would it be legal? It would have to do. She could only hope she would not die before her solicitor came and she could ensure that Benjamina did not thwart this closing act of hers. Then all would be well, the future secured for those who awaited her final deed.

So, the letter to Beatrice and the solicitor's visit first. Then, she must speak with Hettie, for she had something to tell the girl, something only Queenie knew – something that would change Hettie's life forever.

Chapter 14

As the doctor was leaving, he stopped Hettie on the landing and said, 'I was present at your birth, young lady.'

Hettie was taken aback by this. She knew the story, of course, but she did not know it was this doctor who had been summoned by Rose Jenkins to save her life and that of her mother. Her family never had enough money to see him, relying instead on various potions Anny made or bought. She was moved to meet this doctor at last, the man who had ensured that her passage into this world was a safe one.

'Thank you!' she said. 'Thank you so much!'

He waved away her gratitude and bustled off down the stairs saying, 'My pleasure, Miss Jones. I'll see myself out.'

Hettie stood for a moment, thinking how things would have been so different if the Kings had not sent for him that day. She might not have been standing here now. Then she recalled herself and went back to her mistress, the same woman who had paid for that doctor to save her life. How curious and strange life was, its web of connections mysterious.

She found Mrs King quite agitated. First, she insisted that Hettie send a note to the family solicitor, demanding his presence immediately, which Hettie arranged straight away. Next, she feverishly dictated a letter to Miss Beatrice Ashford, her great-granddaughter, requesting her to return home from America as soon as possible, due to her dangerously ill health. Then, she made Hettie sit on the edge of the bed, and said she had something to tell her.

Hettie was wondering what it could be when Clayton popped her head around the door to say that the solicitor had arrived, and Mrs King said that she would speak to Hettie afterwards.

The solicitor, Mr Steadman, was shown in, and Hettie was told to leave and sit in her room to await instructions. She waited there, preoccupied. She could hear the voices of Mrs King and the solicitor murmuring in the next room, but could not make out any of the words. She shouldn't, of course, because it was private business. But she did wonder what it was that Mrs King felt she needed so urgently to tell her. Now she had the time to sit and think about things – unexpected in the daily routine of a lady's maid – her wonderings crowded in. What would happen now? If her mistress died soon, as it seemed she would, what would Hettie do next? Could she go back to her pit life, or would she take her experience gained and go on in service? If her mistress wrote her a reference, she surely could. But she would have to ask her, as she was certain that young Mrs King would not bother or would write her a terrible one; she seemed to hate Hettie so, though Hettie still had no idea why.

For some reason, Mr Lawrence Maxwell Ripley came into her mind, the vision of his handsome face as large as life before her. She had thought of him often since beginning her work here at the King household months before. It was something about being in a well-to-do environment that prompted it. She would enact grand fantasies in her mind, of going to London with Mrs King as her maid and accidentally bumping into Mr Ripley in a restaurant or hotel foyer. He would seek her out again and declare his love, defy society's expectations and ask her to marry him.

It was all folly; she knew that. But it kept her warm on cold nights. At other times, she thought of Evan, his strong arms, the beautifully thick blond hair that she would love to run her fingers through. It hadn't been easy turning him down when they met that day at Southover. She knew he was in love with her. And she loved him – of course she did. But she could not get Mr Ripley out of her mind, and marriage to Evan would mean giving up her post; she could not bear that, not when she had only just started it and her future was shining more brightly.

Since then, Evan had not brought it up again, and she half wondered if he had changed his mind about her.

They certainly were drifting apart. Her new post altered not only her appearance in her finer clothes, but her voice too, as she took on Mrs King's daily advice about her language and deportment. If she married Evan, a life in the pit beckoned – her old life, back again. Sometimes she missed it, but other times she thanked her lucky stars that Mrs King had given her this opportunity and laid her future open to so many new possibilities. Now it seemed it would be coming to an end, and she feared what might happen next.

'Jones!'

Mrs King was calling her from the next room. She went through to find the solicitor packing away some papers and writing materials into his bag. She went to open the door for him, looking briefly at Mrs King to see she was propped up comfortably. She looked better than she had all day. Her face was still odd to look upon, with its slanting left side, all the features drooping. But she had a smile playing about her lips, and looked truly content.

'Show out Mr Steadman and then come straight back to me, Jones.'

Her voice sounded stronger, too. That was good. The solicitor was ready now and followed her out onto the landing.

Once Hettie had shut the door behind her, Mr Steadman turned to her and smiled. He was a short, sturdy man with little remaining hair and spider veins on his cheeks.

'You serve your mistress well, Miss Jones,' he said, a definite twinkle in his eye.

'Yes, sir,' she said, unsure how to proceed. 'I do my very best.'

'Evidently,' he said, with a smile. 'But listen, my dear.' He moved his bald head closer to her, took a quick glance about him and lowered his voice. 'Keep your wits about you. Look out for yourself. And don't let anyone tell you what to do. Strange times lie ahead, and you'll need all of your guile to get through them. Something tells me you'll be fine.'

What in God's name was the man talking about? Hettie just stared at him, knowing she should respond but entirely lost for words. He tapped his nose and winked at her. She had not been winked at by a man since she'd worked at the pit.

'Sir, I . . .'

'All will become clear,' he said and his face changed, from one of amusement to that of utter seriousness. 'I will see you again soon – before too long, I expect. And if you ever need help, you know where to find me. I'll be happy to assist you, at any time. Remember that.'

He did not allow her to reply to this odd statement, and instead turned and trotted down the stairs, leaving her on the landing, agog.

A few moments later she heard Mr Steadman talking to someone in the hallway. She went to the bannister and peered over. It was Mrs King the younger, returned from a ride she had taken out early that morning with a gentle-man friend. She did not even know about the elder Mrs King's condition. Hettie hoped Clayton would inform her, so that she did not have to speak to her. Meanwhile, she saw that Mr Steadman was talking to her in low tones, perhaps giving her the news himself. But at that moment, Mrs King looked up sharply and saw Hettie. She said good afternoon to Mr Steadman and came quickly up the stairs.

Hettie turned away to go back to her mistress, but the younger Mrs King called out to her, 'You. You there.'

She never called her Jones, only *you* or sometimes even just *maid*. Hettie wished she had not been so nosy; she could've been safely back in her mistress's room if she'd not been so stupid as to have eavesdropped on them.

'Yes, ma'am?' she said and turned to Mrs King, who was now at the top of the stairs and making towards her.

'What was he here for?' she snapped at Hettie.

'Mr Steadman, ma'am?'

'Yes, Mr Steadman. Who do you think I mean?'

'I'm sure I do not know, ma'am. He came to speak with Mrs King the elder and then he left.'

'You were not in the room?'

'I was not, ma'am.'

'Are you lying? You're lying, aren't you, you little schemer. You were there or you listened in. I would wager ten guineas you know exactly what was discussed in that room.'

Mrs King's face was now only inches away from her own. Hettie had always thought of Mrs King the younger as a handsome woman, but now her viciousness showed in her twisted expression and Hettie wanted to get as far away from it as possible. But she stood her ground and did not flinch. Something told her that battle lines were being drawn. She did not know how or what would become of this, but she sensed that her mistress needed protection from this woman.

'Indeed not, ma'am. I was in the next room and heard not a word.'

Mrs King gave a dry bark of a laugh, with not one ounce of humour in it, only mockery. Then she turned and marched downstairs, her fine riding clothes rustling expensively as she went.

Hettie gathered herself and went back in to her mistress. Mrs King the elder was clearly waiting for her, as she reached out with her right hand and patted the bedspread.

'Come sit with me. I must speak with you now.'

∞

The child sat on the bed beside her. Queenie still thought of her as the child, for Hettie was so young. Eighteen in July. Not so young, perhaps. But at ninety-seven, everyone seemed like babies to Queenie, even the doctor and the solicitor. Besides, Hettie was the child of the baby on the bridge, the child of Blaize's prophecy, the child who would bridge the divide. Queenie felt as if the past seven decades of her life had somehow been leading to this moment, ever since she had watched her long-dead husband rape the poor maid Blaize, and Queenie had stood by and done nothing. Now, finally, she was able to make amends. Now, perhaps, the ghost of Blaize would approve and leave her in everlasting peace.

'My dear,' Queenie began, suddenly feeling very weary. She wished to sleep, after a busy day of visitors and the settling of affairs. But she had no idea how much time she had left and this last duty must be done. 'I have something to tell you. When you hear it, it will change you. But I hope it will do so for the better. Your life now will alter immeasurably, as will your future. You must listen carefully and not interrupt. Do you understand?'

Hettie's green eyes were narrowed with curiosity, her brow furrowed. She nodded.

'Many years ago, when I was a new young wife, my husband used to assault the servants that worked in our house. One day, I found him forcing himself on a young maid called Betsy Blaize. Later, that maid left our employ. No, I must be truthful. I dismissed her. I regret this deeply. But there it is. Betsy Blaize had a child, the bastard child of my husband, Ralph King senior. She carried it across the iron bridge and gave it to a passing Quaker man, and then she died. The Quaker was called

Beddoes and he brought up the baby on the bridge with his wife, as their own. This baby was Martha, your mother.

'So you see, my dear, your grandfather was Ralph King senior. You are related to the Kings. You are a King, more so than myself or my daughter-in-law Benjamina, for we are Kings only by marriage, not by blood. My granddaughter, Margaret, was your cousin, and her daughter Beatrice is your first cousin, once removed.

'When Beatrice comes here from America, you will be reunited as the family you are. She was present at your birth and she cared deeply for you, your mother and father, as well as the Malones, whose son Owen she was in love with before he died. So, you see, the Kings, the Malones and the Joneses are all intimately connected, though it has brought us nothing but trouble. The feud has raged on these sixty years or so, but now you are the one to bridge that divide and bring harmony to these families. You are the one true connection between us all. *The child will cross the bridge. The child will make one house from two. The child is the answer.* That is you, my dear Hettie. *You* are the answer.'

The relief of having said it all in one speech was immense, but so was the effort expended. Queenie closed her eyes, inhaled deeply and breathed out slowly, her breath slightly ragged. She had watched Hettie's eyes grow wider and wider as she listened. Now

Queenie had said her piece, she felt so exhausted, she decided not to open her eyes again. She had no energy left to answer the child's inevitable questions. She heard Hettie's breathing, but she kept her eyes closed.

A peace had come upon her the likes of which she had not experienced for a lifetime; the last time she felt like this was in her youth, with her sister. But Selina had gone strange, been put away in an asylum and killed herself. And Alice had married Ralph King, a cold, cruel rapist of young women. She had sacrificed any peace she might have had for a marriage to a monster. He made her pregnant and she lost twin girls to tuberculosis before they were six months old. Eventually, she produced her son Ralph junior and from then on, she devoted her life to this family, to making it the greatest in the county and beyond.

But oh, what terrible losses they had suffered along the way. Now, in her final days, she could see at last that everything was coming to fruition. The King fortune was considerable, but almost all of its descendants were dead or had abandoned the family. Yet this child, this baby of the baby on the bridge, this Hettie Jones, would be Queenie's final act. Queenie smiled inwardly and felt a great wave of peace wash over her, as if she lay at the bottom of the River Severn, the water flowing over her lazily, as her mind drifted away from consciousness and she slept.

⁓

Time passed. It might have been hours or days or even weeks, Queenie had no idea. She was just so tired, so very, very tired. Sleep felt like a comfortable bath, continuously topped up with more deliciously warm water. She had no inclination to leave it and step out into the cold glare of waking life.

Her dreams were muddled and shifting, scenes from her long life filing past her like a motley parade. She was aware of Hettie at times, Benjamina and Clayton at others. She believed the doctor was there at points, but couldn't swear on it. He might have been another dream.

But then, one night, she opened her eyes and the room was bathed in a bluish-white light. She knew that light. It was the spectral garb of her old companion, the ghost of Betsy Blaize.

She's come for me, thought Queenie.

She forced herself to focus and moved her eyes lazily across the room, seeking the source of the light. And there she was, the spirit, clothed in a brilliant white gown, her hair flowing in a gentle zephyr, her blue eyes shining out and gazing upon Queenie with infinite pity and love.

'*It is time*,' a voice spoke in Queenie's mind, the voice of the spirit.

'*I am ready*,' answered Queenie, without moving her lips.

'*Look*,' said the spirit and raised her hand, gesturing towards the bed where Queenie lay.

Queenie saw the forms of others materialising, coming into being as if a fog was lifting. First was Jenkins, her beloved Rose, her smile knowing, mischievous and yet kind, just as she often looked on her mistress in life. Beside her were the beautiful blonde locks and large blue eyes of her granddaughter Margaret, who clasped her hands before her and nodded at her grandmother, smiling. Beside her stood two identical little girls, ribbons in their hair, both broadly grinning, their teeth a brilliant white – Queenie's daughters, lost as babies, grown into the girls they would have been. Queenie's heart overflowed with joy.

Then, last, came the one she lost the longest ago, a slim, willowy figure with the same large blue eyes her great-niece had inherited; it was Queenie's dear sister Selina. In life, those eyes had been clouded with trouble, but now, in death, they shone clearly and brightly.

Selina held out her hand to Queenie.

Chapter 15

The morning was an extremely cold one. Hettie shivered as she went to her mistress's fireplace to remake the fire. She cleaned out the ashes and lit a new one, all the while expecting her mistress to wake at any moment to complain that Hettie was making too much noise.

But Mrs King did not wake up and berate her as she usually did, and once finished with the fire, Hettie approached the bed slowly. As she drew back the bed curtains, a chill ran down her spine, which at first she thought must just be the cold. But something stopped her, and as she looked up at Mrs King's face, she saw that her eyes were open, staring to the side of the bed. Her arm was outstretched, her palm open. There was that chill again and as Hettie bent over Mrs King, she knew immediately that she was gone. The dead look in the eyes was beyond that she'd seen when her mistress had been very ill. This was death and it was unmistakable.

Hettie stood still and looked down upon her mistress. She had never seen a dead person before. She didn't know if this was the correct thing to do, but she felt very strongly that she should close her mistress's eyes. She gently did so. Then she placed her arm beside her body, so that it was not outstretched. The skin was ice-cold.

Hettie knew that Mrs King the younger must be told, and that the woman would be delighted; everyone in the house knew that she wanted her mother-in-law dead. As Hettie stood next to her mistress's small, slight figure, dwarfed by blankets, and looked down at her still, pale face, she felt a wave of sadness overcome her and her own eyes welled up. She would miss her mistress very much. She would miss her company, her stories and the twinkle in her eye when she smiled at Hettie. And though she knew it was selfish to do so, she also worried for her own future. With old Mrs King gone, Hettie knew that her work here was done. She would have to move on and find another position. She had not even had the heart to ask her mistress to write a reference for her before she passed away. Now she would be stuck with no reference, or a very poor one from the younger Mrs King.

Hettie thought about the pit bank and returning to work there. It felt like another country now. She could move back in with her father and resume her job – but how would the others be with her? She had barely seen Ada and the others since she left. She had been in service, working at the big house, as a lady's maid, no less. She knew she could be a pit girl again – that girl had never left her – but she also knew that she had moved on from their world and would not easily be accepted back, perhaps ever. She was caught in between two worlds, with nowhere to go except the uncertain future.

With a heavy heart, she went back to her room, dressed herself quickly and walked through to find Kezia to tell her the news, so that Mrs King the younger could be informed. She stood by her mistress's bed and waited until the doctor came to pronounce her formally gone. Hearing his words brought the truth of her loss closer. Somehow it wasn't real until Dr Fitzgerald said it. He shed a tear too.

Once he was gone, the reality of Hettie's situation sank in and she expected at any moment to be dismissed from the premises. But before the undertaker arrived to take Mrs King away, a note from the solicitor came, informing them of a two o'clock meeting, which he summoned Mrs King the younger and Miss Hettie Jones, lady's maid, to attend, in order to discuss an urgent matter relating to the death of Mrs King the elder.

At two o'clock, Hettie found herself sitting in the most uncomfortable of silences in Mrs King's study, awaiting the solicitor's arrival. She sat bolt upright in the chair she'd been given. The atmosphere in the room was so thick with menace, Hettie was sure she could have cut it with a cheese knife. Benjamina King could not keep still. She kept shuffling in her study chair, the rustle of her silk gown slicing through the air. She was pretending to look at papers on her desk, but Hettie, even without looking directly at her, could tell it was all for show. Hettie stared straight ahead at the wall, desperate not to catch Mrs King's eye.

Hettie's mind would not keep still. It was filled with the events of the last few days – old Mrs King's revelation, old Mrs King's death. Her mistress was dead, and Hettie was a King. She was the daughter of a woman whose mother had been raped by Ralph King senior. Just being the product of such violence was disturbing enough, but to discover that she was related to the hated Kings was another matter entirely. The new knowledge of her origins burned a hole in the fabric of her mind. Her overwhelming feeling was of shame. Utter shame. She felt embarrassed and appalled that her mother was not only a bastard in the eyes of the law, but also a product of rape. It seemed that this despicable fact somehow followed her through the generations and infected her, too. She felt disgusted to be related to a man who could do such a thing to an innocent young girl. She wondered if she would ever tell anyone: her father? Anny? Evan? She could not imagine framing the words. She did not want them to look at her differently, or to look at her mother differently. No, she would keep it to herself always. Nobody should ever know. It was her shame and she would carry it for the rest of her life. The only people who knew the truth were now dead.

Hettie looked up at the sound of footsteps, and the butler Busby finally showed Mr Steadman in. They had been waiting for him for only five minutes or so, but it felt like an age.

Pleasantries were exchanged between Mrs King and Mr Steadman, who took a seat next to Hettie.

'I must say,' began Mrs King, splendid and regal behind her enormous desk, 'that the haste in which you have demanded to be seen is very unusual, Mr Steadman. It is only a few hours since we found that my dear mother-in-law had passed away during the night, and yet here you are.'

'I understand your concern, madam. But I must tell you that the elder Mrs King's instructions were absolutely clear,' said Steadman, confidently.

Hettie had no idea why she'd been summoned to this meeting, but she was glad that Steadman wasn't afraid of Mrs King like everyone else was.

'She clearly stipulated that I must attend as soon as possible after her death, in order to give you and Miss Jones fair warning.'

Mrs King shot a glance at Hettie, who unfortunately caught her eye, then looked away swiftly. What was happening here?

'Warning?' said Mrs King, in a low, almost threatening voice. 'Of what?'

'The reading of wills is always a delicate matter. Under normal circumstances we would schedule this meeting in a few days in order to let . . . the dust settle, if that is not an unfortunate metaphor to use . . . but Mrs King made it clear that she wanted the contents of her will to be revealed within a day of her death to the two parties hereby present, so that one of the parties did not unwittingly throw the other party out of the house at the first opportunity.'

Now the atmosphere was thicker than ever. Hettie could feel the anger and confusion emanating from Mrs King in waves. Her own mind was racing. Why on earth was she in this room with these people? She should have been packing her bags to leave by now.

'What the devil are you talking about, man?' Mrs King's mask of respectability was slipping.

'I must inform you both that Mrs King the elder was the sole owner of the King fortune, stock, businesses and houses. Therefore, upon her death, it was her duty to dispose of these riches as she saw fit. She had a will drawn up some years ago that left all of this to you, Mrs King, on the proviso that if her great-granddaughter Beatrice ever returned from America to seek her fortune again, the whole must be given up to her. However, Mrs King the elder called upon me very recently and drew up a new will. This is the document I have here today and will make known to you presently.'

'If my mother-in-law has in her final days made this ... maid ... a beneficiary of some trifle in her possession, surely this could have waited? I am a very busy woman, Mr Steadman.'

'I will read you the main points first,' said Steadman, ignoring Mrs King and looking straight at Hettie, who met his gaze. He gave her the briefest of smiles, which only confused her further. Then he took out a document and held it up to read from it. 'This being the last will and testament of Alice Mary King, née Hinton, on this day, et cetera, et cetera ... Ah, here we are. That the entire King fortune owned solely by the aforementioned Alice King is hereby bequeathed upon her death, in whole, to Miss Hettie Jones.'

There was a low guttural noise from across the desk. Hettie realised it was Mrs King saying, 'What?' For herself, Hettie did not believe the words she was hearing. None of it made sense. It created a kind of schism in her brain; on one side was common sense, telling her that what was happening was real. On the other was the certainty that this was a daydream and she would come to her senses at any moment.

Steadman went on. 'Thereby Miss Hettie Jones is the sole heir of all monies, businesses, stocks, houses, other goods and chattels, et cetera, et cetera. Nothing will go to Mrs Benjamina King, apart from the clothes, jewellery and other trinkets she already owns. The will stipulates that Miss Jones is now the sole manager of the King businesses, that she can employ Mrs King to run said businesses if she wishes, but is under no obligation to do so and can choose to turn Mrs King out of the house immediately if she wishes to. However, on the occasion that Miss Jones refuses the inheritance or passes away without issue, rather than the inheritance going to Mr Adam Jones or to the crown, the sole heir will be Mrs Benjamina King, being the last living survivor with that name.'

Hettie sat stock still and so did Mrs King.

'I refute this madness,' said Mrs King, slowly and carefully.

'You may do as you wish, but the meaning of the will is transparent and was drawn up by myself very recently. Your maid Kezia Clayton was called in to witness the signatures and therefore the will is valid and legal. You may contest all you like, but you will not change one word of the meaning of this last will and testament. Mrs King the elder knew her own mind . . .'

'That is where you are wrong, Steadman,' spat Mrs King. 'The old woman's mind was failing her, for months, if not years, before her death. The servants heard her talking to someone when in her room alone. She then hired a pit girl as a lady's maid, further evidence of her addled mind. So if you think I'm going to sit back and allow this travesty to . . .'

'And now,' said Steadman loudly, cutting off Mrs King, which left her agog, 'we come to the reasoning behind Mrs King's decision. Miss Jones is aware of this information already. But it is time to reveal the reason why Miss Jones is named as sole heir.'

Hettie felt as if all the blood drained from her head and pooled in her feet. Surely Mr Steadman didn't know . . . surely?

'Sir . . .' she began. But Steadman was already speaking.

'The fact is that Miss Jones is . . .'

'No!' cried Hettie.

Mrs King glared at her, then her expression changed to a kind of evil fascination. 'Do go on,' she said, smiling disgracefully.

'Miss Jones is in fact a King heir,' said Mr Steadman. 'She is related in blood to Mr Ralph King senior. He had relations of a forcible kind with a maid, Miss Betsy Blaize, which produced a child, Martha, who married Mr Adam Jones, and thus Miss Hettie Jones was born. Therefore, she is a King by blood and due her inheritance, gifted by Mrs King senior.'

Hettie wanted the ground to open up and swallow her. The shame dripped from her like sweat. To have known this fact was bad enough, but to have it paraded so gaily before an enemy was too much to bear.

'Well, well, well,' said Mrs King and stood up from her desk. 'We have a bastard in our midst.'

Mr Steadman stood up too. 'Now then, that's enough, Mrs King. And inaccurate. Miss Jones's mother may have been born out of wedlock – through no fault of her own, I may add – but Miss Jones was born firmly within wedlock. I am sure that if any one of us were to look back into our own ancestry they'd find a bastard or two along the way. Even amongst royalty, as history clearly shows!'

'But she had no claim,' said Mrs King. 'There is no proof!'

'I have Mrs King the elder's word and that is enough for me. In any case, it is of no consequence, as Mrs King could choose to leave her fortune to whomsoever she desired. She could leave it to your little dog if she wished. But she did not. She left it in whole to this young woman, whose kindness she hugely appreciated these past months. And that is something that could never be said of you, Mrs King!'

'How dare you!' she cried.

Hettie felt as if her head would split open if she had to hear any more of this. She felt so hot in this room – the atmosphere was so close. She wanted to run.

Steadman was putting his papers back into his briefcase. 'I must confer with my client now. Miss Jones, will you take a turn around the garden with me? We can talk there.'

Hettie glanced at Mrs King, whose cheeks had two round red spots of rage blooming upon them. Her eyes were like ice. Hettie wanted nothing more than to get out of that room, so she nodded meekly and stood up. She had no idea what to say, so she said nothing.

'This is not over,' said Benjamina, staring down at the desk now.

'That is your opinion, but not a legal fact. I will provide more details in the coming weeks of the extent of the King fortune, of course. But for now, Mrs King the elder made it very clear that I must give the two of you this news within a day of her death, so that you,

Mrs King, did not force you, Miss Jones, to leave the house in the mistaken knowledge that you were now in charge. It is you, Miss Jones, who are in charge now. Come, let us walk and I will explain things further to you. I take my leave of you, Mrs King.'

With that, Steadman went straight to the door and held it open, nodding at Hettie. She did not look round at Mrs King, but could feel the hatred flowing from her, as real as a roaring fire. She left the room and then Mr Steadman walked before her silently, leading her across the hallway and through a side door, out into the grounds. As she followed him, her mind was screaming. Mrs King had left her entire fortune . . . to her. To Hettie Jones, pit girl, strawberry picker, maid. Everything: the houses, the businesses, the money. To her. It was daft. It was impossible.

Once outside, Mr Steadman turned to Hettie and smiled.

'Good to get out of there, hm?' he said, and gave a sly look towards the house.

'Mr Steadman, please,' said Hettie, her voice shaking.

His expression changed and he reached out and patted her on the shoulder. 'It's a shock for you, I know. But you must bear up under it. Your life has changed in a moment. Do you feel faint, Miss Jones?'

Did she? Perhaps she did. Her head was swimming. But he was right, it was good to get out of the house.

'Could we walk a bit?' she said and stepped onto the path away from the house that led into the woodland. She needed time to think, to breathe.

'Of course, my dear. We shall walk and talk a little.'

Steadman explained to her what would happen next. He would arrange for her to sign some papers at his office. He said something about 'probate', but she didn't know what that was, so she just nodded. He explained some details about the businesses and who ran each one and what Mrs King wanted, but he lost her after the first few seconds and she just let his voice flow over her and she walked slowly onwards, the birds chirping around them in the trees, oblivious.

'Excuse me, sir,' she said, interrupting. 'Surely it's a mistake.'

'In what sense?' he said.

'All of it. Mrs King must have been losing her mind to do this.'

'Not at all, my dear. She was absolutely lucid. She knew exactly what she wanted to do and why. She explained it all to me. And do not fear: Mrs King junior's bark is far worse than her bite. She can do nothing to refute this. The will stands. You inherit, and Mrs King does not.'

'You said something about "issue". If I "pass without issue". What does that mean?'

'If you die before having a child, the heir will be Mrs King junior.'

'I see.'

'Yes, Mrs King senior added this stipulation to the will for a particular reason. You see, she originally wanted Miss Beatrice Ashford to be the sole heir, but Miss Ashford refused it, and she wondered if you might do the same. Also, she feared that if you passed away before your time and had not yet married and had children, that the estate would go to your father – with which outcome I'm afraid she was not happy – or to the crown. She could not bear that idea. She wanted the King name and houses and businesses to live on in perpetuity. Is there any risk that you will do that, Miss Jones?'

'Die without children?' she said, shocked at such a question.

'Ah no, my dear. I meant, that you might refuse the inheritance.'

Hettie had not considered it. The Malones would, she was sure of that. And Beatrice had, for all the right reasons. Should she herself refuse it too?

'Can I use the inheritance in any way? In whatever way I see fit?'

'You can do whatever you wish, with the businesses, with the money, with Southover when it is completed and with the old brickmaster's house here, as we still call it. You are in control of the entire estate, and may use it or dispose of it as you will.'

Hettie stopped walking and turned back towards the old brickmaster's house, her home for the past five months. She stared at it, outlining with her eyes the windows, doors and bricks that built it.

'Are you feeling ill, Miss Jones? Can I assist you?'

'No, thank you. I am well. But I have a question. I have plenty of questions. But one in particular is gnawing away at me.'

'Never fear. In a day or so, you can come to my office and we'll go through it all together. I will see you through this strange time. But what is your question?'

'When can I move my father into this house?'

Chapter 16

Benjamina still sat at her desk, rigid with shock. She could hear her dog Drina barking intermittently upstairs. It was time for her walk, after which Benjamina would normally take her afternoon nap. That was the unchanging pattern of her life for the past few years: up early, business in the morning, luncheon, dog walk, nap, dinner, entertainment, bed. She had taken the monotony for granted. She had sometimes complained of it, to her dog, to her acquaintances, to her lovers – how hard she worked every day to manage the businesses, how little time she had for shopping, or socialising, or dancing. But she'd been happy with it, too – delighted, in fact. After all these years of being an ornament, she had finally had a use. And it all had a higher purpose: it led towards the conclusion of the inheritance. One day when the old bitch had died, Benjamina would own everything: from the mines to the forges and the brickyards, every wine glass in the cupboard and tulip bulb in the garden. It would all be hers. She had no child to leave it to, but she didn't care. She had no interest in what happened to the King name after her death. It could go to the dogs for all she cared. But she had waited for this all of her adult life.

And now it was gone, in a moment. To this slip of a girl, this pit-wench, this *maid*.

Her thoughts fell heavily on Hettie Jones, the object now of all her hatred. Hettie was the same age now as Benjamina herself had been when she was given to Ralph King. Given, like a gift, like a possession, like a transaction. She'd never had her own life until now. And this child had strolled in from the pit bank and taken it from her. One girl was sold to a man and the other girl was given a fortune. The comparison gave her physical pain, a gnawing in her gut that had just begun. The injustice of it! Benjamina could well imagine the pleasure Queenie must have felt as she added that stipulation to the will, that if Hettie refused or passed without a child, the next heir would be herself. So close and yet so far. The old witch must have delighted in knowing how much that would torture her. Benjamina clenched her fists and looked down at them, her perfectly manicured nails digging into her palms. She felt positively murderous.

She heard someone enter the house from the garden door and assumed it must be the girl, back from her walk. Benjamina had to face up to her situation. She would contest this will – of course she would. But in the meantime, she had to deal with the girl. Shouting and screaming would get her nowhere. And the horrible truth was, the girl could have her thrown out. That very day, thrown out of her home, the house she had renovated in every detail, down to the spoons and the vases and the other thousand tiny details of a home. Benjamina wasn't going to lose all that because of anger or pride. She would have to be clever now.

She left her study and went into the living room, where there was a door out to the garden. There she found Hettie, standing by the window, looking out at the woodland beyond. The girl turned swiftly upon her entering the room. Her face looked shocked and pale. Her eyes darted about the room, before looking back at her.

Benjamina guessed the girl must feel awkward and even a touch guilty about standing in a room that had so recently been the leisure room of her employers. She wondered if the girl would dare even touch a chair, let alone sit in one, leaning her head back on an antimacassar. Benjamina realised she could take advantage of the girl's astonishment at her new situation. She was a babe in the wood. Benjamina still had the power here.

'Miss Jones,' she said and forced herself to smile.

The girl looked at her blankly, then tried to smile as well.

'Mrs King, can I speak a bit with you?'

Ah, so the girl had more nerve than she'd given her credit for.

'Of course, my dear. Won't you sit down?'

'Oh no, I couldna do that.'

Benjamina noted that, in her nerves, the local dialect was coming back, after weeks of Queenie schooling her against it. Well, the girl was rich now. Benjamina supposed she could talk however she pleased.

'But you must,' said Benjamina, forcing another smile. 'This is all yours now. You must make yourself comfortable.'

But the girl was not comfortable – far from it, standing stiffly by the window, her eyes still wide with the surprise of it all. She reluctantly came forward and chose a chair to the side that was not generally used by either Queenie or Benjamina and sat awkwardly on the edge of it.

'Thank'ee, ma'am,' said Hettie.

Benjamina's mind was feverish with plotting. How should she handle this girl? She could steamroller her into agreeing with her terms, which would be quite easy, she felt, as the girl was so confused she would probably defer to her on anything at this moment. But Benjamina needed to know her intentions, so it might be best to play the subtler game and let the girl talk a while, to see where her thinking lay.

'No need to thank me. Now, you wish to speak with me. I think that is a capital idea. We have much to discuss and organise. So, please, do begin.'

The girl sat bolt upright, as if a broomstick were strapped to her back.

'I want to say plenty of things, ma'am. It's hard to know where I should start. But the very first thing to tell you is that I had no clue that anything like this could ever happen to a girl like me. I didna know a thing about my mistress's plans. I promise you that. But I mun confess I did know about my origins. Mrs King told me about it the day before she passed. I couldna ask no questions, as she slipped into sleep just after and never awoke. So I'm as perplexed by it as the next person.'

She still had those frightened rabbit eyes, but once she started talking, her demeanour changed and she seemed to grow in confidence. Benjamina needed to assert some control over this now, as the girl was dangerously close to being assured, and Benjamina couldn't have that.

'My dear, it must have been a terrible shock to you, to understand that you came from . . . well, such inauspicious circumstances.'

The girl looked blankly at her. Benjamina knew how to use words as weapons.

'I inna sure I know what that means. But yes, it was a dreadful shock. And I want to say summat else. The idea that I own this house and everything in it and all the businesses and all that – it boggles my mind, it does. And I know that you, ma'am, have been in charge of all this for many a year, and that is your world, not mine. There was summat Mr Steadman read out, summat about you running the businesses or being thrown out onto the streets.'

The girl stopped talking. Benjamina felt the blood rush to her cheeks. Was she trying to humiliate her? Was she playing with her? She had to remember that not everybody thought as she did, in a scheming manner. She must control her own anger and resist striking this girl down with it. She had to be cautious and courteous.

'Yes, Miss Jones. I recall it very well.'

'Well, ma'am, I want you to know that this idea of you, the mistress of this house and family, being thrown out onto the streets is a heartless thing. Of course that mun never happen. Everyone in the county knows you and admires you for being so clever at your business. And you mun carry it on and be paid a fair wage for it. No question of that, ma'am. The thought that you, at this time of your life, would lose your home and all you are used to, in an instant, and because of me – well, it inna right. And though I was proper fond of my mistress, I believe this a cruel thought and one I want no part in.'

For once in her life, Benjamina didn't know what to say. The girl had disarmed her. She'd only known of this extraordinary change in her circumstances for such a brief time and already she had come to terms with it and was beginning to make decisions about how to proceed. This was not what Benjamina expected and it unsettled her greatly. Perhaps this girl would not be as easy to mould as she had thought. But she was not giving up as yet.

'Miss Jones, I can see that my dear, departed mother-in-law made a wise choice when she gave you the role of lady's maid. You have a natural refinement that belies your origins. I thank you for your kind remarks regarding my . . . new situation. And of course, I would be delighted to remain here, in my family home, as I believe is right and proper. I have designed and refurbished every inch of the interior of this house. It is my home. Southover is being rebuilt presently, as you know. You may find that residence more to your liking, perhaps, when it is ready. But until then, I can see from your courteous demeanour that you and I will get on famously.' She paused. 'But there is something else I feel I must put to you. Something about your family.'

'My family? I have little. Only my father. I'll be moving him in here tomorrow.'

What was this? The girl had already planned this out? Benjamina knew about Adam Jones, the man who had been transported for burning down Southover, whatever he claimed about his innocence. Benjamina always quizzed the servants for their gossip, as knowledge was power, so she knew the rumours about Hettie's father being a hopeless all-day drinker. It reminded Benjamina of her own father's violent drunken bouts. It brought an old fear back to her, clutching at her heart, of hiding under the stairs with her mother, awaiting his terrible fists. She felt a tightness in her chest at the mere thought of a drunk living in her beautiful house, let alone one who had committed arson against her family. But she must remain in control.

'That is one idea and a good one. I'm sure it will be a great relief to you to provide a stable environment for your father. But . . . a thought occurs to me. This will be a great change in your life, and in his life. As you say, I will be running the businesses and carrying on my life as before in many respects. For you and your father, this will be an enormous challenge, a metamorphosis in comparison to the way you've previously lived. So, let me make a suggestion. The money that is coming to you from the will . . . I am sure that Mr Steadman could forward you an advance, which would allow you and your father to seek alternative accommodation, perhaps a nice, cosy house in Ironbridge. Something that would suit you both well. I would continue to reside here, in my home and to continue my work to keep the King name and businesses thriving. You could live at your leisure, in town, amongst . . . your people. Indeed, you may find that the idea of accepting this will and becoming the sole heir is not to your liking, that it will remove you from the bosom of your family and, as I say, your people. Miss Ashford made a similar choice, when she emigrated to America and started a new life.

She knew where she wanted to belong and it was not here, in this house. And I know you admire Miss Ashford hugely and one must admit, she certainly seems to have thrived after such a wise decision. Mrs King senior was well aware of this fact, mentioning in the will that you might follow suit. And . . . if you were . . . to *refuse the inheritance*, you would not be going against Mrs King's wishes, as she predicted in her will that you might indeed do so. I wonder if you understand how much your life will change – being the sole heir – and whether you are ready for that change? Might it not be better for you, for your father, for your adoptive family and your friends, if you refused this inheritance and instead I make a generous donation to you for your services here? It would be more than generous, enough for you to live comfortably for the rest of your lives with . . . your people.'

Benjamina was unsure if she had pushed things too far. But the thought of this wench and her drunken father living here, under the same roof as a King, was utterly ridiculous. And more importantly, perhaps she could turn the girl away from the inheritance altogether, upon which happy day she herself would become the heir and all would be as it should be again. Surely, the girl had to see that. Hettie had looked down at her hands, clasped in her lap. Now she looked up and met Benjamina's eye.

'There is a part of me that is a King. I know that now. I was born a Jones. Then I grew up as a Malone, but apart from them, not being of their blood. Now, for the first time, my mistress has given me a chance to make myself anew, to become the person maybe I was always meant to be. And I mean to grasp it with both hands, Mrs King. I will not be refusing the inheritance. And I will be staying here. And my father will live here with me. And we will all have to do our best to get along.'

Damn this child!

Benjamina managed a simpering smile. But this was not over. Not by many a mile.

'Of course, my dear. Whatever you wish.'

'But I would ask one thing of you – that you dunna tell a soul about my . . . about how I came about, how I'm related to the King family. It inna a fact I wish to be gossiped about by all and sundry. It is my business, and my business alone.'

Oh, the little, trusting fool. Now she had shown a weakness. Still, it would not strengthen Benjamina's own case for it to be common knowledge that the girl was related to the Kings. She had already decided that tomorrow she would travel to Shrewsbury and see her own solicitor, and ask him to bring a suit against Hettie Jones, claiming that Hettie bewitched Queenie and preyed upon a weak old woman, that the will was changed through coercion upon a very elderly lady who was not of sound mind. If Hettie was keen to keep her relation to the Kings quiet, that would only serve Benjamina the better.

Still, it was good to know that the girl was ashamed of it. Benjamina might be able to use that against her one day. For now, she slipped it into a mental pocket for another time.

'Why, of course, my dear. It would never cross my mind to speak of it. It would be better all round if enquiring minds who wish to know why this extraordinary event has come about be instead directed towards the idea that the late Mrs King was aged, infirm and confused in her last days. That would explain everything to our satisfaction, don't you agree?'

Hettie shook her head. 'No, it wouldna, ma'am. I spent every moment I could with my mistress and I am sure this was her choice and one she made with a clear head. Mr Steadman says the same and he has the law on his side.'

It was time to end this meeting. Benjamina was tired and running out of parries for this surprisingly feisty pit bank wench. She knew now what she was up against. This was no village idiot. The girl had a brain and she had spirit. A troublesome combination, but not a match for Benjamina King. The girl might have been thinking she had won this battle. But this was a war.

So Benjamina smiled at the girl and took her leave, claiming a need to get back to business as it wouldn't run itself. She left the room determined to go to any lengths to beat this upstart and to win this war, by any means fair or foul.

Chapter 17

As much as Anny loved raising all of her children (and Hettie – she always considered Hettie one of her own), she was delighted when they began to develop more independence. It made her life easier but also gave her a mother's satisfaction of knowing she had nearly achieved her goal of getting them through childhood and into early adulthood without disaster befalling them. Or death. After Owen had *left them* (to that day, she could use few other words for it, as it still hurt so much), she had such a fear of losing her children. As each completed the next stage of development, it was as if a checklist was ticked off in her mind on the journey towards adulthood. Each goal reached settled her fears somewhat. Once they were grown and gone, she would still worry for them, but her charge of keeping them alive would not feel as urgent.

So when Hettie had talked about going to London and Anny could see her spreading her wings, she had been all for it. It would be marvellous for her independence. But then Adam Jones came into her life. And then the job from Mrs King. These unexpected twists of fortune had forced Hettie suddenly to complete her final stage of growing up. Hettie not only moved out of the house, but out of the family too, somehow. Living with the Kings was the final insult.

Now that old Mrs King had died, Anny wondered what would happen to Hettie. She would be out of a job, surely. Anny didn't think the younger Mrs King would want to keep Hettie on, after the gossip she'd heard about how mean she was to Hettie. Anny dearly hoped that Hettie would be back to work in the pit and all would be as it was. Perhaps she'd even come home, tired of her father.

One chilly Sunday, Hettie turned up with Adam unannounced at the Malones' door. It was wonderful to see her. She had filled out a bit, her cheeks fuller and her hips dipped in a greater curve. She looked like a woman now, confident and well dressed in her Sunday outfit. Anny saw that Evan found it difficult to keep his eyes from her, but also that he was awkward in her presence. Anny's heart went out to her son. She knew this separation had been hardest on him.

She looked back at Hettie, who was staring at her. There was something wrong. Anny knew it from Hettie's eyes the moment she looked at her. Hettie had news to tell them, and it looked like the telling of it would be uncomfortable. Was she moving away? Please let it not be that. Anny had always feared that

Adam would find slotting back into his old existence in Ironbridge impossible, that he might use the King money to move on elsewhere and start his life anew. Anny wished he would – but not with Hettie in tow. Now Hettie had had a taste of the service life, maybe she would go with him, looking for another post as a servant elsewhere.

No, it looked worse than that. Adam had gone to stand by the fireplace, looking smug. Oh Lord, what was it? Anny caught Hettie's eye and saw her hesitate.

'I have news, for all of you,' said Hettie.

Anny glanced at Evan, whose eyes were round and worried. Peter looked over at her too, and fielded the twins to sit down on the hearth rug to keep them still, while Flora perched on a chair, excited to hear the latest turn in the fortunes of Hettie Jones.

'Go ahead then, lass,' said Anny. She could not sit down herself; she was too agitated to move.

'Summat has happened, summat unexpected and . . . well, strange.'

'Spit it out then,' said Evan gruffly.

Adam was still preening at the fireplace.

'I'm sure you've all heard about Mrs King's death. As it turns out . . .'

Hettie paused and her cheeks flushed. She faltered. Nobody spoke. It was as if everyone held their breath.

'Well, I'm her only beneficiary. She left it all to me. All of it. The house, the businesses, the money. All of it.'

There was a moment's stunned silence.

'What's a ben-fish?' asked Lily, unusually speaking before her brother.

'Oh, everyone knows that,' scoffed Billy, but he looked uncertain.

Anny stared. Was she hearing right? Could it possibly be true?

'Are you sure, lass?' said Peter, standing up now, his eyebrows furrowed in confusion. 'It inna some mistake?'

'It be true, all true,' said Adam. Anny could hardly bear to look at him, now she knew the reason for his complacency.

'It is all confirmed by the solicitor, Mr Steadman,' Hettie explained. 'He helped Mrs King draw up the new will near the end.'

She looked intensely uncomfortable. She did not look like a young woman who was in receipt of astounding good fortune.

The room was utterly silent. Anny glanced at Evan, whose face was a picture of confusion. He was in shock and could not hide it.

'Congratulations, Hettie,' said Anny. Somebody had to speak.

'Is Hettie rich now?' asked Flora, the gravity of Hettie's announcement finally beginning to weigh.

'Rich?' said Billy.

'Rich?' said Lily. 'What's that got to do with fish?'

'Yes,' said Adam.

Anny refused to look at him; she knew that his face would be trained upon her, lording it over her. 'It is astonishing news, Hettie. Truly astonishing. And I'm happy for you, love. Truly happy. Congratulations.'

'Yes indeed,' said Peter, and went over to Hettie and hugged her. 'Congratulations, lass!'

The children were still unsure as to what was happening, but they were happy to join in with the general air of good news and they hugged Hettie too, said, 'Well done,' and did a few little jumps afterwards.

Hettie looked painfully at Anny and gave her a lopsided smile. Anny came and put her arms around Hettie, though she felt stiff as she did it and knew that she was withholding herself from fully embracing her dear girl. The truth was, this latest news was more than a wedge between them. Her previous post of the King servant had been bad enough, but now there yawned a chasm. It was Evan she worried for most. He looked as if he had been punched in the stomach.

Hettie explained to everyone about what had happened in the days leading up to Mrs King's death, about the will and Mr Steadman the solicitor, about the younger Mrs King being disinherited (*which will cause no end of trouble*, thought Anny warily).

'Hettie, I know you are the best kind of person and it is no surprise that others think the same,' said Anny. 'But did you have any inkling that Mrs King was going to do such a thing? Did she give you any warning of her intentions?'

'Not at all. We had grown closer in recent weeks, that was all. She relied on me a lot. I was . . . fond of her, I was. And I believe she was fond of me. But no, I had no idea.'

'What will Mrs King the younger do about all this?' said Peter, echoing Anny's thoughts.

'It is said she wonna let it lie. So we shall see,' replied Hettie.

'Watch out for that one,' said Anny. 'She could cause you grief and no mistake.'

Hettie said, 'I have Mr Steadman in my corner. I believe he will see me right. And that's something else I wanted to say. I want to see you all right. All taken care of.'

Another silence fell then. Peter glanced at Anny.

'We have no need of anything,' said Anny, aware her voice sounded cold.

'I know that, but I will have surplus and I want to use it wisely. I want to help. I want to change your lives, if you will let me.'

Peter was watching his wife closely and Anny looked away. She knew they would be discussing this later, perhaps even arguing about it. But she was resolute. She had guessed, moments after Hettie revealed her news, that this would be coming.

'Hettie, you know I'd accept any gift from you but this. We will never accept King money. It is blood money. We've said this before and so I say it again.'

Hettie looked physically pained by Anny's words. 'But it is not King money anymore. It is mine. And I want to repay the love and kindness you have shown me all my life.'

'You think we want your money for that?' said Evan, speaking up at last. 'You think we want paying for loving you?'

'No! Course not!' Hettie's tone was exasperated.

'Let them refuse it,' said Adam, still leaning infuriatingly on the mantelpiece. 'Bloody fools.'

'Now then,' said Peter. 'No need for that.'

'Father, please,' said Hettie. She looked back at Anny. 'It would grieve me sorely if you did not take what I am offering you. Money is not evil in itself. Only what is done with it can be called a good or evil thing. And this would be a good thing.'

'We dunna want it,' said Evan, folding his arms. 'Any of it.'

'That's right,' said Anny. 'Thank you for thinking kindly of us. But we respectfully decline.'

Now the atmosphere had moved beyond strained to soured. Hettie looked at Evan, then at Anny, then at her father. Her face remained confused, her hands twisting her gloves round and round. Anny just wanted to hug her, to tell her not to fret, that she was still their dear girl. She took a step towards her and put her hand on Hettie's arm.

'We are happy for you, love. It is marvellous news. And a testament to the good work you have done for that lady, no doubt about that. Your kindness and companionship have been rewarded. It is wonderful. Be happy and enjoy it. We will always be here, if you need us. But we are not part of your world now, nor shall we ever be. Go freely into it and never fret for us. We are doing well and we shall prevail, without help from any quarter. You can rest assured of that.'

Hettie still looked pained but she gave a weary nod. 'It is as I suspected. And I respect you for it. But let me assure you that none of this turnabout in my fortunes will affect the love and regard I have for you all. I wish us to be easy with each other, as we always have been. I intend to remain unchanged by it and to be true to myself always.'

'Good girl,' said Anny. She reached out and hugged Hettie again, this time full of proper feeling, and it was returned heartily.

But over Hettie's shoulder, Anny glanced at Evan and saw in his face that his dreams had been crumpled up like autumn leaves held in the hand, crushed to smithereens.

Chapter 18

Stockings, knickerbockers and a chemise came first. Hettie asked Kezia to help her with the stockings as Hettie's hands were still rough from her working days and snagged on the fine material. Kezia tied up her corset next, pulling the laces quite tight and crossing them at the back, then bringing them round to tie them in front.

Next, Kezia helped her lift the crinolette over her head, a caged and fabric construction that had a bustle on the back. Hettie buttoned it at the waist. Kezia threw over a white petticoat with lace at the hem, which Hettie pulled down and arranged neatly over the crinolette. Then came the camisole, a sleeveless cotton top, buttoned at the front, which hid the corset ridges. The skirt, made of green silk with maroon piping, was pulled over her head and put in place, buttoned at the back by Kezia. At its base was an extra row of detachable ruffles designed to protect the skirt from the dusty, dirty ground; she'd need this later, as she intended to go for a walk that afternoon.

On top of this came the overskirt, in maroon silk with yellow bows, cut away at the front to reveal the green skirt beneath. Then Kezia helped her on with the bodice, a waist-length silk jacket, with frilly cuffs and fitted style, in matching maroon and green. First a waist stay was fastened to keep it in place, then Kezia started buttoning at the bottom and Hettie at the top, meeting in the middle. Each tiny button had a perfect five-pointed star embroidered upon it. Hettie pinned on an extra yellow bow at the waist to complete the outfit.

It was a pleasure to put on colourful clothes again. The household had been in mourning clothes for a month until the end of March, but now it had been decided that it was seemly to wear the full wardrobe again, since no one in the house had been a blood relation of Mrs King. If she were going out immediately, she would have added a hat, her little boater with yellow ribbons perhaps – but the meeting she was going to attend was here at home, so she did not need to leave the house as yet. Kezia had pinned up her hair at the sides, which fell down at the back in a waterfall of ringlets.

Throughout this long procedure of dressing, Hettie and Kezia, her newly appointed lady's maid, gossiped and laughed and chatted the time away. Hettie knew that custom dictated she should call her maid by her surname, but Hettie refused to call her Clayton. She considered Kezia a friend, not a servant. How grateful she was to have Kezia here with her, helping her learn the ways of this new world, not in order to be a maid to another, as in her previous life, but in order to be the lady herself. For that was what Hettie had to be now. A lady.

And a businesswoman, or at least, the owner of the businesses. Benjamina, as Hettie now called her, was still in charge of running the businesses, but Steadman had insisted that Hettie attend a monthly meeting with Benjamina and the managers of the three industries – iron, coal and brick – in order to keep her hand in and hold Benjamina to account. Steadman attended too and gave Hettie a debrief after each one. Hettie dreaded them. She had been to one in March and she was about to attend her second. She had sat through the first in utter confusion, listening to the numbers being thrown around that meant nothing to her. She'd tried to keep up and nod politely from time to time, always hotly aware of Benjamina's smug face watching her. The woman knew that Hettie had no idea what they were talking about.

Their relationship was strained further by the fact that Benjamina was suing to have the will overturned. Steadman had told Hettie that nothing would come of it, that she would never prove that Mrs King was not of sound mind. But it was a constant worry, of course. Hettie's relationship with Benjamina was a seething mass of resentments topped with a thin veneer of courtesy.

At least Steadman was there for Hettie. He was her one friend in this echelon of society. Hettie smiled at the thought. Friends came from unexpected places when you most needed them. When she had been a new maid, it was Kezia. Now she was a new lady, it was Steadman. Her only friends in her new life.

She thought of her old friends, Ada and everyone else at the pit bank, Evan and the rest of the Malones. She thought of that awful day in late February when she had walked to their house from her father's, after giving him the news about the inheritance. He was full of it, crowing and whooping about their good fortune. He had warned her not to see them, as they would disapprove and put a dampener on it all. He'd said she should write to them instead, but Hettie knew she couldn't just write. She had to tell them in person, because they were family. Two months had passed since she'd told them, and she had not seen them once. It was as much her fault as theirs, perhaps hers more so. She had not sought them out and it was hardly likely that any of the Malones would troop up uninvited to the old brickmaster's house for afternoon tea. She decided she must rectify this soon, but truly, she did not know how. It was easier to put it off and think about something else, like this fearsome meeting she was about to attend. Or like her father.

She had moved him in within days of the announcement. He had turned up sheepishly at first, but once

269

installed in his rooms, with his own valet, he soon acclimatised himself to his new position and began enjoying himself immensely. The truth was that he was enjoying himself far too much, with the brandy and whisky kept at home, and in the taverns he still frequented, now dressed up in his new gentlemanly finery, from which his valet had a damnable job of removing stains after his nightly excursions into town. With more or less unlimited funds, he had run up huge bills at various establishments and would not stop doing so, despite Hettie asking him to steady himself.

She had discussed it with Steadman, who came up with a plan. He had her father come to his office in town and informed him that he would be giving him a weekly allowance, to be collected by him from the office every Monday morning at 9 a.m. sharp. If he did not arrive, he would not receive it, and he was told that all of the shops and public houses in town had been informed not to give anything on account to him. Her father was livid and shouted the house down when he heard this plan. He called it a humiliation, said he was being treated like a child. And what was the point of all this money if he could not spend it how he wished? He had been through hell, he told Hettie, and now his reward should be to do whatever he liked.

But Steadman stuck to his guns and so did Hettie. Adam lived on his weekly allowance and it meant he could not perhaps get as drunk as previously, not if he wanted to drink every day anyway. Hettie felt that at least he had some portion of control exerted over the worst of his nature, which gave her some relief. It was not enough, of course, and she still feared for him, but it was the best she could do for now.

In the last few weeks, Hettie had spent her time learning more and more about the etiquette of ladies from Kezia and about the businesses from Steadman. She had also tried to learn how to control her father, though she felt she was failing at this. He was as drunk as ever, but at least there were days when he ran out of money and could not go out to disgrace himself. Then he'd take a decanter upstairs to his room instead.

Benjamina ate all her meals in her room, so often Hettie ate alone, her father out or ensconced in his quarters. Of course, Kezia could not come to eat with her, though Hettie wished she could. She had never felt more lonely in her life.

Now she picked up her fan from her dressing table; although it was only April, the sun was warm that day and she knew she would feel it, especially in the dreaded meeting that was to come, with all those people she did not understand packed into Benjamina's study.

Just as she was about to leave the room and face the music, she heard the sound of carriage wheels approaching the old brickmaster's house. Hettie went to her bedroom window and saw an unfamiliar coach arrive and pull up to a halt, the horses stamping and shaking their heads. She presumed it was one of the business managers, perhaps come in a new coach as his was being repaired. But out came a woman in her thirties or thereabouts, with a shapely form and a beautiful face. She stepped down from the carriage and stood very still, staring up at the house, wide-eyed and pale, as if she were looking at a ghost.

Intrigued, Hettie left the room and headed downstairs. As she reached the front entrance hall, Benjamina's office door opened and her disagreeable face appeared.

'Didn't you say you wrote to Beatrice Ashford about Queenie's death?' said Benjamina to Hettie, walking towards the sitting room, scowling.

Hettie replied, 'I did. Two days after Mrs King's passing.'

'Well, it clearly didn't get there on time. Or else the girl was determined to come anyway. Blast it. I could do without entertaining her for God knows how long. We never liked each other.'

'That lady outside is Beatrice Ashford?' asked Hettie.

'Yes, of course it is. Come, we shall await her.'

Hettie had heard much of Miss Ashford from her mistress – and she had held a fascination for her long before, since Beatrice had been present at Hettie's birth and had had a love affair with Evan's older brother, Owen. As she had assured Benjamina, Hettie had written to Miss Ashford informing her of Mrs King's death, and Mr Steadman too had written, explaining about the change to Mrs King's will. But now Hettie was secretly pleased that it seemed both letters had not arrived in time, as Beatrice cut a romantic figure and she was eager to meet her.

Normally, visitors would be greeted by the butler and brought into the sitting room, but Hettie was not as interested in custom at that moment as in meeting Miss Beatrice Ashford. She went straight out of the front door herself, to find Busby greeting Miss Ashford. Busby turned in surprise to see the lady of the house approaching them across the driveway, but when Hettie told him she would take care of it, he took his leave.

Miss Ashford look tired and yet so handsome, her brown eyes and brown hair shining in the April sun. She looked curiously at Hettie and raised her eyebrows.

'Miss Ashford?' said Hettie. She did not know whether to hold out her hand or curtsey, but she had heard so much about Beatrice from her mistress that she felt like they were old friends already.

'Yes,' she replied, hesitantly, her face tired and slightly confused. 'And you are?'

'I'm Hettie Jones.'

Now Miss Ashford looked positively shocked. 'Are you really? Little Hettie Jones? Why, you're all grown up!'

She had a tinge of a foreign accent about her voice. It might be the American influence, but she'd also been told Beatrice had been raised in France, so maybe it was a mixture of both.

Hettie replied, 'Well, yes, I reckon I am! I'll be eighteen in a couple of months.'

'My great-grandmother told me in her letter that you were now her maid, which astonished and delighted me. I am also most eager to see her. How is she?'

'Miss Ashford, I am so sorry to be giving you bad news, but Mrs King passed away back in February.'

Beatrice's eyes dimmed and she nodded her head. 'I suspected as much. I came as soon as I could, but I was not sure if I would make it in time.'

'I wrote to tell you, and so did the family solicitor, Mr Steadman, but I think the letters must've arrived after you left. I am truly sorry you've been put to all this bother of coming, only to find ... Well, I am sorry.'

'Please, do not apologise. It is not of your doing.'

'You'll stay with us a while, though, Miss Ashford? Come in, please.'

Beatrice did look weary and nodded firmly. 'I would love to stay. And to get to know you, Hettie.'

They crossed the driveway, and Beatrice stopped just before the front door. 'I suppose Benjamina is still in residence.' This was said with a slight grimace, which gave Hettie a thrill. It seemed she might just have a supporter in her ongoing war against Benjamina.

'Yes, she is. She now runs all of the King businesses.'

'Indeed,' said Beatrice thoughtfully. 'Hettie, I hope you don't mind me asking, but I cannot help but notice you are not dressed in a maid's uniform. Can you explain to me what has changed in your situation?'

Hettie felt a slight dig of shame. Perhaps she was still an interloper, dressed as a rich lady but still a poor girl inside. But she knew that Miss Ashford approved of such things as poor folk bettering themselves; her mistress had told her all about Beatrice's kind ways.

'That's what the solicitor wrote to you about. Mrs King left her fortune to me. I know it must be a proper shock. Nobody expected it. But it is legal, I assure you. Mr Steadman the solicitor will be here soon, as we have a business meeting planned for today. I'm sure you could ask him any questions you want and have it all explained.'

Beatrice stared at her in amazement, the O of her mouth expanding into a delighted smile. 'Why, my dear! This is most welcome news! Good old Queenie! What a marvellous final gesture!'

To hear Beatrice's approval was much more than Hettie could have hoped for. She had worried that Beatrice might argue with it, as the old will had mentioned that if she changed her mind about renouncing the King fortune, she could inherit everything. But she seemed to have no interest in that whatsoever.

'Really? You dunna mind? I mean to say, you do not mind, miss?'

Beatrice took Hettie's hand and held it between her own. 'Firstly, never apologise for speaking in the way you were raised. To hear the Shropshire dialect again after all these years gladdens my heart.' At this, her eyes filled and she glanced round at the house. 'And secondly, many years ago, when I first left Ironbridge, I wrote to my great-grandmother and asked her to look out for you and others like you. I'm thrilled to hear that she took my advice to heart. To think, little Hettie Jones is the sole heir of the King fortune. It's a stroke of genius. Well done, Queenie!'

Beatrice laughed, yet the tears were falling down her cheeks now.

'Oh, Miss Ashford, I dunna know what to say. You are as kind and beautiful as my mistress said you were, even more so. I know we dunna know each other, but I am proper glad you're here. It's . . . been hard, miss. So hard these past weeks.'

Beatrice retrieved a handkerchief from her pocket and dabbed her eyes. 'I imagine that Benjamina has been appalled to be disinherited. I am sure she has not made things easy for you. But I am here now. And we will talk of many things. And you will stop with this "Miss Ashford" and so forth. You shall call me Beatrice.'

'All right, I will!' said Hettie. 'Now, you mun be tired and needing of rest. Come in, do.'

Hettie watched as Beatrice and Benjamina met again for the first time in years and saw there was no love lost between them. They were stiff and formal with each other and both looked as if they could not wait to escape the room.

Hettie was glad her father had gone out early and had not yet returned, yet she dreaded him coming back. She was aware that Beatrice and her father had known each other back in the old days, and didn't know what kind of reception he would give her. Those stories were all wrapped up with pain and resentment, with her father's false conviction, with Owen Malone's death. It was a heavy burden for any new friendship to bear. But Hettie felt freer of it than most, only being a baby when it had happened. She took to Beatrice immediately and was overjoyed to have her here, a reminder of her mistress and an ally against Benjamina.

Soon, the carriages began to arrive for the monthly business meeting, and Beatrice went up to her room to rest. She said she was too weary to meet anyone unknown to her, but asked Hettie to pass her regards on to Mr Steadman and thank him for writing. She would visit him in due course during her stay. She told Hettie she would stay around a week or ten days, after which she would be going on to Paris to visit old family friends. Hettie wished that Beatrice could stay forever, but was at least glad it would be a week or so.

The meeting went well, particularly as Beatrice's arrival had given Hettie such a boost that she felt more confident in this meeting and actually spoke twice, giving her approval to certain items. She could see this was infuriating to Benjamina, whose response to Beatrice's arrival was clearly severe displeasure.

Afterwards, Steadman congratulated Hettie on her success at the meeting. Beatrice slept in her room all afternoon, then came down for some afternoon tea. Benjamina took it in her rooms as usual, leaving Beatrice and Hettie alone together.

What a delight it was to have a female companion to talk to, other than her dear Kezia. Beatrice told her stories of America, of her work there as a journalist, of the fact she had decided not to marry thus far and instead still lived with her friend Dinah, an artist, who had once been her maid. This fact fascinated Hettie. Dinah had graduated from maid to lady's companion, to now having a career in her own right, and it made Hettie feel as if she were not such a freak of nature after all. It taught her that the strict lines of separation between the classes were not as set in stone as others would have her believe. It was freeing to think on it. In fact, everything about talking to Beatrice was freeing. Hettie felt her mind being opened wide, as if she could step out of it into a new world.

After eating substantially at afternoon tea, Hettie and Beatrice had decided to forego dinner. Hettie told the cook to only provide meals for Benjamina and her father that night, in their rooms, and she and Beatrice remained in the sitting room, where they talked into the early evening. The topic of conversation eventually turned to Hettie's father.

'He lives here with me,' she told Beatrice. 'But he's out just now.'

'Ah, Adam Jones.' Beatrice nodded thoughtfully.

Hettie wondered whether to keep his drinking quiet for the moment, but she was worried how Beatrice would react if he came home appallingly drunk, as he sometimes did. He wouldn't know they had a visitor, of course, so would not think to curb his behaviour.

'I mun tell you that he is not the man you once knew. The years havna been kind to him. The time in Australia broke his body and nearly his spirit. And then, once he came home, the demon drink has taken him and he canna escape its clutches. I do what I can to discourage but I am afraid to say he is a heavy drinker, and it pains me every day.'

'I am sorry to hear it, though considering his experiences, I suppose one could say it is understandable, though selfish. He should be supporting you, Hettie, not causing you more problems. I must be honest and say that I have complicated feelings towards your father. I do believe he was innocent of the charge of arson made against him. Queenie at least did what she could to lessen his punishment, and indeed saved his life – but he was there that night when . . . the fire happened. And some say he should not have been and that he should have protected Owen Malone . . . who died, as well as my mother, of course.'

'It must've been awful,' said Hettie quietly. All of these events took place so long ago, before her memory began, but she saw how such happenings scored their place deeply into family history and remained a scar upon the memories of others. 'Do you mind me asking, what was Owen like? I grew up with his family after my mother died, but Owen was gone when I were a babby. They never talk about him. I think it's because it's too painful for them. I've seen Anny's eyes fill up just at the mention of his name.'

Then Hettie was surprised to see that Beatrice's eyes were full of tears, too.

'Oh, I'm so sorry! I've caused you great upset. I'm a fool.'

'Oh, no, not at all. It is nearly twenty years ago, give or take a year or two. I really should be able to think of him now without blubbing. But it is being here with you, in this place. The memories are crowding in. I do feel somewhat overcome by them at times. But I am fine, I assure you.'

'Let's speak about summat else then,' said Hettie.

'No, no. It's good to air these things. And you must be very curious about these events. They happened when you were an infant but they still play out now in your adult life.' Beatrice smiled. 'Owen Malone was a good person, the best person I ever knew, I think. And so handsome. My, he was a fine-looking man. And I loved him. I loved him very much. I wanted to build a life with him. You know yourself the barriers that are in place even today for those from different classes. In fact, you are living it yourself, at this moment! So, you will know that the odds were utterly against us. But love knows no barriers and will range freely, where it will. I lost him and I lost my mother in that fire. It created a deep hollow in me that took years to fill, with work, with friendship and with a new life. Oh, it is strange to be back here, haunted as it is by the past. I am glad to see it again. It seems smaller, somehow than it has been in my memory. I'll visit the graves tomorrow. And I'm so glad to have met you, Hettie. Perhaps knowing you and being back here will help to exorcise those ghosts a little, who knows.'

'We both lost our mothers, then,' said Hettie. It had slipped out without her meaning it to. It was a thought that became words. She looked swiftly up at Beatrice to make sure she hadn't been too forward to say it.

'Yes, so I heard from Queenie. I am sorry to hear about your mother. I met her twice and she was a good, strong, fearless woman. And you have certainly inherited her beauty, especially those magnetic green eyes of yours, Hettie. I'm sure you're the belle of Ironbridge now and the young men will be swarming round soon.'

'I mun say, I canna think what it must be like to lose the man you love. I'm proper sorry it happened to you.'

'Is there not a special young man in your life, Hettie?' said Beatrice, smiling.

Hettie thought of Evan and Laurence Maxwell Ripley in the same moment. She had sometimes thought recently that now she was a lady, she should write to Mr Ripley and inform him. But every time she thought of doing so, she was crippled by embarrassment. How would he view her now? With fascination as an object of study, or as an eligible young woman? Was it even proper to write to him? The rules of propriety confused her. She kept putting it off, aware too that she felt guilty for even considering another man when she thought of Evan. She knew some part of her loved him, but it was now more complicated than ever considering her new position in society. Hearing Beatrice talk of her love for Evan's brother brought her own feelings for Evan to the surface and she missed him with a twinge in her heart, like a deep hunger. But would he want to see her now? Would he judge her harshly in her finery? She looked down at the yellow bow on her bodice and wondered if he'd hate it and say it was foolish, or think her prettier than ever.

She did not know Beatrice well enough yet to explain any of this, so she simply replied, 'No, not yet.'

At that moment, Hettie heard her father arrive home. Her throat felt tight as he began arguing with Busby in the hall. When he'd first moved in, he'd made a big show of treating the servants as equals, but this soon dissolved into them becoming scapegoats for his changing moods. And it sounded as if his mood tonight was a bad one.

'That'll be my father. I'll just go and see what is vexing him. I'm sure it's nothing.'

Beatrice smiled at her, but her eyebrows showed she was perturbed by the noise.

Hettie rushed out into the hall to find her father remonstrating with Busby about his hat. Apparently the butler had taken it roughly from him.

'Father,' said Hettie and put her hand on his arm, trying to keep her voice sweet. 'We've a visitor. Please, calm yourself.'

'What visitor?' he said. He was not as drunk as he could be. He was able to stand up straight, talk coherently and walk. But he was in a foul mood.

'Beatrice Ashford, come all the way from America. She's a lovely person, Father.'

'Beatrice . . . what, the King girl?'

'Mrs King's great-granddaughter. Maybe you're tired and you'd like to meet her tomorrow. Maybe you'd like to take your dinner in your room. We inna having ours now, you see, as we had a big tea earlier. So, would you like to go upstairs now, Father?'

'No, I would not. I would like to see this King girl. What's she doing back here after all these years?'

'I told you that before. Mrs King wrote to her before she went, urging Miss Ashford to visit before she died.

But she's got here too late, of course. Father, surely you'd rather . . .'

But her father was striding forward to the sitting room and it was too late to try and stop him now.

'Miss Ashford,' Hettie heard him say, as she came in behind him to watch things unfurl.

'Mr Jones,' she said and stood, offering her hand for him to shake in manly fashion. He looked awkwardly at it for a moment, then decided to shake it. His face showed his begrudging respect for such a move.

He flicked his coat-tails back and sat down heavily on the settee opposite Beatrice.

'It's been nearly twenty year,' he said.

'It has,' said Beatrice.

'And you look so much the same as the last time I saw you. It puts me to shame!'

'You are too kind,' said Beatrice, smiling gently. 'I have aged and yet I would recognise you anywhere, Mr Jones.'

'You are the one being kind now. I am a wreck of a man and I know it. I weathered those years on a chain gang in Australia. And since, I have been ravaged by drink – by my own hand, I'll not deny. I know I am not what I was.'

Hettie had sat down, her bustle dictating she must perch on the edge of an armchair. But she felt as if she would faint with embarrassment if her father carried on roughly like this. She wished he would vanish in a puff of smoke.

'You have suffered much,' said Beatrice. 'And I am sorry for it. But you are right that some of your suffering has been of your own making.'

'And what do you mean by that exactly?'

Hettie swallowed hard. Things were heating up between them already and she felt powerless to stop it.

'I believe that a man who has been given a second chance in life should not abuse it by drinking it into oblivion. You have a duty to your daughter to be a good father to her and help her, not drink yourself to kingdom come.'

'Well, well, if it isn't Miss High and Mighty come all the way from America to teach us foolish country folk how to live.'

'Father, please,' said Hettie, reaching out her hand towards him.

'Father, please, what?' he cried, his face reddening. 'She's insulted me and I'm meant to stand for that?'

'I speak the truth and that is all,' said Beatrice.

'Well, missy, try this truth on for size. I suppose being back here has brought back memories for you. I suppose you've been thinking on Owen Malone and your great love affair. There's summat you dunna know about all that and it's this. Owen was only ever with you for me. He worked for me, as a spy for the strikers. I told him to befriend you and win you over to our cause. He used you to get information. That's all.'

285

Hettie watched Beatrice's face fall. She looked down at her hands, then back up at him.

'That may be how it started. And I see now how you used his good nature to suit your own purposes. But it was not how it ended. Owen and I loved each other, that I know. You were not there in our secret meetings, you did not understand the workings of his heart. I did. And I know he loved me.'

'He was playing at it! He got carried away, is all. Dunna flatter yourself.'

'But he saved her life!' cried Hettie. 'He ran into a burning building for her!'

Her father looked shocked to hear her jump in to defend others. 'That's because he were a good lad, that's all. He'd'a done that for anyone.'

'But he did it for me!' cried Beatrice, her eyes shining with emotion. She fought to control herself, but her breathing was heavy. 'I live with his sacrifice every day of my life. Since then, I have striven to make my life worthwhile, so that his death was not meaningless. Through my writing, I work hard to bring ideas of democracy to the public, to argue for equal rights for all. But none of this will ever assuage the guilt I carry with me every day that Owen Malone gave his life so that I could live. The only thing that helps in some small part is the knowledge that he acted out of love. And nothing you say, in your petty, mean need for absolution, will ever take that away from me.'

Hettie saw her father shake his head, but he seemed a little chastised by her words. 'Well, that's not how it began, even if it ended differently. The fact remains if he hadn't gone in after you, he'd'a been here today, a fine grown man.'

Beatrice countered with, 'And there were those who say that you should never have allowed him to come that night to Southover, that you were his father's cousin by marriage and should have known better than to put him in harm's way, an innocent young man as he was. So perhaps there is blame on both sides, Mr Jones.'

Hettie felt pity for everyone involved, for the suffering of the families and the two people in this room. What a mess this feud was between the two families! How much misery it had triggered and was still causing.

In the silence that fell between them, Hettie spoke quietly but firmly. 'There are losses on both sides. I've seen it from the Malones, from my father, then from Mrs King and now from Miss Ashford. Everyone has suffered through these terrible things that have come to pass between these families: the Kings, the Wood-vines, the Malones and the Joneses. But here we are, sitting together in a King house that I now own. And whatever power I have due to my inheritance, I want to end this feud and go forward into a brighter future, where old miseries are laid to rest, where new friend-ships are made and old ones are made like new again.'

287

Beatrice nodded at her and smiled. Her father sighed and looked up at her.

'You've become a poet,' he said. 'A good one. And a wise one.'

'I dunna think so, Father,' she said gently.

He clapped his hands on his knees and stood up. 'I find that I've outstayed my welcome, as usual. So I shall off to bed and sleep off this rotten mood of mine. Miss Ashford, Hettie, I take your leave. Dunna stand up. Not for me.'

And with that, he left the room and closed the door behind him.

'Beatrice, I'm so . . .' began Hettie, her voice apologetic.

'He is a good man, deep down. And he loves you more than anything in the world, Hettie. Despite his problems, he is still your father. I never knew my father, and since my mother's death, I am of course an orphan. You at least have him and he has you. Never forget that.'

Beatrice took her leave of Hettie, claiming tiredness from her journey. Hettie sat alone, cursing her bustle for making her seat so uncomfortable. She missed her old clothes. She missed Anny and Peter and the little ones. She missed Evan.

She was feeling sorry for herself and found tears building in her eyes when the door opened and Beatrice was back.

'Do you need summat?' said Hettie, standing up and walking to meet her at the door.

'No, my dear. I am fine. I just wanted to say something else to you. I am so very glad that Queenie made this decision and named you as her sole beneficiary. I think it is an act of genius.'

'Oh, that means a lot, coming from you. I wondered if you might feel . . . cheated. It should be you in Mrs King's will. Not me. I'm nobody.'

'No, my dear. I made it very clear to Queenie years ago that I wanted no part of the King fortune. It was poisoned for me by the terrible losses I suffered. And I was determined to make my own life, and I have certainly done that. So yes, it is right and proper that it should go to someone deserving. If anyone can bring these families together and help atone for the past, it is you. You're a good, kind soul, but you're also clever and determined, in a quiet, calm way, which is necessary. I was always a hothead, and that has gotten me into no end of trouble. But it won't be easy for you. You're living between two worlds now, that of the rich and that of the poor. It won't be easy. Neither side will accept you easily. But I believe you'll find your way. You will make a success of this inheritance, I am sure of it.'

'Thank you,' said Hettie. 'Your words are kind and mean so much. But it may not be mine for much longer. I havna had a chance to tell you yet, but there may be trouble ahead. Benjamina is suing to change the will, saying I made Mrs King do it and she had a weak mind.'

'Sounds ridiculous,' said Beatrice. 'It will be thrown out, I'm sure.'

'Well, it's made me wonder whether I should leave this place and set up elsewhere. It was Benjamina's house for years. Maybe a house in town. Maybe Southover, when it's rebuilt.'

'They're rebuilding Southover?' said Beatrice, shocked.

'Oh yes, I'm sorry. You didna know. Mrs King ordered it last year.'

'Such a strange idea. I think it would have been better left a ruin.'

'We played in it as little'uns,' said Hettie. 'Me and Evan. That's Owen's brother.'

'Did you?'

'Sorry,' said Hettie, suddenly realising how heartless that must sound to Beatrice, who had lost both her mother and her lover there. 'That was a stupid thing to say.'

'Not at all. I'm glad to think of you playing there, shooing away the old ghosts. Perhaps that's what Queenie had in mind. Perhaps Southover is the place for you, Hettie. Once you've decided what you're going to do with the rest of your life. What will that be, I wonder?'

'Oh, Miss Beatrice, I am running to keep up with my present life, let alone make plans for the future.'

'But one day you will. And I predict you will do something extraordinary, Hettie Jones.'

Beatrice smiled warmly at her.

Hettie hesitated. Now would be the perfect time for her to tell Beatrice the whole story: not only were they connected by their past and by Queenie's regard for them both, but they were also linked by blood: Hettie had worked it out in her head while they were talking. She was Beatrice's mother's cousin. But the thought of the good news of that connection strengthening their bond was scarred by the fact of how it happened: a product of rape. Hettie opened her mouth to say it, but faltered and stopped.

'Are you quite well, my dear?' said Beatrice.

'Oh, yes. Proper jam,' said Hettie and smiled.

'Good. Now, Hettie, I was there at your birth and believe me, heaven and earth were moved to bring you into this world. You've earnt your place in it. Now I have no doubt you will do something wonderful with your life.'

Beatrice then bade her good evening, turned and crossed the chequerboard hallway. She stopped for a moment and Hettie watched as she looked about her at the floor, reliving something perhaps. Then she shook her head and wearily mounted the stairs.

Hettie was left with a mind riddled with thorny thoughts, and yet glimmering behind these was something new and warm and comforting. Instead of seeing her origins and the inheritance as an unending series of problems, Hettie saw that her life really was open-ended now. With this money, she could do anything, for good or ill. She had the freedom of the woodland birds she'd seen fly away as she walked by. And it was Beatrice who had shown her this. She saw now that Beatrice had given her two marvellous gifts: hope and wonder.

Chapter 19

Beatrice stayed eleven days, and she and Hettie became fast friends. Beatrice showed her such kindness it gladdened her heart and gave her courage to go on. Even Hettie's father seemed to come round to her a little. He sometimes stayed at home and had dinner with them, which was a nice change. He was begrudgingly polite to Beatrice at first, then seemed to warm as the days went on.

But the day she left, he fell into a black mood once more. Hettie tried to talk with him about it, but he refused. All he would say was that her coming 'stirred up bad old memories.' Hettie had been hoping that this would help her father to heal, but it seemed to have the opposite effect. When Beatrice left, it was a terrible wrench for Hettie and she too felt saddened and downhearted. She did not want to go on alone with this strange new life.

Soon after, Hettie was on her own in the sitting room one day, reading a book of poetry she used to read to Mrs King, strange little poems by John Donne, that made her mind wander along unusual paths. She was thinking about this and feeling a little sad, when her father came in, dressed smartly and newly shaven by his valet. She hadn't seen him look so well in ages.

'Hettie, can I speak with you a little?'

'Course, Father. What is it? You look as if you've an appointment somewhere.'

'I inna going anywhere, but I wanted to look the part. For this very morning, I have made a decision and I wanted to share it with you. Seeing the Ashford girl had a bad effect on me for a while, as you know. And I am sorry for it, for my black moods. But this morning I awoke with a clear head and I had cause to think on my turnabout in fortunes and everything it meant. And I decided to turn over a new leaf. I have been self-indulgent and weak.'

'No, Father,' said Hettie, reaching out to him.

'No, no, dunna interrupt, child. It is the truth. I have been weak. And Evan Malone was right that I have been a burden to you. No, let me finish. That all ends now. I am going to embrace my good fortune – not the money, but finding you again. You're worth more to me than any heap of gold. I will give up the drink and find a useful occupation to fill my days. I dunna know what it shall be yet, but I shall use my clear head to think on it. And you will be proud of me, Hettie. That is my dearest wish.'

'Oh, Father!' she cried and threw her arms about him. How often she had wanted to hear such words from him. How many times she had rehearsed such a speech in her head, imagining that the day would come when she would hear him come into his own and change himself for the better.

∽

In the days following, he was true to his word. He stopped drinking and got up each morning. He went for long walks and came back weary yet with a look of satisfaction on his face. The walking was good for him, anyone could see that. It was such a relief to watch her father leave the house without the fear that he would return in a terrible state. The weather matched her mood and all through April the sun shone down on the spring flowers. Everyone said how strange it was that it was the warmest they could remember for many a year.

But then, at the beginning of May, heavy rain came. It came down hard and it did not leave. It poured down solidly for days on end. At first, it was somewhat of a relief to see it, as Hettie always loved the sound of the rain and had missed it. But this rain seemed unnaturally prolonged, making the paths and roads churn with mud and become almost impassable. Her father's mood was affected by it too. Trapped in the house, he began to look depressed again. More worrying still, the river was rising and there was fear in town of flooding.

One night, the wind got up and buffeted the house. Hettie lay in bed listening to it whistling through the eaves and making the walls creak and groan. Then came a new noise, one of commotion downstairs. She got out of bed and went to her door, met there by Kezia who had awoken too. Hettie said she'd deal with it and told Kezia to go back to bed and get some sleep.

With a sinking heart, Hettie headed downstairs. She knew it must be her father. She had heard him come in like that so many nights in the past. Though Kezia was kind and never judged him, Hettie was still embarrassed by him and wished to deal with him herself. She could hear him shouting now and hurried her step down the staircase and towards the kitchen, from where the noise emanated. Her heart felt heavy in her chest, crushed by disappointment. All his fine words and long walks and lighter moods had come to nothing. He was a drunk again, and perhaps he always would be.

Then she was shocked to hear him call out a name, a name that was very dear to her.

'Evan!' he cried. 'Leave me be!'

Hettie rushed into the kitchen and found them there, Evan holding her father up, as he pushed him away, a rash of vomit down his front, remnants of it clinging to his mouth. A look passed between Hettie and Evan, a complicated look mingling shame, frustration and acceptance. Hettie took up a kitchen cloth and came to her father, wiping his mouth and trying to clean down his front. Evan took one arm and she the other. The butler Busby and her father's valet, Towers, appeared on the stairs and Hettie shook her head at the butler to tell him that he was not needed. He retired, while the valet and Evan helped her father mount the stairs and stumble towards his room. He was singing an old Shropshire folksong now. Once they'd got him into his room, he seemed to come to himself and realise what was going on. As they tried to manoeuvre him onto the bed, he pushed them both away, complaining bitterly.

'I dunna need your assistance. I dunna need any of you. I survived by my wits alone in the Swan River Colony, all those years living hand to mouth in the damned desert with chains about me. And you think I need you now? A slip of a girl and a stupid servant and a village idiot?'

'Father!' cried Hettie. 'Behave yourself, I beg you. I am so sorry, Evan.'

'Dunna be sorry about him, the stupid old drunk,' said Evan, crossing his arms and shaking his head.

Towers, a tall, long-faced, sombre young man, said, 'If I may, ma'am, I shall prepare sir for his bed, shall I?'

'Get out!' yelled her father at Towers. 'I dunna require anything from the likes of you.'

Hettie was exasperated. She feared her father might strike Towers, so she whispered to him to go back to his room and said she would call him to clear up the clothes and the rest of the mess later. He left unwillingly, and Hettie turned to see her father leaning forward with his head in his hands, starting to weep. She went to him and placed her hand gently on his shoulder.

'No pity for me, my dear,' he said morosely. 'No pity for the convict. I let that boy die.'

'What boy?' she said gently, thinking of some lad in the colonies perhaps, another cryptic reference to his convict days he sometimes threw out but never explained.

'My brother,' said Evan, still standing with his arms folded. 'Is that who you're going on about, Jones, eh? My brother Owen?'

'It was all my fault,' sobbed Adam. 'I was the man. He was only a boy.'

'It was all an age ago,' said Hettie, trying to curb this conversation before it got out of hand.

'Not to my parents,' said Evan. 'It lives in them to this day, every day.'

Hettie said, 'Oh, please, now is not the time, Evan!' She tried to cajole her father into removing his waistcoat so that she could give it to Towers to clean. All his clothes were wet and muddy from the rain and his trip to the gutter, and they were soiling the bedsheets. But she'd have to deal with that tomorrow – or rather, his poor valet would. Hettie wondered if Towers would stay much longer; her father was such a handful to manage. His face was in his hands now and she couldn't wrest them free to remove his clothes. Instead, she sat down next to him and put her arm about his shoulders, as she had done many a time. It always seemed to calm him, but tonight it had the opposite effect.

'No, my dear!' he cried and flinched from her. 'No sympathy for me. I mishandled everything. The strike, the ones who starved. All my fault. Then Owen, who should never have been there, in that danger with those ruffians determined to cause trouble. Again, down to me. My own conviction was not of my doing, but it was my punishment for Owen's death. I see that now.'

'No, Father, you are too hard on yourself. We all make mistakes.'

'Him more than most,' muttered Evan.

Hettie shot him a look, which he took and looked down sheepishly.

'But, you see, my own life was ruined when Owen died. If he had lived, he would've testified for me, that I wasna part of the plot to burn the house down. He was my only salvation. I would've gone free. I would've come home. Martha may still be alive, who knows? I was out cold, on the ground. I wasna strong enough to wake up and stop him going in that house. It's all down to me. I ruined my own life.'

'Enough of this now, Father,' Hettie said and put both arms about him. 'Nothing is solved by harping on in the small hours this way, and certainly not when you are that far gone. You wonna recall a word of this in the morning. Let us get you to sleep and we shall talk it all out tomorrow.'

'I dunna wish to sleep – or rather, I wish to sleep and never wake up. I dunna wanna live further, child. I dunna wanna exist on this earth. My life is forfeit. What is the point in my living further? Even this new life, this fortune, has made no difference to me. I detest myself in my very bones. I promised you I would give up the drink. I have promised it so many times, I have forgotten how many. I am a liar and a fraud. I had purpose once. I had a cause and a wife and a child. I had a life. Now I have no life worth living. I canna mix with my old kind in town, and I wonna mix with the new kind. If I went to fine establishments, I would be laughed at and banished. I am at home nowhere. I am a nowhere sort of a person, a nothing.'

'And yet you have this gold!' cried Evan. Hettie looked up at him, shocked to hear such emotion in his voice. 'You have a daughter, mon. She loves you far more than you'll ever deserve. She is here beside you at this minute. The finest wench in all of Shropshire, in all of England. You have more money than you could ever use. And you're pissing it all away! The things I'd do with your fortune. Why, the very first thing I'd do . . . I'd . . .'

Evan looked directly at Hettie, a yearning look in his eye. But he could not finish his sentence, and instead made a noise of frustration and ran his hands roughly through his hair, leaving it sticking up on end. He turned away and rubbed his eyes.

Then Adam groaned and slumped forward. He seemed to lose consciousness for a moment. Then he came to and looked around, confused.

Hettie took the opportunity to persuade him to lie down. He did so, led like a sickly child into lying on his side. Hettie removed his muddy shoes and placed them on the floor beside the bed. He was sleeping soundly now, snoring noisily.

Then she glanced at Evan and beckoned for him to follow her in leaving the room.

She closed the door behind them and turned to Evan. 'Come to the kitchen. You're drenched. I'll warm some milk up.'

'I wonna say no to that,' he said.

Downstairs, Evan seated himself at the large oak table in the centre of the room. Hettie was suddenly aware that she was dressed only in her nightgown. She knew Evan had seen her many a time in her nightclothes, but somehow it felt quite different now. She felt him watching her as she stoked up the range and put a pan of milk on to warm slowly. She sat down at the table as they waited.

'Thank you for bringing him home,' she said.

'I was out with some lads. I found him in the street. I couldna leave him there. Much as he deserved to be left in the gutter.'

'Let's not fight about that,' she said and sighed, suddenly very tired. 'Let me just say thank you and be done with it.'

Evan was leaning his chin on his fists, watching her closely. 'You've changed,' he said.

'Course I have. My life has changed.'

'In the old days, you woulda said thank'ee. But you talk different now.'

'In some ways. I felt I had to change myself to fit in. But I might'a changed my mind on that a bit.'

'How so?'

'Miss Ashford came to stay. You know who she is.'

'Arr, she inna a person the Malones like to speak of, as you well know.'

'Well, you oughta change your opinion on that, since you never met her. I spent days with her, and she is the best kind of person you could ever hope to meet. And she loved your brother with all her heart.'

Evan gave a mocking laugh.

This infuriated Hettie. It was just like him, like he had always been when they were children. Always knowing best, despite being ignorant of many of the things he professed to dismiss. 'There you are again, making fun of something you know nothing about!'

'I know all I need to know. My brother's life was taken by that woman.'

'He gave it willingly because he loved her. And she has lived ever since trying to make up for that. She is a good person and she does good things in the world. She tries to make it a better place. You shoulda seen the emotion in her, being back here, the place where she lost both of them, her mother and the man she loved. It was still raw in her, Evan. It would break your heart to see. She's never married, you know. She truly did love your brother and still does.'

Evan looked at her directly and then looked down. She knew of old this was his way of admitting she was right without actually saying it.

Then he looked up again and spoke. 'So, how did she change you then? You said you changed your mind about things when she came.'

'She said she loved to hear the Shropshire way of talking in me. Old Mrs King tried to school me out of it. My maid Kezia Clayton has taught me, too, how to smooth out the rough ways of local talk. But Beatrice loves it. She says it's our character and our soul, buried there in those local words and ways of saying things. She says never to feel forced to change myself to suit others, that they should be more accepting and choose to change their opinions on such things, more than I should change my nature.'

'Fancy talk,' said Evan and sniffed.

'Oh, you drive me to distraction,' she said and got up to check the milk. She poured it out into two mugs and sat back down, pushing his towards him roughly, so the milk slopped over the side a little.

'What are you angry at me for? A minute ago I was the hero of the hour, saving your father from certain death in the streets of Ironbridge.'

'Because you always dismiss things you dunna understand.'

'Your dear father might call me the village idiot, but you know I inna so stupid.'

'I didna call you stupid! I'd never think that of you!'

'And give me some credit, wench. I understand you perfectly about this Miss Ashford. And I'm sure she is honest and believes what she tells you. But the truth is it is easy to have such lofty principles and try to change the world when you are rich. Folk with money can afford opinions. Those without canna and never will.'

Hettie sighed and took a gulp of the warm milk. She knew he was partly right, but she was as stubborn as he was and never enjoyed admitting she might be wrong to Evan Malone. The wind was getting up, rattling the shutters and whistling down the kitchen chimney. A spattering of heavy rain lashed the window and the sound of a downpour filled the room with a smothering, rushing noise that made them sit very quietly and listen.

'Sounds like a storm,' he said. 'I'd best be off.'

'No, Evan, you mun stay. I'll show you to a room and borrow some nightclothes from Towers.'

'No thank'ee. I wonna be doing that,' he said and swigged down the last of his milk, before standing up.

'Dunna be soft-headed. It's blowing a gale out there.'

'I wonna be staying in the house of a young lady. It inna . . . seemly.'

'And when have you ever cared about what is *seemly*, Evan Malone? I know I dunna care. And you and I, we are old friends. And that is enough reason for me to offer you a bed for the night in my house when there is a storm a-raging outside.'

'Friends? Is that all I am to you?' he said, glaring down at her.

'*All*?' Hettie stood up too now. She wouldn't have him leaning over her like that. 'Is that *all* you are? A friend is worth more than gold. A friend is what I need. I had no idea how precious a friend was until I had none.'

'But Hettie,' he said, his face changing now, his eyes burning, 'I want to be so much more than that. Surely you know . . . my regard for you . . . Hettie, you offer me a bed in your house . . . when there is only one bed I wish to have with you.'

At that moment, something crashed upstairs. Then a bang. A sound like the front door opening and being blown back on its hinges. Hettie moved first and Evan followed her. Up the stairs to the hallway they went and found the side table that held the plate for visitors' cards overturned, the plate smashed. And her father's coat was discarded on the doorstep, one arm turned inside out, as if he'd struggled to put it on and abandoned it.

'I'll look outside. You check he's not upstairs,' said Evan. He stepped over the coat quickly and went out into the rain.

Hettie took the stairs two at a time and burst into his room. Her father was gone, his shoes still beside the bed. He'd gone out into the storm without shoes or coat. She went to wake up Towers to ask for his help, explaining that his master was gone. He said he'd get dressed and join her directly. Next Hettie went to her room, pulled on some warm bloomers, stockings and boots. Kezia came and gave her a woollen dress of her own to keep warm, which she threw on over her nightdress. Then she rushed downstairs and retrieved her cloak and bonnet from the cloakroom, tying the bonnet tight onto her head to save it blowing away in the gale. Busby was up and asking how he could assist her. When she told him what had happened, he went to get dressed too.

She ran outside and called, 'Father! Father!' but her voice was lost in the wind. Then she called for Evan, but there was no sign of him either.

Soon, Busby and Towers joined her. They agreed to split and go in three separate directions, though the two men both said she shouldn't be out and they would take care of it. She wouldn't have that, and instead went off in the direction of the woodland path towards town. Evan appeared along it and ran to her.

'Any sign?' she shouted in the wind.

'No, he's proper vanished. Get yourself home.'

She shook her head violently and went forward. He grabbed her arm and shouted, 'Go home, wench!'

But she wasn't having any of that and wrested her arm free, running forward on the path, calling, 'Father! Father!' as she went.

Evan came up behind her and joined the call. Wind-battered trees waved violently in the gale. Just ahead, a branch was torn from its tree and crashed across the path. Evan stopped her again and held her arms fast so she could not proceed.

'It's not safe!' he yelled. 'I'm taking you home.'

Hettie saw the branch whipped up by the wind and smash into another tree. He was right. It certainly was not safe on this path. She nodded and back they went towards the house. All around them, the trees whipped back and forth as if possessed by demons and the wind howled through them. The rain lashed into their faces, almost blinding them by the time they reached the front door.

Inside they went and Hettie rubbed her face with her cloak so she could see. She turned to tell Evan they should call back Busby and Towers, as it wasn't safe for them either – but Evan had already gone back out into the storm.

She could not stop him now. She went to the kitchen to find the cook and kitchen maid up with the house-keeper, preparing a hot breakfast for the men when they returned. Hettie stayed with them. They told her to go, that all was in hand, but she could not bear to. Kezia came and stayed too, all of them bustling around the table as Hettie and Kezia sat and she told her what had happened with her father.

Since Hettie had become mistress, relations with the servants, though cold at first, had eased. She had proved to be a kind and thoughtful mistress, and everyone had warmed to her – except Brooks, the young dark-haired maid who had bullied her at first, and who was now Benjamina's lady's maid. Sitting at the kitchen table, listening to the gossip of the servants and drinking hot, sweet tea prepared by the cook, Hettie felt she would rather be with these fine folk than anybody else while she waited and worried herself sick about her father.

'I fear he will try to harm himself,' she said to Kezia in a low voice.

'He is most likely asleep under a bush and will come to by morning,' said Kezia, but her voice didn't sound convinced and Hettie found little comfort in it.

After an hour or so, they heard the servants' door open in the hallway along from the kitchen and Hettie rushed out to see Busby, Towers and Evan appear. Behind them came no one. Her father was not there.

'I brought these fellows home,' said Evan. 'It's too dangerous out there.'

Hettie agreed and knew it was unfair to ask any of these men to risk their lives further for her father.

'Then I mun go,' she said and stood up.

There was a universal cry of 'No!' Busby told her that she should absolutely not, that her father would find a place to rest and come home in the morning, and the housekeeper and the others agreed. Nobody could convince her this was the case, but she soon found that none of these good people would let her go alone, and she didn't want them in danger either.

Evan accepted the offer of a bed for the night, but not in the guest room. He agreed to sleep on Towers's floor and that was that. Towers arranged fresh clothes for him. The men ate the breakfast of bacon and eggs the cook had prepared first, then everyone trooped up to bed. Hettie bid all good night and went to her room in weary anxiety.

Kezia wanted to fuss over her and sort her damp clothes, but Hettie sent her to bed too. She could sort herself this one time. She became her own lady's maid, removing her clothes and towelling herself down, retrieving a fresh nightdress and wrapping herself in a shawl, as she felt shivery. She opened the curtains to watch the storm and climbed into bed. The sky was lightening, but there were no birds brave enough to sing the dawn in. Hettie leant back on the pillows but did not close her eyes. She would not sleep until her father returned, she thought. And as soon as the sky was light enough, she would get dressed and go out to continue the search.

But her body had other ideas and before she realised it she was fast asleep.

∽

When she awoke, the sky outside was grey, the rain had stopped and the wind had died down. She leapt out of bed and went straight to her father's room. His bed was empty, the room unchanged since she had last seen him there. She knocked on Towers's door and waited. No answer. When she looked in, she saw that both Towers and Evan were gone. They must be out continuing the search.

She went to find Busby and discovered he was gone too. She was descending the stairs to the chequerboard hallway to ask the housekeeper if she had seen the men go, when she heard the front door handle squeak. She turned to see Evan on the doorstep, his cap in his hand, waiting to come in. She knew he wouldn't normally give a damn about ceremony and would walk straight over any rich man's threshold, just to make a point. And especially hers. But he just stood there, his eyes wide and his face white.

'What is it?' she asked as she approached him. 'Evan?'

But all he could do was shake his head. His eyes were filled with pity.

'Tell me.' Her whole body turned cold as ice. She felt as if she were made of glass. One shove and she would fall over and smash into a thousand pieces.

310

'We found him,' he said. 'Too late.'

'What? Too late for what?'

She could hear the words coming from her mouth, but she had no control over them. She knew how pointless they were.

'The river flooded,' said Evan. 'Half the town's been out escaping from their houses. Roads are impassable. Strewn tree limbs are all around, and other wreckage. It is a fearsome mess. Three people drowned in the flood last night. Hettie . . .'

'Was my father one of them?' she said.

But even as she said it, she knew the answer.

Chapter 20

Evan wore his best suit to the funeral. He had scrubbed and scrubbed at his face and hands to remove the coal dust. He wanted to be clean and smart for church and to show Hettie he'd made an effort, for her father, for her. A funeral service was always hard at the best of times, but to see Hettie there, her eyes red from weeping, and to know that he could not cross the church and put his arms around her . . . it was torture. But Hettie was a lady now, and thus sat alone at the front. The Malones came and took their places on the other side, where the general ordinary folk sat. Hettie had greeted everyone at the door, barely able to speak and trying to force a small smile at each person. But it was all very formal, of course. There was no room for comfort or hugs.

As he listened to the few words that were said about Adam Jones, Evan experienced a stab of guilt for the relief he felt that the man was dead. On that terrible night, he had wanted to be the one to find Adam, to deliver him safely back to Hettie. But he still felt infuriated with the man for causing Hettie all that trouble.

Once he had known Adam was dead, he had dreaded delivering the news to Hettie. She wept and wept afterwards and blamed herself. It was torment to watch her suffer like that, and Evan wished he could take that pain from her. To see her now so composed at the church, so stoic and strong, had a tremendous effect on him. He admired her more than ever and it ate away at him.

That afternoon, after the funeral, he moped about at home, stewing in his sorrows. Then, in the evening, he suddenly got up and left the house, saying he was going out to meet friends. But he took the woodland path instead without thinking about how wise the decision was, and somehow found himself at the door to the old brickmaster's house.

It was after nine o'clock on a Sunday. Would they let him see her or send him away? Evan knocked on the servants' door, hoping Busby wouldn't be the one to answer. He wasn't sure the man would let him in, even though they had bonded on the night of the storm. The man would be a stickler for the rules, he was sure, and say it was impossible for the lady of the house to be disturbed. But if a maid answered, perhaps Evan could charm her into letting him in . . .

The door opened. It was a maid. He didn't know her name but she was scowling.

'What the devil do you want this time of night?' she said.

'Urgent news for Miss Jones.'

'Give it to me, then,' said the maid, now looking self-important. 'I'm Mrs King's lady's maid and I dunna have time to be wasting on townsfolk.'

'I was told I mun deliver it in person to Miss Jones herself and Miss Jones only.'

'Concerning what?' she said, and narrowed her eyes at him.

He wanted to say *concerning none of your damned business, wench*. But charm always worked better than anger, in his limited experience.

'Concerning Miss Jones and not for you, I am sorry to say, miss.'

She squinted at him, and he smiled at her. It was not easy to find a female who didn't respond to a smile from Evan Malone. But it never did him much good. He knew the effect he had on girls, but all he did was compare each one to Hettie and find them wanting.

The maid smiled back and dropped her eyes. 'Well then, come in, if you mun. Sit at the kitchen table and I'll deliver news of your arrival to Miss Jones. But I canna think she'll see the likes of you. Even with your Sunday best on, you still reek of the pit.'

Evan had to force himself to keep the smile on his face, when all he wanted to do was slap her. He had done his very best with his suit for today's funeral, and he'd kept it on for this visit, hoping it would show him in a good light to Hettie. He wanted to remind her that he was not always caked in coal dust and could scrub up well when the occasion demanded.

He followed the maid to the kitchen, where the cook was finishing up for the night and nodded at him when he came in. They had an acquaintance now since the terrible night of Adam Jones's disappearance, and though the maid had been a pain, the rest of the house were generally quite warm towards Evan. The maid left and the cook made him a cup of tea and asked, 'What're you doing here then?'

'Message for Miss Jones,' he said.

The cook, Mrs Guest – a short, stocky, middle-aged woman with enormous forearms – winked at him. 'You're sweet on 'er,' she said and crossed her forearms over her bosom, presenting quite the formidable stance.

'Dunna be daft,' he said and took a sip of the welcome tea. 'She's like family. And anyway, she's a lady now.'

'You're still sweet on 'er. I inna blind. And Hettie Jones is good and kind, despite her new airs and graces. Any man would fall for that beauty. But you've no chance, lad. A gentleman will turn up afore long and snap her up.' Then she looked up, raised her eyebrows alarmingly and said, 'Can we help you, ma'am?'

Evan swivelled round and saw Hettie standing in the kitchen doorway. She still wore her black funeral dress from today and despite its sombre tones and her pale face, she managed to shine from it, her green eyes dulled but still wonderful. Evan stood up.

'Evan. Are you well? Everyone at home well?'

It gladdened his heart to hear her call it home, but he knew it was not her home any longer and had not been for a long time.

'Yes, all is well. I came . . . with a message for you.' He glanced at Mrs Guest, who was busying herself putting away the tea things.

'Will you come up to the sitting room?'

Mrs Guest said, 'I'm all done for the evening, ma'am, if you wish to talk here.' She nodded politely at Hettie and left the room.

'The cook dunna approve of me, I wager,' said Evan and grinned at Hettie. He was trying to make her smile, but he realised it was a stupid thing to do on this day and he cursed himself for being so crass.

She took a seat opposite and sighed heavily. 'Thank'ee for coming today,' she said and managed a small smile back. Perhaps it was not such a bad idea to smile at her. He guessed she needed a smile these days.

'Course I came. It must've been . . . a difficult day for you.'

She nodded and drew a hand over her eyes, dropping her head wearily. 'What was the message?'

'No message. I just wanted to see you.'

'Thought so,' she said and smiled wanly. She looked shattered.

'It's late. I shouldna come,' he said. 'What was I thinking? I'll be going.'

'No,' she said urgently and looked up at him. 'I dunna wanna be . . . on my own here.'

'You're surrounded by folk,' he said and smiled at her again, trying to win one back from her. 'At your beck and call day and night.'

'It inna the same. They're paid to be here. They're good people, I know that. But they're not friends. Or family.'

At the word family, her voice cracked a little and she looked down again. Her eyes were brimming, but she raised her head and sniffed, using her hands to dispel the tears that threatened to spill onto her cheeks.

Evan said gently, 'You can weep if you wish.'

'If I start, I fear I shall never stop.'

How he wanted to take her and kiss those tears away. But on the night of her father's funeral? It wasn't . . . seemly. That was the only word he could find in his mind for it. He'd have to be more careful than that, if he was to win her.

'I am here,' he said, simply.

'I know. I'm so glad of it. To see a friendly face.'

Every mention she made of the word friend annoyed him. He did not want to be only her friend. But he understood now that it meant more than anything to her. It was, in its way, a high compliment.

'We will always be friends to each other, Hettie.'

She looked up at him. 'I am an orphan now. I had not thought of it until this very evening. I used to think on it much as a child, when I thought my father was dead and gone, like my mother. I hated the word orphan. It sounded so forlorn. But now I have known my father and lost him, the loss is worse somehow. I wonder sometimes if it'd been better I never knew him. And then I scold myself for my selfishness, for it meant the world to him that he found me again. That is why . . . I dunna understand . . . why . . . oh, Evan . . .'

She could not hold back the tide now. He could not hold himself back either. As she sobbed into her hands, he pushed back his chair and was round the table in a second. He crouched down and put his arms about her. She turned and sobbed into his chest, and he felt her tears on his skin, warm and sacred.

Then, she suddenly sat up and said, 'Do you think he meant to drown himself? It haunts me all day and night. I will never know if it were an accident or if he wanted to die. He said he did, that night, remember? But why, when he . . . why would he throw away his life when he had me?'

Evan wanted to take away her pain with some magic spell. It was too much. Every thought he had about Adam Jones was bad and she wouldn't want to hear that. 'Some people were not meant to live long,' was all he could think of to say at first. 'But there were two others drowned that night. It's just as likely your father was the same as them. An accident. Just an accident.'

Now that she was sitting up, he felt foolish crouching beside her. He stood up and took his seat opposite her again.

'You're right,' she said, looking for a handkerchief in her sleeve and dabbing her eyes. 'I'm sorry about all the upset. I just feel . . . so alone. So very alone.'

'Dunna be daft. You're allowed upset on this day of all days. And you inna alone. You have me and the family with you forever. We all love you and would do anything for you – you know that. We are family. We are bound together by our past, if not our blood. You know, Hettie, blood inna everything. Blood doesna matter as much as you think.'

He watched as her face changed. There came the most extraordinary expression in her eyes, something akin to fear. And shame. She looked away.

'What is it, Hettie?' He knew her so well that every glance was easy to read.

'I canna say,' she said, so quietly he could barely hear her.

'Yes, you can. And you mun say it. Summat awful has come over you. What is it?'

'It's summat I carry with me. Summat I wish I never knew. But it's such a burden. I havna told a soul. Not even my father. Or Miss Ashford.'

'But . . . why would you tell Miss Ashford?' His mind boggled. 'Whatever burden you carry, share the load with me, Hettie. I will not tell a soul either. You know that.'

She looked up and fixed him with her eyes. Those eyes that he adored, shining green, now worried him. There was true fear there.

'If I tell you, you mun promise me that you will never think on me differently. That I will always be your Hettie.'

To hear her call herself this gave him such joy that all thoughts of fear were banished for a moment. 'Course you will. You'll always be my girl!'

'I am a King.'

He frowned at her. 'Not truly. Inheriting their riches doesna make you one of 'em.'

'No, there is more. Mrs King told me afore she died. My mother was a bastard, born of rape. By Mrs King's husband, old Ralph King. He took a maid, Betsy Blaize, and put a child in her by force. That child was my mother, Martha. So, you see, I am joined by blood to the Kings. I am a King.'

As he stared into her fearful eyes, Evan felt as if the room about them tipped to one side. All his life, the name King had been impressed upon him as a wicked word, a terrible thing of monstrous proportions. He had grown up knowing that the Kings had imprisoned his mother and killed his brother.

And now, his best girl, his true love, his Hettie. She was a King? It was unthinkable. He wouldn't have it.

'It could be a lie,' he said slowly.

'Why would Mrs King have lied? What good would it do?'

'Maybe the old bitch was mad. Maybe she made it up like a story in her head.'

'She wasna mad. And she wasna a bitch. Dunna ever call her that.'

'Oh, you would defend her, being a King.'

He had not meant to say it, but Hettie always riled him. He couldn't bear it when she told him off. He always answered hotly. But it was an awful thing to say. He had spat the word *King* from his mouth as if it were bitterness on his tongue.

Hettie stood up abruptly. 'I think you better go now,' she said. She clasped her hands before her, her chin jutting out proudly.

'No, Hettie, please. I'm sorry. I didna mean to say it. I didna . . .'

'Please go,' she said. Her eyes were pleading, yet as she looked away, there was that shame again. She was ashamed of who she was and he had made it worse by insulting her. He could punch himself.

'I will, Hettie. But I mun say . . .'

'No,' she said, firmly and loudly, so much so that it shocked him. 'No more tonight. Thank'ee for coming.'

With that, she left the room, her black gown swishing along the kitchen floor as she went. No goodbye, no kind word. He had hurt her badly and he was a bloody fool.

There was nothing for it but to skulk off out of the house and walk the dark path home. But as he neared town, he couldn't face going to his house. He didn't want to be where his family was, didn't want to have to face his mother. She had an uncanny ability to read his thoughts in his face. She would know something was very wrong from just one glance at him. And he would not be able to hide it.

No, he needed something to distract him before he had to see her. He turned towards town instead and headed for his favourite tavern. He would partake of the local ale, and only then would he be ready to go home and face his mother, so drunk, he hoped, that she would not bother to question him about anything.

As he walked through Ironbridge, Evan thought for the first time in his life that his love for Hettie had changed, not by anything he or she had said or done, but by invisible forces beyond their control. Could he love a King? Should he tell his mother the truth about Hettie? Did he now look at Hettie differently, knowing her mother was a King bastard? He didn't want to think any of these things, but he couldn't help it. Blood had changed everything.

Chapter 21

'You want to get out, don't you?' said Benjamina. 'Not yet, not yet, little one.'

Benjamina fondled Drina's ears. The little dog loved a carriage ride. She would sit on Benjamina's lap and stare out of the window, tongue hanging out, absorbing the atmosphere and intense excitement of the outside world. Now the carriage had come to a halt, Drina's tail was wagging so hard her whole body was lurching from side to side. Benjamina had instructed her driver to pull in to a clearing at the edge of the woodland on a road above Ironbridge. They were parked opposite the Holy Trinity church at Coalbrookdale, the iron railings framing its long, slim grounds, beyond it the thick woodland stretching for miles, punctuated by the steaming trails of chimney smoke and other signs of industry. It was a quiet spot at this time, so early in the morning. It was thankfully cool, as the July weather that week had been particularly hot and uncomfortable. Benjamina had chosen this time of day for its coolness, but mostly to avoid people as much as possible. She did not want any passers-by to witness the meeting she was about to have.

It was not something she would ever have planned, but it had become essential. It was a necessity due to the cruel actions of others. The final straw had been the meeting with her solicitor last week. He had told her that her lawsuit ought to be dropped, that it would come to nothing, that there was no evidence and no witnesses to support her claim that Queenie was losing her mind or that Hettie Jones had inveigled her way into the old woman's affections and subsequently her will. Benjamina had argued with him for some time, but she had not persuaded him. He did not want any more part in it. She could have engaged another legal man, but she trusted his judgement and knew that if he said it was pointless, it must truly be so.

She was bitterly disappointed. And she was furious. She had come home that day determined to scream at the Jones girl, to strike her in the face, even. She did not, of course, but she pictured doing so often as they spoke to each other across the sitting room or wherever it was in the house – Jones's house now, not her own. Benjamina felt that she was no better than a lodger in her own home.

A couple of days after her meeting, the Jones girl came to her directly and said she had been speaking to her own solicitor, too, that he had given her the news that Benjamina was to cease pursuing her claim. Jones had simpered and said how glad she was, that they could move forward and put it behind them. Benjamina had smiled and nodded and agreed with the little fool. But inside, she was wracked with rage. She had gone back to her study and picked up a fountain pen, wanting to stab herself in the hand with it. It was the only thing she could think of to calm her fury, to focus on physical pain rather than her internal storm. But she did not. She had more control of herself than that. Instead, she sat at her desk for hours that day, mulling it over. If legal means would not bring her what she deserved, then she would have to circumvent the law and take matters into her own hands.

She had formulated a plan that grew into a brief note, a letter sent to this man to meet her here.

He was late and Benjamina scolded him into Drina's ear, telling her all about the silly man who kept them waiting. Finally, she heard her driver speak to someone and the carriage door opened. There he was, looking much worse than the last time she had seen him, years before. Drina barked madly at him and he looked alarmed. Benjamina calmed her down and called her driver to take Drina for a walk, so that they could talk in peace.

'Mr Troon,' she said. 'Please.' She gestured to the seat opposite her. He climbed in somewhat clumsily, for he was a man unaccustomed to riding in carriages. He had been fine-looking once, many years ago. But time and circumstance had not treated him kindly and he looked haggard now.

'Mrs King,' he said and nodded. He took off his cap and held it awkwardly in his hands. He was looking at her now, at all of her, a hungry survey of her figure. An image from nearly twenty years ago popped into her mind, of a time he had kissed her neck when they stood in the shadows behind Southover. It disgusted her now, this thought. But that had been in the times when he was the foreman at the King brickworks, often coming for meetings with Queenie and loitering about afterwards to liaise with Benjamina when she allowed it, when he was a younger man, virile and darkly handsome. Now, the thought of this ghost of a man coming anywhere near her made her feel queasy.

'Thank you for coming to meet me. I have a business opportunity for you. Would that be of interest to you?'

'It would, ma'am, yes. I've fallen on hard times since last we . . . knew each other.'

'I can see that,' she said, with some distaste.

'I wasna always this . . . shabby a man. I'm hoping you recall . . . how I used to be.'

'I do, Troon. And I can see that you are in need of a new prospect.'

'I am, Mrs King. All that business at the brickyard broke me. After the strike and that poor lad Brain. After he died, it was never the same. Then Mrs King let me

326

go. I dunna wanna speak ill of the dead, but that wasna fair. I'd worked myself to death in that job, and she just dismissed me. Since Mrs King let me go from the brickyard all those years ago, my life has taken a terrible turn. My wife left me with our children and I've spent a spell in the workhouse. I barely saw my little'uns growing up and now they are grown they will not even speak to me in the street. My life has been cursed, ma'am. Truly cursed.'

'Well, then. Stop your complaints about the past and listen. I do have a job for you. And you're the man for it. The pay will be significant. But you may find it distasteful. It is beyond the law, you see. It is very much against the law. And afterwards, you must leave the area and never come back. But I will give you a year's wages that you would've once earnt at the brickyard. Will that be enough to persuade you?'

Troon leant forward, his eyes like saucers. 'A year's wages? A whole year, in one go?'

'Yes. That is what I said. Are you interested?'

Troon blinked. 'And it is against the law of the land?'

'It most certainly is. But if you are not capable of taking such a risk, then I shall find another who has more about him and . . .'

'No, I am your man for this, Mrs King. I am your man. Dunna deny me. For a year's wages, I'd raise a pistol at the Queen, may God forgive me for saying so, ma'am.'

Benjamina smiled and leant forward, placing her hand carefully on Troon's thigh. 'Good, Troon,' she said, in a treacly voice. 'Good man.'

He was desperate for the money and desperate for her. Yes, he would do nicely.

Chapter 22

July 1876

First class was rather different from second or third. Hettie recalled her strawberry picking railway journey with clarity: the buffeting breeze, the sooty steam and the hard seats. This time, her trip to London was characterised by comfort. Hettie's tickets, as well as those of Kezia and Mrs Elkin were all numbered and reserved, so there was no pushing and shoving to find a seat. The seats themselves were far more comfortable and the compartment had glass windows. For the first part of the trip, a gentleman lit up a cigar, which filled the small space with choking tobacco smoke, especially unbearable in the warm July weather. Mrs Elkin pointedly yet politely informed the gentleman that smoking of any sort was prohibited on the railways, but the man simply flicked his newspaper on his lap and ignored her. Kezia opened the window and everyone was glad when the man alighted at the next stop. Hettie wondered if her clothes might stink of cigars forever.

Mrs Elkin kept up a steady stream of conversation for most of the first half of the journey. For a trip of any length, an unmarried young woman such as Hettie required a chaperone, and Mrs Elkin was an old business acquaintance of Mrs King the elder. She had also once met Beatrice Ashford and extolled her virtues at length to Hettie, which Hettie was able to join in with, and they had a very pleasant conversation as they recalled Beatrice in all her ways. Mrs Elkin was a widow, her husband Edwin – a local tile manufacturer – having died ten years before. Hettie thought Mrs Elkin seemed cheery yet lonely, and she had been eager to join them for the trip, to escape her business affairs and home and get away to London for a few days.

Hettie too was eager to escape. That was the purpose of her trip, though the reason she had given to others such as Mrs Elkin was that it was a treat to celebrate her eighteenth birthday, which had recently passed uneventfully. The truth was that since the news that Benjamina's suit was unsuccessful, the atmosphere at home had been intolerable. It did not help Hettie's spirits that since telling Evan her secret about her origins, he had not visited once. She wondered if he had told anyone: his mother and father, perhaps? What would Anny make of it? Would she detest Hettie now? There had been no news from them, so Hettie did not want to visit and find out. She could not have borne seeing a look of disgust in Anny's eyes. It was bad enough when she was working for the Kings. Now she was one of them, would Anny and Peter ever accept her as the child they'd once raised?

Too many questions plagued her. Instead of facing them, Hettie simply wanted to vanish. She was miserable, stuck at home with a woman who hated her and separated by circumstance from the one person who could ever lighten her mood and truly understand her: Evan Malone. She missed him so, more than she ever had before. She could only hope that his distaste for her secret would have compelled him to keep his mouth shut and not tell a soul. Hettie certainly intended never to tell another living person.

In the second half of the journey, Mrs Elkin's late middle age caught up with her and she fell into a slumber to which the rhythm of the train played useful accompaniment, keeping her snoozing most of the rest of the way. When Hettie heard a snort of a snore from her, she glanced at Kezia and they smirked at each other, then had to cover their mouths to stop themselves giggling, lest they wake up the talkative Mrs Elkin. It was a relief to have some peace. Nobody else in the carriage wanted to converse, thank heavens, so Hettie was able to relax and look out of the window, watching the countryside roll past them.

It wasn't only Benjamina's fury and Evan's absence that she wanted to escape. It had only been two months since her father's death. The night of the storm and its aftermath was like something out of a nightmare to her now, from which she felt she had never awoken. Her father had been a worry from the moment he arrived back in her life, but he had been *her* trouble, and all that he was belonged to *her*. He was her only kin.

She was an orphan now. How she hated that word. It felt so final. She had not seen her father's body; Evan told her not to and she had acquiesced. She wanted to remember him in his best times: sitting by the fire, puffing on a pipe and telling her stories about her mother, the brickyard, her baby days, the old times . . . The years and his woes seemed to drop from him then. She saw him as he could have been, the father he once promised to be, before fate took him and ravaged him, turned him into the half-man he became.

Through it all, despite the evidence before her eyes and the faithless stance of the Malones, she had still believed that one day he would turn a corner and give up the drink for good, settle into a quiet life and become the father she'd always wanted. Instead, he was taken from her too soon and she was tortured by the feeling that if only she had sat with him that night, she could have stopped him leaving, seen him through his dark night of the soul and kept him safe. Perhaps after that, he might have improved. Perhaps she could've taken him away on a trip somewhere – a European tour perhaps, where he would not have the time or opportunity to drink so much, where he could have his eyes opened, his horizons broadened, where he could have realised there was more to the texture of the earth than the landscape of his failures. Perhaps, if only . . . these were the words that haunted her.

Thus, she had hastily planned a trip to London, to escape the house and its memories. She had no particular plan, other than to stay in a hotel recommended by Mrs Elkin and to frequent some of the smart London shops and enjoy some entertainments.

But Hettie was lying to herself. She knew that there was one particular reason she wanted to visit London and it had nothing to do with shopping or museums or parks or theatres. It was Mr Laurence Maxwell Ripley.

On arrival at the railway station, the porters swarmed around them, and they chose one to carry their luggage. Mrs Elkin was in charge of tips, and paid them generously, as the porter was civil and most helpful. He informed them that their residence while in London, The Great Western Royal Hotel, was immediately adjacent to the station, and thus they could walk. He pointed it out and allowed them to walk ahead, to spare them the embarrassment of having to walk with him.

As Hettie approached with Kezia and Mrs Elkin, she looked up in awe at the building. The hotel was a magnificent many-windowed structure, made from a caramel-coloured stone. It was admittedly stained with the sooty deposits of London, but still looked beautiful. Carriages, porters, guests and staff came and went from its doors like busy bees at a hive.

Mrs Elkin dealt with the bookings and before long, they were being shown around by another porter, this one dressed extremely smartly in the crimson and grey hotel uniform. He showed them briefly to the general coffee room on the ground floor, a long room sweeping the whole length of the building, peppered with people enjoying their drinks and snacks. On the first floor, they were shown a reading room, its walls lined with books and its table strewn with newspapers. Next was a music room furnished with a highly polished grand piano, and then they were shown a private coffee room. They were asked to follow the porter to their room along the deep-piled carpets which rendered all footsteps soundless.

Their suite was a series of rooms, one for each of the three women, with a dressing room besides, all spacious with tall ceilings and elaborate stucco work. Heavy silk curtains hung at the windows, and the main one opened on to a balcony. Outside, the view of the street gave Hettie the impression of a postcard depicting a typical London scene, with carriages and horses and omnibuses and hard-working folk going to and fro about their business. Inside the apartment, the furniture was fine and served their every need. There was a writing table, and even a sofa and armchairs for the ladies to use when they wished to escape the hubbub of London life outside. Mrs Elkin, to whom Hettie had given a substantial sum of money at the beginning of their trip in order to take care of tipping and other small bills, gave the porter a prodigious amount; she clearly felt delighted to be able to splash other people's money around.

Over the next few hours, Mrs Elkin rested in her room, while Kezia unpacked the two ladies' belongings. Hettie wanted to help but Kezia refused, as usual, so Hettie went to the writing table and took up pen and ink. Before beginning, she thought for a while about how she should frame this letter to Mr Laurence Maxwell Ripley.

Dear Sir, she began. Was that too formal? They had spoken on two occasions, and she was now a lady, after all. She put that piece of paper aside, cursing herself for the wastage, though she knew it didn't matter. *Dear Mr Ripley*, she wrote. Yes, that would do. She knew his name, after all. Why not use it?

You will not remember me, I'm sure. We met at the strawberry field and you gave me your card. Since then, I have had a very surprising turnabout in my fortunes. I am now an . . .

She had no idea how to spell *heiress*. After all, it was not a word she ever thought she would need when she was learning to read and write. She thought it might start with an *a*, but after that she was lost. And she didn't want to seem like a dunce to Mr Ripley, though she felt like one.

She asked Kezia, who wasn't convinced by the *a* but couldn't think what else it would be, so Hettie went through to find Mrs Elkin supine on her bed, reading a novel. Mrs Elkin told her the correct spelling, which seemed so outlandish that Hettie doubted she could possibly know what she was talking about. But with no other authority to ask, she would have to trust her.

. . . I am now an heiress. I was left houses and businesses and money by my employer, Mrs King, on her death. She was very kind and wanted to see me right. As we have met before and also as I suppose I am now a lady, I wondered if we might meet for a stroll and a talk, if you think such a meeting would be seemly. I can tell you many more things about Shropshire ways for your research and so it might be a useful meeting to you, who can tell? I will be with my friend Mrs Elkin so it will be seemly. If this is not something that you wish to find time to do or if it is not in good taste or seemly or not something you desire to do for any reason, and other things I know not a lot about then . . .

She ran out of steam and read over the last sentence, wondering where on earth she'd been going with it. She'd used *seemly* three times. But it was a good word, and so it should be used as much as possible, she thought. It summed up everything she felt she didn't know about being a lady. But how to finish this stupidly long sentence? The point was, she wanted him to be able to safely say no without fear of offending her. After all, she knew it was probably a ridiculous thing to be contacting him in the first place. It was highly likely he would have no memory of her whatsoever. He was luminously memorable to her, of course, as meeting him was a highly unusual occurrence in her life, but with his work researching women of the working classes, he must come across wenches like her daily – or like the wench she had once been, at any rate. So she wanted to ensure there was ample room for him to decline and not seem ungentlemanly. She decided to abandon that sentence and put a full stop at the end of it, as surely it was long enough now. She then added:

This is all very well understood and not to be questioned by myself or anyone.

Yes, she liked that sentence. Now, it was time to finish this thing off. How to end a letter was a mystery to her, lost in the schooldays that had passed so many years before. She could hear Mrs Elkin snoring again now in the next room, so did not wish to wake her to ask. At last she decided on something which sounded appropriate without being too familiar.

Regarding,
Miss Hettie Jones
The Great Western Royal Hotel
Paddington
London.

Kezia arranged for it to be sent to the address on his card, which Hettie had always kept safe and sound and had brought with her to London. When the letter had gone, she held the card in her hand and looked upon it again. It was creased and worn, now having been handled by her on many occasions since it was first proffered to her by its owner. The thought, however unlikely, of seeing him again perhaps today or tomorrow or the day after that brought a warmth to her cheeks and made her smile.

And it had been quite a while since a thought of anything had made Hettie smile.

༄

The following morning was to be spent in the pursuit of shopping. This was something that Hettie had never done for pleasure, only necessity. At first, she had to be persuaded by Mrs Elkin that it was worth doing at all; shopping had always been a chore to her, not something to be pursued for entertainment. Her chaperone said it would be a marvellous experience for her, as she could spend all she liked. Kezia accompanied them too, at Hettie's request, though Mrs Elkin did not see the need to bring a maid. But Hettie secretly wanted Kezia to enjoy her stay in London, too, for Kezia was much more a friend than a servant, though Hettie could not or would not explain this to the likes of Mrs Elkin. She had been well off all her life and was not a creature of two worlds, like Hettie. She would not understand.

They travelled in the carriage to Regent Street, where some of the best shops were, according to Mrs Elkin. The experience of seeing London from a carriage was vastly different from that of traversing it on foot with a basket of strawberries perched on your head. Walking through the streets made Hettie feel a part of it, but the view from the carriage removed her from the action and made it seem like a puppet show, where the passers-by were there only to furnish the scene with spectacle. Hettie tried to dispel that strange, isolated feeling of distance from these ordinary people by picking one at a time and trying to imagine where they'd been and where they were going. It made her feel more of a connection to them, something she'd felt sadly lacking since she'd become an heiress. At times she felt locked up in a castle; her situation was so removed from that of her previous life and acquaintances. She hoped that London would make her feel part of the world again, but here, in the coach she felt more removed than ever.

Hettie's favourite shop was Liberty. It was like a treasure chest full of pretty things, the likes of which she'd never seen before. Mrs Elkin told her that much of it came from far away, from the East, exotic places like Japan, of which Hettie had so little knowledge she could not even begin to imagine what life was like in such a country. Mrs Elkin, who seemed to enjoy shopping for Hettie more than Hettie did herself, encouraged her to buy some ornaments for the house, but Hettie had no idea what to choose, as everything looked so exquisite. When Mrs Elkin was engaged talking to a lady at the perfume counter, Hettie said to Kezia, 'I want to buy gifts for the Malones, for all of them. But I dunna know what to buy. What would they like from here?'

Kezia thought a moment. 'It's hard to say. Maybe some nice fabric for Anny, tobacco for Peter. Toys for the children, of course.'

'Yes, yes! You're so clever to think of it all, Kezia. But what for Evan?'

They both pondered and decided to find the other items first, while still considering Evan Malone. Hettie wanted to buy him something he would like, that would bring some pleasure to his everyday life, that he wouldn't judge her for or turn his nose up at. She couldn't think of a single thing. A hat or gloves or other item of clothing from Liberty wouldn't fit into his world and would be left on the hook or in a drawer. He didn't smoke much, unlike his father, so tobacco would not suit. It seemed impossible to buy the man a gift! She tried to think through his day at the pit and his time at home. What did he need?

'I've got it!' she told Kezia, and led her back to a part of the shop where they sold tin boxes decorated with attractive scenes. 'He can put his bait in it to keep it safe from the rats.'

'Capital idea!' said Kezia. They looked through the piles of tin boxes, discarding anything with flowers or small animals on. Everything was too feminine. But Hettie found one with a woodland scene painted on it, tall trees and a blue sky behind with cottonwool clouds. It reminded her of their walks in the woods up to Southover when they were children. There was even a hint of a river in the picture, a splash of blue twinkling in the sunshine through the trees. Yes, this was perfect. Big enough to hold his lunch yet small enough to put in his greatcoat pocket.

Hettie was thrilled with all of the gifts she'd selected for the Malones, and once she'd purchased them she turned to Kezia and said, 'Now, what would you like?'

But Kezia firmly shook her head. It was not the done thing. Hettie didn't care and insisted, and in the end, Kezia accepted a writing set with pretty paper and envelopes, to write to her mother in Staffordshire, which she did every week. Hettie was glad to think that Kezia would have a nice thing that she could use, something that would bring her a little joy every time she used it.

Money was a necessity, Hettie realised, but when you had a surfeit, it could bring little joys like these and make life easier and more pleasant. She still worried that the Malones would find her gifts extravagant and ridiculous, and she so wanted to please them. Another unpleasant thought crept into her mind, that they might think she was trying to buy their favour, especially if they now knew from Evan that she was a King. She dismissed the idea, as the gifts were purchased now. And after all, whatever they knew or thought about her, she loved them and wanted to treat them.

When they arrived back in their suite, after shopping and luncheon, Kezia came to Hettie with a letter received that morning at the hotel while they were out. She did not recognise the hand, so turned it over to see the sender had written his full name on the back. In that moment she ripped open the letter with her fingers, not waiting to use the paper knife on the writing desk that ladies were supposed to use.

Dear Miss Jones,

Why, of course I remember you. I recall our meeting and conversations with perfect clarity. To hear from you is nothing short of a miracle. I never imagined I would but I gave you my card in the small hope that one day our paths might cross again. To hear of your change in fortunes is like something from a romantic novel! I am delighted to learn of it. Nobody could deserve such luck more than you, Miss Jones. I could tell from our meetings that you are a good, hard-working person.

I would be delighted to meet with you. May I suggest the Royal Aquarium, which has only recently opened to the public? We could meet there and have a stroll around the exhibits and talk as we do so. I think this would be supremely 'seemly', a word of which you seem excessively fond! I am free tomorrow afternoon, if that suits. I look forward to seeing you again, Miss Jones, very much indeed.

Yours sincerely,
Laurence Maxwell Ripley

⌘

Further arrangements were made by letter and a plan to meet was decided upon, at the hour of three the following day. Hettie and Kezia chose her smartest mourning frock. Something about the blackness of the dress made her eyes shine more greenly than ever, Kezia said, which Hettie was pleased about, as her competition was the dark, dangerous eyes of Mr Ripley. She wanted to dazzle him as much as she knew he would dazzle her, whatever he was wearing.

Mrs Elkin was all a-flutter at the idea of meeting a gentleman, and Hettie hoped she would not take over the entire conversation with him. After some whispering with Kezia, they secretly planned that Kezia would fall behind with Mrs Elkin, pointing out things of interest and thus allowing Hettie and Mr Ripley to converse with each other with a modicum of privacy.

Arriving at the aquarium, Hettie was again astounded by the size of the buildings in London. As with the hotel, it was one of the biggest buildings she'd ever seen, though this was even more spectacular. The main hall was covered by a curved roof of glass and iron. The room was huge and long, filled with tall, exotic plants and sculptures, amongst the many water-filled glass tanks. Overwhelmed as she was by the spectacle, Hettie's eyes flicked from person to person, looking for the one person she wanted to see more than any other at this moment in time. It was the dark eyes she searched for, those eyes she had pictured so many times in her mind. She looked hurriedly about for them, amongst the many hats and bonnets that bobbed along, stopping and starting, admiring the exhibits. They had agreed to meet by the largest tank, so Hettie headed that way, passing by several smaller tanks filled with fish darting to and fro, pointed at by onlookers. Amidst the hub-bub of chatter, the sound of a musical instrument sliced through, followed by others tuning their instruments, ready for a performance. She looked over and saw the musicians seated, chatting amongst themselves and playing snatches of tunes. If she had come here without the plan to meet Mr Ripley, she would have been completely taken up with the spectacle of what surrounded her. But she was intent on only one thing.

And there he was, standing in a leisurely fashion, his back to the main tank, staring at her with a gentle smile on his face. He had seen her first and waited for her to approach, watching her all the way. She had to look away. Seeing those black eyes again did something to her she couldn't explain. He took off his hat as she neared him and she saw that his hair was longer than the last time she'd seen him, curling at the sides about his ears and halfway down his neck, jet black and perfectly outlined against the water in the tank behind him. His smile grew wider and she saw his neat white teeth. He was beautiful; there was no other word for it. He was even more handsome than she recalled, and that was truly saying something.

He stepped towards her, shaking his head, smiling all the while.

'Why, Miss Jones, you are transformed.'

She didn't understand his meaning for a moment, but as he glanced over her figure, she felt a thrill akin to nothing she had felt before. Then she realised what he meant.

'Smarter than last you saw me,' she said and found she was grinning at him. Things felt so easy between them, as if they had spoken only that morning.

He leant in and said more quietly, 'To me, your fruit-picking garb was just as charming. Yet that is not what a young lady wants to hear, of course. Your dress becomes you. I am sorry to see that you are in mourning.'

'My father.'

'Ah, Miss Jones. Please accept my heartfelt condolences.'

'Thank you,' she said quietly, unable to look up at him as she said it. Those eyes made her feel like she couldn't concentrate.

'May I ask, was it a long illness?'

Hettie was about to explain about her father when Mrs Elkin came suddenly was upon them and introductions had to be made. Mr Ripley was so kind and solicitous to Mrs Elkin that she was utterly charmed.

They strolled in a three, Kezia behind, as Mr Ripley pointed out the names of some of the sculptures and the fish in some of the tanks, explaining that the larger tanks were empty as the aquarium had only been open for a few months. He teased Mrs Elkin by telling her they would be housing whales, which she believed for a moment, then collapsed into giggles when she realised what a foolish idea that was. Hettie enjoyed the chance to watch him talk and move, but she was beginning to get frustrated with her chaperone's presence. Then Mr Ripley seemed to read her mind, for he told Mrs Elkin that she looked weary and suggested she might like to be seated a while and listen to the orchestra, which was about to play. Mrs Elkin readily agreed, never refusing a chance to sit down. She agreed that Mr Ripley could show Hettie the other amusements while she was sitting down, as long as she could see them at all times.

346

They readily agreed, and Kezia winked at Hettie as she took a seat beside Mrs Elkin.

At last, they were alone. They were surrounded by hundreds of people, but to Hettie they all fell away, leaving only herself and this man, his hair and his eyes. They strolled slowly, not wishing to complete their circumference of the hall too quickly, for then their time alone would come to an end.

'Now we can speak of our true minds and dispense with small talk,' he said with a twinkle in his eye.

'Dunna be cheeky,' she said, and enjoyed his smile at her Shropshire way of talking.

'Oh, I can be far cheekier than that,' he said, his voice low and delicious. 'But Miss Jones, what I would like to tell you is how much more fascinating you are to me now than before. Not because you are now a lady. No, that is not it, even if that's what you were thinking. It is the process of that transformation that interests me. I see your life as that of two phases: your working phase and your leisure phase. I would love to study the differences between the two, how your daily life has altered, your physical state, even how your thoughts and feelings have changed, if you would be willing to explain such things to me.'

She loved having his full attention, but as they passed by the tanks filled with tiny marine lives, she felt a little like a lobster or limpet or some such specimen, only interesting to him as an object of study, to examine and file away. She wondered if he genuinely liked her as a person, or only as an object of curiosity. She could have given him a long speech about how much her life had changed, but instead she decided to be brutally honest.

'I am more lonely and miserable now than I've ever been in my life.'

He stopped walking. She turned and faced him, wishing she had not said it. She had meant to appear gay and joyful to him, for she assumed that was what a man like him would find attractive in a lady.

'I can see it is true, Miss Jones. There is an intense sadness about your magnificent green eyes. I am much aggrieved to hear it. Please be assured you can speak to me about your father's passing, if it would assist you.'

She looked away and continued to stroll forward and he fell into step beside her. 'My father drowned in a storm two months back.'

'Oh, I am so sorry. How terrible for you. This is awful, Miss Jones.'

'Yes, it was. He was a troubled man but he was my only family. I am alone now.'

'You are an orphan?'

'Yes.' How she hated the word.

'I am an orphan too.'

'You are?' She never imagined rich people as orphans. It often happened to poor folk. but she never imagined it with the wealthy. She supposed she had always thought of them as living charmed lives, though she knew from her own experience how wrong she'd been about that.

'Yes. My mother died when I was a small boy and I was sent away to live with an aunt. I saw little of my father, and then he died abroad the year I turned twenty. So I have been an orphan these seven years. It is a curious feeling, is it not? Like a boat without an anchor.'

'Yes, it's exactly that way. I grew up feeling like that, as my mother died when I was a little'un and then my father only came back . . .' She hesitated. She certainly did not wish to tell him that her father had returned from Australia as a former convict. '. . . from being away, and we spent a year and a half together. But then . . . I lost him.' That was how she still felt about it. *She* had lost *him*, for if she had only stayed with him that night, she would have kept him.

'I know how hard that must have been for you. I am sorely sorry to hear it. At least you have your friends to sustain you at this difficult time. I know I have relied on my own friends far too much these past years. But they don't seem to mind. They indulge me.'

'I never see my old friends now. We canna be easy with each other, like we would in the old days. And I canna make new friends, for folk look at me as an odd thing, without a place. I feel as if I live between two worlds and I canna be in either without wanting the other.'

'I see. I am ashamed of myself, Miss Jones.'

'What for?'

'When I asked you to tell about your experiences, I imagined you regaling me with amusing anecdotes about how strange it has been to discard your old ways and adopt new ones, how using the right spoon at the dinner table or negotiating the vagaries of a lady's dressing routine had flummoxed you. And that we would chortle about such things, and I would see delight in your eyes at your new situation and enjoy it with you. Now I see I was a blind fool. Of course the truth is that such a drastic change in anyone's life brings with it trauma. And my heart aches for you, Miss Jones, for the loss of your father, for the estrangement from your friends and everything sorrowful that has befallen you since we last met. Please accept my apology.'

'No need to say sorry,' she said quietly. His words had moved her very much, though she had not understood every one. But she knew he was humbled by her suffering and that was enough. 'It inna your fault, Mr Ripley.'

'Please, won't you call me Max now, as I asked you to all that time ago? If we are to be friends – it is what my friends call me.'

'I'll call you Max if you'll call me Hettie.'

'Agreed,' he said and beamed a smile, which she shyly returned. 'It is good to see you smile. I am hoping that the very least I can do is offer my friendship. If, as you say, your old friends have abandoned you . . .'

'Oh no, not abandoned. It's not like that.' She thought of the Malones and particularly Evan, and wondered if perhaps it *was* like that. Had Evan abandoned her? Could he still love her now he knew who she was? Maybe he had abandoned her. Maybe it was true.

'Of course not, I did not mean to judge harshly. Let me rephrase. If you feel that relations with your old friends are troubled and you have not yet found new friends, then let me be your new friend. In fact, I am your old new friend, as we met over a year ago, did we not? I hope you will always look upon me that way, as your new old friend or your old new friend, it matters not. The key word is friend.'

'Yes, I need a friend more than anything in the world,' she said and looked round at him. He was staring at her so intently that she held her breath.

'None of my friends have your honesty, Hettie. Not only in your directness and your words. It shines from your eyes somehow. They are so clear. So beautiful. So purely and perfectly . . . green.'

By now, their circle around the hall was complete and the orchestra had just finished their last piece, the audience before them erupting into applause. Hettie had not heard a note of it, had not taken in a single thing in the aquarium. All that she saw and heard was Laurence Maxwell Ripley.

Mrs Elkin was up now and coming at them with overtures of rapture about the music and how she hoped they had enjoyed their stroll, and saying that there was now a performance of bell ringers which was not her favoured instrument, it always sounding a bit tinny to her ears, and perhaps they would be better taking a look at the aquarium's gallery room, which housed some fine art, apparently ... and so she rattled on, while Hettie glanced up from time to time at Mr Ripley, who was not listening to a word Mrs Elkin said and instead was gazing at Hettie. She drank it in, that look, those eyes. She wanted the world to freeze in time – like the merry-go-round at Oakengates came to a halt and the passengers clambered off the galloping horses, so she wished London would stop, so she could step off with Max, take his hand and vanish into a world of their own making.

Chapter 23

August 1876

It was warm already, even at dawn. The night had been hot and sticky. Evan hadn't slept much. On the walk to work, he clutched his new bait tin in his hand. As it was August, he wasn't wearing his greatcoat to work so had to carry the tin, which invited merciless teasing from his fellow miners. Some of the others had tins, but nothing so fancy, with trees painted on it and from Liberty of London. He knew he'd be ribbed for it, but he didn't care. He wanted it with him all day in that dark place. It gave him a taste of the outdoors, of nature and of Hettie.

He still carried a torch for her, of course he did. It didn't matter that she was out of reach now. He couldn't help the way he felt; he had felt it since before he could remember. She had always been with him, in his heart. The bait tin was physical proof of it and he kept it close to him at all times underground.

When the gifts had arrived – delivered anonymously, though they all guessed they were from Hettie – there was general delight from the kids and his parents were also touched. Billy and Lily were overjoyed with their wooden train set, and Flora adored her fan decorated with pictures from somewhere far away and strange. She treasured it and kept it very safe, barely using it lest it break, instead opening it out carefully to gaze at it every day.

But they were all disappointed that Hettie hadn't visited with the gifts in person, and everyone felt her absence even more. It was nice to know she was thinking of them. But, Evan felt, why couldn't she come herself? Did she believe she was too good for them now? No, he couldn't believe that of her. She'd never be that way. Maybe she was embarrassed, about what she'd told him . . . well, he didn't want to think about that right now. Just the thought of it flushed his cheeks as he strode along the road to work, his father chatting with Socksy and Boxer behind him. He'd done something that night after he'd left her, something he wasn't proud of. But hopefully it would blow over. He brushed it aside in his mind, just as he arrived at the pit and Socksy clapped him on the back with one of his huge hands.

'That tin be proper jam! Wheresoever did you get a winsome tin like that, Scrapper?'

'Jealousy. That be your problem, Socksy. For the rats will carry your bait off, while mine'll be safe.'

He shoved it inside his shirt and wondered if he should keep using it. Did it make him look foolish? Was he indeed a fool, to still hang on thoughts of her, when she could not even bring herself to visit the family?

Maybe he should give up on her, see other girls. There were plenty around, plenty who wanted a taste of Evan Malone, he knew that. He saw it in their eyes when he caught them looking. He could have his pick. He ought to, really. But his heart wasn't in it.

He took a look over at the pit girls gathering for work. There was the odd pretty one, but none of them could hold a candle to Hettie, so what was the point? He had to snap out of it, that was for sure. Or his life would pass him by.

Then, to his surprise, his mother appeared, walking around the girls and coming towards him, looking straight at him.

'Evan!' she called him. His father turned. She was carrying a load of other people's dirty laundry to take home and she looked vexed. Angry, if truth be told. The other miners glanced around.

He walked up to his mother and his father came, too. Evan said, 'We were just about to go down. What's the fuss about?'

'I wanna word with you, Evan Malone.'

∽

Dear Hettie,

I hope my latest letter finds you well and hearty. I have highly enjoyed our correspondence these past weeks. I hope you realise by now that I am eager to see you again. I wish to inform you that on Tuesday next I will visit Shropshire to meet with you. I will send a note upon my arrival to see if you are free to receive me at your home. If not, I will wait at my lodging until that happy moment when you send for me.

Yours in great anticipation,
Laurence Maxwell Ripley (also known as, your Max)

The day had arrived. Hettie read over the letter again, for perhaps the twentieth time since she'd received it a week before. A note had that morning come to announce that Max was staying at an Ironbridge inn. She had replied that the time was perfect, and now awaited his arrival. He had come all the way to Shropshire to see her.

Since she'd seen him in London, she had thought of little else. They had indeed been writing long letters to each other for a month and every time one arrived, she felt a thrill of excitement. But there was something there, something that clouded these happy blue skies a little: a niggling doubt. His letters were charming, interesting, full of his thoughts and ideas. But there was nothing about his feelings for her in them, only about his work and how much she could help him with it. She wondered if he was shy about sharing his feelings . . . yes, perhaps that was it. So, to hear that he was coming all this way to speak with her made her heart soar. Would he now pour his heart out to her? Would he tell her how beautiful she was, how her eyes or her hair or her figure made his heart sing? She knew it was vain to think such things, but she also knew that she wanted to hear those compliments more than anything. She knew she was interesting to him related to his work, but she wanted more, much more. She wanted to be his great love. And she was not convinced yet that she held this place in his affections, or anything like it. That he was travelling all the way from London to see her promised much excitement. Kezia had helped her pick out the perfect dress with just the right amount of bare skin about the neckline, but not too much as to be obvious.

The sound of a carriage pulling into the drive alerted her. He was here. It was time. How would her life change within the next hour or so? She felt light-headed with excitement and sick to her stomach with nerves.

❧

'What is it, love?' said Peter to his wife.

'Evan, you have some explaining to do,' said Anny. 'One of my laundry clients just told me that the night of Adam's funeral, when you got roaring drunk, you blurted out in the tavern to all and sundry and any-one that would listen that Hettie was a King bastard. Everyone is gossiping about it, apparently. Is it true? What does it mean? What do you know? And why haven't you told us about it?'

'What's this?' said Peter. 'What does that mean – a King bastard?'

Evan felt his face burn hot as he recalled his behaviour that night. He sometimes blacked out when he got properly inebriated, but he remembered every little thing he did and said that night, as the shame ran deep. Yes, he'd been mouthing off about Hettie. He'd started on Adam, saying he didn't wish to speak ill of the dead, but it was good riddance to that waste of Shroppie air. Then he'd started on Hettie, that she was all hoity-toity now she was rich. But she had no reason to have airs, for she was a King bastard, after all. Folk had started to ask him questions about it: what did he mean? Whose bastard was Hettie Jones? He'd brushed them off and stood up to tell them all to get lost, when he tripped over and didn't remember much after that, except arriving home at some point and sleeping it off.

''Tis true. Hettie told me, the night of the funeral. Her mother Martha was born of old Ralph King, who took a maid against her will.'

'And why am I only hearing of this now, and from townsfolk, for heaven's sake? Why am I the last to know?'

'I dunna believe it,' said Peter, shocked.

'It makes sense,' said Anny. 'Explains why old Mrs King left everything to Hettie. She was her kin, or at least, kin of the Kings. But why keep it from us, lad?'

Evan heard behind him the bellman ring the bell for the miners to descend the shaft. He looked away from his mother's accusing eyes. 'I didna know how to tell you. It was shameful.'

'How is it shameful?' said Anny. 'How is it Hettie's shame what her grandparents got up to?'

Evan did not know what to say. Whatever the truth was about Hettie's origins, he knew that the shame was with him, for rejecting her for it, for blurting it out to a bunch of gossipy townsfolk and for not having the nerve to tell his parents. Anny pinpointed him with her fierce gaze and added, 'I never raised you to be judgemental, Evan.'

Then Evan heard a whistle from across the way and turned to see Boxer gesturing to him and his father.

'Come on then, lads,' shouted Boxer. 'We're the first lot down today. Look lively.'

Boxer and Socksy climbed onto the doubles to ride down to the coalface.

Peter turned and called out, 'We'll go on the next one. Set Daff and the new boys on. See you down there.'

Evan glanced back and saw Daff, now an old hand and no longer afraid as he had been last year. He helped on three new boys, so there were six riding the doubles. It was too many folk on there, really, but the boys were only small and light, so he supposed it would be all right with one more.

'Coming!' said Evan, glad of the escape. Then to his mother, who he tried never to disrespect, despite her testing him at times like these, he said, 'We'll talk about this later.'

'You stay right here, Evan,' said Anny, still fuming.

Socksy called to Evan, 'You coming or what, Scrapper?'

∾

Kezia had brought tea, cake and sandwiches. Max sat opposite her, talking away about his work and ignoring the food. Hettie sipped at her tea, marvelling in his presence. His letters had been thrilling enough, but to see him again was almost unbearable. His eyes flashed as he described to her the chapters he was writing on the various pit women of the Black Country, Yorkshire and Lancashire, how their clothes and accents differed. It was interesting, of course, but she was eager for the conversation to turn towards her, or his feelings, or their future. Perhaps he was nervous and that made him talk so much on other subjects. Whatever it was, she was tiring of it and decided to take matters into her own hands. After all, even when she was a strawberry picker, she had been quite forward with him. Why stop now that they were equal?

'It's a proper long way from London to Ironbridge,' she said, 'so I'm wondering what's brought you all this way.'

He smiled and his eyes locked with hers. It was so very hard to look into those eyes and not want to drown in them. Now was the critical moment. What would he say next?

∽

The banksman at the pit was a widower. His wife had died in her sleep a few months back. They had been childless and now he lived alone. When he stood at the pit head and did his work, he often thought of the happy times they'd had together, once upon a time. Nobody knew why she'd died in her sleep. It was just God's way. Even the doctor couldn't explain it, muttering something about a weak heart. He was thinking about his wife that morning when he heard Anny Malone calling to her son and husband. She was a fine-looking woman, with that red hair. But even she wasn't a patch on his Sarah.

The men were coming over, climbing onto the doubles. He needed to focus now, so he banished thoughts of his beloved from his mind and concentrated on his work. The hook and chain on the doubles had to be checked, to ensure they were secure. The chain had a ring at its end that connected to the hook. That was the crucial part of his job. He checked it and checked it again, to make certain. Yes, all was good. The doubles began to descend. He glanced back to see if that Anny Malone was still around, as he liked her red hair and it did him good to see it.

That was when it happened.

The engine man, whose job it was to lower and raise the chain, shouted out, 'Gone slack!'

Those two words were filled with horror for every man at the pit head. Something was wrong, very wrong. Everyone around rushed over and looked keenly down the shaft.

'Wind it up!' called the banksman.

'The doubles fell,' said another miner, as the chain was being wound up.

The banksman and others were shouting down the shaft, asking if anyone could hear them, if anyone was there, if they were hurt, if they were in pain. But there was no reply, only the blackness of the shaft looking back at them.

Up came the chain, with the horrifying absence of the doubles. All that appeared from the shaft was the chain and hook, with a short section of chain below it, snapped off. The doubles – and all the men it carried – were gone. The banksman, whose heart had been in his mouth until the chain was brought up, nearly fainted with relief that it had not been his fault. The hook and ring were still intact. It was the chain below this that had snapped. He'd complained to his boss only last week that it needed replacing. A new chain had been purchased but not fitted yet. Whose fault was it, then? The banksman did not have time to think about that. All he knew was that it wasn't his.

And that the men down there must be dead.

They had fallen from such a great height, taller than a clock tower.

Things moved very quickly then. An alternative doubles was brought and four miners volunteered to go down and look. As the men and boys on the broken chain had been the first on their shift, there would be nobody already down there to help them.

A miner said, 'Sure these men are safe to go down? Is the chain weak? Will it hold? There could be four more men dead.'

But the banksman and others said the upper chain was good. It was the chain connected to the doubles that had snapped. Four men climbed aboard the doubles. They were given candles and sent down the shaft. All at the pit head were grim with grief. The banksman was too, but it was tinged with guilt that he had been thinking mostly of his own actions not being the cause of the tragedy. How he wished his Sarah was still with him, so that he could go home and hold her, put his head in her lap as he used to and tell it all to her. And she would stroke his hair and listen and understand him.

❦

'As ever, you are straight to the point with me, and so I shall come to the point with you.'

Max put down the cup of cold tea he had been holding onto for some time. Hettie steeled herself for this moment. She found herself sitting up straighter and her eyes widened, as if to drink in every last drop of his next utterance.

'Hettie, my dear, dear girl, I am in love with you. Yes, it is true. I have thought of nothing else but you since I saw you that day in London. The truth is also that I thought of you for months after I first met you in that field. The memory of you only faded slightly at that time, since I had little if not no hope whatsoever of laying eyes on you again. So to receive your note asking to meet me in London – and the news of your extraordinary change in fortunes – was an absolute delight and, dare I say it, has changed my life. Not only does it promise of joys to come, in the nature of love and marriage and family and so forth, but also in terms of my work. If you agree to be my wife, I foresee a delightful collaboration between us that would enrich my work and make it even more enlightening for the general reader, as well as profitable.'

He stopped then, picked up his cup again, took a sip of its cold contents and grimaced.

Was that it? Was that a marriage proposal? He did mention the word 'wife' in there somewhere, but had he actually asked her to marry him? It did not feel as if he had. Hettie felt deflated. She tried to formulate what she would say next, but it seemed he wasn't finished.

'What I have in mind is this: we could do a series of illustrations – or perhaps even photographs – of you in the different working woman's clothes you used to wear, that of the pit-wench and the fruit picker. We could then compare and contrast these with images of you in your finery as you are today. It would be fascinating for the general public to read your story and see your transformation. I know that this is more than merely a story. It is, of course, your life. And I know it has not been easy for you, and indeed you have suffered great loss and heartache because of it. I hope that marriage would ensure that you need never suffer again for a moment in your life. I would take care of you for the rest of your life. You need never again worry about your Shropshire businesses, as I would ensure that these are well taken care of, too. Instead, you would lead a life of leisure in London with me, with travels to Europe from time to time, dinner parties and balls and exhibitions and oh, so many things to fill your time in our great capital! There would be fun and friends galore for you in London, my darling. So yes, that is what I am offering you if you were to become my wife.'

Instead of the overwhelming excitement she should have felt at hearing a marriage proposal from Laurence Maxwell Ripley, she felt nervous, tinged with disappointment. She had thought of him often these past weeks, of course she had. She had brooded upon his dark eyes many times a day, had imagined his lips kissing hers, his arms touching her back as he embraced her. She had delighted at his letters, full of anecdote and charm. But now, this. She had wondered about his feelings for her, wondered if he saw her only as a friend, or even a curiosity, perhaps part of his work, her story being that much more interesting now it was a rags-to-riches tale. She had hoped that he felt the same desire for her as she felt for him, hoped that the looks he gave her in London that day were reciprocal and long-lasting, evidence of his regard for her and not merely a passing fancy or moment of lust.

Now she had absolute proof of it, an answer to all the questions her heart had been asking for weeks. But what was this? No joy, no excitement. She had built up so many expectations of a proposal from a man she desired that the moment itself was probably bound to fall a little short. But it was much more than that. There was something of the business arrangement about the proposal, as well as a hint of the scientist in there, too. If she married him, would he expect to share her fortune? Might he want to use it for his own work? From her conversations with Beatrice, Hettie had already been toying with the idea that she should do something more useful with the gift of wealth she had been bequeathed, and she did not know what Max would make of that. She had continued the regular donations to charity that Mrs King had begun, but she also had an inkling of what more she could do with it. Perhaps something more useful than mere money ... some sort of organisation that would truly help people less fortunate in practical, everyday ways that were much needed. All of this was just beginning to coalesce in her mind and was far from certain. But it was something she was considering. If she married, that would not be her choice alone.

In scientific terms, his words also disturbed her. From all of her interactions with Max, she knew he was obsessed with his work. It was his one true love. Nothing was as interesting to him as his book, as yet unfinished after years of his studies. She was reminded of the animals in the aquarium, trapped and stared at, taken out of their natural environment and imprisoned for the entertainment of others.

The proposal felt as if it were not a declaration of love; instead he was laying out the terms under which she would spend the rest of her days. She would be given comfort (which she already had, being an heiress) in exchange for her worth as a subject of study. Yes, he was offering far more than that – and the potential pleasures of their companionship were attractive indeed – but there was this niggling feeling that, once she had escaped the misery of being holed up with Benjamina in this comfortable Shropshire prison of hers, she would swap it instead for a London version, complete with a charming, striking husband and all the trappings that would furnish, yet still a prison in its way. He was a handsome man, that was certain and she felt a twinge in her belly when she looked at him. He was beautiful on the outside and he seemed to admire her, but was he beautiful on the inside, too? Of this, she was less than certain.

Suddenly, she felt very hot on this sweltering August day. How much easier it was to cope with the heat in her old poor Hettie clothes, than her new rich Hettie frocks with layers of undergarments!

Hettie tried to focus. What on earth should she say to him, looking keenly at her, waiting for her response?

Then, thankfully, a knock came at the door. In walked Kezia, who Hettie was so pleased to see, saving her from having to answer Max directly. But Kezia's face showed alarm.

'What is it?' said Hettie.

'An accident at the mine. Where the Malones work.'

'Is it them? Is it Evan? Or Peter?'

'No names yet.'

Hettie started up. 'I'm going down there.'

Kezia nodded and said, 'I'll go and make arrangements for the carriage now.'

'You are leaving?' asked Max. In that moment, Hettie realised she had entirely forgotten about his presence.

'I must go, I do apologise.'

'Do you own that mine?'

'No, but I used to work there. These are my friends.'

'Then I shall come with you.'

'No!' she said sharply, then wondered why she had. 'I am sorry for that. I didna mean to snap.'

'Well, you must go. Don't worry about me. Just go and do what you need to do.' His voice was reasonable and solicitous, and she felt momentarily guilty about her own sharpness with him.

'Thank you. I will return presently.'

Hettie got up and went to fetch her hat and purse. The carriage was ready outside. She walked away from Max and did not have a single thought in her head but the lives of Evan and Peter, and the horror that they might have ended while she took tea with a London gent.

Chapter 24

Once out in the carriage, Hettie's imagination took full flight. She could picture the dead bodies of her loved ones stretched out at the pit head, all the miners and pit bank wenches standing about, heads down with sorrow.

She told herself that there were many men who worked at that mine. It could easily be someone else. She did not wish death on any of them, but she prayed in her carriage, so hard she screwed her eyes shut and clasped her lace-gloved hands tightly together, that the deaths were not Evan or Peter Malone. *Anyone but them*, she thought, *and may the Lord forgive me for that*.

She arrived at the mine and swiftly descended onto the dusty ground. There were many people milling around. The pit-wenches and the miners who would normally be hard at work on their shift were standing about in groups, talking in low tones. It seemed all work had halted for the day. This was not a King-owned mine, so Hettie had no influence here, but she noticed as she walked forward that many eyes were on her. People parted like a wave as she walked towards the pit head, where she could see the owners standing, marked out by their suits rather than working clothes. Her eyes were scanning the folk for the faces of her beloved ones, but she could not see them. As she walked closer she feared she would faint if the answer to her question involved their names.

Her old foreman spotted her and stepped in front of her, stopping her progress towards the mine owners.

'You're not needed here,' he said roughly.

She had never liked him much when he was her boss, but now she didn't work there anymore, he seemed to hate her.

'I heard some have died,' she said.

He nodded.

'Evan and Peter Malone. Were they . . . ?' She could not finish her utterance.

'Hettie,' came a voice behind her and she turned to see Anny. Hettie stared at her face, so beautiful in its familiarity. She ran towards her. Each step seemed to take an age.

⁓

The men on the doubles watched the flickering candle-light as they went down. They all guessed this would most likely be a retrieval situation, not a rescue. But you never knew for sure. It all depended how far the men fell. Perhaps they had broken limbs and had been in too much pain to call out. Maybe they had been knocked out by the fall and could not reply to the shouts above. All four men on the doubles stared down into the gloom to try and catch a glimpse of what they were facing. None of the men spoke.

As they neared the bottom of the shaft, they lifted their candles to throw light at the base. The first thing they could make out was splinters. The oak planks that lined the base of the shaft had been smashed. The remains of the doubles were half in and half out of the hole, and wrapped inside them was a pair of legs, the torso that belonged to it buried beneath the smashed planks. Everyone knew that beneath the floor of the shaft was a sump, where many feet of water accumulated. They could see now that all of the men had smashed through the planks and must now be underwater. Only one was halfway out, but his head must be submerged. The moment they were close enough, all four men wriggled out of the doubles and leapt to the site of the accident.

Peter and Evan got there first and glanced at each other. Without saying a word, both knew the meaning of that look. They knew that if Peter had not stopped Evan from going down on the first descent, along with Socksy, Boxer, Daff and the others, it would be him in that sump, broken and drowned. It was only Peter's insistence that Evan respect his mother and finish their talk that had saved Evan from this fate. But there was no time to think on that. Who knew if one or more of the men could still be breathing?

They quickly began the grim task of lifting up the fractured planks to get to the bodies. They pulled out the doubles, and tangled with them were the top man's legs. Evan hoped against hope that once freed, perhaps the man might breathe again. It was Socksy, those huge arms trailing out of the water last as they dragged him onto the shaft floor, his face deathly pale and his hair dripping with filthy sump water.

'Put him on his front,' said Peter, who knelt down and started to push against his back rhythmically.

Evan knelt down. 'Socksy? Socksy, mon? Wake up. Wake up, mon.'

The other two were looking down into the hole between the broken floor and the sump. There was no sign of any of the other men. They must have sunk into the sump and were completely submerged. There was no question that all would be drowned, if the fall hadn't killed them first. Socksy, Boxer, Daff and three brand-new boys, their first day down the mine. All dead, in an instant.

Men above were shouting down the shaft for news.

Evan called up, 'All dead. Six dead.'

There was only silence from above.

'We'll need ropes,' said Peter, who had given up on trying to pump the water out of Socksy. 'Ropes and hooks to drag 'em all out of the sump. We'll have to go back up. We'll take Socksy.'

One of the other men stayed below, in order to be the hooker-on, in charge of supervising the connection of the hook and chain for the doubles to ride back up the shaft. Evan and the other man helped Peter take Socksy over his shoulder as he sat on the doubles, then he climbed aboard and helped his father keep Socksy's body balanced. They rose up the shaft, Socksy's drenched body dripping down into the darkness, Evan's hand aching from holding him steady on Peter's shoulder.

As they ascended, Evan felt a wave of nausea wash over him. He swallowed and screwed his eyes shut to stop himself from vomiting. He thought of his mother, whose face always calmed him down in moments of panic and realised with a shock that not only had his father unknowingly saved his life by making him stay, but his mother had too, by coming to talk to him at all. If she hadn't come to ask so urgently about Hettie, he would be dead in that sump right now. And so would his father.

He felt a cold chill on his neck so clearly, so tangibly that he turned his head to see if some spirit with icy breath was floating behind him in the gloomy shaft. He used his upper arm to wipe away from his eyes the damp hair that was plastered to his forehead. He thought, *It's as if Hettie's secret saved our lives.*

∽

Hettie held onto Anny, not wanting to let go. Anny's embrace held years of comfort in it. Hettie was determined not to cry with relief at the news that Evan and

Peter were alive. All around her were the friends, colleagues and family of the six who had died, and her tears of relief would not go down well. As she pulled away from Anny, a look passed between them that expressed all of this and more. Being here, amongst her people, was overwhelming. She hadn't realised until this moment just how much she had missed them all.

They turned to watch the grim spectacle of the first body retrieved from the mine being brought up. Hettie saw Evan and Peter carrying the body, which was taken by other miners at the pit head and placed on the ground with infinite care. The foreman tenderly draped a jacket over the dead man's face. Hettie watched Evan and Peter climb out of the doubles and stand beside the body, shaking their heads. After that, they went down again and brought up more bodies. Hettie waited with Anny, arms linked, quiet and watchful as the grim recovery operation unfolded. Six bodies were brought up, three of them small. When the mothers and fathers of the boys arrived, their grief was dreadful, the sound of their sobbing piercing the thick summer air.

There was nothing more for Evan and Peter to do to help. Hettie watched as they looked about for Anny and then spotted Hettie beside her. Evan came first, striding towards them, Peter following wearily behind.

Evan came close to Hettie and said, 'So glad you're here.'

'I had to come,' she said. 'I had to know. I'm so happy it inna . . . I mean, I'm so sorry . . .'

She felt the tears of relief build again in her eyes and lifted her gloved hand to wipe them away. Evan's face showed signs of exhaustion and struggle, dark patches under his eyes, his hair plastered to his head, as if he'd been dunked in a dirty pond. But his eyes showed pity for her and concern for her feelings, which made her want to let those tears fall even more. As she smiled at him, Anny and Peter came closer.

'Hettie, it's good of you to come,' said Peter, smiling. Now his kindness would set her off again, but she knew she mustn't cry in front of these brave people. This was their struggle, not hers.

'I was so worried,' she said, and tried to smile back at them.

'Dunna fret,' said Peter. 'Evan is all in one piece.'

Hettie smiled at Peter, Anny and Evan in turn. She wanted to throw her arms around them all and sob with relief. But then she heard her name.

'Miss Hettie Jones. Miss Hoity-Toity.'

It was a woman's voice. She looked to see that it was Nora, her leader on the strawberry trip, standing nearby, next to Hettie's other hut mate, Edna.

'Miss King, more like,' said Edna.

'Yeah, the King *bastard*,' said Nora, spitting the words as if they tasted bad.

Hettie shot a look at Evan, who shook his head hurriedly, his pale cheeks blooming red.

'You're not wanted here, bastard,' continued Nora. 'You always thought you were better'n us. Well, now we all know. You're nothing but a bastard. A King bastard at that. Why dunna you run off back to yer mansion and leave us poor folk be?'

Hettie wanted to run. How could this be? How could Nora and Edna possibly know her secret?

'Hettie, I didna mean to,' said Evan, and she looked at him, horrified. 'I were drunk and I blurted it out at the tavern. I didna mean to. Please, Hettie.'

'Bastard!' said Nora again.

'That's quite enough of that rubbish,' said Anny, striding towards Nora with her hands on her hips. 'This is not the time and the place for any of this. And what's more, that girl is a good girl. I know because I raised her myself. It matters not where she came from, only how she acts in her time. And she is a good, kind person, as you all know. She came down here today out of concern for her loved ones, as anyone with a heart would. And you judge her. For what? For what her grandparents did scores of years ago?' Anny raised her voice and turned to address all the onlookers. 'And anyone who has a problem with Hettie Jones has a problem with me. So, anyone else like to open their stupid damned mouths to me, eh? Anyone?'

The huddles of people shifted uncomfortably. Nora turned away and marched off in the direction of the pit bank, Edna following her dutifully.

'Thank you, Anny,' said Hettie quietly.

'Come on home with us, love,' said Anny. 'Come and have a drink and a pie with us, like old times, eh?'

'Yes, I'd love that,' she said.

'Hettie, I'm so sorry,' Evan said. 'Can yer forgive me, Hettie?'

She looked up into his face, wracked by fear and worry, already exhausted by the events of the day.

'There is nothing to forgive,' she said quietly. 'What happens here is important. This is life and death. Who knows or doesna know who my grandfather is . . . well, what does it matter? I'm glad it's out now. I dunna have to worry about it no more.'

Evan and Peter had to stay at the mine, so she bid them farewell, so glad to see Evan's face smiling at her through the grime and tiredness. She told the coachman to go home, that she would send for him later. The walk back to the Malone place with Anny was wonderful, just like old times. They linked arms and Anny told her all the gossip about Flora, Billy and Lily and the scrapes they'd got into, while Hettie told her the particulars of her life, about Beatrice's visit back in May, about Benjamina's failed suit and Hettie's trip to London. But she stopped short of telling Anny about Max. She knew that Anny knew how much Evan loved her. And she loved him back, more than she loved her own self. Her crushing fear at the possibility of his death had taught her that, if nothing else.

Once back at the Malone house, the children greeted her with the most effusive hugs and whoops and cheers. How good it was to play with the feisty twins and chat with Flora about her hopes and dreams! Hettie helped Anny bake a batch of pies for the miners and then all of them went back to the mine, the twins tagging along behind, finding items of interest on the ground as they went, bringing each little thing to Hettie as a gift.

The pies were handed out and, though she received a couple of sidelong glances, Hettie was more or less ignored, as she had hoped to be. The Malones all walked home together, along with Hettie. She found herself feeling more at peace than she had in weeks, if not months, despite the horrors of the day. In fact, seeing the dead brought up from under the ground had made her feel keenly grateful for her own life and those of the ones she loved, her dear Malones.

Back at their home, they invited her to stay the night, but everyone knew it was not 'seemly', and instead Evan offered to walk her home, which she accepted gladly.

On their walk, she asked him to tell her about the accident, if he wished to do so. He said it would help him, if she didn't mind, and he told her the whole story, how they'd used hooks and ropes to secure the bodies from the sump and drag them up. She learnt the names of the men and boys who'd died. She shed a tear for them all. And as usual, Evan wanted only to comfort her.

When they arrived at the old brickmaster's house, she turned to Evan and touched his face. He stood stock still and let her do it.

'You are the best of men,' she said.

He shook his head violently. 'No, I inna. I let you down, Hettie. Badly.'

'No, you didna. I told you, I'm glad the truth is out. It were a terrible burden to carry alone. Now everyone knows, it canna hurt me no more. That's a good thing. You did me a favour, Evan, in a way.'

'I'm proper glad you feel that way. But I still know it were wrong. Thank you for being such a forgiving person. I dunna deserve it.'

'Will you come in and sit with me a while, Evan?'

He looked up at the house and down at her. 'No, I dunna think so. This be your world, Hettie. I oughta go back to mine.'

'Are you sure?' She wanted to keep looking into his blue eyes; she was beyond happy to see they still looked upon the world and were not glassy in the sump at the bottom of the mine.

'Yes. I am glad you came. To the mine. And home. We've waited for that.'

'I'm glad too. And Evan, about the mine – I want to do summat.'

'What?'

'I want to give some money to the families of those that were lost. A gift, not charity. To see them right. And I want to pay for a memorial stone to be placed in the graveyard where they are to be laid to rest. The town should remember them and what they gave up for the mine.'

'That is proper jam, Hettie Jones. Proper jam.'

With that, he gave her a little bow, then turned and walked away. She watched him go, the evening sun throwing shadows of the shifting trees onto the ground behind him as he disappeared along the woodland path. Then she went into the house and stood in the hallway for a moment, looking down at the black and white chequered floor.

She knew now that she would never fit into either world, the rich or the poor. They were as opposite as the black and white squares beneath her feet. She inhabited the grey area in between. It seemed an impossible place to survive, but she knew at that moment that it gave her distinct advantages, too. She could use her knowledge of the working folk and her resources of the wealthy to effect real change. She could do this small thing for the families of the miners who were lost. But she could do more, much more than that. She could use her money to do real good in the world. If she married Max, surely her future would look very different. She would be a married woman, with responsibilities to her husband. For all his interest in working women, she had no idea if Max would approve of her schemes. But if she stayed a spinster, she would always have full control over her life – and her money and the good it could do.

She looked up around her at the old brickmaster's house – Benjamina's house, as she still thought of it. It would never feel like home, and she did not want to stay in it any longer than she had to. It was time to make a decision. She had been informed recently that the building of Southover was now finished and ready to sell or occupy, whichever she preferred. Now she knew what she wanted to do. She was going to move out of this place and into Southover. It would become her home. She would arrange a meeting with Steadman and think about some organised way she could do the good in the world that she wanted to achieve. Southover would be her base, and she would use it to create something that would change the lives of needy people in the local area and, who knew, perhaps even further afield. She didn't know what yet, or how it would be shaped, but the idea was blooming in her mind. So she was the pit bank wench, the strawberry picker, the rags-to-riches girl, the daughter of Adam and Martha Jones, the King bastard. She was all these things and more, much more. She was Miss Hettie Jones, and she was going to stay that way. And now, she had a plan for her future.

Busby appeared, full of concern for his mistress and clearly eager for news from the mine. Hettie told him everything she knew and they spoke in hushed tones about those who were lost. Again Hettie felt more at home with the servants than the new class she was supposed to now be a part of.

Max! Thinking of his proposal, she suddenly remembered that she had left him to go to the mine.

'Is Mr Ripley still here?'

'No, ma'am. He left just after you did. Let me fetch the note he sent for you.'

Busby went over to the hall table and handed her the note, then gave a small bow and left. Hettie opened up the note.

My dear Hettie.

I waited for a time at the inn, but then felt it would be best to take the evening coach back to London. I am about to board it now. I will await news of your response to my proposal there. It was unfortunate that we were interrupted by such tragedy, but I am glad I managed to say what I needed to. I do hope you look upon my offer favourably. As I hope I conveyed to you, I do think we would make a marvellous team.

Yours in anticipation,
Max

She thought back to the moment he had said he'd come with her to the mine and she'd snapped at him. She hadn't had time to understand it then, but she did now.

Firstly, the pit was not his place, it was hers. Or at least, it used to be hers. Secondly, she feared he would be seen as some sort of ghoulish tourist, turning up to witness the tragedy of others. And she didn't want to be associated in any way with that. Lastly, and most importantly to Hettie, she did not want the Malones – and especially Evan – to know about Max, to even be aware of his existence. The thought of Evan and Max coming face to face was unbearable.

As she pictured this fictitious meeting, she compared the two men in her mind. Evan, tall, blond, muscular, a proud working man; Max, the small, slight, dark-eyed gent from the big city. Thinking of him again gave her that familiar lurch in her stomach. She still had a pang for him – of course she did. Could she really turn down a proposal from him, after wanting him for so long, since that day in the strawberry field? Could they be a team, as he suggested, and really make it work? But what about Evan? Wouldn't they make a better team? Could Evan accept her now she was a King, after everything he'd said?

So many questions, and no answers. Only the wash of relief that her loved ones were safe and she was thankfully alone with her thoughts once more. She ascended the stairs and fell on her bed.

Soon, she slept. It had been an exhausting day.

Chapter 25

It was a sultry September morning, the air heavy, the atmosphere stifling. A sticky, uncomfortable day. Benjamina stood at her bedroom window, waiting for the carriage to leave with Hettie inside it. There was a haze of sweat on her forehead. She was so hot, she wished she could tear all her layers of clothes off and plunge into the River Severn. But a lady would never do such a thing. And anyway, she had work to do. Today had come at last. It was the day when her plans would come to fruition.

Finally, Troon had agreed to her plan. Once he'd heard the precise nature of it, she had to raise the payment to two years' salary for him to acquiesce. No matter. Once the plan had been executed successfully, she would be independently rich. And Troon would earn his money, of that there was no doubt. He'd need a decent amount to hide afterwards, somewhere very far away. Benjamina didn't want Troon hanging around like an idiot waiting to be caught and confessing all. The fee would be worth it, in the end.

Benjamina heard footsteps outside her room. She had listened to Hettie and Clayton packing all week, ready for the move to Southover. She was delighted when Hettie had told her the plan a month back, just after that pit incident. Whatever happened, Benjamina would have her house back and the little interloper would be gone.

That morning at breakfast, Hettie had informed her that she was going over to Southover that afternoon to supervise the arrival of furniture and where it was to be placed in the house. As usual, Hettie Jones had mistaken her role and taken on activities that only a maid or servant should be doing. But the stupid young woman could not leave her lower-class origins behind. This was another reason why the girl should never have become an heiress. Benjamina remembered her own transformation from shop girl to lady of the manor. She had had to learn fast and adopt the airs and graces of a lady quickly, in order not to embarrass her new husband, Ralph King junior. She had been desperately lonely, without a soul to advise or comfort her. And she had managed it magnificently.

This one, this Jones girl, had moped about the house for months and made a mess of everything, including the death of her wastrel father. Now at least she had made a good decision: to move out. But, Benjamina reminded herself, none of that would matter after tonight. She looked down at the driveway before the house and watched the landau carriage leave, Hettie inside. Now, it was time to act.

Benjamina left her room and went to find Clayton, who she discovered in Hettie's room, cleaning one of Hettie's hats. Hettie had such crass taste in millinery that it would be an embarrassment to be seen with her, if Benjamina ever bothered to accompany her anywhere. Benjamina smirked as she thought of it. At least as a shop girl she had known about fashion and used this to her advantage when she became a rich wife. Hettie always looked like a jumped-up poor child mimicking wealth.

Clayton looked up as Benjamina entered the room without knocking. She put down the hat and brush, then stood up immediately. 'Ma'am?'

'My dear,' said Benjamina, using a term of endearment she would never normally adopt with an inferior, 'I bring news of your mother.'

Clayton looked confused. 'My mother?'

'Yes. I was outside taking the air and a boy approached the house, saying he brought news of Kezia Clayton's mother. He said that she is gravely ill in Staffordshire and that she has requested your presence as soon as possible.'

'Oh, my word! Thank you, ma'am. May I have your permission . . . ?'

'Of course, Clayton. I will arrange for transport for you to the coaching stop just outside town. I understand there is a weekly service to Staffordshire that leaves later this afternoon.'

'That is so kind of you, ma'am, but I couldn't accept . . .'

'Oh, but you can and you will, Clayton. We always look after our own in the King household. And you have been with us some years now and have always proven yourself to offer good service. Now, do go and pack a bag and I will organise your transport.'

'Thank you so very much, ma'am. May I ask, did the boy say who he was? Is he still here? I would like to reward him if I can for his kindness in bringing such a message. I can't imagine who he was or where he came from, Staffordshire being such a trip. '

'Ah no, I gave him a coin and sent him on his way.'

Benjamina knew that when Kezia arrived at her mother's house and found her hale and hearty, the falsehood would be revealed. But she relied on her position in society to be assured that nobody would believe a servant's doubts over her word, and that she could easily claim there had been a misunderstanding or even a prank of some sort and blame the phantom boy. After all, nobody could prove he did not exist.

'Thank you for that kindness, ma'am. I'll pack directly. Please, you do not need to concern yourself any further with this family matter of mine. I am so grateful for the solicitude you have already shown.'

'But I would be remiss if I did not assist any person under such circumstances. I will tell Busby to prepare the cabriolet to take you to the coaching stop. You pack your things now. No need to find me to say goodbye, my dear. I will inform Miss Jones of your departure.'

Then Benjamina gave Clayton her best approximation of a sympathetic smile and left the room.

Good, she thought. *That's the first obstacle out of the way.*

Benjamina went back to her room and rang the bell for Busby, who arrived within less than a minute. She informed him that she had decided to visit friends in Shrewsbury. She would take the barouche and would be gone for two days, taking her maid Brooks with her. She informed him also of Clayton's imminent departure and that Miss Jones would be without a maid.

'However,' she explained to Busby, 'Miss Jones has often said to me in the past that she is in no need of a lady's maid, being aware of all the accoutrements a lady requires, having once been a maid herself. I am sure she can manage without one for a day or two. May I suggest that Towers, our former valet and now footman, be assigned to be on hand to assist Miss Jones if she needs any particular jobs doing – other than dressing, of course?'

'Yes, ma'am,' said Busby, although he did look alarmed at the thought of Towers serving as lady's maid in any capacity, however temporarily. 'I will instruct

Towers accordingly. I will prepare the barouche for your departure.'

'I will be taking Drina with me, so make sure there is a blanket for her on the seat. And send Brooks to me. We need to pack for Shrewsbury.'

Her maid came, and was all a-flutter at the thought of a couple of days in the county town, away from the boredom of her usual routine. Benjamina feigned tiredness and let her fuss on, lying down and watching her plan unfold. Soon, Clayton would be gone to Staffordshire, and she would be gone to Shrewsbury. When Hettie came back from Southover later, nobody would be present in the room next to hers for the whole day and night to come. This was what Benjamina needed and it was all nicely coming to pass. This night was what all these years of struggle had been leading to, and Benjamina was delighted to be on the cusp of success at last. Tomorrow would be delicious. The first day of the rest of her life.

Drina ran in from wherever she'd been creating havoc and leapt on Benjamina's bed. The dog had cottony fluff all around her chops, suggesting she'd been destroying some item of furniture or clothing somewhere in the house.

'Good girl,' said Benjamina, and gave her a kiss on her wet nose.

❧

In the early evening, Hettie stepped down from the carriage and thanked the coachman. She looked up at the sky, where dark grey clouds were gathering in the distance. There had been some rumbles of thunder far away as she'd been coming home, and now it looked as if the storm was heading her direction. She welcomed it in one way, as rain would hopefully dispel the humid heat that had felt stifling for days. But storms brought sadness with them, reminding her of the night of her father's passing. She associated them with melancholy.

She tried to put this from her mind as she walked towards the front door of her old house, and instead filled her head with visions of her new one. Seeing the writing desk and bookshelves being delivered, and supervising their placement in her new study was an absolute delight. This study – which she learnt had once been the site of Mrs King's office when she lived at Southover – would be Hettie's base of operations for her new endeavours. She had had meetings with Steadman these past weeks, firstly outlining her vague plans to him and then discussing possibilities for how best she could bring them about.

They had come up with the idea of a foundation, an organisation she would run from Southover that would require funding not only from her own fortune but from a wide range of donors. Steadman was delighted to be involved and gave her many ideas about how the foundation could be managed and become successful. They discussed at length which kind of recipients would be most in need. Hettie was adamant that charity must begin at home, and that the first groups of people to be helped should be Ironbridge folk and those of the locality that found themselves out of work or otherwise incapacitated, who would otherwise be forced to starve or end up in the dreaded workhouse. Money could be used to set up a hostel of some sort, or two, one for women (and their children, if they had any) and one for men. Her other concern was that of men or women who had had their lives blighted by alcoholic abuse. She wanted a safe place where people could go to save themselves from the ravages of drink, stop their drinking and recover. This could be situated in Ironbridge or another town nearby. These were her first two plans. Steadman said that was quite enough and would be very expensive as it was. Hettie had so many ideas in her head of how she could help people further, but Steadman was right. The King fortune was finite and needed to be treated carefully in order for it to be managed well and for the charitable endeavours to become successful.

For the first time since the arrival of her father in January of the year before, Hettie felt that she had some modicum of control over her life. At last, she had a purpose in this world. It felt wonderful.

Hettie was met by Busby as she came into the house. He informed her of a number of unusual events that had occurred in her absence. Firstly, Benjamina had gone to Shrewsbury, taking her maid Brooks with her. Secondly, Kezia had received a message stating that her mother was gravely ill and thus had left on the afternoon coach for Staffordshire. Apparently, Benjamina had suggested that Towers wait on Hettie in Kezia's absence. Hettie could see how worried Busby was about this last case in particular.

'Please dunna fret,' she said to Busby. 'I'll be fine without a maid for a day or so. Tell Towers I'll call on him for anything I might need, but other than that, I'll make do.'

'Yes, ma'am. Please be assured that under my watch, this household will always exceed any idea of "making do". We will always do our utmost to serve you, ma'am.'

'Oh, I know that, Busby. And I thank'ee for it. But I will be fine.'

Hettie went to her room, full of concern for her friend Kezia. When she arrived at her writing desk, she saw a note in Kezia's hand and also a letter from Max. She took up Kezia's first and read of the same particulars Busby had already told her. She decided that in the morning she would arrange for flowers and wholesome fruit to be sent to Kezia's mother's house, as well as some extra money for Kezia in case she had medical expenses.

Then she turned to Max's letter. She almost wanted to leave it unopened, for she was unsure how to face whatever it contained. She had not replied to his suggestion of marriage and had further left a subsequent letter from him unanswered. More rumbles of thunder came and she looked up at the sky, those storm clouds now closer than before. A knock came at her door and Towers appeared, looking ill at ease in his new role of lady's maid. Hettie assured him that she would most likely be in no need of him tonight, except to bring her dinner in her rooms. She didn't want to dine formally tonight downstairs, as the house would be mostly empty except for herself and the servants.

'I think it'd be a nice idea for some of the servants to have the night off. What do you think, Towers?'

'If that is what you require, ma'am?'

'Yes, it'd be good for them. I'll just need you and Busby and the cook here. Everyone else can go out or visit friends or family if they want to. I'll give you a night off another time instead, Towers.'

'Thank you, ma'am!' he said, very pleased, and she sent him off to deliver the news.

So, it would be a quiet house tonight. That suited Hettie. She had so much on her mind that she liked the idea of a mostly empty house to think in. Now it was time to open Max's letter.

My dear Hettie,

Firstly, I am concerned that a previous letter I wrote to you has perhaps not arrived, as you have not replied to it, and I am certain you would have if it had arrived. Therefore I can only assume it was lost in the post. It has been a month since my proposal and though of course it is the woman's prerogative to keep a man waiting, I must say I grow anxious at the lack of news from you. Indeed, I would say that keeping a man waiting this long is decidedly 'unseemly' – to venture a play on one of your favourite words, I seem to remember! What a funny little thing you were in that first letter you wrote to me, the new heiress. How far you have come, my dear! So, please put a gentleman out of his misery and tell me you will marry me, darling. If I hear nothing more in response to this letter, I will hereafter complain most vociferously to the postal service, which has caused me such distress. And then I will forthwith take another coach to Shropshire and press my suit in person again, hopefully not interrupted by local matters once more!

Yours in rather desperate anticipation,
Max

Hettie didn't know if he was trying to be clever, or stupid, or what he was being. The letter felt crass and unfeeling, even selfish in the extreme. Perhaps it was arrogance; a gentleman like Max had probably never had to wait for anything in his life. And a man as handsome as him had never had to wait for an answer from a woman. All she knew was that, despite his beauty, she did not possess the feeling for him she once had. On first meeting, their situations had been so different that she was in awe of him. Once she had become an heiress, their levels were more equal in society, and she had been blinded by his eyes and his hair and his skin and his frame and everything that made him irresistible.

But now, the truth of what their marriage would be – and all she would stand to lose if she went through with it – suddenly lost him his sheen. She began to see him in a new light, that of a gentleman who lived a life of leisure, whose good fortunes had always fallen into his hands. He was not a bad person. He wanted to study working women and thereby enlighten the world of the good they were doing by their hard work. But she felt she would always be an object of curiosity to him, rather than a wife. And the final nail in the coffin was that in this letter he had again teased her about her use of the word 'seemly'.

'Enough of this,' she said aloud. She did not want to be married to a man who constantly sought to remind her of her little flaws, however amusing they might be. And he could not truly understand her if he thought that mocking her speech might endear him to her. She hated the way he teased her about the word *seemly*. This annoyed her more than anything, as small and insignificant as it was. For it was Evan's word, and she felt that not only was she herself being ridiculed, but her dear Evan too. And she would not stand for that. One joke was more than enough, but to continue the joke on and on went beyond funny to something akin to scorn. All of these things could have been borne, she realised, if she really loved Max.

As the first spots of welcome rain spattered against her window pane, she took up her pen and ink to write him a letter thanking him for his kind proposal but turning it down, as she wished to remain a spinster.

But the truth was that she did not love Laurence Maxwell Ripley. She loved Evan Malone. She always had and always would. Marriage between them was impossible – she knew that – so she would remain a spinster and dedicate her life to deserving the good fortune that had been given to her.

❧

Troon had been told to wait until the cover of darkness to approach the old brickmaster's house. As it was August, this meant waiting until eleven or twelve at night. He was already feeling sleepy at nine. He had been drinking too much those past few days, using the money Mrs King had given him as an advance. But tonight was the night she'd said and he must do the deed.

When the rain started at seven or so, it soon became heavy and the skies darkened so much that night came early. Troon left the one room he lived in and trudged through the rain to the woodland path to the old brick-master's house. He thought of his children, now living in Wales with his wife, who had left him all those years ago. Mrs King had told him he must meet her in Shrewsbury on the morrow to collect the rest of his fee and there-after flee the country and never come back. Well, he could go to Wales first, couldn't he? How would anyone know to look for him, anyway? He could go to Wales, spend some money on his wife and children, see if his new-found wealth might encourage them to accept him again as father and husband. His children were now grown, but everyone needed money. Yes, that's what he'd do. Mrs King did not need to know.

This thought bolstered him as he slogged on through the woods, every inch of him drenched, looking up from time to time to see the lightning flash and hear the thunder rumbling about him. To be out on such a godforsaken night was foolishness, but he had a job to do and after all, the storm gave him the perfect cover. As he saw the house looming ahead in the darkness, he went into the trees to get a better look. He didn't want to be seen by someone watching the storm from a window.

Once he'd decided that nobody was present, he skirted the house at a distance and saw the back door for which he'd been given a key. He crossed over, slotted the key in the door and turned it. He opened it slowly and quietly. Thunder crashed behind him and made him flinch. As another boom came, he quickly shut the door, using the sound to mask its closing. The storm was serving him well.

He was inside the house now, and nobody would have heard a thing.

Chapter 26

Evan sat in the chair by the fireplace. The little ones were in bed, but nobody was asleep, as the storm kept them all jittery and nervous. His mother and father were at the table, sorting through a series of bills and organising their accounts for the next month. He knew he should be helping them, but his mind was filled with other things – namely Hettie, as usual.

Seeing her again recently had been an absolute tonic, especially watching her here in his home, playing with the children and helping Anny with the pies, just like old times. The only thing that had been out of place was her fancy frock. Other than that, she slotted right back into her old ways and he hadn't seen her smile and laugh so much in a long time. Walking her home, he had felt their old closeness was there again. When she'd invited him to come into her house, of course he'd been desperate to agree – but every time he was there, he felt like the hired help. It did not suit him for her to see him there, in his poor excuse for clothes. And he figured it would do her good to have him say no to her for once, so that she would think of him in his absence and perhaps call on him again.

She hadn't called on him again, though. His plan had not worked. Ever since, he had been ruminating on how to solve this conundrum. He loved Hettie, he always had. And she loved him, in her way, he was sure of that. But they lived now in two separate worlds. How could he bridge that divide, in a way that would make both of them happy?

Another crash of thunder made the children call out from their beds, so he got up and went through to comfort them. Once they were settled, he went to the kitchen window and watched the storm for a while. White sheets of lightning lit up the ground outside, rendering it bright as daylight for a split second. Evan realised its significance with a pang. The storm would remind Hettie of Adam and the night of his drowning. She'd be sitting there right now, in her house, thinking of that night, sad and utterly alone. Evan's heart ached to be with her, to comfort her. But what could he do for her, truly? He couldn't bring her father back. He could not offer her a thing. She had everything she needed, didn't she? She was an heiress, after all.

But he remembered something she once said to him, that a friend was worth more than gold, more than anything. After a lifetime of friendship, obstacles had piled up between them in this past year or so. She was a King, he was a Malone. She was rich, he was poor. But really, what did any of that matter? The one thing they had in common was their feelings for each other. And surely that was enough to declare his love for her, to marry her. He didn't want any other girl, ever. He only wanted Hettie Jones. He was sure now that she loved him back, he was sure she would be sad this night and he was sure it was the right time to go out and find her. He was going to Hettie's house and he was going to ask her to marry him.

At that moment, as the storm raged around his house, he decided that he couldn't live without her and he needed her to know it. He wanted to tell her that her relation to the Kings meant nothing for him, that he would always love her, and that they should marry and damn what people think, and damn the money! He had to be with her, on whatever terms.

'Off out,' he said, grabbing his coat and cap.

'On a night like this?' his mother cried. 'No, you're stopping in, lad.'

'I wonna be long,' he lied and opened the front door.

'Dunna be daft,' said his father. 'It's treacherous out there!'

But he was already out, slamming the door behind him. He did not want to hear their reasons why it was ridiculous. He ran away down the path before either could come after him. He glimpsed the front door open as he turned the corner onto the next path and away down into town. Now sopping wet, he went across the bridge and into the woods, on his way to the old brick-master's house, to Hettie. His ambition to marry her kept him warm and dry in his heart. And somehow he welcomed the rain, as it seemed to wash away all his old pride and leave him fresh and clean of excuses, ready to make her his wife.

∞

Hettie was at her writing desk, the curtain open to see the storm. When something frightened her, she'd rather see it than hide from it. She liked to have the lightning about her, as somehow it was more disturbing to hear the thunder without it. The room itself was dim, as she had only a small lamp on her desk, and without Kezia here to light the other lamps around the room, she had not bothered. She sat in a small pool of lamplight, the rest of the room shrouded in darkness.

She was trying to decide how to sign off her letter to Max. She knew now that 'Regarding' was wrong. He'd told her that in another letter. *Always correcting me*, she thought. He was probably trying to help her, by telling her what she was getting wrong. But it was another indication to her that she was making the right decision in turning him down. She didn't want a teacher for a husband. She wanted an equal, someone she felt comfortable with and could share her failures and successes with, as well as his own. She decided to sign off with *Yours sincerely*, as she knew now that it was

403

correct when you were acquainted with someone. They were more than acquainted, of course, but she felt it was right to begin to distance herself from him. After all, she never intended to see Mr Laurence Maxwell Ripley again after this letter was sent. She would never see those dark eyes again. *Good*, she decided. They were far too dangerous.

She was folding the letter when she heard the creak of footfall behind her. She turned round swiftly to see a pair of dark eyes coming at her through the dim room. For a crazed moment, she thought it was Max, come to propose. But it was not Max. It was a man she'd never seen before and he was lunging towards her.

She went to stand up but he was upon her before she stood fully, his full weight forcing her back onto the desk. His body was sodden and she felt splashes of water land on her skin as he grappled with her. His hands were about her throat and as she twisted away from him, the single lamp was pushed to the floor and extinguished, the room thrown into utter darkness. Her hands grasped at her throat as the man's closed about them. The strength in his fingers was intense and she could feel the air being squeezed out of her.

But she was a pit girl and a strawberry picker and she'd always had the upper body strength that had kept her going through the long days of work. She called on it now and grabbed at his arms, twisting her body violently to the side, which dragged him across her as they slipped from the desk and collapsed onto the carpet.

In the moment of confusion, she tried to cry out for help, but one of his hands was on her neck again, the other hand forcing its way into her mouth, the taste and texture of his three thick fingers on her tongue gagging her with disgust and terror. He pushed himself onto her and she bit down hard on his fingers. He cried out and she yelled, 'Help me!' But the storm was raging and her voice was lost in the thunder that crashed about them. He grabbed her head with both hands, one now bleeding from her almighty bite and smashed it backwards. She felt it crunch into the lamp behind her head and a searing pain took over her consciousness.

She heard him whimper and say, 'My hand!' in a pathetic voice, but her own pain was too much and she blacked out for a moment. But her body felt him reach for her again and reacted, kicking away at him through her skirts, causing him to cry out again. It gave her enough time to scramble up, but he was coming up with her, and now he had her against the window. She was flailing her arms at him. The pain in her head and the darkness of the room rendered everything like a dream, and as in dreams, she found she could not speak or cry out.

Instead, time slowed to a crawl, as she saw a flash of lightning create his outline for a moment, his black eyes like pools of ink on his face as he threw himself towards her again, his arms outstretched. And a thought came to her that this was the last thing she would see. She would die here, now, on a stormy night, just as her father had.

∽

There was only one light in a window of the front façade of the old brickmaster's house. Evan knew it was Hettie's room, on the right-hand side of the house, as she'd told him about it before. He smiled at the sight. It felt as if she had left a light burning for him alone. All the other rooms on this side of the house were in darkness. He guessed the kitchen would be lit at the back of the house and perhaps some of the servants' rooms, but from here it looked as though Hettie was upstairs and everyone else was out or asleep.

Then, suddenly, the light disappeared. Had she blown it out? He hadn't seen her at the window before, but now there was someone there. Not someone – two people. There were two people struggling in the window. Then he saw that it was Hettie, her head being pushed back against the glass.

Evan broke into a frantic run, the likes of which he'd never felt. His legs seemed as if they were flying off in all directions and he nearly fell flat on his face as he hurtled across the frontage to the kitchen door at the back. He threw himself at the door, not waiting to see if it was locked or to bother knocking. Someone was attacking Hettie, and no other thought was in his mind but to stop it.

He turned the handle and it opened. He nearly fell again getting across the step, so violent was his forward momentum. His legs pushed him onwards as he ran into the front hall, one dim lamp in the hallway lighting his approach as he hurtled up the stairs, taking them two at a time, and then he was on the landing and heading for Hettie's room.

He threw open the door and there they were, a hunched, dark form by the window, the man's hands around Hettie's neck as her arms slapped wildly at him. In two strides Evan was there. His fist landed heavily on the man's lower back, making him loosen his grip and reach for the site of his pain. In that moment, Hettie dropped down, and Evan landed another punch on the man's side, winding him until Evan could grab him and drag him away from Hettie, whose hands were now around her throat as she coughed and gasped. Even when he hacked the coalface with his pick, Evan had never felt such strength as now when he grabbed this man, surely as tall and broad as himself, and dragged him away from his beloved.

The man stumbled and Evan laid another punch in his gut. He fell backwards as Evan rammed into him, punching for all he was worth. He pummelled the man's stomach, making him stagger backwards towards the far wall. Evan rushed forward with him, landing punches wherever he could. But the man had broad arms and still some strength, for he landed a punch on Evan's jaw which rattled him for a moment. Then the man stood upright and Evan saw he was even taller than himself. He threw another punch, catching Evan on the ear and making him see stars. Then came another punch on the side of his head and he felt his body bend at the waist like a hinge. He must stand upright, he must! He had to finish this bastard.

As Evan opened his eyes to throw another punch, a flash of lightning lit up the room, and he saw Hettie with a smashed lamp in her hands, the glass jagged in the white light. She raised it above her head and brought it down with brutal speed onto the man's ear and down he went like a skittle. Evan stepped forward and brought his boot down hard on the man's genitals, causing him to double over and curl up, whimpering and blubbering like an infant.

The man was no threat for the moment and so Evan turned to Hettie. She stood beside him, breathing heavily, her hair wild, her dress ripped. Another bolt of lightning lit her up like a picture and he saw a trickle of blood running down her neck into her bodice.

Evan said, 'You're hurt.'

The man groaned and tried to move, but Evan lifted his boot and kicked him back down at the chest. He didn't move then.

'I'll survive,' Hettie said, her voice croaky.

A thin moaning now came from the man. He was still alive, but incapacitated now. Lightning came and in the same moment thunder crashed again and the very house seemed to shake. The storm was immediately above them now.

As they stood there, gasping to get their breath back, Evan and Hettic glanced outside at the raging storm and saw a perfect zigzag of forked lightning rent the sky, a strange pinkish tinge to it. And as the thunder shook the house again, their eyes met in the dim moonlight and they laughed with the madness of it all. They actually laughed.

Chapter 27

A light threw two shadows on the wall at her door and Hettie started. Would it be friend or foe? Nothing would surprise her tonight.

'Ma'am, sir!' came a voice. It was Busby, with Towers close behind. They came through the open door, both carrying lamps. 'Are you well? Oh, my word! I did not hear this. An intruder! Towers, go fetch the constable and the doctor, for heaven's sake – hurry, man!'

Hettie's throat ached horribly. Her love was standing before her also the worse for wear, and at their feet was the man with the black eyes who had tried to kill her, still breathing, but otherwise motionless. And all she wanted to do was reassure Busby. She tried to speak out but it hurt, so she motioned for Busby to come closer.

'The man came in the storm,' she croaked. 'Evan helped me.'

'I must offer my most humble apologies, ma'am. I am the keeper of safety in this house and I have let you down most heinously. I will tender my resignation on the morrow.'

'No, you wonna be doing that,' she said hoarsely. 'You didna do a thing wrong. The storm drowned everything out. I need you, Busby. Dunna desert me now.'

Busby's face was a mixture of pride and mortification. 'Of course, ma'am. I see you have been injured. Please sit down or lie on the bed until the doctor arrives. You must rest, ma'am. Please.'

'He's right. Come on,' said Evan.

'I'll sit here. Something tells me if I lie down, I might not want to wake up.'

Evan righted her chair that had been pushed over in the fight. As she sat down, she saw Busby peering closely at the intruder.

'Well, I never. It's Troon. He was the foreman at the King brickworks years ago. Mrs King senior dismissed him and he went to the dogs, so they say. What on earth was he doing here?'

'Trying to kill me,' said Hettie.

Evan said, 'Most likely robbing the house. Maybe he had a grudge against the Kings.'

'No,' said Hettie firmly, her throat twinging with pain in response. 'He was trying to kill me. He had no other intent. He could've robbed the house easily under cover of the storm, but instead he came to me and went straight for my neck. He wanted to murder me. There inna a doubt about it.'

Mrs Guest, the cook, was up and about now. Hettie was brought warm milk with honey and a little rum in it and Evan was given a glass of whisky, which he seemed to particularly savour. Mrs Guest brought warm water and washed the blood from Hettie's neck and inspected her head. There was a wound there but it was mercifully small and she would leave the doctor to dress it, as he would know the right way. She also had some cream in a small jar she said was arnica for bruises, which she dabbed on Hettie's neck. She offered some to Evan, which he refused. Busby did not want to leave the room while Troon was still there, and nobody wanted to move him lest he should wake. He stood guard by Troon's sleeping form, as Evan sat in an armchair and Hettie drank her milk slowly, each swallow an effort. The storm was moving away and she watched the rain subside, as the rumbles of thunder grew quieter.

The constable arrived first. Hettie told him the bare facts, to which Evan added his part in it. When Troon was lifted up by Busby and Towers, he began to grumble and moan. Hettie flinched at the sound of him, terrified he should wake up, despite the room being filled with people to protect her. She knew she'd never forget the sight of those black eyes coming at her.

Evan was suddenly there, crouched beside her chair, his hand on her arm, looking up at her with concern.

'He'll never get to you. He'll never get anywhere near you again. I'll make sure of that.'

Everyone had left the room now and they were alone. Hettie looked down into Evan's blue eyes and was overcome. Her own eyes filled with tears.

'My darling girl,' said Evan and put his hand on her cheek.

'Dunna ever leave me again,' she said.

'Never. You know it. You've always known it.'

'Stay with me, Evan. Stay forever. For the rest of our lives.'

'I will. Oh, my love.'

He leant in and kissed her tenderly. How she had imagined this moment over and over; her first kiss. She had imagined it chaste or filled with passion, but never had she pictured that it would be so tender and full of love that it would make her weep with emotion.

The tears were flooding now as Evan put his arms about her awkwardly, still crouched on the floor at her side. She held onto him and sobbed. The feel of his cheek against hers, the strength of his arms around her, the smell of his damp hair, mingled with blood and whisky and honey. She would never forget this moment.

As her sobbing subsided, he pulled back to wipe the tears from her face and he smiled at her. Evan was often scowling at things, often dissatisfied or annoyed. It was a long time since she'd seen his face at peace like this. It reminded her of the look he had as a child, at the end of a carefree summer's day, when they were exhausted from playing out but utterly happy. She went to stand up and he said she mustn't, but there were some things that needed to be said standing up and this was one of them.

Hettie stood before him, his hand reaching tentatively for her to catch her should she fall. But she felt stronger than ever, for love was coursing through her.

'Evan Malone, will you be my husband?'

He looked shocked. Then he grinned. 'Course I will. It's what I came here this night to ask you.' He grasped her two hands. 'And as usual, you've shown me up. I was gonna ask you first.'

'Ask me then,' she said.

'Hettie Jones, will you be my wife?'

'Yes, I will. We be quite the team, eh?'

'Yes, we be that all right. We can beat anything, face anything, take on anything. As long as you're in my arms, Hettie.'

'Take me in your arms then, Evan.'

And he did. Their next kiss was long, slow, deep and glorious.

Epilogue

October 1876

Anny Malone was tidying her desk. Every item on it delighted her. She counted back the years, to the last time she had sat at a writing desk in an office. It was back in 1839, thirty-seven years ago. Back then, she had worked in the Kings' estate office and had her whole life ahead of her. She'd had visions of promotion to a legal clerk or something of the sort in Shrewsbury. But then the curse of the Kings came upon her and her life was blighted. Now, here she was, back on King property – but inside Southover this time, rather than banished to an estate office – back at a desk, ready to start her new job as clerk of the Hettie Malone Foundation. At the age of fifty-three, she had finally achieved her dream of an office job.

She thought about the events of the past months, how much had changed, the shocking events of that night on which she feared her second son might be lost to the storm. She had spent that night wracked with fear at Evan's absence, remembering the death of her firstborn, Owen, all those years before. Peter had gone out to the taverns to look for Evan, but he was nowhere to be found. After the storm had subsided, still no sleep came for her. She had worried herself sick for hours, until she heard the sound of carriage wheels and a horse, and went outside, thinking it would be some official telling her that her son was dead. She was stone-cold sure of it. But out of the carriage stepped Evan, looking like nothing on earth. Bruised and beaten, hair sticking up in a thousand directions. He had been brought home in Hettie's carriage. Anny's mind had filled with questions, but her body was weak with relief. She took him inside and cleaned him up, listening to the extraordinary events of that night.

As the days followed, more revelations came thick and fast. Troon had recovered and told the whole story to the police, who arrested Benjamina King in Shrewsbury. She had hired Troon to murder Hettie so she could inherit the King fortune. She had sent away Kezia Clayton on a false errand, telling her that her mother was ill in order to get her out of the house, so Hettie would be unguarded. The malice of it was wicked. Anny had never liked Benjamina King, but to hear of this cruel plan was shocking in the extreme. Troon was charged with attempted murder and Mrs King with conspiracy to commit murder. Both were in prison, awaiting trial.

It was the scandal of the decade. All tongues were wagging about it for weeks – until the wedding of Hettie Jones and Evan Malone, that was. Then they had something else to gossip about.

The wedding was a beautiful yet simple affair, as they both wanted. It took place in the local church, attended by family, friends and assorted pit workers. Hettie looked a picture in her dress, her green eyes shining with love for Evan, who had never looked more handsome. Anny's heart had nearly burst with pride and joy that day.

Now, Evan and Hettie were living at Southover. On their wedding day, instead of being the ones to receive gifts from her, they told Anny that they wanted to give her a gift instead: the old brickmaster's house now belonged to her and Peter. They were to go and live there with Flora, Billy and Lily. They could retire from their long years of work and live in peace.

Peter adored his new life of leisure, spending his time developing a new vegetable and fruit garden in the grounds of his new home. But Anny at first missed having a purpose in life and needed industry to make her feel necessary. Then, she and Hettie came up with the plan for Anny to help her with the running of the foundation.

And here she was, at her desk, beginning her first day of clerical work in decades.

Anny thought back to the time she sat with Martha Jones, Evan and Hettie at their feet. Martha had said they were proper sweethearts already and that maybe they would marry one day. Poor dead Martha's prophecy had come to pass. For Anny back then, Owen's death was still raw in her mind. And she had said to herself that this would not come to pass, that she would raise Evan to want more from life than she had had. She promised herself then that she would raise him to leave this place forever and forge a new life away from the daily grind, away from servitude to rich masters, away from the Kings and away from the secrets and lies of Ironbridge.

But, as more children came into her life and they settled into a routine of contentment, her feelings had subsided, though she often wished her son had a better life than toiling underground all the livelong day. And when Hettie had become entangled with the Kings again, Anny had felt the old shadow looming over her, this fear she'd carried for years that the Kings and her family would never escape each other, and that one day it would bring her death, or worse than that, the mortal hurt of those she loved.

But it had not come to pass. Anny realised now that Ironbridge and even the Kings were never the problem, that it was some curse that hung over them all that now seemed to have lifted.

Anny had no time for ideas of the invisible world, but she did feel as if other forces had been at work, and that somehow now they had moved on. She felt lighter than she ever had; all those years carrying a worrisome burden since Cyril's attack, the loss of her father, through her imprisonment, Margaret's disappearance and taking her sweetheart Jake away from her, her mother's passing and Owen's death. All of these felt like a heavy sack, heavier than any load of laundry or trayful of pies, that she carried with her always, that she had dragged behind her for years. Yet now, it was as if the load had dispersed like soap bubbles on the wind and Anny was free to go on her way, lightened and at liberty.

Without fear, Anny was content and had achieved her goals at last. She had work that finally utilised her intellect. Her family were safe and provided for forever. Her husband would never have to work down the mine again and could tend the garden at the old brickmaster's house for the rest of his days. Her son was happily married to the girl he loved. Anny could finally contribute towards helping others poorer than herself. And lastly, the feud between the Kings and her family had been vanquished forever, not only by Benjamina's incarceration, but also by Hettie joining the two houses together.

Anny took up a pen, dipped it in the green ink she had ordered to keep a record of accounts and began to write. She could not be happier.

ᑫᕫᕽ

October 1877

Hettie put her baby girl in the pram. Though Kezia fussed her and wished to help, Hettie told her friend that she was quite all right and so was baby Martha.

She was well-named, for she had her grandmother's green eyes, just the same as her mother's.

Kezia helped Hettie down the steps with the pram and Hettie set off across the grounds. It was a misty autumn morning, wisps of fog still lingering in the trees around Southover, and she wanted to take Martha to meet someone. She pushed the pram across the bumpy, grassy ground and rounded the house, heading for the graveyard. Last week, she took baby Martha to visit her mother and father's graves in the local churchyard and now she wanted to do the same here. She came to Queenie King's grave and stopped. She looked down and saw that Martha was already asleep.

'Well, you'll have to listen in your dreams then, little'un. For as Anny always told me, never wake a sleeping baby.'

Hettie put a hand into the pram and tucked the blanket more closely around her beautiful child. She caught her breath in a little gasp at how overwhelming her love was for this tiny person.

Then, she turned to the grave and she spoke to it.

'Now then, Queenie. I think we know each other well enough for me to call you by your nickname. And you certainly earnt that name, didna you? You ruled the Kings like a Queen and you were never beaten, not even by Benjamina, who now rots in gaol, you'll be glad to hear. Well, Queenie, this is my daughter, Martha. I married my love, Evan, and here is our child.

'I want you to know that we are all well, that my family prosper and that we have put your fortune to good use, just as your great-granddaughter wanted. Beatrice is coming to see us in the spring, in fact, to meet Martha and to write about our foundation. We are helping many people hereabouts and further afield. We are living good lives and strive to be good folk in our hearts. I hope you'd be proud of us, Queenie. I think you would. For we're happy, and everything is proper jam.'

Hettie found there was a tear in her eye. She missed old Mrs King. As she stood by her grave, listening to the sound of the autumn wind lifting the tree boughs in the woods beyond, and hearing her sleeping daughter snuffle, Hettie thought she heard a whisper of an answer in her ear. She looked about her, but dismissed it as a natural thing, leaves falling from the trees perhaps and rustling on the woodland floor. She nodded at the grave of Alice King and turned the pram around and pushed it back to the house.

The front door opened before she got there and out stepped Evan, his blond hair thick and brushed back, his blue eyes shining at her. He was dressed in a simple yet smart pair of brown trousers and a cream shirt, tucked in to reveal his fine chest and strong, flat stomach, his sleeves rolled up to show his broad, muscled arms. Ah, he was a fine figure of a man was Evan Malone. And he was all hers.

He smiled at her and took the pram with infinite care to carry it up the steps, placing it carefully down inside. Then he leant over and kissed her tenderly.

Hettie smiled and closed the door, safely inside Southover, away from the autumn chill.

⤳

And if the good ghosts of Southover could see Hettie go inside her house that day, what would they think of how things had come to pass? Perhaps they would gather about the graveyard – Betsy Blaize, John Woodvine, Queenie King and her twin daughters, Margaret Ashford, Owen Malone, Martha and Adam Jones, and even Rose Jenkins might be there, shining in a blue-white spectral light. They would see this happiest of couples and their new child inhabit this once fire-ravaged house, now built anew, order restored from chaos. The feud was no more, the divide had been bridged. And perhaps the spirits would smile on this, and at last leave this place, vanishing into the mist, finally at rest.

Acknowledgements

Shroppiemon, for continuing dialect and historical help, for again reading the early draft quickly, as well as moral support when I really needed it.

Katie Lumsden and Claire Johnson-Creek at Bonnier Books UK, for providing such expert edits and support, as well as Tara Loder for commissioning the trilogy and believing in it all the way. Brilliant, insightful editors are a gift to any writer and I have been blessed in this regard with Bonnier! Particular thanks also to the wonderful design team for producing such gorgeous covers.

Lu Corfield, for doing a perfectly beautiful job of narrating the previous *Ironbridge* books and bringing the characters to glorious life.

My excellent agent Laura Macdougall and also Olivia Davies at United Agents for their constant support and vigilance.

Memories of Shropshire Facebook group, for helping with my post about coal mining places to visit in the area: in particular, comments from Colin Armfield, Kate Cadman, Geoff Fletcher, Margaret Sheridan,

Rosemary Perry, Graham Hickman, Gareth Maverick, Nicola Edwards and Louise Bremner. Also, Juanita Gennard from the group for sharing the story about her father as a child listening to the clogs of miners walking past his window. Also, thanks to Alison Utting from the same group for telling me about the term 'clog chorus'.

Oakengates History group on Facebook: Gwyn Thunderwing Hartley, for help on pit girls' dress as well as on the Oakengates Wake; Dave Baker for excellent, detailed help on the railways, particularly the route from Ironbridge to Oakengates and the trip to London.

All the members and administrators of the various other Shropshire Facebook groups who have continued to give great advice on the subject as well as support the *Ironbridge* saga:

- Shropshire Tales, History and Memories
- Telford Memories
- Ironbridge and Coalbrookdale pictures
- Ironbridge through the Dales

Bill Scriven, ex-miner and font of knowledge about mining, with whom I had a fantastic phone conversation listening to his memories of working down the pit.

Joanne Smith and Sarah Roberts at the Ironbridge Gorge Museums Trust library and archives. Joanne, for finding materials on coal mining that were waiting for me when I arrived, and Sarah, for looking after me when I was there and showing me where all the coal mining materials were.

The Friends of Ironbridge Gorge Museum Trust, for inviting me to do a talk in November 2019 on the research for the *Ironbridge* saga. The audience's enthusiasm and help with coal mining research was awesome.

Ray Farlow, who I met at the IGMT talk, for sending me news articles from 1870s newspapers.

Steve Dewhirst of Broseley Local History Society, for articles about local fairs.

Andy Rose of Madeley Town Council, for resources on the pit girls and pit conditions.

Martine Bailey, for direction to useful resources on transportation to Australia.

Jé Maverick, for info and ideas on convicts.

Essie Fox, for information on the London Aquarium.

Early readers – my darling friends Lynn Downing, Pauline Lancaster and Lucy Adams, for reading so quickly and enthusiastically, as ever.

Melissa Bailey, Lynn Downing, Kerry Drewery, Kerry Hadley, Kathy Kendall, Bee Lewis, Fiona McKinnell, Beth Miller, Jamie Pearce, Louisa Treger and Sue White, for always indulging this chatterbox and drama queen.

Sumaira Wilson of SpellBound Books, for the best memes and moral support when any normal human would be focusing on their own battles. An absolute queen of a woman, publisher and friend.

My dear Facebook friends, for seeing me through difficult days and always making me laugh, for messaging me to check how I'm doing, as well as shamelessly encouraging me to post ever more highly inappropriate memes.

Readers, reviewers, book bloggers and booksellers for reading, selling and sharing your thoughts on the *Ironbridge* saga. A particular thanks to every single reader who has contacted me via social media to tell me how much they've enjoyed the books. Your messages and comments mean the world to this author.

Bev Johnson, for keeping me healthy.

Clément Barbin, for bringing me the sweetest of treats.

Fiona Cooke – you know why, babe. Suffice to say, the greatest and truest love story of lockdown. Grateful forever for your friendship.

This book was written and edited throughout the Covid pandemic, from first lockdown to third. I'd like to take this opportunity to thank my daughter, Poppy, and our family, as well as all our lovely friends, who helped me get through this period with camaraderie, humour and patience. Let's hope that by the time this book goes out into the world, there is hope on the horizon of a return to some semblance of normality. Love and gratitude to all of you.

·MEMORY LANE·

Welcome to the world of Mollie Walton!

Keep reading for more from Mollie Walton, to discover a recipe that features in this novel and to find out more about Mollie Walton's inspiration for the book . . .

We'd also like to welcome you to Memory Lane, a place to discuss the very best saga stories from authors you know and love with other readers, plus get recommendations for new books we think you'll enjoy. Read on and join our club!

www.MemoryLane.Club
f /MemoryLaneClub

Dear Reader,

Thank you for reading the third instalment of the *Ironbridge* trilogy. If you're new to the *Ironbridge* saga, then welcome. And if you've followed all three books, then I hope you've enjoyed them all. I must say I've loved writing them.

For this book, some aspects of the research could not be as hands-on as usual, as it was mostly written during the Covid pandemic. However, luckily, before the first lockdown, I was able to visit Ironbridge and nearby Coalbrookdale and spend some time in the Ironbridge Gorge Museums Trust archives, to learn about mining in the nineteenth century. Through a Shropshire Facebook group (one of my most treasured resources) I was put in touch with Bill Scriven, an ex-coal miner from the area. We had a phone call that lasted hours, where I mercilessly quizzed him about his career. Luckily, he didn't seem to mind! His reminiscences were marvellous and gave me a fascinating, luminous image of these brave men and the work they did underground.

I've found that throughout the writing of this trilogy, my research into the lives of working people – such as ironworkers, brickmakers and colliers – have transformed my understanding of the industrial revolution and earned my eternal respect. It's one thing to be aware of their hard work and sacrifices; it's another to try and put yourself in their shoes. Not only did they suffer, but they also lived with camaraderie and community spirit which can sometimes feel lacking in this day and age. I will always feel grateful to them and in awe of the difficult lives they led.

So, it's with a heavy heart that I say farewell to the *Ironbridge* saga with this third and final book in the trilogy. I first had the idea for this story five years ago, when standing on the iron bridge itself. To see that story come to fruition is a very emotional moment for any writer. I must confess I did have a little cry when I finished this book. I've lived with these characters in my head for all those years, following their fortunes and – let's face it – putting them through hell! To say goodbye to them and see them go off into the world without me is a very peculiar feeling – part relief, part sadness. I've grown excessively fond of them all. I like to think of them living their lives into the rest of the nineteenth century and beyond. Maybe, we'll revisit them one day, who knows . . .

Looking back over the last five years of writing about these characters, one thing above all else stays with me and that is the delight of discovering

Shropshire and its people. I'd like to sign off with a thank'ee to all the folk of this beautiful county that I've connected with, and I hope to visit you soon, when lockdown lifts. I miss my Ironbridge friends and I will be back. You're all proper jam.

Best wishes,
Mollie

Glossary of Shropshire Dialect Terms

Arr: yes
Babby: baby
Bait: packed lunch
Butty: mate, friend
Coulda: could have
Couldna: couldn't have
Crowsty: bad-tempered
Cwtch: a cuddle or sitting up close to someone
Daff: someone who is shy, silly or inexperienced
Didna: didn't
Doesna: doesn't
Drodsome: dreadful, alarming
Dunna: don't
Frit'ee: frighten you
Hadna: hadn't
Hasna: hasn't
Havna: haven't
Inna: isn't or am not
Little'uns: babies or children

Lollocking: easy, idle

Mon: man, a term of address for males

Mun: must

Owd: old

Proper jam: lovely, really good

Scuffling: weeding with a hoe

Shoulda: should have

Sniving: overrun with

Summat: something

Understrapper: boy

Wasna: wasn't

Wench: used for a young woman in a similar way to 'lass', in no way derogatory to females

Wonna: won't

Woulda: would have

Wouldna: wouldn't

Strawberry Ice

At the Oakengates fair in Chapter 8, Hettie and her father, Adam, eat a strawberry ice each from a glass cup. An 'ice' was a Victorian precursor to ice cream, and would have been made with fresh strawberries such as the ones Hettie herself picks in the earlier chapters of the book.

You will need:

2 lb fresh strawberries
¾ pt cream
3 oz caster sugar

Method:

1. Cut the stems off the strawberries, slice them into small chunks, then either mash or blitz in a blender.
2. Push the mashed fresh strawberries through a sieve, getting out as much juice as you can.
3. Pour the sugar into the strawberry juice and stir until the sugar dissolves.
4. Whip the cream in a separate bowl until it forms stiff peaks, then slowly stir in the strawberry juice.
5. Spoon the mixture into individual glasses.
6. Freeze these overnight, then eat with a spoon.
7. Enjoy!

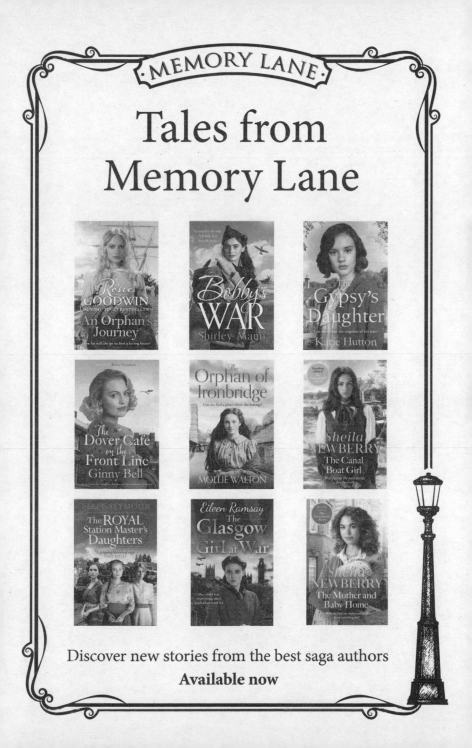

MEMORY LANE

Tales from Memory Lane

Discover new stories from the best saga authors

Available now

·MEMORY LANE·

Introducing the place for story lovers – a welcoming home for all readers who love heartwarming tales of wartime, family and romance. Join us to discuss your favourite stories with other readers, plus get book recommendations, book giveaways and behind-the-scenes writing moments from your favourite authors.

·MEMORY LANE·

www.MemoryLane.Club

f /MemoryLaneClub